REMEMBER ?

Forbidden Series ~ Two

Cynthia B. Ainsworthe

Other Works by Author

Front Row Center's Passion in the Kitchen,
2015, 2014 Words and Passion Publishing

Front Row Center,
2015, 2014 Words and Passion Publishing

When Midnight Comes and *Characters*
Two short stories in the horror anthology *The Speed of Dark,*
2013 Chase Publishing Enterprises

This is a work of fiction. Names, characters, businesses, organizations, places, events, and incidents either are the product of the author's imagination or are used fictitiously. Any resemblance to actual persons, living or dead, events, business establishments, or locales is entirely coincidental. All people and plots in this book are fictional. None of the medical procedures or medical diagnosis in this book are to be taken as medical treatment or medical suggestions, nor is it meant to represent the "state of the art" treatment at the time of publication. No responsibility is assumed for any medical information or procedure described in this book. See your own primary care provider for diagnosis and/or treatment.

Copyright © 2015 Cynthia B. Ainsworthe
All rights reserved. 2015 Words and Passion Publishing, first edition,
Florida, United States
Cover design: Trish Jackson
No portion of the text, graphics, or other content of this work or its dependant websites may be copied, reproduced, stored, or transmitted, in its original form or in a derivative, electronic, digital, or modified form, without the written permission of the copyright holders. *"Taylor"* song lyrics ©2008 used by permission of composer Mark J. Dye.
ISBN: 0980245974
ISBN-13: 978-0-9802459-7-4

IN DEDICATION

To Mitch and Cindy, my loving husband and daughter, whose steadfast encouragement spurred me on to write from my heart. Their love and support is my strength to face life's difficulties.

To my dearest friends, Mark and Adrienne Dye, who have always been in my corner and cheered me on to accomplish my goals.

To all my fan readers who enjoy my writings and have remained loyal and encouraging.

REVIEWS

5 Stars! Review by Trish Jackson, editor

"Follow famous singer Larry Davis on his desperate quest to find his missing wife, Taylor.

Cynthia B. Ainsworthe has done it again! *Remember?* -- Book number two in the Forbidden Series, and following the IPPY award-winning novel, *Front Row Center*—will take you on a journey fraught with danger, passion, and shocking surprises.

Famous singer, Larry Davis' tour schedule has brought him to London, England, where he continues his desperate search for Taylor. His chances of finding her seem bleak, until he discovers a woman named Tiffany, who has lost her memory, and has no recollection of her life before her marriage to the titled and world-renowned neurosurgeon, Clive Bradford, the Earl of Latham.

She looks exactly like Taylor. She speaks like Taylor. Could it be possible she really is Taylor? Or is that just another illusion?

You won't be able to put it down until you know the truth."—Trish Jackson

5 Stars! Review by Alexandria Matthews, editor

"'Remember?' by Cynthia B. Ainsworthe, the sequel to the IPPY award-winning 'Front Row Center', is a fantastic contemporary romance novel following the lives of Taylor Allen and the world-famous singer and icon Larry Davis. Cynthia is a very gifted storyteller who effortlessly creates well-developed characters and engaging storylines. You are quickly drawn in and kept guessing about what will happen next. If you enjoy a dramatic and intriguing fast-paced love story that you can't put down, then this is the book for you!"—Alexandria Matthews

IN ACKNOWLEDGMENT

My heartfelt thanks to those who assisted me in the creation of *Remember?*~~

To Trish Jackson my wonderful editor who realized my vision and guided me through the process of turning a rough manuscript into a well-crafted and enjoyable read. I am immensely grateful for her attention to detail and keeping me on track.

To Alex Matthews, my UK editor, for her in depth research dealing with English culture, dialogue, forms of address among titled characters, customs, London's landmarks, my numerous questions, and first editing of this work.

To Julie Lowe, my immense thanks for traveling to London to meet with me and my husband, generously sharing your knowledge of English culture during a wonderful drink and dinner, and for revealing the intricacies of maneuvering London's bus system. Your contribution heightened this novel.

To Vivienne Roberts, my sincere gratitude for sojourning to London to meet me and my husband for a glass of wine at a local pub. Sharing your insight on British royal heritage enhanced the authenticity of my story's setting. Your encouragement and support of my writing is treasured.

"The end of their torment ...

lies in remembrance ..."

~~ CB Ainsworthe

REMEMBER ?

ONE

"PULL OVER HERE! Now! Quick!" Larry Davis exclaimed. "That face. The woman adjusting the scarf on that mannequin."

Joe Winton raised his bushy black eyebrows in astonishment. "Chief, what's goin' on? You saw a ghost or somethin'?"

"Not a ghost. It's Taylor! I'm sure of it." Larry's eyes remained fixed on the dark haired beauty in the store window. "After all this time and the endless searching, I've finally found her in that boutique. In London. Where are we exactly?"

"On a side street in the West End, near Mayfair. Lar, don't jump the gun." Joe must have seen his desperation. "It could be someone who looks like Taylor. Remember, Interpol didn't turn anythin' up after eighteen months. I'm your bro and your friend, not to mention your right-hand man. I'm only lookin' out for y'."

Joe's words faded as Larry's mind whirled with anticipation. The limousine driver pulled over to the curb in front of the dress shop. Larry's heart beat faster as he anticipated reuniting with his lost love. He flung open the door and extended his long legs onto the slush-covered sidewalk. The brisk, cold air reddened his cheeks and a light breeze tousled his dark blond hair.

Joe sighed heavily as he followed his longtime friend to the store entrance. A crowd of fans quickly formed. They had caught sight of their American idol. Larry was oblivious to their squeals and cheers. He focused on his sole quest.

The shop doorbell cheerfully chimed announcing Larry's entrance. All eyes turned toward his commanding, yet boyish stature, and then settled on his sparkling and piercing blue eyes. The dark-haired woman came from the display window as if curious from all the commotion. Her quizzical eyes froze on the good-looking stranger before her. As voices called out requesting autographs, Larry remained silent and mesmerized at the sight of this woman. He tentatively took a step toward her.

"Tay, is that you?" His voice quivered. "I've been looking for you for so long. I can't believe I've finally found you."

"What did you say?" Her words caught in her throat.

"I said *'Tay'*. Aren't you Taylor?" *Doesn't she recognize me?*

"That's not my name. I'm Tiffany, Tiffany Bradford." Her eyes held confusion. She shyly extended her hand.

Autograph seekers closed in around him as he sought her hand. Their fingers met briefly. Larry rejoiced in her fleeting touch. Her fingers slipped away. Joe did his best to hold the British fans at bay as they busily tapped the keys of their cell phones and sent messages on social media to spread the news.

His eyes fixed on hers. Larry didn't hear the fans bombard him with questions and comments.

"Mr. Davis, may I please have your autograph?"

"How long are you staying in the UK?"

"I just love your music!"

"I've been a fan of yours for so many years."

"Are you recording a new song?"

Joe countered the queries in his usual unflappable style. "Mr. Davis is tourin' the UK for a couple of weeks. A new song is on the horizon. He loves his British fans. Most likely a return visit will be in the distant future."

Larry's voice was soft as he spoke to Tiffany. "I'm sorry. You look so much like a woman I knew." He tilted his head boyishly. "Funny, you don't sound English—your accent, I mean."

"I'm not," she replied. "I'm American. My home is here in London."

"How about coming to my concert tonight at the Royal Albert Hall?" Larry turned to Joe. "Give Tiffany one of those backstage passes and that reserved ticket you keep in your pocket."

Joe did as requested and handed the treasured document to Tiffany. Cheers came from the surrounding fans.

"Thank you Mr. Davis ..." She fingered her hair. "I don't know if I'll be able to attend. Wouldn't you rather give this to one of your fans here?"

I know you're Taylor. You have to be! I don't understand any of this!

"No. It would make me so happy to see you there tonight at the concert.". He stumbled over his words, "Please say you'll be there."

REMEMBER ?   11

"Maybe I can make it." Her blue-green eyes looked up at him with an expression of remote recognition.

"Great!" Joy radiated from Larry. "I'll be looking for you—front row, center seat."

"Chief," Joe interjected. "We need to get back to the hotel. You've got a press conference to get to."

"Yeah," Larry replied as he continued to look at her. "I'll leave in a moment. Gotta sign a few autographs first." *I know she's Taylor. It has to be her!*

As he signed various pieces of paper, his eyes returned to her at every chance as if drawn to her beauty by a magical force. A small smile peeked from the corners of her mouth and a faint pink glow came to her cheeks.

Larry's mind went into a whirlwind. *Why doesn't she recognize me? What is wrong with her? This isn't at all like Taylor!*

"C'mon, Chief," Joe reminded. "We need to go! Can't be late for the press."

"Yeah, I hear you." Larry reached for Tiffany's hand and gave it a reassuring squeeze. "I'm counting on seeing you tonight at the Albert." He punctuated his last comment with a smile and wink. "I'll be disappointed if you're not there."

Tiffany looked up at him from beneath her long black lashes. "Maybe. We'll see."

Oohs and aahs rang throughout the room. Larry wedged through the throngs of female admirers.

Larry turned briefly at the entrance and called out to Tiffany, "I'll be looking for you tonight. Don't forget." He quickly left, leaving shoppers buzzing about this impromptu visit from the famous American idol.

~~***~~

A blast of cold air entered with his exit. Tiffany stood in the middle of the room mesmerized by the experience as others asked a multitude of questions, their voices muted—her mind awash with confusion. Karen approached and placed her hand warmly on Tiffany's shoulder while studying her face with wonder.

"Tiff, how does Larry Davis ever know *you*?" the shop owner inquired with the tone of a loving mother.

"That's just it." Tiffany wrung her hands as questions formed in her mind. "I barely know of him, let alone, ever meeting him."

12   *Cynthia B. Ainsworthe*

She walked briskly to the back counter.

Karen followed and continued, "He bloody well thought he knew you. I think he was downright genuine—not one bit cheeky."

"Yes, Kar. He did act as if he knew me." Tiffany's brow furrowed as her eyes narrowed. Her mind searched to make sense of this chance encounter. *Who is this Taylor woman? He thinks I'm her. I wonder why they're not together now. What could've happened? Does he only want me at his concert because I look like this lost person?* "I know I shouldn't ask this. But, can I leave early today? Penny and Liz are here to close up."

"Sure." Karen's reply was easy. Her eyes held a devilish glint. "Need time to get ready for Larry's show?"

"No. I don't even know if I can go. Have to check with Clive first." Tiffany reached for her heavy wool coat. "I wanna grab a cup of coffee at the corner pub. Need to gather my thoughts." She felt a little breathless and for some reason her hands were shaking.

"Oh, the Hare and Hound?" Karen automatically reached for her plaid coat and wool scarf. "I'll tag along. Don't mind havin' a spot of tea. After seein' the likes of Larry Davis, I might even have a pint. My God, that man can get to a woman with his wonderful blue eyes." Karen brushed away her pure white bangs that framed a youthful face of fifty years.

Tiffany chuckled softly. "That's why I like you, Kar. You tell it like it is. No pretense—you just come right out with it."

"C'mon, deary." Karen grabbed her arm gently as they walked to the door. "We'll have a nice long chat and figure out how you can get *Mr. Handsome* to ask you to his dressing room after the show. Might as well make the most of that backstage pass!"

"Kar, I didn't say I could go." She stopped abruptly in front of the shop window and cocked her eyebrow. "Didn't you forget a little thing—my husband, Clive?"

"Put that American puritan look in your pocket," Karen chided humorously, then chuckled, "I didn't say you should let him into your knickers—unless you want to."

Tiffany's eyes grew large with amazement. *If it wasn't for Clive, I wouldn't mind the possibility.* She pensively bit her bottom lip. "That's your fantasy, Kar. Not mine."

REMEMBER ?   13

"Not at all." Karen flung her scarf around her neck without a care. "I don't take to his music much—just his bum."

"No wonder Clive feels you're a bad influence," Tiffany countered. "You have the thoughts of a teenage girl."

"Women are all the same deep down," Karen remarked as they approached the corner. "I never much liked keeping me feelings to meself. Blimey, I'd never fit in with the posh crowd—all stuffy, sipping brandy after dinner. Give me a good pint and a strong bloke who'll last the night—that makes me one happy woman …" She paused a moment in thought. "I worked hard in those early years. Climbed out of that East End hole. I'm proud of that, I am. The cream now come to my shop."

"I think the upper crust would enjoy your brand of humor. They'd find it refreshing." A gust of wind tousled Tiffany's hair. "You're fun to be with. Not a bit like Clive and all his protocol."

~~***~~

In his lavishly appointed hotel suite, Larry sat on a dark brown leather upholstered chair. He stared in deep reflection at the heavy brocade drapes flanking the large window. Late afternoon sunlight laced patterns on the Persian carpet. Joe went to the wet bar for his usual can of beer and flopped on the sofa.

"Chief, I don't mean to trounce on your thoughts," Joe remarked in his usual deep voice, "you're sittin' there like the weight of the world is on your shoulders." He swallowed some beer and placed the can on the antique coffee table. "Wanna talk about it?"

"Nah, I already know what you'll say." Larry shifted his gaze to the carpet. "That I'm seeing things that aren't there."

"Or, a person who's not there," Joe quipped.

Larry raised his eyes to his old buddy. "You can't resist—jolting me back to reality." He let out a breath of frustration. "For the past year and a half, Taylor has been on my mind constantly … ever since she disappeared. It's as if she was only a dream to me. One minute she's in my life, and the next … she's gone without a trace."

Joe leaned forward resting his arms on his knees while his brow rutted with concern. "Lar, I know it's been tough on you.

14   *Cynthia B. Ainsworthe*

I think you've done remarkably well holdin' the whole damn thing together—goin' back on tour and all that—but you gotta let go of this fantasy that Taylor will return to you. Who knows where she is…or even if she is? That dame in the shop could merely be Taylor's double. She never recognized you. If she is Taylor, she wouldn't deny knowin' you."

"Joe, stop it!" Larry rose from his seat. He felt his heart pound with restrained anger. "I don't want to hear one word about Taylor being dead! I refuse to believe it! I can't believe it!"

"Calm down, Chief," Joe offered meekly. "I didn't mean to get you riled up."

"Well, you did!" Larry paced the floor. "For that matter, I *know* that this Tiffany woman is Taylor—she has to be. I can feel it in my bones."

"I think that woman in the shop got to more than your bones." Joe smiled slyly.

"She touched my heart." Larry fingered his wedding band. "That's why I *know* she's Taylor. I could never love another woman but her."

"Lar, you gotta stop obsessin' 'bout Taylor and begin to accept some facts," Joe stated softly in a brotherly tone while his buddy paced the carpet. "The last you knew of Taylor's whereabouts, she was on a freelance business trip for Gérard's in Paris. Even those bigwigs at Gérard's couldn't locate her. She was last seen in that artsy district."

"Montmartre," Larry said wistfully. "I remember the first time we went there. She showed me the sights …. What a wonderful and beautiful time we had."

"Chief, you have to accept at some point, Taylor won't return." Joe spoke with a soft firmness.

"You're asking me to give up on her—I won't do that!" Larry's voice raised an octave. Frustration burst from every pore. He stopped short in his tracks. "I can't do that!" He thought aloud, "Why in hell did I ever agree to her crazy idea to go back to work for Gérard's? We were only married less than a year, and she gets this itch to return to the business world."

"Chief, Taylor was her own woman," Joe offered with up-turned palms as if pleading his case. "You wouldn't been able

REMEMBER ?   15

to control her. Even her first husband, Paul, said as much before he left her."

"Joe, there you go again, speaking of Tay in the past tense." A sense of desperation crept into Larry's heart. "I refuse to think of her in those terms—Tay's *alive* until I have proof otherwise."

"Look, ol' buddy," Joe stood up and walked to his brother, "I saw the same woman as you in that dress shop." He took a deep breath. "I admit she's a spittin' image of Taylor—but that's all—it's not her. Tay would never leave you, and start a new life with another man—not with all it took for you two to end up together."

Larry spoke with the fire of conviction in his eyes. "Joe, trust me. I know it's her."

"Chief, I've heard Taylor say many times…" Joe placed his hand on his buddy's shoulder. "'There's always a twin of someone walkin' around', and you found Taylor's."

Disgruntled and frustrated, Larry walked to the large window and looked at the street below. Pedestrians hurried to their various destinations bundled in heavy coats, scarves, and carrying protective umbrellas from the icy cold rain. Deep in his own tormented thoughts, he didn't notice the large crowd of females who held sentry on the sidewalk. They stared at the hotel windows in hope of catching a glimpse of their idol. Their squeals fell on deaf ears. All the love and adoration of his fans couldn't fill the aching emptiness deep in his heart. Thoughts of Taylor occupied his every waking moment.

~~***~~

Karen Edwards took a long puff on her cigarette, then lazily exhaled. The smoke traveled upward outside the noisy pub. Tiffany inhaled the secondhand smoke as if some forgotten pleasure came to her. With half-closed eyes, a gentle smile crossed her lips.

"I don't know if I smoked or not. There's …" She looked skyward. "Something familiar about the odor."

"By the way you look," Karen flicked her ash onto the sidewalk, "I'd swear you did smoke." She quickly stomped out the cigarette.

Tiffany followed her friend into the pub where they found a window table near the entrance. Karen went to the bar to place

16   *Cynthia B. Ainsworthe*

her order—a pint for her and coffee for Tiffany. She returned with the beverages, grabbed a napkin, and wiped the dripping ale from the glass mug.

Karen sat at the table. Tiffany leaned on her elbows and spoke in a near whisper, as though to reveal a secret. "I wish I could remember something—anything before the accident. A face, a name, cities. Anything about my past."

"You really don't remember a single thing?" Intrigue spiced Karen's voice. "If you ask me, I'd be bloomin' bonkers. I'd want to know every bloody detail about my past. How can you accept everything Clive tells you?"

"What choice do I have?" Tiffany watched the brown liquid swirl in her cup as she stirred her coffee nervously in rapid circles. "Clive's been so kind, and I believe he must really love me. It can't be easy on him—to have a wife who doesn't remember the courtship or even our first date, let alone a marriage ceremony."

"Yes, yes … I know all that." Karen probed further, "But … do you love Clive? If you can't remember datin' the bloke, then how can you feel love for him?"

"What I feel must be love or something close to it." Tiffany sighed as she tried to make sense of her words. "I don't think I would marry a man I didn't love. I'm sure, in time, my memory will return with the deep love I felt for him. Right now, Clive gives me a comfortable feeling—like a comfy bathrobe or slippers."

"Aye, 'bathrobe or slippers', you say." Karen took a large swallow of ale. "It'd be a bleedin' blizzard in hell before I'd be happy with a man what only made me comfy like bloomin' slippers! I want hell's a blazin' passion with a man before he'd get into my knickers."

"Kar, I'm sure Clive and I had that type of relationship before we married." Tiffany nervously twirled her plain gold wedding band around her finger. "It'll just take time. I'm really very lucky he's so patient."

"Tiff, at least you know you're a Yank." She aimlessly looked at the men standing casually at the bar. "I suppose that's something to hang on to."

"Yes …" she agreed with a vacant stare. "It's all I have at the moment—a shred of who I was or who I am." Tiffany sipped

REMEMBER ?   17

her coffee, then bit her bottom lip in thought. "Kar, why don't you come over for dinner sometime? I've mentioned you quite often to Clive. We've been friends for nearly a year. You rescued me from those boring flower shows."

"What? Me? In that posh house of yours in Mayfair?" She chuckled loudly. "Are you daft? A common shop owner sharing dinner with the likes of Clive Bradford, the Earl of Lantham, the famous neurosurgeon and you—Countess of Lantham? That would be a bloody laugh! Him entertaining a woman who's only one step up from the streets in his eyes—go on, will y'. I won't have more than three words out of my mouth before he'd be correctin' my grammar like Henry Higgins in that play."

"Clive's not like that at all. My title means nothing to me, and he knows it." Tiffany's arched brows reflected that she believed every word she spoke. "He's very kind to everyone. Look at all the hours he spends at the free clinic—the NHS walk-in center in the evenings when he could be home relaxing with a brandy? He doesn't have to give his services to the poor in society, but he does."

Karen twisted in her seat as if her friend's words hit a nerve. "I hear what you're sayin', and I'm sure he genuinely wants to help those less well-off." She touched Tiffany's hand. "Givin' help to those unfortunates is a far cry from spendin' a bleedin' evening with one. I know my place, and I don't cross social lines. Owning a shop doesn't raise me much higher in the eyes of the likes of him—it's part of the social structure. We all know our places and keep to 'em."

"Those are a silly bunch of rules!" Tiffany's eyes hardened as she tried to understand the reasoning. "We are all the same. I'll never understand this class thing. I can't believe that Clive takes his title seriously. He has his humble moments. I don't think Americans are so class conscious over there as you Brits." *Could it be something I remember from my past in the US?*

"It's been the same for centuries," Karen commented with an understated firmness, "and I can't see it changing much in the future." She took another sip of ale. "Back to Mr. Wonderful. Going to the Albert Hall tonight to see him?"

"I really don't know." Tiffany glanced out the pub's window at the passersby. "It all depends on how Clive feels. I only have

18   *Cynthia B. Ainsworthe*

one ticket, so that could pose a problem. He might not want me to go alone."

"If I were you," her friend affirmed, "no man would keep me from an experience like that! I'd go anyway. To hell with Clive."

~~***~~

Two hours before Larry's concert. Tiffany stood in Clive's library. He sat on the dark brown leather sofa catching up on the latest news from the paper. Wood paneling accompanied by floor-to-ceiling bookcases gave a formal feel to their Mayfair townhouse.

She approached tenuously and sat next to him. Her face held a hint of anxiousness. She interlaced her fingers in her lap.

"Clive, I want to talk to you about something." She placed her hand gently on his arm.

He didn't take his eyes off the newspaper. "About what exactly, my pet?"

I hate it when he calls me his "pet." I'm not a poodle! "There was an odd occurrence at the shop today." Tiffany chose her words carefully. "Larry Davis came in and gave me a free ticket for his concert and a backstage pass."

Clive put his paper on the seat beside him and raised his eyebrows. "Really? Are you referring to that hip-swiveling Yank who has all the women drooling as if he was the last man on earth?"

Her voice quavered, "Yes. He's the one."

"You're not considering going, are you?" Clive sat straighter. He ran his fingers through his iron gray hair. "You're too sensible to do a thing like that. My God, what would our friends think?" A condescending smile came to his face as he patted her hand. "I'm sure you're flattered, but don't let yourself be used for any publicity stunts. It was very clever of him to offer a free ticket to you, Countess Lantham. If you attend, I'm sure your picture will be in all the London rags tomorrow."

"Clive," she began softly. "Mr. Davis doesn't know who I am, or that I'm married to an earl. He was just being kind."

"I can hardly believe that. Everyone in society and such knows who you are." He made a face. "It bothers me that you insist on working in that shop—such a prosaic position. I don't know why you feel you need a career. I make a good living. You working gives the impression that I have you on a pauper's allowance. I tell you, it can be very embarrassing down at the club." Hurt came from his voice. "It gives the impression I don't treat you properly."

"Don't be silly," she replied with a tone of reserved commitment. "I work there because I want to, and I like the people at the shop."

"That may be true." His eyes pleaded, "I should think you could find some charity work to do, as that would be more befitting your social standing."

"I don't care about social standing." She pouted. "It's important to you—not to me." Tiffany placed her hand on his in a pleading gesture. "Please, can't I go to the concert tonight? I might never get this opportunity again."

"Definitely not!" His face hardened. "No wife of mine will be seen attending such a vapid concert like that! If it was a performance of classical music or an opera—well, that's different."

Determined, Tiffany's lips thinned. "I don't need your permission, Clive. Don't fight me on this. No one will know who I am, and if they do, what of it? It's not like you'll be there!"

"I *forbid* you from going to that bloody concert!" he nearly yelled.

"I don't care." She angrily yanked her hand away from his. "If I decide to go tonight—then *I will!*"

TWO

"JOE, HAVE YOU seen Taylor, I mean Tiffany in the audience?" Larry anxiously paced in his dressing room.

"Lar," Joe replied with an apprehensive brow, "you sound like you did years ago when you were wonderin' if Taylor would show up for your Vegas show." Exasperated, he upturned his palms. "This woman is *not* Taylor. She may look like Taylor and sound like Taylor, but that's where the similarity ends. You know nothin' 'bout this dame. She has her own personality and *isn't* your lost love."

"How can you be so damn sure?" Larry's eyes popped in disbelief at his brother's words. "You don't know for a fact she's not Taylor. Maybe something happened to her—and that's why she doesn't recognize me."

Joe's voice rose with frustration. "Tiffany don't know you 'cause she's never been in your life!"

"Until I know different," annoyance colored his reply, "I'm not giving up the notion she could be Taylor." Larry scrutinized his show costume in the wardrobe mirror and adjusted his shirt cuffs for a comfortable fit. "Getting back to my original question—Joe, has she shown up or not!"

"Sorry, Lar." His kind eyes held disappointment for his friend. "No one has filled that center seat." Joe shook his head despondently. "Looks like all those front row center seats you've been savin' for Taylor has gone to waste…this one included." He placed his hand on Larry's shoulder with brotherly affection. "I know you keep hopin' she'll show up at one of your concerts." Joe gave a heavy sigh. "After eighteen months, it's time to move on."

A demurred mask with a hint of deep sadness came over Larry's face. His jaw tightened. "Never, Joe. Never. My heart will never be free of her."

~~***~~

Filled to capacity, the Royal Albert Hall's audience waited for their American idol to make his entrance. All eyes scanned the stage. Excited voices rang from the crowd. Fervor buzzed.

REMEMBER ?   21

Strident voices of ardent proclamation for their love and support of Larry Davis obliterated the background music. Numerous posters touted the affection held for this world-famous singing idol. "Larry, Larry, Larry," the chanting crowd echoed all around the vast arena.

A musical medley of his famous songs heralded the long awaited entrance. Houselights dimmed, then the curtains parted. A cloud of smoke veiled a black silhouette of the performer atop a platform with steps leading to the stage.

Applause and cheers overflowed, nearly annihilating Larry's band as they played the first strains of his opening number. He stood strong and steadfast. He waited for the audience's roar to fade. A warm and gentle smile embraced his face. Twinkling clear blue eyes held excitement and anticipation.

Larry started the refrain of "Love on the Line" as his eyes adjusted to the lights. His steps were quick and sure. He effortlessly strode down the steps to the stage floor. Closer to the edge of the stage, he immediately focused on the first row. His voice never wavered. His eyes darkened with tormenting sadness. *She's not here! Taylor never showed up. Joe was right again. I've been chasing a dream.*

His background singers unobtrusively entered the stage. The spotlight followed his every movement.

Remaining true to his high professional standards, Larry gave the performance of his life. His long strides commanded the stage, while his endearing facial expressions captivated the mostly female crowd of all ages. In every audience member he sang to, he saw Taylor's face beaming back at him. When he sang of love, his words were for her. His whole existence centered on her memory—memories that tore at his heart. How he wished to have her in his life once more.

Near the end of the first half of his performance, Larry began his well-rehearsed monologue, "I'm so glad you enjoy the music I bring to you." Cheers abounded with applause. "I sing to each and every one of you." *I'm really singing for you, Tay, wherever you are.* "That's the real joy for me ... knowing I can take you to beautiful places in your heart." He strolled to the side of the stage with the mic in his left hand while his right hand rested comfortably in his pants pocket.

A voice called out in the audience, "Sing 'You Were the Only

One'."

Larry turned his attention to the unknown voice, paused, then replied solemnly, "I can't. No more sad songs for me." He shook his head. "No, sorry. There's so much sadness in the world …. Happy songs make us feel great … anyway, makes *me* feel better."

A remorseful "aah" came from the crowd.

He continued, "I have an upbeat tune I think everyone can move to." Larry nodded to Tom Anderson, his music director. "Hit it, Tom."

The introduction to "City Beat" began. His high energetic movements, captivated hearts, and further cemented the idol-fan bond that had propelled and now maintained his superstardom status. Larry ended the song on a high note with outstretched arms, embracing the resounding love and admiration

~~***~~

In the dressing room, Joe handed Larry a glass of water, which he quickly gulped down. He stared at the empty glass as if it expressed the emptiness in his heart. His strong hand grasped the vessel tighter. Sadness filled his eyes.

Joe cleared his throat. "Chief, I know you got your hopes up again…hopin' this Tiffany babe would show up—turning out to be Taylor. Don't torture yourself. Be thankful for the time you had with Taylor. Hang on to that."

"I can't give up—that's what you're asking me to do—give up on Tay. I only had less than a year with her since our marriage." Muscles in his face twitched. His jaw set in reservation. "For all I know, she could've suffered a heart attack on her last trip. Maybe she's somewhere in Europe in a hospital or a convalescent home."

"Chief, if that was the case, then why hasn't she called y'?" Joe stoked his chin with concern. "Taylor wouldn't just pick up and leave y' hangin' like this? It's not her style."

"Maybe she got depressed, like she did when she lost Paul." Tears rimmed Larry's eyes as he remembered seeing Taylor at her lowest. "She might've felt the old feelings of guilt over Paul. If I hadn't gotten to her when I did, she would've drank herself into the grave."

"Yeah, I hear y'." Joe offered a warm smile. "But Taylor was crazy for you—right from the first time you met at the Tampa concert. No amount of guilt would keep her from you." Joe sighed heavily and gave Larry's shoulder a squeeze with his beefy hand. "Accept it and move on. If you don't, your music will suffer—right now, music is the only thing that's keepin' you together."

"Joe," Larry wiped a tear from his eye, "*hope* is what's keeping me together—not music. It's hope that one day I'll find her."

A makeup artist patted Larry's forehead. His eyes held a vacant look of despair and loss—a loss that emanated from his every pore and eroded at his emotional core. He glanced down at his gold wedding band. *I remember Tay's face so clearly and her words when she placed this ring on my finger. Am I destined to spend the rest of my days searching for her? Or, will some unexpected event bring her back to me?*

Joe brought him back to the present. "Chief, you're at ten. Better get back to the wings for the second half."

"Yeah …." Larry sighed with the weight of ten tons. "I'm ready—manufactured smile and a face of warmth and love—right on cue."

Larry stood up from the chair, took a deep breath for courage, and walked confidently toward the stage wings. He wouldn't let his audience see the pain in his heart. He was a professional showman and always gave his audience more than their money's worth.

~~***~~

Houselights dimmed. The audience hum softened to an awe-anticipating silence. A bright spotlight swerved to the left. The vamp of another Davis hit welcomed him. An energetic smile framed his striking white teeth and hid his pain. He strode with the confidence of a conqueror to the waiting microphone that rested atop the black grand piano. Stage lights blinded him. He looked out into the crowd of adoring fans. Larry placed his hand to his forehead as his eyes adjusted to the glare. Flashes from handheld cameras came from all directions.

"Welcome back," he announced, "glad to see I didn't run anyone off to the restrooms or to get a drink." Chuckles came from the crowd. "Great! I could sing to you all night. You make what I do s damn enjoyable! I should be paying you guys—but my accountant wouldn't like that." Cheers and laughter

24   *Cynthia B. Ainsworthe*

rang out. "Let's keep this party going! I'll sing every song I know."

Larry briefly turned to Tom and signaled for the song to begin. The spotlight sharpened to a narrow beam, highlighting his face.

He began "Lost in the Feeling". This song held special meaning for him and Taylor. It was the first melody he had written to express the deep love in his heart for the woman of his dreams. Larry looked out at the nameless faces in the crowd and beyond to the back of the house where only tiny exit signs punctuated the blackness. He saw Taylor in his mind's eye while diverting his attention from that one empty seat in the first row.

Toward the end of the song, before the last refrain, his eyes skimmed over the seat. The vacant one in the center of the front row. He did a double take. Joy filled his heart as the last note escaped in a long, resounding sound. While he took his bows, his mind raced.

He couldn't keep his gaze away from the captivating face. *She did come! Taylor, Tiffany, whoever she is—she came tonight. I knew it! I just knew it! She felt something when we met. I know she did!* His heart pounded with elation and hope. *I don't give a damn what Joe says—she is Taylor. No one can convince me otherwise.*

Larry's energy soared as he went through his well-honed routine. Not one step was missed, nor a gesture forgotten. Swiveling and pumping hips abounded to thrill the female audience members. *It's the Tampa concert all over again—only this time, she's my wife and not someone else's!* He stuck to his Set-List and didn't throw a curve to his musical director, at least not until the very end.

After he took what seemed to be his final bows, Larry strutted back on stage with exuberance to grab the waiting microphone from the piano top. Cheers and joyful shouts greeted him as he made his way to the stage edge, where he sat down in front of his mystery woman.

A warm, boyish smile lit up his face and he ran his hand through his hair in a casual, endearing fashion. The roar of the crowd simmered to hushed murmurs in eager anticipation of what was to come.

"I don't usually give encore performances." His eyes looked

REMEMBER ?   25

deeply into Tiffany's. "But, you all have been so great tonight—I just couldn't leave—not yet, without singing one last song." Oohs and aahs chimed out with loud applause. Larry turned his head to his musical director. "Tom, get the song 'Taylor' up." Band members scrambled for the selected number. "Y' know, this song is very special to me. It speaks to my heart and maybe, it will speak to yours."

The band began the heartfelt ballad. Larry took a deep breath. His eyes and heart focused on Tiffany. Her gaze remained on him as she listened to the words from his heart.

"When the world has come between us,
The truth will lie beneath us.
No one can know you,
The way I know you.
My love will always be with you.
Ohhh, Taylor,

He noticed a small smile come to her lips. By the end of the song, it widened into a beam of appreciation mixed with embarrassment. Her chest heaved while Larry sang the final words from his soul with an outstretched hand.

"With these words you know I care
In this song I'm always there for you
There for you."

After the last note traveled through the excitement-laden crowd, a deafening din rewarded him, but not the reward he sought.

Larry stood near the edge of center stage. He took his bows, and then motioned for his band and backup singers to receive their well-deserved applause. All bowed in unison. His mind raced. *I hope she uses the backstage pass. What if she leaves? She can't. I have to find out what happened during all these months! Why doesn't Tay act like she knows me? What's wrong with her? What if she's not Taylor? She has to be Taylor!*

Larry reluctantly left the stage and grabbed the bottle of water from Joe, where he waited in the wings. His speech was rapid and pressured, "Joe, don't let her go. Get her right away. Bring Tay to my dressing room!"

"She's not Tay!" Joe retorted stubbornly. "Got me runnin'

26   *Cynthia B. Ainsworthe*

after her like I did when y' fell for Taylor."

"Stop it, Joe!" Larry remained in control. His voice raised an octave, "Just go! Get her before she leaves! Run!"

~~***~~

Joe made his way to the center section of the front row as he mumbled, "Makin' a damn fool of himself. This dame is gonna think he's a nut—a talented nut, but still a nut! She might not wanna meet him. She didn't act thrilled to see Lar in the dress shop." He breathed heavily. Perspiration trickled down his forehead and neck. Her back was to him as he approached and gingerly tapped her shoulder. She turned around briskly. Her eyes grew wide with surprise.

"Yes?" Tiffany responded softly.

"Mr. Davis would like you to come to his dressin' room." Joe took another labored breath. "He really wants to see y'. It would make him so happy to speak with y'."

Tiffany's mouth opened slightly with hesitation, "Really? I didn't know the backstage pass was for a personal meeting with Mr. Davis. I don't know what to say."

"Y' can say 'yes'." He grabbed Tiffany's hand firmly, clearly not giving her the possibility to refuse. "C'mon. Larry's waitin' for y'."

"Well, it shouldn't take too long." Her red high heels made a high-pitched noise as she scurried behind Joe. "I can't keep Clive waiting. I don't want him to worry."

Joe's mind went into overdrive. *Holy shit! This dame's married or goin' with some guy! If she really was Taylor, she wouldn't be hooked to another man. Tay would never do that to Lar, or would she? Nah, this broad isn't Taylor. Poor Lar. It's Vegas all over again when he didn't know Taylor was married to Paul. He's gonna fall like a ton of bricks! Hope he doesn't cancel the rest of his tour.*

~~***~~

Larry paced anxiously in his dressing room. He hadn't taken time to change his clothes or remove the remnants of makeup at his temples. He repeatedly fluffed the small accent pillows and rearranged them on the sofa in his sitting area.

Thoughts spun in his head with neither rhyme nor reason. *What if she doesn't recognize me as her husband? What if it's not Tay? This poor lady will think I'm deranged or something. What should I say? How should I start? Can't just jump the gun and dive headlong into the subject. Better not scare her off. There could be a medical reason for all of this.*

Larry opened his wallet and gazed at Taylor's picture. *I don't dare show this photo to Tiffany. She might be fragile and run away out of fear and confusion. I gotta be careful.* His movements quickened. He arranged waiting glasses of champagne on the coffee table for the fourth time. His palms grew moist and quickly grabbed a nearby tissue and wiped the sweat away from his forehead and hands. *I'd better start off slow. Make small talk, see where her head's at.*

A manly knock sounded on the door.

THREE

"CHIEF, YOU READY?" Joe's voice called out from behind the door.

"Yeah, be right there!" Larry exclaimed. Hope and anxiety filled his being. *I hope Tay's with Joe. If she's not, where do I go from here?* He took a deep breath before firmly turning the knob.

Joe stood behind Tiffany. Larry welcomed her and pointed to the waiting sofa. "I'm so *glad* that you took me up on my offer. Seeing you in the audience made my night! Sorry you didn't get to see the first half of the show." He inclined his head with an unspoken request. Obviously, Joe understood his cue and left quietly. Larry said, "I've been thinking all day about this! I can't believe you actually came to see my show! God, I'm blessed!"

"Mr. Davis," she started tentatively. "I don't know what to say to all of this. I don't know you and barely know your music…though, what I heard tonight, I truly enjoyed. I wish I had listened to your songs before."

His eyes popped. "You don't know my music? Never heard of the songs I sang tonight? Not one of them?"

Tiffany bit her bottom lip as color rose from her neck to her face. "I'm sorry. No, I don't listen to music much. By the time I leave the shop every day, there isn't much time left in the evening."

"That's too bad." Larry offered her a crystal flute. "Champagne? It's quite good."

"Thanks. I do know I like the bubbly." Her fingertips grazed his hand. "That's very kind of you."

I love the feel of her touch. "Don't mention it." Larry sat close to her on the sofa. "Now, Tiffany. Do you have a last name?"

"Yes, Bradford. The Countess of Lantham to be exact." She sipped the pale liquid as her eyes met his.

"Sounds impressive." Larry frowned momentarily. "I thought you said you're American. How did you obtain a royal title?"

"Oh, that!" She chuckled lightly. "I don't take much stock in that. It's only a title by marriage."

Larry coughed loudly. Painful visions ran through his mind.

REMEMBER ?   29

Marriage! Holy shit! She's married! How did this happen? Is she or isn't she Taylor? What in hell am I doing?

The trace of her charming smile softened his heart. "I've only been married for less than a year to Clive, officially known as the Earl of Lantham."

"Tiffany, that's interesting, *very* interesting." Larry hid his disappointment. "Please, continue. You're fascinating."

"Not much more to tell." Her manner was casual and nonplus. "I'm married. I work at a dress shop to fill my time. Really, quite ordinary."

Uncomfortable, he quickly changed the subject. "Have you eaten dinner? Would you like to come to my suite for a bite? Nothing fancy, just a light meal."

"I don't know." Tiffany wrung her hands. "I'm married. I noticed you're wearing a wedding band, too. People might talk."

"I'm Larry Davis," he replied with cool confidence. "I know my way around all the obstacle courses. I'm not about to seduce you—I like to get to know my fans. Nothing more than that."

"If you're certain none of this will leak out." Plainly, she had qualms. "Maybe, just this once. Besides, I doubt I'll have another chance to be with a famous singer."

"Great!" Delight lit his eyes and masked his yearning to know her deepest thoughts. "I'll have Joe call my driver."

Larry grabbed his cell phone and relayed the necessary information to Joe.

~~***~~

At midnight in Larry's suite, a bottle of Dom Pérignon champagne chilled in an ice bucket on a nearby table in the sitting room. Tiffany sat on the inviting brown leather sofa. Larry hung up her cashmere coat in the foyer guest closet. His manner was unsure and spoke of inner fears.

He walked into the room and gestured with his arm. "This is home for the next night until I move on to another city. What do you think?"

"It's very plush." Tiffany eyed the sumptuous surroundings. "You must have a wonderful life, all glitter and glam."

"Don't let first impressions fool you!" He shook his head and chuckled. "This is all superficial—means nothing to me. Music

30   *Cynthia B. Ainsworthe*

and love is what matters in life. The connections we make in our lives—that's where the truth is."

"Yes. I agree. You have to admit, all of this adds to the enjoyment," Tiffany stated as she crossed her legs, apparently unaware the hem of her red skirt seductively revealed her shapely thigh. "How could anyone feel sad for very long with such fine living?"

Larry expertly opened the bottle of champagne and poured their glasses. He handed her the crystal flute, fine exquisite bubbles rose to the surface.

He sat next to her, restraining the urge to touch her hand. "It all depends on the cause of sadness. There's pain that can never be softened by material things—pain that runs deep and dark."

"How sad for anyone in such agony. Luckily, I've never suffered such sadness—at least, none that I can recall." Her gaze ran over his face, as if in search for the truth of an unknown question.

"You're very fortunate," he remarked. *Why do I feel you're Tay? This feeling grows stronger with each passing moment.* "I've had my share of heartache." *My heart's aching now.* "So, Tiff, if I may call you that?" She nodded. "Please, tell me more about yourself. I'm truly interested."

"Like I said, I'm married and live a simple life." She smiled and placed her hand on his. *Tiffany's touching my hand! Does she feel a connection? My feelings don't make any sense. Why don't I feel awkward around another woman? If she's not Tay, why don't I feel guilty?* Tiffany continued, "I work, then come home. No ups or downs. A pretty mundane existence."

"Where did you grow up in the States?" *I have to know more.* "Any brothers, sisters, or children?" Larry tilted his head boyishly.

A shadow of confusion rested in her eyes with a slightly furrowed brow. "I don't think I have any family, besides Clive."

Sparks of intrigue darted from his eyes. "What do you mean you *don't think* you have anyone besides Clive? I don't understand." Larry lightly placed his hand on top of hers.

"Just what I said." She sighed deeply, as if glad to unburden her confusion to another. "I know I shouldn't be confiding in someone I just met—but, you seem so warm and genuinely

REMEMBER ?   31

wanting to know everything about me. I feel I can trust you."

"Tiff, you can trust me *completely*." Larry inched closer. He inhaled her lingering fragrance. *She's wearing "Forbidden". She has to be Tay!* "You have my complete confidence as, I hope, I have yours?"

"Of course you do." She laughed lightly. "We Yanks have to stick together."

He eagerly encouraged, "Continue. You were saying…."

"I don't remember anything of my past. Not my parents, if I have any siblings, children, places I've visited, or things I've done." She paused to sip the exquisite tasting liquid. "Everything's a complete blank. If it wasn't for Clive, I wouldn't know my name. I'm very lucky to have him."

Larry's heart sank at these words. *Clive again. How in hell did he get a hold of Taylor? What has he done to her? This is madness! Wait! Maybe she's not Taylor.*

He couldn't resist asking, "How does Clive fit into your life, other than being your husband?"

A knock sounded on the door. The unnamed voice called out, "Room service, sir."

Larry quickly excused himself to open the door. The waiter pushed the cart into the room and quickly set the small table with a white cloth, two silver domed plates, and linen napkins to complete the setting. Before leaving, he asked in a refined British accent, "Sir, is there anything else I may do for you?"

Larry replied softly, "No, thanks. Everything looks great."

"If there is anything you may require, the Royal Arms is at your disposal."

"Yes, yes," he answered hurriedly in an effort to swiftly dismiss the waiter.

Larry walked over to Tiffany with his hand extended. "Dinner is served, Lady Bradford, or is it Lady Lantham? Please do me the honor of assisting you."

"Officially, Lady Lantham." Her small laugh escaped. "Now you sound like Clive. All stuffy and proper."

He adjusted her seat. "Stuffy? That adjective has never described me. I'm one of the most down-to-earth guys in the world—almost anyway." Larry sat opposite her. Taking his napkin he asked, "So, tell me more about how you and Clive came to be."

32   *Cynthia B. Ainsworthe*

"I only know what Clive has told me." She took a sip of the white wine. "We were married on a boat in the Mediterranean somewhere. I guess, it was a short courtship."

Larry lifted the domes from their plates. "Mediterranean? Very romantic." *If she tells me Clive is a Brit singer—I'm gonna freak! This is some kind of nightmare! Tay and I married on a boat in the Mediterranean. Is someone else living my life?* "What else has he told you?"

"Only told me what he knows." She eyed the waiting entrée. "Umm, lemon chicken, rice, and haricots verts. Very nice."

"Glad you approve." Larry noticed her innate flirtatious gaze beneath her long black lashes. "Does this meal mean anything to you?"

"Other than chicken in a lemon sauce?" Surprise colored her words, "Why? Should it?"

He stammered nervously, "No, no, no, no, no, just wanted to make sure I chose something you'd like." *Don't you remember? That's what I served when you and Paul had dinner in my dressing room. She can't remember. What if she's not Tay?*

"What I would really like—is a steak with a load of herb butter, a baked potato with all the trimmings—not to mention a piping hot cup of coffee and a cigarette for a grand finish. Though, I don't remember smoking."

Her food choices and wanting a cigarette sounds like Tay. "If you want, I can order something else up."

"Not at all." She reached over and touched his hand warmly. "I'm not allowed red meat, fats, or smoking anymore." She sighed deeply. "Clive says I've got a heart condition and must stay away from all the bad stuff."

"I hope it's not serious!" Larry's eyes moistened as he remembered his wife's cardiac close calls. *This is too unbelievable! She's got Taylor's health history! How can this be? What in hell is going on here?* "Tiff, what did Clive tell you about how you met and married?"

She began slowly as if relaying a grocery list, "Well, it seems we met while I was in Paris, though I don't remember this— fell in love, and impetuously decided to marry on a boat."

He desperately tried to put the pieces together. *Tay was last seen in Paris. What could've happened to make her lose her memory of us?*

She took a bite of chicken and closed her eyes as if savoring

REMEMBER ?   33

the delicate taste. "I'm told while we honeymooned in Paris, I suffered a nasty fall, went into a coma for a month or so, and…" Tiffany took a swallow of wine to wash down her chicken. "And nothing—I woke up to see Clive's smiling face looking down at me—complete with wedding bands."

"Did you believe him?" Larry replenished her glass.

"I saw no reason not to." Her tongue slipped along the edge of her bottom lip. This didn't go unnoticed. *Tay always did that gesture.* "I can't imagine why Clive would lie to me. From what I can tell, he would have nothing to gain. It's not like I came with a big bank account. I don't even know if I have any assets, and to the best of my knowledge, Clive never said I came from a family that was wealthy, though he certainly is."

Larry probed further, "What does Lord Clive do?" He leaned closer as he hung on her every word.

"He's a famous neurosurgeon. Been published and all of that." She took a forkful of the delicate beans to her mouth, chewed, and swallowed quickly. "I'm very lucky. He's been incredibly patient with me. It can't be easy having a wife who can't remember her past."

"Aren't you curious?" His interest piqued. "Have you tried to put the pieces together?" Larry took a sip of wine. "I know if it were me, I wouldn't stop searching until I could fill in the blanks."

"That may be true for some …" Tiffany wiped her lips as she finished her last mouthful. "But not for me. I'm quite content with Clive's explanations. Besides, he gives me pills to keep my nerves under control."

Larry's eyes widened. *What in hell has he been giving you? Being a doctor, it could be anything!*

Conviction rutted Tiffany's brow. "I completely trust him. He wouldn't give me anything harmful. They're just mild tranquilizers and, of course, my heart medication for high cholesterol."

Larry's lips thinned. *Taylor had high cholesterol. A coincidence is one thing, but this is not to be believed! How can she be anyone else but Tay?*

He rose from his seat. "Shall we have coffee on the sofa? It's decaffeinated."

"The coffee or the sofa?" Tiffany quipped playfully.

"The coffee, of course." *My God, she jokes like Tay.*

34   *Cynthia B. Ainsworthe*

She eased down into the soft's yielding cushion and clearly relaxed in the comfortable surroundings. Tiffany looked about the room while Larry poured their coffee.

"I must say," she started, "I could never warm up to the stuffy British décor. It's so dark and looming. I prefer light lines and touches of gold, though Clive won't let me redecorate."

Larry sat beside her. Their thighs touched. She neither pulled away nor outwardly acknowledged his contact.

"Let me guess." A lock of hair fell to his forehead. "I bet you would like French provincial with crystal drops hanging around?"

Her full lips curled in a flirtatious smile. "Why, yes. How did you know? Have a sixth sense or something?"

"Maybe we met in another lifetime." *This is bizarre.* "Someone who's close to my heart said those very words to me."

"Your wife?" Tiffany asked, almost in a whisper.

Larry extended his arms around her shoulders. "Yes." He felt restrained tears at the back of his eyes. "I've lost her. My life has only been a vacuum of performances. I've never been complete since she's been gone. I keep hoping she'll return one day."

Tiffany leaned toward him. She gently placed her hand on his chest. Her voice was soft and low with compassion. "How very sad for you. I had no idea. Any chance of getting back with her?"

"There's always a chance." Impulsively, Larry lightly kissed her temple. "I'm sorry. I shouldn't've done that. You must think I'm very forward—using my stardom to take advantage."

"Strangely, no." He saw her eyes glisten. "In a very odd way, I feel like we've shared this moment before, as if … I don't know what to call it…a déjà vu thing."

"I feel exactly the same way." His finger ran gently along her chin. "As if we connected before, shared our lives before." *Dare I believe she is Tay? I must! It's all I've got left to hang on to. If she's not Tay … then how can I pursue her further? What a damn mess!*

"I wonder …" Tiffany looked pensively straight ahead to avoid his gaze. "I wonder if you're a relative of mine from my forgotten past."

I am your relative. Tay, can't you see me? I'm your husband. You're my wife. I want things back the way they were! Why in hell did I ever agree to you working freelance for Gérard's? I was a damn fool.

She jarred him from his thoughts. "What do you think? Could you be my relative? You seemed to recognize me in the shop today."

"Yes." His words caught in his throat. "You didn't remind me of a relative. It was someone I love."

"Your lost wife?" Plainly, her curiosity drove her questions.

"Her name is Taylor." His tone cloaked despair.

"Ah, so that's it." Her face assumed a look of discovery. "That's why you wanted me to come to the show and have dinner with you—you thought I was Taylor."

His fingers drew aimless patterns on her palm. "No, that's part of it..." Larry's words came slowly as he looked deep into her eyes. "I was drawn to you. I genuinely wanted to know you. I felt a connection from the start ..." He hesitated a moment, "Tell me, Tiff, did you feel a tugging, too?"

She bit her bottom lip as her brows drew together. "I think so, but I'm not sure. Maybe I felt nothing more than curiosity. I really can't put a name to it." Her tongue lazily moistened her lips as her fingers interlaced his and gently gave a squeeze. "I don't want to bring up questions about my past or my feelings. If ... if I do, it might destroy my world as I know it. I can't risk that. I can't risk losing Clive. I know he loves me, and that's all I have to hang on to."

He drew her closer. "But, Tiff, if you asked all those hard questions—the answers you find, could bring such joy to your life and a feeling of completeness."

She looked down at her wedding band with a sad and pensive expression. "That may be true. Right now, I'm content with my life now. I've picked up the pieces, and I don't want to go back. I must concentrate on my future."

"Your future with Clive?" Larry searched her heart as he gazed into her eyes.

"Yes, Lar." She looked startled by her own words. "Sorry, I didn't mean to be so familiar. I meant to say 'Mr. Davis' or 'Larry' at the very least."

She automatically called me "Lar." Like Tay did. "'Lar' sounds perfect to my ears. It's a nickname I've grown up with all my life."

36   *Cynthia B. Ainsworthe*

Big Ben rang out three chimes in the London mist reminding her of the time.

"Mr. Davis—" she began.

"Please, call me 'Lar,'" he requested with adoring eyes.

"Lar, I've got to go. I had no idea how late it was." She grabbed her red purse from the coffee table. "Clive must be in a stew by now. I forgot to take my cell so he could call me. It's a wonder he hasn't called the police—what am I saying? Maybe he has."

She stood up to leave. Larry quickly followed. At the door, he helped Tiffany with her coat.

"I can have my car drive you home," he offered. *Then I'll find out where you live.*

"Don't bother. A cab is better for me." Tiffany smiled warmly as she held his hand for a long moment. "Your driver would just raise unnecessary questions from Clive." She sighed with a tinge of regret. "He didn't want me coming to your concert anyway. It wasn't easy for me to get free to see you."

He stepped closer and placed his hands on her shoulders. Their bodies nearly touched. His restraint was close to breaking.

Larry nervously cleared his throat. "Tiff, I have another ticket for tomorrow night's performance … if you would like to see it again, see me again …. You could see the entire show this time."

"That's a very nice offer." Her brow furrowed and her eyes clouded for a moment. "I think I'd better pass. It's been a wonderful evening. You've given me a beautiful new memory I can share with the girls at the shop."

"Please reconsider," he implored. "It would make me so happy…and it will be my last night in London before I move on to Glasgow."

"Sorry," Tiffany replied quietly. "Give that ticket to another fan who knows all your songs."

"Never," Larry replied with soft determination. "The seat is yours—a special seat for Lady Bradford, the Countess of Lantham."

Her shy smile warmed his heart. "Truly, I don't dare. I can't."

"If you won't come to my show again, can I give you a parting gift?" His blue eyes combed her face with heartfelt love.

REMEMBER ?   37

"Yes, I guess that would be all right." Her words filled his hopes.

Without hesitation, Larry embraced her closely and relished the feel of her body next to his. Her fragrance intoxicated him. He placed a tender loving kiss on her cheek.

A smile of embarrassment brightened her twinkling eyes. Her gaze wandered about his face.

"Lar, I liked that very much." She searched his eyes. "I shouldn't've liked your kiss—but, I did. Please don't think ill of me."

"Think bad of you?" He threw his head back with a laugh. "Not a chance. You're a wonderful and vibrant woman, who's down to earth with a kind heart." He tried again."Now, won't you reconsider? Come to my last London show tomorrow night?"

She raised her eyebrows playfully. "I really don't see how I can. But," she made a face and thought for a second, "if I can, then I will."

"Fantastic!" Larry's voice rang with joy. "I'll be looking for you."

"I really need to be going. It's late. I make no promises. I probably won't be able to attend tomorrow's show."

"Can't blame a guy for hoping." *Please find a way.*

He quickly grabbed the treasured ticket from his shirt pocket and pressed it into her hand. Tiffany quietly left his suite.

Larry was left with his thoughts—thoughts that added to his confusion. *Tiffany is Taylor. There are too many similarities for her not to be.* He shuddered. *If she's not Tay and merely has this uncanny resemblance to her, then if I get involved, it will be the same as when I was seeing Tay when she was still married to Paul.* His rambling steps kept in time with his rambling thoughts. *But this time, it could be worse. I'm still married and in love with Taylor! If Tiffany is truly who she says she is, then I could end up cheating on Tay! How am I ever gonna get at the truth? Somehow, I feel Tiff has the key—but the key to what?*

FOUR

THE MUTED LIGHT from the street lamps faded into the surrounding darkness as Tiffany gingerly opened the front door of their townhouse and stopped to listen. No sound came from the upstairs bedroom. She fervently hoped Clive slept soundly in bed, and prayed Rodney, their brown and white Cavalier King Charles spaniel, wouldn't come running down the stairs to greet her. She closed the door carefully and, with shoes in hand, tiptoed on the foyer's cold marble floor, hardly daring to breathe. As she passed the library's doorway on the right, a looming voice called out to her.

"The concert lasted a bit long, don't you think?"

The clock chimed four from the fireplace mantle.

Her stomach clenched. "Is that you, Clive? You startled me." Her voice sounded tenuous. She squinted to see the form sitting in a chair outlined by dim moonlight.

"I stopped at a local pub after the show," she lied with restrained nervousness. "Hailing a cab wasn't easy."

"Oh, that ought to make a right good read for the morning tabloids! One can see the headlines now." Rodney jumped off his lap as he leaned forward and raised his voice. "'The Countess of Lantham carousing in a pub without her husband!' Don't you have an ounce of decorum running through you?"

She entered the library. "Don't worry, there wasn't anyone who gave me the slightest attention. The family name will remain intact."

He jumped from his chair with raised fists as he approached her.

"I remember telling you not to go to that ruddy concert." He grabbed her shoulders firmly and snarled, "Why did you disobey me?" His eyes blazed.

"Clive, let go of me." She struggled against his grasp. "You're hurting me."

"I'll ask you again." His grip grew firmer. "Why did you go against my wishes?"

She wiggled away from his confining hands. "I'm my own

REMEMBER ?   39

person. What makes you think you can tell me what to do? I have a mind of my own. and it was just a concert. Nothing to get riled about!"

"Don't take that insolent tone with me!" His angry eyes narrowed. His jaw twitched with seething emotion. "You need to be reminded who runs this house and who you belong to!"

He seized her upper arms more firmly. His fingertips dug deep into her soft flesh.

Tiffany shouted, "Clive, let go! You're hurting me!"

He didn't obey. "You go where I say and do what I tell you!" he exclaimed though clenched teeth and eyes incensed with contempt.

Clive kissed her fully on the mouth as he roughly embraced her. Clearly, his anger morphed to fiery passion and control. Overcome by his strength, she gave way to his desire and nearly tumbled to the rough carpeted floor. He quickly removed her hindering panties as he sought his own satisfaction. His touch was ardent and hungry. It was obvious to her that his feelings ran deep, with insecurity at the core. She didn't resist or respond with passion. Her reaction was that of a warm corpse.

Afterwards, he stood up without uttering a sound and went to his bedroom, leaving Tiffany lying there alone to absorb his unspoken message—a message that raised more questions in her mind.

~~***~~

Tiffany broke the long silence at the breakfast table. "Clive, why were you so rough with me last night? You hurt me. You've never treated me like that before. You've always been loving and understanding."

"I told you before—you stepped out of line and needed to be reminded of your place." His words were controlled with an icy calmness.

"I'm your wife, not a servant. I'm your equal." Tiffany spoke softly with a hurt tone.

"It seems to me, my pet, there's too much bloody Yank in you." He sighed heavily as if he was explaining simple facts to a child. "*You* are Lady Lantham, and it doesn't do for royalty— no matter what the rank—to be seen at night unescorted, in particular without his lordship! As far as being my equal—one

40   *Cynthia B. Ainsworthe*

doesn't see any blue blood flowing through your veins. It's because of our marriage that you have the privilege to be referred as *Lady Lantham*."

Tiffany pushed the food around on her plate. His words burned in her mind.

Clive took a bite of his kippers. "Furthermore, I won't tolerate this outrageous behavior again. What do you want to do? Make me the laughing stock at the Kings Club? One has a reputation at stake."

Tiffany looked sincere. "Who am I? I have so many unanswered questions about my previous life."

He remained aloof. "You're who I say you are."

"You can't make up a past for me," she retorted firmly while noticing his hardened expression.

"I'm not making up a 'past' for you, as you call it. I'm merely telling you what I know before your dreadful fall on our honeymoon in Paris." He shifted uneasily in his seat. "*You* were the one who told me your brief history."

"Clive, tell me again," she pleaded, "maybe it will help with my memory."

He threw his napkin onto the table with vexation. "All right. This is the last time. I'm tired of repeating myself." A stony, cold look came over his face. "As I said before. We met in Paris. You told me you were there on business from the United States, and that you had no family and were raised as an orphan. We fell in love immediately, got married on a boat off the south of France, toured the Riviera, and continued the last days of our honeymoon in Paris. You took a nasty fall and suffered a coma. I brought you back to London. You woke up without any memory."

"Clive, you make it sound all so simple," she remarked softly.

"It is simple." He took a sip of hot tea and stared at Tiffany's finger drawing an imaginary design on the tabletop. "Why do you Yanks always have to make things so complicated?"

"What was my name before we got married?" She studied his expression in search of the truth.

"Tiffany Clayton or Andrews or whatever." He avoided her gaze. "What does it matter? I don't remember your blasted last name. You're Lady Lantham now, so what of it?"

"My name is an important part of my past—of who I was."

REMEMBER ?   41

She fostered a hunger to know more. "Isn't my name on our marriage certificate?"

"Look, Tiffany." He spoke softly as if to ease her concern. "Yes, it is. I have the document locked away safe at the club." He sighed deeply and said with condescension, "I fully understand how you want to know more about your previous life. You need to give your recovery time, time to heal. It's only been a little over sixteen months since you came out of the coma. Some people never completely recover. Be happy with the life we share." He leaned forward on his elbows. "I must say, one could have ended up worse than being Lady Lantham."

"But, Clive, I—"

He cut her off, "What I think, my pet, is you need a stronger dose of your medication. All these senseless questions are proof of that! Remember, I'm not only your husband, but your doctor. I know what's best for you."

"Do you really?" Doubt filled her eyes.

"Of course I do." His snide smile sickened.

He rose from the table, presumably to leave for the Kings Club.

Tiffany interrupted his movement when she asked, "I thought it was unethical for a doctor to treat members of his own family."

"That only applies to the States," he quickly retorted. "Now, be a dear and take your medicine. Elizabeth has it waiting for you. I'll adjust your dosage tomorrow."

"Clive, why don't you give me the medicine directly instead of having a servant do that? After all, you *are* my doctor." Tiffany sported a perplexed look.

"Always questions coming from you!" He walked over to her shaking his head, and chuckled lightly. "Elizabeth has my complete instructions and confidence. Doctors don't *dispense* medicine, we *prescribe* it. The way your memory has been lately—you might forget to take the tablets."

Before Tiffany was able to utter another word, Clive left the room. He grabbed his coat and umbrella as he headed out.

Elizabeth entered the dining room. She held a silver tray laid with a small plate that held two white tablets.

"If I may, milady, I have your medicine. Lord Lantham was

42 Cynthia B. Ainsworthe

very specific with his instructions." Her manner was sweet and innocent.

Tiffany looked at Elizabeth's kind young face, gentle blue eyes, and her blonde hair pulled back to reveal a fair porcelain-like complexion. She took the tablets from the plate and held them between her fingers. She scrutinized the pills looking for any distinguishing marks. She found none. *I wonder why these pills don't have pharmaceutical markings. Why can't I take these with my heart medicine in the evening?*

"Please, milady." Elizabeth broke her train of thought. "His lordship was very strict in his direction. You need to take your medicine."

"I will." Tiffany didn't put the pill to her mouth. "I'll take it after I finish breakfast. You can go now."

"I'm sorry. I can't." The servant explained, "Lord Lantham told me this morning and instructed that I must watch you take your medicine. He's afraid you might forget."

"Ridiculous!" Tiffany exclaimed. "It's my past I can't remember—not the present."

"Yes, milady." The girl hesitated. "Milord said he was not certain you would remember to swallow the tablet." Elizabeth made a slight face. "Please, milady. I don't want to get into any trouble—I don't want to make milord angry and risk losing my position. I enjoy being in service."

Why are these pills so damn important? It's not my heart medicine. Can I believe Clive? Do I really have a heart condition? She blew her questions aside. *Silly of me. He loves me and wouldn't do anything to cause me harm. Guess Clive is right. I do need to take these pills. I always feel calmer when I take them.*

Tiffany put the tablets in her mouth and promptly washed them down with a large swallow of water. Elizabeth sighed and sported a look of relief.

"Right, then," the servant remarked sweetly, "you'll feel much better and less nervous in a little while."

"Elizabeth." Tiffany furrowed her brow. "I wasn't nervous before."

"Well then, it will keep you calm," she answered. "Karen Edwards called while you were taking breakfast. I told her you were indisposed, and I would give you the message. Here's the number, milady." The servant reached into her pocket and produced a piece of paper with Karen's cell number scribbled on it.

Tiffany took the wrinkled paper and pondered, *What could be so important that Karen would call me at home? She's never done that before—always been afraid to approach me at my residence because of my ladyship status. I'm not supposed to be working at the shop today, or is Clive right about my memory? Did I forget to show up to work? This must be important!*

FIVE

"HELLO, KAREN," TIFFANY said with concern, "is there anything wrong? I didn't forget to come to the shop, did I?"

"No. It's Saturday." She noted slight amazement from Karen's voice. "Why do you ask?"

"Clive thinks my memory might be slipping…" Tiffany screwed her face with worry. "I thought I'd forgotten to come to the shop."

"That's not why I'm ringing you up," she answered. "Have you or Clive seen the morning paper?"

"No. We haven't." Her forehead creased with worry. "Why do you ask?"

"There's pictures of you and Larry Davis entering his hotel, and more of you leaving at three thirty in the morning! You're on the front page of every tabloid!" Karen's voice nearly rang with joy. "Very sensational, if you ask me!"

"Oh my God, no!" Tiffany's eyes widened in disbelief. "I cringe to think how Clive will react to all of this. He already gave me a lecture over breakfast about me coming home so late."

"Tiff, I don't want to tell you everything I've read over the phone," Karen explained. "Let's meet at the Hare and Hound in thirty minutes."

"Good idea," Tiffany sighed. "I need to get a full picture of the damage." *Why on earth did I ever go to his hotel? What a stupid decision!*

~~***~~

In his suite, Larry sat at the small table as he enjoyed his morning tea. Joe relaxed in a chair opposite. A vast array of papers rested on the centerpiece. Joe held a half-eaten scone slathered with Devonshire cream and jelly in his left hand and a newspaper in his right. Morning sunlight dappled a bright pattern on the carpet.

"Chief, take a look at this!" Joe handed the tabloid to him.

"What?" Larry asked with a broad smile. "Did I get a good review from last night's performance?"

REMEMBER ?   45

"Yeah, the review was great!" Joe's voice bounded with both excitement and concern. "But read about you and Tiffany Bradford! They're askin' if you two are lovers or anythin'!"

"What!" Larry's eyes frantically searched for the article. "Joe, *nothing* happened between us last night—absolutely nothing!"

"Well, that's not how the newsboys see it." Joe chuckled. "Read on."

The singer remained quiet as he absorbed every word. Images of possible repercussions filled his brain. *What will Tiffany think about this? Hell, what will her husband think? I never wanted to cause her trouble! My curiosity has really created a hornet's nest!*

After a few moments, Joe broke the silence. "Lar, how are y' gonna do damage control? Any ideas?"

"Damned if I know." His face hardened with concern. He stood up from the table and started pacing the floor. "Maybe Tiffany, Clive, or both haven't seen the paper or don't even read the news. If they have, maybe they'll throw it off as sensationalism."

"Yeah, right!" Joe responded, "Don't count on that one!" He persisted, "So, Lar. What did you and Lady Lantham talk about?" He snickered. "Some sales at Harrods? The goin' price of sheets these days?"

Larry didn't appreciate Joe's humor. "Stop it right now! She's a lady, and I was a gentleman." His pacing became faster as his monologue took over. "We talked about a lot of things …. Found out she has no memory of her past, is married to a doctor, has some sort of heart condition, and he's feeding these pills to her for a nervous condition."

"Sounds a bit mysterious if you ask me." Joe took a bite of his scone with a look as if deep in thought. "If you get involved with Tiffany, you'll be cheatin' on Taylor."

"Not if Tiffany *is* Taylor!" Lar exclaimed with wide eyes. "I can't be cheating on my wife *with* my wife."

"Lar, you don't know Tiffany is Taylor." Joe took a fatherly tone, "Look, all you know about this woman is she looks like your lost wife—that's where the similarity ends! I'm not gonna support you in this Tiffany thing. If I hadn't encouraged you to see Taylor in the first place, Paul wouldn't be gone. I'm not gonna make that mistake twice!"

"Joe, I don't wanna hear it!" Larry stopped short. Hands on

46   *Cynthia B. Ainsworthe*

hips emphasized his words. "I've been living with that guilt, too! I liked Paul. Such a wonderful person—kind and genuine."

"Sorry, Chief." Joe hunched his shoulders. "I only wanted you to know how I felt. Are you ready to take the chance of cheatin' on Tay?"

"When I'm with Tiffany, talking with her, I don't feel as if I would be cheating if I made love to her. I have this nagging sensation that Tiff *is* Tay." Larry looked out the window, as if the answer rested on the London rooftops. "I can't shake it. It's something I know in my heart—but I don't know why I know."

"Lar, you're imaginin' stuff you *want* to believe—not the truth." Joe took a sip of coffee and studied Larry's reaction.

"Guess she won't be coming to the show tonight." Despondency colored his words.

"You gave her another ticket?" Joe sat straighter in his chair.

"Yeah, and a backstage pass, too." His voice trailed off into space. "Just the same, Joe. I want you to be on the lookout for her. This is my last London performance before Glasgow."

"Whatever you say, Lar," Joe replied flatly. "But, I still think you're barkin' up the wrong tree."

~~***~~

Tiffany scurried into the pub. She spotted Karen in the far corner sipping a cup of tea with an expression of exited concern. Patrons glanced at Countess Lantham, then quickly turned their heads and whispered in hushed tones of her suspected liaison with the famous American entertainer. She slid onto a seat beside Karen.

Without letting Tiffany speak, Karen started. "Tell me everything. I want all the bloody details! Did you and Larry do the nasty?"

"No." *Why would Karen think such a thing?* She breathed deeply. "I went to the concert, even though Clive didn't approve, then to Larry's hotel where we had a very nice conversation. There was nothing out of the way with his actions. Larry was a complete gentleman. I enjoyed his company so much that time slipped away, and I left later than I should have."

Karen probed, "You mean … he didn't act romantic? Go on will y'! I can't believe that hunk of American masculinity didn't take a fancy to *you!*"

REMEMBER ?   47

"If he did," Tiffany answered softly, "then I didn't sense it." She paused, "Now, tell me about the tabloids. How bad does it look?"

"Ruddy bad. Like I said on the phone, your picture is all over the place—going in his hotel with him and then leaving alone." Karen's eyes narrowed with worry. "How are you gonna handle Clive? I imagine he'll be boilin' like a tea kettle."

"I haven't figured that one out yet," Tiffany answered pensively. "After the greeting he gave me last night, I shudder to think how he'll act when he comes home from the club today."

"It was that bad? Was there a row then?"

Tiffany's words came in a near whisper, "Clive was not happy."

A waiter stood at her elbow. She quickly gave her order for coffee with cream and sugar. After he left, Tiffany's jaw tensed with apprehension. "He quickly let me know he was in charge and reminded me that I had disobeyed him."

"How did he do that?" Her friend listened closely.

Tiffany's eyes widened. "Clive took me on the library rug when I came home, then gave me a verbal lashing this morning."

"Hot passion!" Karen licked her lips. "Sounds like Clive doesn't like a man takin' a fancy to his bird."

"I didn't appreciate it—not one bit." Tiffany looked absently toward the crowded tables. "I can do without that form of affection. He doesn't own me."

"Ah, that's the Yank in you coming out." Karen said with aplomb, "You forget that you're *Tiffany Bradford, The Countess of Lantham*, and with that title comes responsibility."

"Now you're sounding like Clive." Tiffany looked at her friend with bewilderment. "Whose friend are you? Mine or Clive's?"

"I'm yours, of course." She chuckled. "Just reminding you of the culture you married into."

"Well, don't." Tiffany twisted her napkin.

The server placed Tiffany's coffee on the table, then left. She took a sip of the steaming brew. "Clive hammered that point home quite sufficiently."

"If you didn't do that Larry bloke, did you at least get his

48   *Cynthia B. Ainsworthe*

autograph?" Her friend sported a devilish look.

"Better than that." Tiffany stirred her coffee quickly, as if the mere thought of Larry created inner excitement. "He gave me another ticket to his show tonight and another backstage pass."

"That's bloody fantastic!" Karen reacted as if she lived vicariously through her friend's experiences. "You're going aren't you?"

"I don't know yet. Larry wants to see me again one last time before he moves on to Glasgow." Her eyes took on a dreamy expression. "He seems so genuine, caring, and compassionate. There's something about that man, just draws me in—as if I've known him somewhere before. I can't explain it. Larry gets to me, somehow."

Karen grinned. "I can. It's his great bum and those blue eyes. I wouldn't think twice before having him in my knickers."

Tiffany spoke as if transported to another place in time. "Kar, I don't see him that way. It's a deeper feeling I can't put into words …. A connection of some kind."

"Tiff, if you ever need a stand-in for that connection you talk about—I'm your girl." Her friend laughed softly. "I'll connect with him anytime. If I have him, I might even start to like his music. If I were you, I'd go to that ruddy concert. I say, to hell with Clive and all his stuffy protocol. You won't get another chance like this."

Easy for you to say. Kar, you don't know how Clive hurt my feelings.

Her friend continued, "It's a once in a lifetime experience. Blimey, he's got them queued up in the streets waiting to get a glimpse and hoping to see him leaves his hotel."

Tiffany leaned forward on her elbows. "If I *do* decide to go tonight, there will be hell to pay when I come home—and hell's name is Clive."

~~***~~

Clive sat in an overstuffed wingback dark brown leather chair in the club's common room. He felt at home here with the comfortably masculine décor of forest green leather sofas and chairs positioned throughout the sitting area. He liked the way the deeply hued Persian carpet in shades of burgundy muted the footsteps of the members.

Soft, well-modulated conversations, just above a whisper, provided an ambient background hum. Frequently, other club

REMEMBER ?   49

members glanced at him, but none had ventured forth for any conversation. Small smiles escaped from the corners of distinguished mouths when they looked in his direction. *What's so funny with my appearance? Am I wearing the wrong tie with my waistcoat?*

His longtime, cousin-in-law, and business associate, Alistair Hollingsworth, the Duke of Steffenfordshire, approached and pulled his chair closer. He hunched his shoulders in anticipation of striking up a conversation.

Clive looked up and gave a small reserved smile. "I'm glad you don't feel I've broken one of the social commandments." He sighed. "If I didn't know better, from the reception I've received, one would think there was a picture of me running naked along the Thames in the morning paper."

"Funny you should put it that way, ol' chap." Alistair brushed away the strands of gray flecked dark brown hair from his forehead. "Have you seen the morning news?"

"No. Not yet. Why do you ask?" Clive's posture straightened with concern.

"I'll put this as gently as one can." His voice lowered an octave, "The Countess of Lantham is on the front page—pictures of her going into Larry Davis' hotel with him, and she was snapped leaving alone around three thirty this morning."

Clive gritted his teeth. His fingers dug deeply into the arms of his chair. He let his friend continue.

"All the chaps are talking about her little indiscretion." Alistair searched Clive's face. "I didn't know quite what to say to them. I did my best, ol' man. Remarked it might have to do with some charity function Tiffany is involved in."

"Yes. Quite right." Clive's voice took on a steely edge. "It was charity all right. A bloody charity called *Tiffany Bradford*. One wonders what type of donation he made to her!"

Alistair's black eyes widened with disbelief. "You don't mean to say you think her and Mr. Davis—"

"I don't know what to think." Disdain hardened Clive's face. The crease from his nose to his mouth deepened while his nostrils flared. "Lady Lantham will need a drastic adjustment to her medication."

"Ol' man, are you giving her that experimental drug we're working on for MI6?" Alistair's expression spoke of horrified

50   *Cynthia B. Ainsworthe*

and devastating amazement. "Say it's not so. We haven't cleared it for human trials."

"Shush. Keep your voice down." Clive glanced around the room to check for possible eavesdroppers. "I didn't say I did. Since her recovery from that coma, she hasn't been herself. I just give her something for her nerves. A bit of diazepam now and again—keeps her on an even keel."

"Glad to hear it. You had me going there for a minute." He let out a relieved sigh.

"What type of man do you take me for?" Clive asked indignantly "I have my principles. Besides, I would never do anything to harm Tiffany."

Alistair offered his apology, "I should have never doubted your integrity."

"Now, I have to figure out how to subdue this bloody news item." Clive's expression turned sinister. "She could ruin my career and my standing within the family." His lips thinned with a granite determination. "No woman, not even Countess Lantham, will ruin things for me."

"Sooner or later," his friend advised, "the Palace will be contacting you. She won't be happy with the news. At least you've got a bloodline to her—that may give you some insulation. It's not like they can disown you."

"Maybe not. But they can make it ruddy uncomfortable for me." Clive interlaced his fingers as he stared down at the carpet. "They haven't gotten over the fact that I married a commoner—and a Yank at that!" He sighed, then muttered, "My God, man, it's not like I'm the next in line to the throne— I'm so far removed from that esteemed position—five hundred relatives would have to die off before it would be my turn."

Alistair patted his good friend on the shoulder with unspoken empathy. "Give it time. This will blow over. The fickled press will strike in someone else's garden in a few days."

Clive looked up at his friend and colleague. "I hope you're right." *Tiffany needs to be dealt with. She has caused me irreparable damage. She can't go on with her foolish actions!*

SIX

TIFFANY ASKED THE cabbie to take the long way home from the Hare and Hound. She didn't want Elizabeth encroaching on her solitude and needed time to mull over everything Karen had said, as well as Clive's violent reaction, and his coldness at breakfast. Deep in the pit of her stomach came the nagging feeling of a strong attraction for a man she barely knew.

On impulse, she instructed the driver to drop her off at Green Park on Piccadilly across from Mayfair. Tiffany tipped him and didn't look at his face as she stepped onto the sidewalk. Thoughts pounded her brain like relentless drops of water in Chinese torture.

Why do I feel this confusion? What's wrong with me? I think I love Clive. How could I not? After all, I did marry him. I don't think I'd marry a man I didn't love. I'm so tired of not having a past. I'm nothing more than those mannequins I dress in the shop window. The only identity I have is what Clive tells me.

Harsh crunch of gravel echoed her uneasiness as she walked down a path lined with evergreen scrubs. A pleasant, wandering path that reflected her own meandering thoughts.

Why do I feel such a strong attraction for this man? I knew nothing of him before our brief encounter in the shop. Still, his magnetism is electric and seems so familiar to me. Could we have shared our lives in another lifetime—if such a thing is possible?

The skies clouded. Raindrops started falling gently. Tiffany opened her umbrella and strolled back to the park entrance. The wind grew colder. She wished she'd taken her scarf as Elizabeth had advised. She turned up her collar to stave off the cruel wind and held her head downward to avert the coldness that seeped to her core—a coldness she dreaded as much as the cold stare Clive would give her when she misspoke at a social event. To prolong the inevitable meeting with her husband, Tiffany chose to walk the rest of the way to their Mayfair townhouse. *I can only imagine how he'll react when he comes home from the club. If I'm lucky, he'll merely give me the silent treatment.* Her

52   *Cynthia B. Ainsworthe*

thoughts took a step backward. *No, I won't be that lucky. Clive will let me have it with both ugly barrels. Angry or not, I won't let him treat me like he did last night! Never again will I accept his hostile advances. Sex should be tender and loving—not used as a club for submission.*

Tiffany rounded the corner. Her steps slowed as she arrived at the front door. A heavy breath escaped. She stared at the key before inserting it into the lock. Her hand warily turned the knob. Sound of rolling tumblers reflected the tight nervous rumbling in her stomach. *Is he home? All I hear is Rodney's scampering feet.* Another deep breath came from her as she heard the creaking of the opening door. No looming voice greeted her, only the whimpering cries of Rodney wanting attention. He sat by her feet with energetic and loving eyes accompanied by a happily wagging tail. From the back of the house came the sound of a blender in the kitchen. The whirring stopped and was replaced by soft, hurried footsteps that grew louder.

Elizabeth greeted her, "Hello, milady. I expected you home sooner than this. The hour is growing late, and I was concerned about you."

"I decided to take a walk in the park—needed to think a bit." Tiffany removed her coat and handed the garment with her umbrella to the servant. "Is Clive home?"

"Yes, milady. Lord Lantham is waiting for you upstairs." Elizabeth lifted her head in the direction of the staircase.

"I see." Tiffany bit her bottom lip. Her brow wrinkled. "Well, I might as well get up there. No sense in prolonging the agony."

"Milady, if I may." Elizabeth spoke with a kind hesitancy as she lightly touched her mistress' hand. "I don't think milord is in very good spirits. He hasn't spoken one word since he came home. Didn't even thank me for the tea and biscuits."

"Don't worry. I can handle him." Tiffany started up the stairs, then turned toward the young girl. "If you hear anything being thrown about, I want you to call the police."

"Are you certain, milady?" Elizabeth looked simultaneously surprised and concerned. "Lord Lantham has never been like that in the past."

"Yes. I'm very sure." Tiffany looked up toward the staircase landing with an ominous feeling. "He's never had a wife who's embarrassed him before. Heaven only knows what his reaction

REMEMBER ? 53

will be."

"Yes, milady. As you like," the servant replied softly.

~~***~~

Clive sat in the velvet upholstered chair by the roaring bedroom fireplace He glared at the flickering, dancing flames that matched the anger in his eyes. He clearly heard Tiffany's entrance but didn't acknowledge her presence.

She stood rigid at the doorway before tentatively taking a step closer. The profile of his strongly set jaw and firm grip on a glass of scotch sent shivers down her spine. Her stomach tightened. Tiffany inhaled deeply to muster courage. She took a few cautious steps toward him. Clive continued to stare at the flickering flames. Crackling wood was the only sound. Her heart pounded in her ears.

"Clive, you're so quiet," Countess Lantham began softly. "Is there anything bothering you?"

He remained silent. His eyes narrowed with contempt.

"Do you want to talk about it?" she probed further.

Clive spoke with a quiet, despotic control. "Talking can't repair the bloody damage you've done."

"I don't understand," she answered in a near whisper. Her heart beat faster. Flashes of his outburst the night before pierced her brain.

"One isn't surprised—you not coming from a proper upbringing," he curtly replied.

"Clive, why do you hurt me at every turn?" Tiffany bit her bottom lip. Confusion swept over her face. "I don't know anything of my past."

"Really?" He turned his head to face her. "Going to see that Yank singer against my wishes didn't jog a thought or two from your single brain cell?" Clive's coldness made her inwardly shudder.

"No. I had no return of my memory." She took two more steps with a stiff posture that belied inner tremors. "It was a nice evening, that's all."

"My pet, that's not what the papers are blasting!" Clive's voice raised an octave as he sat on the edge of his seat. "A very compromising situation you've put me in. Countess Lantham seen with Larry Davis entering his hotel and then leaving alone at three thirty in the morning!"

Tiffany sat down timidly on the chair opposite him. She took a deep breath in preparation to answer.

Clive cut her off. "Tiffany, what the hell were you thinking? Or weren't you thinking?"

"It was just an innocent visit." She tried to sound confident as she interlaced her fingers in her lap.

"Innocent, you say?" Clive's fist tightened around his glass. "I, and the entire bloody United Kingdom, believe my wife is having a tryst with that damn Yank singer."

A flushed color came to his face. With teeth clenched, his breath grew rapid. The glass in his left hand shattered loudly and the alcoholic contents along with fragments of glass and blood, splattered to the floor. Tiffany stared wide-eyed. She couldn't believe it when Clive ignored his self-inflicted injury.

"Clive, you're hurt!" she exclaimed. "Let me help you."

"I want no help from you! My God, woman, I've had a taste of your help," he shouted. He retrieved a handkerchief from his pocket and wrapped it around the oozing wound. "Hear me, and hear me good—I absolutely forbid you to have anything to do with Larry Davis!"

"Clive, I can't—no, I won't obey you!" Tiffany retorted. "You are not my father! I have my own mind and my own thoughts!"

"Well, not for long if I have anything to say about it!" He nearly lost further control.

Tiffany's anger met his. "And what's that supposed to mean, if I may ask?"

"You'll find out soon enough, soon enough." He sneered and stomped out of the room. Blood drops followed on the floor.

~~***~~

Larry sat in his dressing room, tapping his fingers nervously on the arm of his chair as the makeup girl patted on the last touches of finishing powder. He repeatedly glanced at his watch in eager anticipation. Joe sat in a chair to one side and watched Larry's reflection in the mirror.

"Chief, y' gotta get a hold of yourself," Joe commented.

"Yeah, I hear y'." Larry adjusted his seat. "I hope to hell Tiffany will show up tonight—though, after those photos in the paper, I suppose that's a long shot."

REMEMBER ?   55

"That's beyond a long shot," Joe agreed knowingly. "You might've screwed up ever seein' her again—could've got her in big trouble with her ol' man. Bet there were more than a few hot words between the two of 'em."

"Exactly! Why was I so stupid to keep her so late?" Larry's fingers tightened around the arms of his chair. His clear blue eyes held a twinge of fear.

Joe answered offhandedly, "You thought she was Taylor."

"She *is* Taylor. I'm certain of it," Larry affirmed.

"Yeah, right." Joe gave a disbelieving glance.

The dressing room door opened abruptly and Robby said, "Boss, we're at ten."

Larry glanced in his direction. "Got it. I'll be on stage in five."

Swiftly, he removed the paper drape that surrounded his shoulders and left the room with Joe not far behind. In the wings, a stagehand waited with microphone in hand. Larry quickly took it without a look or word. His entire focus was on one woman—Taylor, who he believed with the utmost certainty, was now known as Tiffany.

The singer took two deep breaths as the fanfare began. Once more the familiar refrain echoed in his ears as the crowd chanted, "Larry, Larry, Larry!" Under different circumstances, this would have been an added source of energy, instead, this adulation heightened his hopes that his lost love would go against all obstacles and be in the center seat of the first row. Each minute dragged on like an hour for him as he waited for his cue.

Larry stood on his mark with a wide and forceful stance as he waited for the stage manager to point in his direction. The orchestra began the overture to his opening number. A translucent smoke screen veiled his entrance as a backlight illuminated his powerful outline and obscured his features. The curtain slowly rose to reveal the audience's cherished performer. With outstretched arms and mic in hand, Larry walked powerfully with deliberate steps to center stage. This was his realm. He cherished every blissful moment. The audience was his and he knew it. He started one of his well-known upbeat songs that burst with energy and life, and sang lyrics of joy and hope. He smoothly went into a ballad of

56   *Cynthia B. Ainsworthe*

unrequited love.

As his eyes adjusted to the bright lights, Larry spotted an attractive woman scurrying to the front row to sit in the center seat. He motioned for the orchestra to continue the vamp of the next song.

He began a monologue to the audience, "Welcome everyone! It's great to be here in the UK again. You all make me feel so loved."

Applause and approving cheers rang out in response.

"As you know ..." His eyes focused on the dark haired woman. A broad smile immediately emerged. "This is my last show before moving on to Glasgow, and I have a few surprises for my UK fans."

More cheers rang out.

"Great! You like that idea!" Larry chuckled. "So sit back, relax, and enjoy the show. If you feel like singing along—go right ahead!"

He nodded to his music director, Tom Anderson.

The lights dimmed to one center bright light. Larry began "Lost in the Feeling." His sole focus was on the woman in the center seat of the first row—Tiffany, the woman he had craved for over a year. She was so close and yet so far away from sharing his life. Larry sang the words with emotion from his soul. He desperately wanted her to hear his unspoken message. *Taylor, it's me, your husband. Why don't you recognize me? What has happened to you?*

Larry began the second chorus. Tiffany mouthed the words as if in recognition of some kind. He noticed this and repeated the chorus. Her eyes sparkled briefly, giving the hint of a glimmer of lost memory, but then quickly faded. His focus remained on her face, drinking every facet of her beauty. By the end of the song, she stood up, which resulted in others doing the same. A standing ovation was his reward for a superb delivery of gut-wrenching emotion coming from the depths of his heart and soul.

As the concert continued, the famous singer poured his deepest inner love and feelings into every lyric, musical phrase, and crescendo. There wasn't an audience member untouched by his interpretation of love and longing. All felt that he was singing to them alone—the one special person in his life—such was his talent to captivate his fans. A talent he had honed early in his career and kept his popularity steadfast in the hearts of millions. Larry's broad and dynamic stride across the stage emphasized his command of the crowd, as well as his confidence and ownership of his musical style.

Midway through the concert, Larry sang "Love on the Line." A song that spoke joyously of love found and the irresistible hope of lasting love beyond all times and tides. He again communicated to Tiffany though the lyrics all his heartfelt emotion. He saw her as his Taylor and desperately wanted Tiffany to understand how his soul was shattered from the loss of her from his life.

With each new song, applause and cheers reward him as the periphery spotlights merged into one single bright light illuminating the idol who so many adored.

Throwing caution to the wind, Larry kept his gaze on Tiffany at every opportunity. If gossip ensued, he didn't care. This was his last performance in London. He took every opportunity to instill his unending longing for her. All too soon, the last song on the Performance List, "You're The Magic", would begin. It started out slow with dramatic lyrics of pure love and physical wanting of a woman. As the song built to a resounding crescendo, Larry accented a man's physical desire with numerous hip thrusts to the audience. He wanted to give them a thrill, but more importantly he wanted Tiffany to know how every fiber of his being desired her. She blushed and glanced up with a sly smile. Their eyes never wavered as hearts defied common sense. If only in song, Larry made her his.

At the last refrain, he came dangerously close to the stage edge. He bent down on one knee and with outstretched arms invited Tiffany to join his heart. She inched forward in her seat and clearly understood his silent message of love and longing. Everyone could see the hunger in his gaze as he sang the last note.

Larry took his bow, then hurried off the stage to the wings. The orchestra played a vamp to one of his famous songs. Larry took a large gulp of water Joe provided. The crowd again chanted loudly, "Larry, Larry, Larry." Clapping hands echoed their desire for his return.

"Chief," Joe began as Larry patted his brow, "you've got 'em

58   *Cynthia B. Ainsworthe*

goin' out there! Great show! Too bad it's the end."

"It's not the end yet." He gave a mischievous wink.

"What do you have in mind?" Joe questioned.

"Wait and see." Larry smiled broadly. "I have a surprise for them."

He nearly ran back on the stage and took additional bows with welcoming arms. His fans loved him, and he loved them back. After more than twenty-five years of entertaining, Larry was amazed and grateful for the adoration, yet still couldn't understand how he deserved their loyalty.

In response, Larry motioned for the applause to die down before he began his impromptu monologue. The audience took their cue as the theater came to a hush of silence. Larry smiled broadly in appreciation.

"What I'm about to do, I haven't done in years. So, bear with me." He paused to wipe a drop of perspiration from his left temple. "In years gone by, I thought it would be fun to bring a lady up on stage to sing to. Well, since this is my last concert in London for a while, I'd like to try that again …. A blind date, if you will."

Cheers and pleas immediately filled the arena as fans shouted, "Pick me, Larry!" and "I'll be your blind date!" He put his hand to his forehead to shield against the blinding lights, as he walked from one side of the stage to the other in search of the special someone who would share the experience with him. Larry glanced to the wings where Joe stood. He ignored Joe's eye roll.

As Larry approached the steps from the stage leading to the audience floor, security immediately flanked his sides and another stood in front of the singer. He strolled directly to Tiffany and reached for her hand. Without reasonable explanation, she took his hand as he quickly escorted her to the steps and onto the stage. She squinted momentarily from the bright lights and clutched her purse. A stagehand quickly provided a stool for the well-known countess.

"Have a seat on this stool while we get to know each other better," he began. Laughter from the crowd filled the theater.

Tiffany's face turned red in response to their outburst. Her fingers fidgeted nervously in her lap. Her eyes cast downward as though embarrassed by his attention.

REMEMBER ?   59

Larry continued, "Tell me about yourself. What's your name and where do you come from?"

A voice rang out from the audience, "She's Countess Lantham, lives in Mayfair with his lordship."

More laughter came from the crowd as if Larry should have known the identity of his famous blind date.

A faint red color came to his cheeks as he quickly explained, "Well, I wanted to hear her beautiful voice say those words."

Tiffany's shaky voice confirmed, "Yes, I'm Tiffany Bradford, um, Countess Lantham. But I think of myself as an ordinary person—no one special."

You're very special to me, Taylor. Larry cleared his throat. "You're far from ordinary. Lady Bradford, if I may, Tiffany." She nodded in acceptance.

"Lord Bradford, or Lantham, is very lucky—very lucky indeed."

Another audience member called out, "She's Lady Lantham—not Bradford."

Larry chose to ignore that outburst as he noticed another blush from his heart's desire. Her blue-green eyes searched his with a hidden question. Larry caught her message and held it in his heart. Now was not the time to delve into personal territory.

He nodded to his stage manager and said, "Tom, get the song 'Taylor' up."

Tom took his cue and gave a swift direction to the band.

In the wings, Joe mumbled, "Oh brother, he's not gonna give up on this thing. Lar, she's *not* Taylor! Drop your foolish hope."

The introduction of "Taylor" began with soft and sweet strains of pure love. Only briefly did Larry's eyes leave hers as he glanced at the audience. His magnetism for her was nearly dizzying. In a trance, his memories took over as he sang,

"When the world has come between us.
The truth will lie beneath us.
My love will always be with you.
Oh Taylor, with these words,
You know I care."

His arm slipped around her waist as he inhaled the sweet

fragrance of her perfume. It was a scent indelibly engraved in his mind—the intoxicating aroma of "Forbidden", habitually worn by Taylor.

As if by some unseen force, she mouthed the words as he sang—words to a song she had never heard before. A broad, joyful smile graced his face. Her recognition was evident. He didn't know why she knew the song, nor did he care. For a brief moment in time, Larry felt he had Taylor back in his arms. He placed a gentle loving kiss on her temple as he closed his eyes and remembered their first meeting at a Tampa concert.

Larry repeated the closing refrain a second time to prolong the feel of her in his arms. Audience members, caught up in the same rapture of emotion with many tear-rimmed eyes, understood the pain in his heart. After the last note escaped his lips, Larry gave her a gentle kiss on the cheek. Plainly, his outpouring of emotion swept through Tiffany. A single tear fell to her cheek.

"Thank you," Larry commented softly, "for bringing this concert to a beautiful conclusion. You have given me a very special treat."

"You're welcome," she whispered as her eyes sought his with a glint of confusion.

He helped her from the stool and escorted her to the wings where Joe stood. Consternation clouded her face as her brow furrowed.

Larry said briefly away from the mic, "Stay with Joe. I'll explain later."

Tiffany's eyes widened with surprise. She remained with his dear friend while Larry returned to the stage.

"I want to thank you all for a wonderful evening! It's been great! That's why I do this—because you enjoy what I do. Thanks again! Good night everyone!"

After taking his final bows, he quickly returned to Joe and Tiffany.

Her mystified expression hadn't subsided. She partially opened her mouth to speak.

Larry cut her off gently, "Not here. We'll talk in my dressing room."

Joe led the way through the maze to Larry's sanctuary, free from prying eyes and unwanted questions. Security men

REMEMBER ?   61

encircled the famous trio.

~~***~~

"Your dressing room is very nice." Tiffany eyed the plush surroundings of a leather sofa, chairs, and coffee table. She noticed a screen separating the private dressing area. Joe and the security men quietly left the room.

"It will do," Larry replied casually. "I don't take much notice of it—comes with the territory." He removed his sweat-laden jacket and placed it on a waiting hanger. "So, how did you like the performance? Did I meet your expectations?"

He motioned for her to sit on the sofa, filled two glasses with Dom Pérignon, and handed her a glass as he sat down close to her. He automatically extended his arm around her shoulder.

"It was wonderful. You were wonderful—I mean, you *are* wonderful." She bit her bottom lip. "But I don't understand why…why you're treating me so special."

"Because, you are …" he paused before adding gently, "to me."

"Mr. Davis—" she began.

"Please, call me Larry or even Lar, like you did before. I'd like that." His hand sought hers with a tender touch.

Her words caught on a stifled breath in her throat. "I feel all I am to you is an illusion of someone you want me to be."

"Tiff, that's not true. I know, and I don't know how I know…but you *are* Taylor." He looked earnestly into her eyes as he searched for some glint of recognition. All he found was compounding confusion. "Please, humor me in this. Since you've been gone, I haven't had a moment's peace."

"But, Larry…" She paused to carefully gather her thoughts. "I can't be more to you than a fan. I'm married and have a life that's separate from yours. The most I can offer you is friendship."

"Don't say that," he implored. "I *know* you understand none of my ramblings, but in time the pieces will all fit together. I don't know how, but I'm confident that they will." His gaze danced around her face in search of her heart. "There's more to you than you remember. There's a past with me, and for whatever reason, that memory has been wiped clean."

Her demeanor was straightforward. "I told you before—I had an accident and hit my head. Nothing more complicated

62   *Cynthia B. Ainsworthe*

than that."

"If what you say is true, that you merely resemble my lost wife, Taylor, and you're not her, then, why did you know the words to the songs I sang? Tell me that. How could you know the words to songs you've never heard before?"

"I have no answer, Lar." Her eyes held onto his gaze as her fingers caressed the hair by his temple. "I can't explain it. With all of my heart, I wish I could remember. There are times I feel like a shell with nothing inside other than a beating heart—a large vacancy occupies my soul."

"Let me fill that vacancy, Tiff," Larry whispered gently in her ear. His hot breath caressed her. Plainly, the near feel of her tender flesh tore at his very foundation.

"I wish I could." Her eyes searched his for an unspoken answer. "It's so strange for me ... being here with you. I feel as if I know you so well. As if ... as if we were related in some way, as friends, or—"

He silenced her by placing his finger gently on her ruby lips. "Lovers, maybe?"

A slight blush came to her cheeks as she whispered, "Yes, Lar ... lovers."

"Tiff, let me awaken the lost memory that lives in your dreams," he suggested quietly.

For a long moment, no words were said. Larry caressed her cheek with the tenderness of handling a fragile vase. He continued to look deeply into her eyes with unfathomable longing for the wife he had told her about. Without further hesitation, his lips sought hers as his warm embrace encircled her. She yielded fully, as if her body had a will of its own. Her parted lips invited his tongue to search her recesses. It was a kiss of love for the woman he had known. Tiffany kissed him back as she stroked the hair at his collar.

"Taylor," Larry whispered, and his lips met hers again. Their long passionate kiss spoke of two lost souls, once again found.

She whispered, "I wish that kiss was for me and not your lost wife."

A loud knock came from the door, abruptly ending the treasured moment.

"Chief," Joe called from the hall. "There's a bunch of paparazzi at the stage entrance and at the front of the theater too! They're gonna wonder what you and Lady Lantham are doin' for so long! What y' want me to do? Better open the door. Y' gotta make plans!"

On impulse, Tiffany reached into her purse. She thrust a small calling card into his palm and gave a gentle squeeze, her way of expressing her own silent yearning.

Larry glanced at the printed words. He smiled, then securely placed it in his wallet. "I never wanted it to end," he said.

SEVEN

LARRY RUSHED TO the door and opened it briskly to let Joe into the room. He burst in with face muscles twitching nervously.

Tiffany sat frozen envisioning Clive's wrath and the never-ending barrage of reporters.

Joe's. dark eyes were round and full of fear. "Chief, the place is crawlin' with reporters. Already the word is out that you're cheatin' on Taylor with Lady Lantham. What a damn mess you've created."

"There must be a way out of this." Larry rubbed his forehead in thought and paced. "There has to be." He glanced at Tiffany. She knew she probably resembled a lost and helpless kitten.

With a glint of nonchalance, she offered quickly, "Why don't I wear a wig, big hat, and sunglasses like I did before?"

"What do you mean '*like you did before*'? Why did you say that?" Larry came to a dead stop.

"I don't know. It just came out." *What is Larry getting at? And why did I say such a thing?*

"Tiff, that's what Taylor did in Bel-Air so she wouldn't be noticed by the news media." Larry spoke as if joy bubbled from within.

"Lar," she replied matter-of-factly, "I wouldn't make much of it. Isn't that a common assumption anyone would make in this situation?"

He scrutinized her look, as if another piece of evidence confirmed his feeling that Tiffany was his. He then quickly turned his attention to his friend.

"Joe, get a blonde wig, large sunglasses, and a big hat from wardrobe." Joe started on his appointed errand. Larry added in a heightened tone, "Get a big coat and have my driver ready at the stage entrance. Make sure my security is alerted, too."

Tiffany forced herself to look relaxed, and casually sipped her champagne. Larry scratched his head with a look of confusion, clearly unable to comprehend her calmness.

"What?" *Why is he looking at me like that?* "I'm enjoying this fantastic champagne."

"Tiff, aren't you concerned about Clive?" he asked with subdued alarm as he sat beside her.

"I guess I should be, but ..." she sighed. "I'm not. What's the worst he could do? Rant and rave for a while?" Tiffany didn't reveal the depth of Clive's anger. "He'll get over it." *Larry's right, Clive could be a problem, but I can't drag him into it.*

Donning the appropriate disguise, Tiffany, Larry, and Joe entered the limousine while reporters hailed them with a multitude of camera flashes and unanswered questions. Joe quickly gave instructions to the driver to lose the paparazzi before driving the countess to her Mayfair residence.

~~***~~

The intense drive to Tiffany's home included detours to nearly every district in London including Greenwich. Luck was on their side. The driver managed to escape the pursuing entourage when the car of one reporter slammed into the side of another causing a mass pileup of frustrated gossip mongers. The couple looked back through the window at the subsequent chaos.

Tiffany knitted her brow and bit her bottom lip as she witnessed the shouting paparazzi yelling profanities at each other.

"I hope no one was hurt," she stated with true concern.

Larry casually commented, "Looks like egos and disappointments were the only injuries, thank God. I hate the idea anyone would be hurt because of me." He gazed at her tenderly. "Still, I had to protect you. I feel responsible for your safety. I don't ever want any harm to come to you."

"Lar, you can't go there .... I'm not yours," she said, nearly in a whisper as her fingers interlaced with his.

"Yes, you keep telling me that." His eyes delved into hers. "Somehow, I don't believe it."

"You must," Tiffany affirmed. "It can't be any other way."

~~***~~

Clive approached Alistair with a glass of scotch.

"I say, ol' man," Alistair said, "what happened to your hand?" His friend and colleague eyed the bandage on his left hand while sitting down on a chair.

"A minor accident," Clive answered blandly. "Tiffany got the better of my anger. It was either striking her or crushing the glass."

"What was the row about, if I may intrude?" Clearly, Alistair plainly saw a new dimension to Clive's emotions. "That Yank singer?"

"I'd rather not discuss it, but ...."

Alistair drew his chair closer in the club's drawing room to hear more clearly.

Clive hung his head as he swirled the ice cubes in his glass before taking another swallow. Unable to remain silent, he spoke in hushed tones to Alistair. "I don't know what's happened to her. Since Larry Davis has come to town, Tiffany's an entirely different woman." He paused a moment, gathering his words, "I can't control her anymore. She doesn't listen to my advice or follow the rules. She's not acting like a proper wife."

Alistair remained silent.

"She acts as if she doesn't care how her actions impact my life and all the negative consequences from my family—she's turned into a bloody freethinker."

"How are you going to handle her?" he asked cautiously. "You could scare her off if you hold too firm. Can't have her running off like Penelope did."

"Penelope was entirely different," Clive affirmed. "Nothing like Tiffany. She was a stupid little airhead who had poor judgment."

"It's getting a bit late, ol' man." Alistair glanced at the clock on the mantle chiming midnight. "Aren't you going home?"

"No. I've booked a room here. Let Tiffany think that one over for a while." Clive looked at his friend in earnest. "Teach her a lesson. Wonder where I am and what I'm doing."

His friend replied with a chuckle, "I've done the same, though for different reasons. Amelia is on holiday with one of her friends up country. The house is too large and empty for me to rattle around in all by myself."

A good-looking young waiter refreshed their drinks. Alistair gave him a sly wink with no verbal acknowledgment. This didn't go unnoticed, but Lord Lantham decided to ignore it.

Clive rested his elbows on his knees to edge closer and whispered, "Have you heard anything from the royals about the

REMEMBER ?   67

tabloids? Will this cause problems?"

"It's been skirted about in polite conversation—nothing has been mentioned directly." Alistair eyed the same waiter from across the room. "I wouldn't worry about it just yet. It's not like she's having an affair with the man. True, Tiffany didn't use the best judgment, but I think the family is making allowances for her lack of breeding. You can't expect her to be aware of all the social graces expected of us."

Clive nodded in agreement. He finished his drink in one large gulp before saying goodnight, leaving Alistair in the drawing room to seek other diversions to fill the remainder of his evening.

~~***~~

The following morning brought new energy to Tiffany. She was very relieved to discover Clive hadn't returned home during the night and oddly, only momentarily worried about what his reaction might be upon his return. *If I'm lucky, he won't carry on about me seeing Larry's performance again. What am I worried about? Clive left for the club before I went out last night. He doesn't even know where I was or who I was with.* Tiffany slipped on her lavender satin robe. She loved the silky feel against her soft skin. *Larry is so kind and gentle. I know I shouldn't feel this way, but his kiss touched me deeply—as if I've kissed him before. That's ridiculous! I'm letting my emotions take control. He's just a fantastic entertainer. His looks aren't bad either. What incredible blue eyes—eyes that see into my soul. I know I should feel guilty, but I don't—why is that? What do I really feel for Clive? Do I love him? I thought I did. Now...I just don't know.*

A faint knock came to her door. Elizabeth called out, "Milady, I have your breakfast."

"Come in, Elizabeth," she replied cheerfully.

The young servant quietly entered the room and closed the door behind her. She gave a small curtsy before walking with the skillfully held silver tray holding a steaming coffeepot, cup and saucer, and a dry slice of whole-wheat toast.

"I wish you wouldn't curtsy every time you serve me. It makes me uncomfortable." Tiffany explained, "I'm not Clive. I don't expect you to treat me any differently."

"I'm sorry, milady," Elizabeth apologized. "It's the way I've been trained. It doesn't feel proper for me to address you any

68   *Cynthia B. Ainsworthe*

other way."

The servant walked to the window and placed the breakfast on the small nearby table. She then arranged the napkin alongside the cup and prepared the coffee to her ladyship's liking. Tiffany followed and took her seat.

"Clive didn't return home last night," she stated to Elizabeth as she reached for the toast. "Do you have any idea where he was?"

"Can't really say, milady," the servant said tentatively. "His lordship only mentioned if the hospital needed to reach him that he would be at the Kings Club."

Tiffany took a sip of the brown creamy brew. "Hmm. I see. Well, I guess he's still stewing over the photos of me and Larry Davis in the papers. In time, he'll get over it—I hope."

Elizabeth cleared her throat. She nervously fingered her apron. "Milady, if I may be so bold …"

"Go on," she encouraged. "Elizabeth, you can say anything to me. I'm no different than you."

"Lady Lantham, there are new pictures of you in today's news. Pictures of you entering the Albert Hall last night. All those awful reporters are asking how you left the theater. No one saw you leave, so now there are rumors that you and Mr. Larry Davis left the theater secretly and you're up in Glasgow with him."

"Oh, if that were only the truth!" Tiffany exclaimed with devilish delight and twinkling eyes. "Wouldn't that frost his lordship's ass?"

"Milady!" Elizabeth looked at her with near horror. "That's a terrible thing to say! Think of poor Lord Lantham! He could never live down the scandal. The family might disinherit him, and he'd lose all his money and backing."

"Calm down." Tiffany laughed lightly. "I didn't say I would do such a thing. It's just a lovely thought."

Elizabeth waited by the table as she watched her take a small bite of toast.

Tiffany glanced up at her. "What is it? You can leave. I don't need anything. I can dress myself."

"You haven't taken your medicine." The servant glanced at the unmarked white tablets that waited on the table.

"What? You still have to watch me swallow these pills?" Tiffany looked mildly alarmed. "That's ridiculous! If I can dress myself, I can certainly take medicine without supervision!"

"Lady Lantham, I'm sorry," Elizabeth offered. "His lordship said I was to make sure you took your medicine."

"Tell *his lordship* that I took my medicine," she replied with irritation. Her eyes popped with a hint of outrage.

Tiffany put the tablets to her mouth and followed with a swallow of coffee. It tasted strangely bitter on her tongue. Satisfied with what she saw, Elizabeth again curtsied, then left the room.

EIGHT

LARRY RECLINED ON the sofa of his Glasgow hotel suite while Joe called room service for a quick lunch before traveling to the venue. The singer felt restless and confused. His recent encounter with Tiffany brought worry and more unanswered questions. *Tiff didn't hold back when I kissed her. Why is that? She seemed to melt in my arms, as if she felt our embrace was a safe haven. And she kissed me back! How could a woman who loves someone else react like that?* He sat up and stared into space. Joe read a local paper. Larry shifted his long legs with an irritated movement. *Tay was able to react to me in the same way when she still loved Paul. Am I living Paul's past? Can she reconcile her feelings, to love two men at the same time? What a damn mess! Tiff is Tay, and she's somehow married to Clive.* Tormented images plagued his mind. *God! Tiff is sleeping with another man. She's cheating on me and doesn't even know it! Wait, what if she's not Tay? Then we are both cheating on our spouses. No, I know better. Tiff is Tay!*

"Chief," Joe interrupted Larry's thoughts, "whatcha thinkin' about? You've been mighty quiet."

"Tay, Tiff…whatever her name is now." Disgusted, he started his familiar habit of pacing. "I haven't had a day's peace since Tay's disappearance."

"Yeah, I know." Joe looked kindly at him with fatherly eyes. "You gotta get a hold of yourself. You gotta show to do."

"Two hours on the stage is the only sanity I know these days." Larry flopped down in the chair opposite his friend. "Tay and I are a unit, a machine that runs so smoothly. My life is out of step without her. There's a vacancy inside of me— deep and gnawing. It grows larger every day."

A knock came to the door as a polite voice called out, "Room service."

Joe let the hotel employee into the suite. Larry remained silent as the waiter efficiently set the table. If the member of staff recognized the famous person he served, he gave no indication. Joe signed for the room charge, and the young man left.

REMEMBER ?   71

Larry looked at the waiting crustless chicken sandwich, then pushed it away. He took a sip of hot tea after preparing it with cream and sugar.

Joe eyed his boss. "Lar, y' gotta eat somethin' before the show. You're doin' mostly upbeat numbers tonight. Y' need your energy."

"I know. Just not hungry." His reply was banal.

"Chief," Joe began slowly while he reached for his hamburger. "I understand how this Tay-Tiff thing is eatin' at y'." He took a bite of his burger. Ketchup dripped onto the plate. "But, have you fully realized the situation you've created for Tiff? She's a royal countess linked to a possible scandal. With all your well-meanin' intentions, you could've put her in a pit of hell, not to mention what it might do to your career. Your fans are loyal, but how long will that last when word gets out 'bout you and Lady Bradford, I mean Lady Lantham? They're gonna think you're steppin' out on Taylor. Sales could plummet down the toilet."

Larry sat straighter as his eyes sharpened. "Have you heard any bad stuff from the PR group?"

"Nah, they're handlin' the damage control okay. Passin' it off as a possible charity event you and the countess might be discussin'," Joe assured. "But, that story will fly for just so long before someone gets wise. I dunno if this Lady B is involved in any charity, but it reads well with the press."

Larry breathed deeply. "That was quick thinking from my PR staff."

"That's why you pay 'em." Joe washed down his burger with a large swig of dark ale.

~~***~~

The long, rambling gravel driveway, flanked by expansive pristine green lawns, brought the Bradford's Bentley to Alistair Hollingsworth's manor house. He was commonly referred to as the Duke of Steffenfordshire. Glittering lights shone through the tall Georgian windows that were decorated with creamy beige damask drapery. Tiffany shivered inwardly despite her luxurious, full-length ranch mink coat. This was an unofficial cocktail party that Clive insisted they attend.

As they sat in the car's comfortable leather seats, he remarked, "It is high time the rest of the family met you. For the love of

72   *Cynthia B. Ainsworthe*

God, don't bore people with your recount of that Yank and his concert. The family's taste in entertainment is far too refined for that," and "Don't babble, my pet. I can speak for both of us".

This last comment wore her nerves raw with irritation. Her forced smile with a hint of cynicism was his reward.

The car pulled smoothly up to the main entrance. A finely dressed servant opened the door and greeted the guests with a discreet and polite smile.

Clive didn't look directly at the man, but gave his usual condescending nod and mumbled a courteous, "Good evening."

The footman offered Tiffany his hand as she left the backseat, her mouth curled at the corners as she replied, "Thank you." Her downcast eyes attested to her less than happy humor.

Alistair stood at the doorway by his wife, Amelia, who was beautifully dressed in a bright blue peau de soie cocktail dress of simple designer lines and a scooped neckline. A single brilliant diamond and sapphire pendant adorned her throat, with matching earrings, bracelet, and a ring completed the look. Her style spoke of old money from generations of English aristocracy.

Amelia immediately extended her hand to her second cousin. "Clive, how nice of you to come. It's been too long. You're such a bad boy staying away from the family." She brushed a strand of chestnut hair from her shoulder. "This must be your lovely bride, Tiffany," Amelia added with a warm smile. "Come in from the cold."

She eyed the long mink coat as the butler helped Tiffany remove the garment. Her gaze fell to her guest's deep purple chiffon dress with matching jacket. "I must say, Clive." Amelia paused before adding, "You certainly know how to dress your wife beautifully." She chuckled lightly. "There has to be a royal affair penned in the calendar before my husband will let me shop for a new dress."

"Now, now," Alistair commented, "it's not as bad as all that. Your closet is brimming with clothes you haven't worn yet."

Clive replied modestly, "Duchess, only the best for the countess. Lady Lantham is far too special to me to deny her

REMEMBER ? 73

anything. I must admit, I love spoiling her. She has me wrapped around her little finger."

Tiffany merely smiled weakly as she looked down at the floor. Knowing she had to support Clive's outward lies pained her. She followed Amelia into the main reception room. A multitude of finely dressed and impressive guests milled about. Discreet footmen with silver trays afforded fare of various exquisite hors d'oeuvres and crystal flutes filled with vintage champagne.

After they entered, hushed tones fell silent as glances took in Clive's new wife. Tiffany felt awkward and meekly smiled to the peering gazes. Her husband had ill prepared her for such scrutiny. Her palms grew moist as a lump of fear filled her throat.

Amelia's sparking green eyes noticed her look of trepidation and whispered warmly, "Tiffany, relax. They don't bite much. You're family. It's not like Her Majesty is here."

Alistair offered, "Well, I dare say, my side of the family doesn't bite—no accounting for Amelia's heritage."

The Duchess of Steffenfordshire ignored her husband's comment. She promptly maneuvered Tiffany among the throng, making introductions as she went. With each greeting, Countess Lantham was met with a warm, polite smile and the usual "Very pleased to meet you. Welcome to our family."

Amelia eased Tiffany away from the others to a corner of the room. Male members of the party had segregated themselves into various clusters, probably discussing politics and sports, while conversations of fashion and gossip of clandestine affairs occupied the women.

"Tiffany," Amelia began out of earshot, "how on earth did stuffy old Clive ever hook you into the family?"

"I really don't know," Tiffany replied sheepishly.

"Really don't know?" Her eyes nearly popped. "What do you mean exactly?"

She bit her bottom lip as if in apology before answering, "Your Grace—"

The chestnut haired beauty interjected, "Please, call me Amelia. I've never been much for titles, though the status impresses Alistair …. He swims in it."

"Amelia," Tiffany emphasized with a small smile "I don't

74   *Cynthia B. Ainsworthe*

remember my courtship with Clive. I woke up one day from a coma and poof! I discovered I was Tiffany Bradford, the Countess of Lantham. I don't even remember my name. I remember nothing of my past …. Only bits and pieces that Clive said I told him before my accident."

"What was the nature of this accident?" Amelia focused on her intently.

"He said I took a terrible fall on our honeymoon in Paris, hit my head, and went into a coma." Tiffany spoke as a child recounting a well-rehearsed nursery rhyme. "I guess we met in Paris, fell in love, and married on a boat by the ship's captain off the south of France."

"Very interesting." Amelia knitted her brow as if in deep thought. "Did you see the marriage document?"

"No, I haven't." Tiffany explained, "I never thought of the need."

"My dear, I don't mean to alarm you," her new friend whispered, "but…you're not the first Lady Lantham—and I'm not talking about Clive's mother."

"Really?" Tiffany stole a glance in Clive's direction and noticed he was busily occupied in male conversation. *What other secrets is my dear husband hiding?*

"Quite right." Amelia touched Tiffany's elbow as she inched closer. "It's been very hush-hush in the family, you understand. But, it seems his first wife took a lover, went away on vacation alone, and never returned. Everyone assumed she met her lover somewhere and abandoned poor Clive. That was eons ago." Both women glanced at the injured man then diverted their gaze. "He sulked around for months before finally getting a divorce."

"I had no idea!" A new understanding came to Tiffany's eyes. "That explains why he's so controlling. He must be afraid another woman would do the same thing." She twirled her wide gold wedding band. "All this time, I've been horrible to him—going to that concert that he didn't approve of—not once, but twice."

Amelia nodded her head with a devilish look. "Yes, I do recall reading something about you and that sexy American singer. I wouldn't mind his slippers under my bed."

Is she serious? "Amelia, you're married to Alistair. How can you think such thoughts?"

"Now that you're in the family, there are some facts you need to know." Her cousin-in-law sidled closer. "Alistair has his stable boys, and I have mine."

Tiffany nearly choked on her champagne. "Amelia, I don't know what to say."

"Say nothing my dear." She cocked an eyebrow. "Marriages for convenience aren't all bad. Alistair has my money, and I improved my royal blood connection. It's all very neat and tidy."

Amelia continued, "Of course, I don't share the same boys as Alistair. My taste is a bit more refined—though, it is tempting.". She winked. "Tiffany, you simply must tell me more about that American singer. What's his name? Oh, yes. I remember, Larry Davis. What was he like? In the papers it looked very compromising. Was it as deliciously wicked as the news portrayed?"

"Not at all," Tiffany replied softly. "He was a complete gentleman. Very nice and kind, I have to admit." Her lips curled up at the corners as she thought of him. "I do find him terribly attractive. It was almost as if we knew each other from another time. I know it sounds crazy, but I felt a real connection with Larry. Even more of a connection than I feel with Clive. I've been telling myself I must feel this way because of the medicine Clive has me on."

"What medicine is that, my dear?" Amelia's curiosity piqued higher. "Why are you on medication?"

"Clive says it's for my nerves," Tiffany explained in a matter-of-fact way, "He doesn't want me to go into a relapse."

"What is the medicine called?" She probed deeper.

"I don't know that either." Tiffany shifted uneasily. "Why do you want to know?"

"No particular reason." Amelia tilted her chin and made a small gesture for the waiter to bring over the tray of hors d'oeuvres. He was promptly at her side with an array of expensive delicacies. "I would want to know exactly what I was taking before I swallowed a tablet, even if it was my husband who prescribed it."

"I completely trust Clive," Tiffany proclaimed. "He would never harm me."

76   *Cynthia B. Ainsworthe*

"Trust no man." Amelia spoke as a woman who had been hurt before. "Deep down, most of them are cads. I say to hell with the lot of them. Enjoy their company for the moment and then move on. Life is too short to allow a man to sap the best years and then only to find he has replaced you with the latest diversion."

~~***~~

In the midst of the cocktail party, Clive and Alistair moved to the sanctity and security of the Hollingsworth library. They quietly discussed their mutual research project, free from prying eyes and eavesdropping ears.

"Clive, when do you think we'll get the okay from the big boys to start the human trials?" Alistair swirled his scotch before taking a drink. "Have you heard anything from your end?"

"Not a ruddy peep." He looked at his friend with cool calculation. "Who says we need their go-ahead? We know the project inside and out. All the results have proved foolproof with primates—their past memories have been erased with no hints of recollection."

Alistair stroked his chin with mild worry. "Yes, I understand all that. But, ol' man, these things have to be approached delicately. Even if we get the go-ahead, there's the massive screening process of possible subjects who must all be volunteers and well compensated for the risk."

"Alistair, you're a relative and a friend." Clive furrowed his brow as he began to pace the floor. "But some projects would never leave the bloody drawing board if everyone played by the rules."

"What are you saying exactly?" His eyes widened as if he realized his colleague's train of thought. "Surely you don't mean we should conduct our own human trials privately?"

"Alistair, just think of it." His voice lowered an octave as he continued, "If we go ahead with this, prove that we came up with a solution for the burnout of the MI6 agents out there— our names would be on a proverbial research map. If the agents can't remember killing a rival, then they're virtual killing machines with no conscience—no sense of guilt to deal with. Think of how our research could expand to benefit the poor souls who suffer from memory lapses? The possibilities are

REMEMBER ?   77

endless. If we know how to control and limit memory, then why not the reverse? Dementia could be a thing of the past. Oh, God—I can feel the Nobel Prize in my hands." Power and control consumed Clive.

"It all sounds a bit far-fetched to me, ol' man." Alistair looked at him with mild worry. "Just where are you going to find these willing subjects?"

"Who said they have to be willing?" His friend's jaw dropped. "There are plenty of unfortunates who would gladly sign up for the price of a pint, and if they don't—they don't care what pills they take as long as they feel better. I deal with them every day at the NHS clinic."

"Yes, that's true," he conceded. "But, they are far from the intellectual candidates we're looking for. We need people who have been well educated, like MI6 agents."

"They can be found." Clive looked smug as if he held a secret. "That candidate may be closer than you think—though she doesn't know it."

"What are you saying?" Alistair exclaimed with near horror. "You're not already conducting your own experiment are you—on a female?"

"I didn't say that." He finished his drink triumphantly, then gave a wink. "Assume what you like." *I wish my bastardly father was alive to see my success. He'd have to eat his words. I'm the smartest in the world—but the world doesn't know it yet,*

~~***~~

That same night, Larry sat in his dressing room after his sold-out Glasgow performance at the Scottish Exhibition and Conference Center. He remembered being the opening performer when this venue first opened years ago, a definite career coup for him.

Joe sat in a chair as he watched his boss remove his makeup before the post performance reception that followed in the greenroom.

"Chief," Joe rejoiced, "you had the audience on fire tonight. The press will be singin' your praises for days, if not weeks."

Larry grabbed another tissue as he wiped the remnants of makeup from his forehead. "You really think so?"

"Sure do," he replied, then a look of worry took over. "There's this one item that could cause trouble for y'."

"What's that, Joe?" Larry turned to his friend with mild concern. "Something in the papers?"

"Yeah." Joe shifted uneasily in his seat. "Seems some sharpie out there has made a connection between Lady B lookin' like Taylor. Sayin' Taylor left you to be a countess in the royal family." Joe sighed heavily. "That kinda press you don't need. People'll start askin' questions about what you did to make Taylor leave y'."

Alarm covered Larry's face. "I did nothing! Tay didn't leave me—she's lost, that's all—a pure case of a missing person, nothing more!"

"Calm down, Chief." Joe tried to sooth his budding anger. "I'm only tellin' y' what the buzz is."

"Why in hell did I ever agree to Tay returning to Gérard's?" His voice rang with frustration. "If I had stopped her, she'd still be by my side."

"You couldn't stop her," Joe said with a fatherly tone. "Tay was her own person with her own ideas. Remember, she insisted on returning to work, even if it was only freelance."

"Yeah, I know." Anger softened to one of melancholy. "Joe, don't use the past tense when you speak of Tay. Tay lives, not only in my heart, but somewhere out there. I know she's waiting for me to find her—she just doesn't know it yet."

Joe met his comment with a kindly nod as he placed his hand softly on his friend's shoulder. "I sure hope you're right on that one."

"I have to be correct." Larry's eyes moistened. "It's all I have left, except for my memories."

NINE

AMELIA AND TIFFANY took Elizabeth to Karen's dress shop as a special birthday treat for the servant. Tiffany had told Amelia that her boss, Karen, had gladly given her the day off when she mentioned the 'Duchess of Steffenfordshire' would accompany her on this excursion. Clearly, Karen hoped Amelia's patronage would bring in favorable future sales.

Ever since the cocktail party, Amelia and Tiffany had become fast friends, as if an unseen bond cemented their relationship— or perhaps it was their mutual freethinking that drew them together.

Tiffany had insisted that Elizabeth choose an outfit she liked. She smiled at the young girl. "Found anything that takes your eye?"

"Everything is *so* expensive. I'm afraid his lordship wouldn't approve." Her eyes downcast with timidity.

"Don't worry about him," Tiffany assured.

Amelia chimed in, "Quite. *She's* the lady of the house. If Lady Lantham wants to give you a present, then a present is what you shall have."

Karen approached the three women and immediately curtsied before Amelia.

The duchess waved her hand. "Don't bother. Save that for my husband. I, like Tiffany, don't see myself any different to you. We all pay our dues to the Crown in one way or another."

Karen replied respectfully, "That's very kind of you, Your Grace."

"My name is Amelia. None of that *Your Grace* for me."

Embarrassed by her lack of social protocol, Tiffany blushed. "Where were my manners? I'm so sorry. Let me introduce you. Amelia, this is Karen Edwards, my dearest friend, boss, and the owner of this dress shop."

The duchess extended her hand. Karen gave her a warm grasp that oddly communicated a female bond on this first meeting. A sense of comradery from the three women filled the room.

80   *Cynthia B. Ainsworthe*

"Tiff, you are so kind," Karen replied and then looked at Amelia. "I am so very honored to have you visit my humble shop. Blimey, I wish the camera on my phone was working properly. I could have a picture of you on my wall. Oh, the customers would like that—they would all right."

"Say no more," Amelia offered, "I'll have an autographed picture dropped off straight away."

"You're so kind," Karen beamed.

Tiffany left the two women and assisted Elizabeth with an outfit choice. Karen noticed this and whispered to Amelia if she may have a private moment of her time. The duchess nodded, then followed her to the back of the store.

"I know we've only just met, and I shouldn't be talking about her ladyship." Karen took a deep breath before continuing, "I'm worried about Tiffany. Sometimes she comes into the shop looking ruddy exhausted. I have to repeat myself two or three times to her. This isn't all the time, mind you, just every now and again."

"Really?" With a surprised look, Amelia glanced in Tiffany's direction. "She was spot on at my cocktail party. Didn't seem off at all."

"I know Lord Lantham has been giving her medicine—for her nerves, says she. But Tiff doesn't know what she's taking." Karen didn't take her eyes off Tiffany.

"Interesting, *very* interesting." Amelia's eyes took on a sinister gaze, one of solving an untold mystery. *Tiffany mentioned those pills she was taking. Now I'm really intrigued.*

Karen continued, "The only time I've seen her happy is when she's talking about that American bloke, Larry Davis."

"Yes, she told me something about that." Amelia explored further, "Do you think she fancies him?"

Obviously delighted, Karen's eyes sparkled. "Blimey, that's an understatement. She has her ears plugged into her media player, listens to his music when she's not waiting on customers, she does, with this dreamy look on her face." She motioned for Amelia to come closer as she whispered in her ear, "If it wasn't for being married to his lordship, Larry Davis could be in her knickers. I'm sure of it—but so would thousands of other birds."

Tiffany and Elizabeth walked by with three outfits to the

dressing rooms. The two women paused their conversation before continuing. A devilish sparkle came to Amelia as her lips curled into a smile. "Karen, I have an idea. I can't talk here. Can we meet somewhere to chat about Tiffany? Perhaps for lunch? It'll be my treat. Will you ask Elizabeth to join us?"

"You want to have lunch with the likes of me?" Amazed, Karen's lips parted. "I'd be honored to be in your presence. Of course I'll ask young Elizabeth."

"Tell her not to say a word to Tiffany," Amelia instructed. "I don't want her to know I'm discussing her situation."

"Mum's the word," Karen affirmed. "Won't be a word from my lips."

Tiffany and Elizabeth came from the dressing room. The young girl glowed. She held three outfits in her hand, then blurted out, "Her ladyship said I could have all three of 'em! What a wonderful pressie for my birthday!"

"You deserve them," Tiffany remarked. "It's high time we show our appreciation for your loyalty. Elizabeth, you're a very sweet girl and deserve nice things."

"Oh, thank you, milady." Elizabeth grinned from ear to ear as she stroked the garments. "I won't forget this. I'm very lucky, milady. Any girl in service would love to have you as their mistress."

Amelia interrupted, "Quite right! Tiffany is very generous and kind. Although, I fear not everyone in her life appreciates her fully."

Karen looked mildly concerned by this last comment.

"I hope you weren't referring to Karen," Lady Lantham quipped. "I couldn't ask for a kinder friend and employer."

"Of course not." The duchess explained, "There are others in your life."

"Just Clive," Tiffany replied flatly.

"Quite. You get my point." Amelia revealed she knew a morsel of truth.

"Ridiculous." Tiffany affirmed, "He's been a wonderful husband. Very patient and kind."

"As you will," the duchess acquiesced. "Now, let's have tea. My present to Elizabeth for her birthday. Some posh hotel, I think."

The young girl was speechless. She looked at Tiffany, clearly

82   *Cynthia B. Ainsworthe*

not believing the generosity of her mistress' newfound friend.

To Karen, Amelia added, "I'll ring you up in a few days." Countess Lantham's curious expression posed a silent question. "Tiff, it's about bringing some of my friends by to shop—there are many nice clothes here—every woman needs something new to wear."

Karen's jaw dropped. "Thank you so much ma'am. This is a humble shop. I truly feel honored by such generosity."

"Make no mention of it." Amelia added with pride, "I enjoy helping a friend of Tiffany's. You're also my friend, my dear."

Karen's eyes lit up with delight as she rang up the purchase with a fifty percent discount as her kindness to Tiffany.

Amelia's driver took the three women in the Rolls Royce for their final excursion.

~~***~~

Clive dined in the upper dining area at Nicholson's off Piccadilly near Mayfair. Elizabeth had the day off for her birthday, but he didn't mind. It provided solitude where he could think clearly without his wife's tiresome questions about her past. *Do I love Tiffany? Her zeal for life is beyond me.* As he sank his spoon deep into the sweet chocolate steamed pudding, unsettling questions plagued him. *How am I ever going to truly control her? I feel I've married all the terrors of Pandora's Box. She can be so beguiling one moment and then a tormenting nightmare. What a paradox—heaven and hell in one beautiful body. Why couldn't I have fallen in love with a simpler girl, like Penelope? She never questioned me, always followed my lead.* His eyebrows knitted as he remembered his first wife. *No, Penelope wasn't easy to live with, in the end—she had to take a damn lover!* His grip on the spoon tightened, nearly bending the silver implement as forgotten anger rose to the surface. *She had the unmitigated gall to challenge my authority and cause me embarrassment! In the end, she got what was coming to her. It serves her right. She lost her title and everything that goes with it.*

~~***~~

Clive entered their home just before ten o'clock that evening. Rodney greeted him enthusiastically at the doorway with a wagging tail and gleeful whimpers. He bent down and effortlessly picked up the adoring pet before returning him to the floor. He noticed Tiffany. She sat silently on the sofa in their sitting room. She didn't acknowledge his entrance. Her attention seemed diverted by the melodies of Larry piping into her ears from her portable player.

He approached and stood in front of her. She immediately pulled out her earphones and turned off the device.

"What time is it?" Tiffany inquired.

"You're more concerned with the time, than greeting your husband?" A glimmer of steel grated his voice.

"Of course not. I'm happy to see you." She hid a yawn with her hand. "I just lost track of time."

"No wonder, listening to whatever that music is." He sat beside her. "Tiffany, we need to talk. I'm dead serious with everything I'm about to say."

Concern and confusion came over her. *What bomb is he going to let loose with now? Is he tired of me?* "Go on. Please don't drag this out. Just come out with it."

"I feel you're drifting away from me." His eyes held a kindness she remembered when she first awoke from her coma. The same kindness she fell in love with. "I'm ruddy frustrated and don't know what to do about it. I can't tolerate you leaving me. One won't tolerate it."

Sounds like the old Clive to me—always laying down the law. "Clive, I never said I'd leave you." Her hand sought his. "I've given you no reason to feel this way."

"You may not think so, but you have—when you went to that bloody concert—not once, but twice." The hint of tears rimmed his eyes. "It was as if my wishes meant nothing to you—as if our marriage meant nothing to you. Haven't I been patient during your long recovery? I've only forced my affection on you once—and I'm sorry for that. I acted like a ruddy cad. I was acting out of fear—fear of losing you. You believe me, don't you? You must."

"Clive, I didn't realize you were so deeply hurt." She kissed his cheek softly. "It was just a couple of innocent concerts—nothing special to me. I had a chance to meet someone famous."

"That may seem simple to you, darling, but he's an *entertainer*. In our circles, that makes him common and definitely undesirable. You must be careful whom you're seen with. We, in the family, are always under scrutiny by being in the public eye. One has a responsibility to act appropriately when in

84   *Cynthia B. Ainsworthe*

public, and like it or not, that includes who you keep company with."

"Well, at least my friendship with Amelia can't be objected to," she replied with relief.

"Amelia!" His eyes grew wide with disdain. "For God's sake, no! Don't strike up a friendship with *that* woman! She's no better than the likes of Larry Davis. Royal or not, she's brought enough scandal to the family—nearly as infamous as Catherine Howard."

"Who?" she questioned simply.

Exasperation colored his face. "The fifth wife of Henry VIII! Have you forgotten basic British history as well! Your time would be better spent learning our history instead of listening to soppy love songs. Maybe then, you'd be able to hold your own at parties in our social circles."

Tiffany sat straighter in her seat. Her voice tightened with restrained anger. "If there are so many things wrong with me and my upbringing—which I can't recall—tell me this, why in hell did you marry me in the first place if I'm so beneath you?"

"No need to use profanity, my pet. One is being prosaic again." Clive's tone took on a controlled coolness. The muscles in his jaw twitched. "I married you because I wanted to. And, I could."

"What am I to you, Clive?" She searched his face to find the truth. "Am I nothing more than an object you own? I'm out of your favor because you realize you can't control me?"

"You're talking like an idiot." He went over to the bar and poured brandy into an expensive crystal glass. "I have never treated you with anything but kindness. You have the complete run of the house. You can buy anything you want, provided it's not the crown jewels, and I even let you work at that loathsome shop to fill your time."

"Those are things, Clive. Merely things." Tenderness filled her eyes. She craved most what he hadn't given her. "What about love? Your love?"

"Silly woman talk." He sat in the chair opposite and crossed his legs as if her prying words made him ill at ease. "Being my wife should say it all. What more do you want from me?"

"I want you to say you love me," she implored as a tear graced her cheek. "I remember you said those words a long

REMEMBER ?   85

time ago, when I first woke from my coma."

"Love talk, love songs, romance—all empty-headed notions women embrace." He took a large gulp of his drink. "I won't submit to such banter."

"Clive, I haven't changed. You have," Tiffany said nearly in a whisper.

He remained firm in his conviction. "Changed? Not ruddy likely."

"Yes, you have." She paused a moment, "Ever since you took more of an interest in my recovery—changing my medication every now and then—as if I'm some personal experiment."

"You sound as daft as that woman you work for." Abruptly, he stood up and finished the brandy in one gulp. "I'm not continuing this conversation. I'm going to bed. You can join me or not. That's your wish—not mine."

"Fine!" Tiffany yelled out as he left. "I just might sleep here or in my bedroom. Since I'm of no consequence to you, it doesn't matter where I sleep!"

She sat there for two hours contemplating Clive's outrageous remarks. *How could he have treated me so harshly? If he really loves me, then why talk to me so cruelly? If Larry was my husband, my life would be filled with love. He's a sensitive man. Wish Clive had some of Larry's qualities. Now, I have a master to contend with—closed minded and pigheaded! Larry's music is my only refuge. I doubt I'll ever see him again. No, that won't happen. Clive will watch my every move. Still, it's a lovely thought, a beautiful thought—one I will dream about.*

TEN

AMELIA, KAREN, AND Elizabeth sat at a private table in the lower level of Grumbles, a well-known restaurant in Belgravia. The duchess enjoyed the old history of this location and brought to mind memories of her childhood. *I remember hearing that the Prime Minister would dine here in a secluded area.* She looked at an isolated table in a corner flanked by curtains. *I wonder if that was where secrets of the Realm were discussed.*

"Elizabeth," Amelia touched the young girl's hand denoting an air of trust, "how did you come to join the employ of Lord Lantham?"

"Nothing mysterious about that," the servant replied cheerfully. "I had the good fortune to be sent out on interview by an agency. I was all nervous and such, but his lordship was so kind and willing to give me a chance."

"Yes. That was a bit of luck for you." Amelia leaned toward Elizabeth. "Tell me, if you can, do you think he loves Tiffany? I mean, Clive has always been so reserved. I must admit, I find his choice in a new wife extremely opposite to his last."

Karen's eyes widened as she sipped her tea. Clearly, she found this subject fascinating.

Elizabeth hesitated, "Well, I dare say … Lady Lantham is nothing like his lordship. She is free and lighthearted. It's almost as if she's a frail little bird in a cage—always looking out between the bars as others live their lives—always wondering what lies beyond but never really knowing."

"Yes," Karen chimed in, "well put. I feel that same way about Tiffany. If she's happy, then she's very reserved about it. The only time I saw her really glow was when she described her experience of meeting Larry Davis—that dashing bloke from the States."

Amelia's ears perked up and a sly smile emerged. She leaned closer to the two women across the table. "You have my rapt attention, ladies. Please continue. My lips are sealed. You have my complete confidence."

Karen began first, with a miniscule of hesitance, clearly

enjoying the attention that the Duchess of Steffenfordshire bestowed on her. "To be completely frank, Tiff was completely taken by him. She went on and on, with her eyes bright and shiny. A totally different person, she was." She paused a moment to sample a lemon biscuit, then lowered her voice to a whisper, "She confided to me that they even kissed! That was the second time they met. Oh, I envy her. I can tell you this— she really fancies that American bloke. My guess is, it wouldn't take much for him to explore her knickers."

Elizabeth appeared eager not to be outdone. "I totally agree. Lady Lantham shined every time she returned home after meeting Larry Davis. She would only say it was a lovely concert and the like. She never shared any particulars, but I'm merely a servant."

"Ladies," Amelia inquired, "has she mentioned how she feels about Clive? Any hint of discord?"

The young girl quickly answered, "I can tell you about that." She paused to sip her tea. "His lordship was cold and silent. Didn't say more than one word to me when she was at the Albert. The next day, milady was quiet and sad. Oh, she tried to act like herself, but I could tell she was most unhappy. Then Lord Lantham had me increase her medicine, he does. Says it's for her nerves."

"Really?" Amelia gave a quizzical glance at Karen.

"Yes, quite right." Elizabeth added, "I hate to give them to her. After a while she acts dazed and knackered. Sometimes, I wish I could just forget to give them to her—but I'm afraid milord would find out and I'd lose my situation."

The Duchess patted the girl's hand. "Don't worry about that. If Clive releases you, I'll gladly take you on." Elizabeth beamed. "Would you be willing to do me a favor?" The young girl nodded. Amelia directed her attention to Karen, "I may need your assistance also."

"Of course," the two women answered in unison.

"I would like to try a little experiment of my own. Clive isn't the only researcher in the family." Amelia took a deep breath. "Elizabeth, would you be willing to substitute her ladyship's medicine for sugar tablets? Only those special tablets Clive insists she takes?" She remained silent with a sideways glance to Karen. "I have my reasons—nothing concrete you understand—

but I do believe Tiffany would be much better served by stopping the medicine Clive is giving her. There could possibly be side effects from her nerve medicine that is preventing her from regaining her memory."

"She does seem to answer questions slower after she's taken her tablets," Karen offered. "As if she's had a pint or two. What can I do to help? She's my very best friend."

"For the present, just watch out for her. Encourage her to talk about her past." Amelia looked back and forth between the two women before she continued in a hushed tone, "Clive seems just too ruddy content with Tiffany's lack of memory, and I just can't fathom out why. I keep asking myself, how does he benefit from her continued affliction?"

Elizabeth and Karen appeared stumped and offered no answer. Amelia retrieved her calling card from her purse and handed one to each of the ladies. "Ring me anytime."

"Duchess, I feel honored you would want to associate with me, a simple shop owner," Karen expressed with delight sparkling from her eyes.

"Please, call me Amelia," she said warmly to the kind woman and then added, "and you, too, Elizabeth. I don't wear my title as a tiara. I'm quite down to earth."

"Thank you." The young girl hesitated, not accustomed to addressing royalty in a common manner. "Amelia, I am so tremendously pleased. You have my complete trust. I will gladly do anything to help Lady Lantham."

"You've got me, too." Karen held a hint of smug delight. "I want only the best for Tiff."

"Brilliant! We're all agreed?" Amelia asked with a triumphant smile. The newfound friends nodded enthusiastically. "I insist we celebrate our new pact with champagne. We must make a toast to Tiffany and her new adventures." She motioned for a waiter to approach.

Karen knitted her brow. "What new adventures?"

"Let me worry about that one," the duchess answered with cool confidence. "Every vivacious lady has adventures of one sort or another." She bit her bottom lip. "Hmm, some experiences can be quite interesting … quite interesting indeed."

~~***~~

Larry gazed out the window in a hotel suite in Dublin, yet

REMEMBER ?   89

another city on his international tour. The rooftops and charm of the city monuments lost their luster as his thoughts whirled around his lost love. Feeling she was so near and yet intangible spurred more torment in his soul. He pulled out her card from his wallet and looked silently at the numbers printed in an elegant script. *I know I shouldn't call Tiff, but I feel I must. Will she reject me? No matter what her reaction is, just to hear her voice would be wonderful.*

Joe noticed what his friend was about to do but held his words. The expression on his face denoted his disapproval.

The phone rang once, twice, three times as Larry began to pace the floor. The untouched tea and toast waited to be consumed. His mind was not on his empty stomach.

Why won't she pick up? What's wrong?

On the fifth ring, Tiffany's soft and inviting voice answered, "Hello?"

"Tiff, this is Larry," he began. "Larry Davis. I'm here in Dublin and wanted to see how you're doing."

"Lar, it was so nice of you to call," her tone signified restrained joy. "How is the tour going? Keeping all those ladies happy?"

His voice was smooth and inviting. "There's only one lady on my mind—Lady Lantham, who I want to keep happy."

"Hmm … very intriguing," she purred softly. "Do you think Lady Lantham would be accepting of such an innuendo?"

She sounds like Taylor—starting her famous word games. "Tiff, you tell me. You know her better than I."

"Maybe I do." She paused a moment, as if enjoying this verbal play. "In what way do you intend to amuse Lady Lantham? Some romantic diversion of song, or something more serious?"

"Whatever the lady wants." Larry swallowed hard. He envisioned Taylor in his arms. "I aim to please."

"What a lovely choice of words, and so powerful in their unspoken message," she cooed in a near whisper.

"Tiff, to get serious for a moment, I have a month off after this tour before I have to return to Vegas. I thought we could connect. Maybe you could show me around a bit? Nothing serious, just a couple of friends doing the sights."

"What about the news media?" she asked wisely. "They could

be a problem for both of us."

"I'll find a way around that." *Is she trying to back out?* "Leave the details to me. I thought a visit to the famous countryside might be nice—less recognition that way—plus I'll have my security with me."

"Let me think about that for a few days." She sounded serious. "I don't want Clive getting upset over nothing. Give me your number so I might call you."

Larry gave her the requested information. He then added, "Tiff, please keep in touch. Even though our meetings have been brief, I feel we have a real connection."

"Lar, I feel that way, too." *Is there a glimmer her memory is returning?* "I can't explain it, and there's no logical reason for it, but I find myself thinking of you nearly every day. You're so very nice and genuine—not at all like Clive and all his pompous protocol. I feel I can be myself around you."

"That's exactly how I respond to you, Tiff." Larry breathed deeply as if a weight was lifted. "I can be the real me when I'm with you. You don't expect an onstage performance."

"Heavens no!" She added, "I'm not that sort of person. For the life of me, I can never figure out why I married Clive in the first place. I must've loved him at some point in time. If I ever get my memory back, maybe I'll have that answer."

Sounds like she doesn't love Clive. If she gets her memory back, will she discover she does love him? "I hope the pieces come together for you. It must be hell not remembering."

"It is," Tiffany confessed. "The only thing that keeps me sane is your beautiful music. I can imagine wonderful images of places and situations …. It helps me escape my reality."

"Tiff," he said with earnest, "I wish I could erase all your worries."

"Thanks, Lar," she uttered softly, as to a lover. "That means a lot to me. I have so few friends."

"I'll be the best friend you'll ever have." He fought back the urge to disclose his deeper feelings. "I'll call you again in a few days. Give some thought to how we can meet again."

"I will, Lar," she ended, "you can count on that one."

ELEVEN

CLIVE HUNCHED OVER his lab desk. He tried to answer a multitude of questions running through his mind. *I don't understand it. The subject has been taking increased dosages of the test drug and there's no effect. If anything, the opposite is true. There seems to be increased mental focus and acuity. Why the paradox response? Something must be wrong with the formula—but what?*

As he reworked the mathematical equations hastily on a piece of paper, Alistair came up behind him.

A frown came to his forehead before inquiring, "Clive, anything wrong?"

"Quite right," he answered without looking up. "I just don't understand it. I've increased the dosage of M43, and there has been a reversal of the expected results. Short-term memory is sharpened along with increased attention span—completely opposite to the predicted results."

"Are you absolutely certain about this?" Alistair queried. "You haven't changed the compound in any way?"

"Never!" He looked at his friend sharply. Lines of frustration etched his face. "I'm too particular about the bloody details to make any rash adjustments." He rubbed his chin deep in thought. "I can't fathom out what has gone wrong. The subject is reacting as if she is taking a placebo."

"You said *she*?" Alistair questioned, "You *are* referring to a primate subject, aren't you?" Clearly, disbelief consumed his thoughts. "Ol' man, please tell me you're not carrying out this experiment on a human!"

"Of course I'm referring to a primate!" Clive responded with near outrage. "I would never jeopardize my integrity with a clandestine experiment! What do you take me for? A dis-reputable scientist?" *I can't trust Alistair. He's loyal to the ruddy rules. Wouldn't ever do anything that wasn't cricket!*

"Steady on, ol' man. For a moment, you gave me a start." A veil of relief rested in his eyes. "I should have never entertained such a thought."

"Instead of questioning my integrity," Clive suggested, "help

92   *Cynthia B. Ainsworthe*

me with this problem. The answer has to be here in black and white—I just can't seem to find it."

~~***~~

A new hire to the Bradford home, Piers Andrews, strode into the kitchen where Elizabeth busily prepared breakfast for Tiffany. In his early twenties, the servant girl felt he projected himself as much older.

"I'll take breakfast to Lady Lantham." His tone of authority matched his tall stature and looming presence. He glanced at the young girl's trim figure with definite approval. A small lock of black hair fell to his forehead.

"You will, will you?" Elizabeth brushed him off curtly with her eyebrow arched. "I've been in service to milady since my first day here. I see no reason to change the routine. Besides, I know how she likes to be served." *Why do all the good-looking blokes have to be so damn cheeky?*

"Lord Lantham instructed me to serve her ladyship all her meals." His authoritative pitch matched the stern look in his black eyes.

"I don't much care for your tone." She stood pencil straight as she placed a cup and saucer on the serving tray. "You're no better than me. Milord didn't give me those instructions personally, so until I hear them words from him—I will continue to serve Lady Lantham." *Of all the bloody nerve!* "Besides, milady might be indisposed. It would not be proper for you to see her in nightclothes. You just tend to the needs of his lordship."

"Lord Lantham instructed me to give her ladyship her medicine, *personally.*" His smug smile screamed confidence.

Elizabeth held firm. "Like I said, Piers, until I hear those words from *his* mouth, I will be the one to give milady her medicine." She placed the remaining breakfast items on the tray along with a single rose in a vase. Two unmarked white tablets waited on the plate with a buttered crumpet. "Now, if you'll excuse me, her ladyship will be wanting her breakfast."

He called out after her, "You will address me as Mr. Andrews. I'm your superior."

She left in a flurry and headed for Tiffany's bedroom. The quickness of her steps echoed her seething irritation. Piers stood in the kitchen as his clenched jaw matched his tightened

REMEMBER ?   93

fists. Like his employer, his demeanor indicated a sense of inner restraint and the urgent need to control others.

~~***~~

Elizabeth knocked softly on Tiffany's bedroom door. No answer returned. She opened the door softly and found her mistress sitting at her dressing table staring at the image in the mirror. A faraway look occupied her eyes, as if deep, dark thoughts traveled in the recesses of her mind.

The servant girl cleared her throat. Tiffany didn't move nor did she show any expression. She was unaware of anyone other than her sense of loneliness and the great void within her.

"Lady Lantham," Elizabeth hesitated. "I have your breakfast." She looked at the pillow next to Tiffany's on the bed. It was plainly not rumpled and suggested Clive hadn't slept there.

"Sorry, Elizabeth," she apologized automatically. "My mind was wandering …. I was someplace else. A nice warm place, with love and hope."

"No bother," the young girl offered. She placed her breakfast quietly on the small familiar table. "I do hope I haven't upset you in some way."

Tiffany's kind face looked at the young girl as she rose to walk in her direction. "Don't be silly. You've been nothing but a source of comfort to me." She secured the lavender satin robe around her slender form. "I wish I could say the same about Clive."

"I know of no such things between you and Lord Lantham," Elizabeth spoke a half-truth. "He never comments on details of a personal nature."

"Of course not," Tiffany agreed. "His insane protocol must always come first—even at the expense of his own wife." She buttered her crumpet. "Elizabeth, do you know anything about his first wife?"

"Heavens, no!" The young girl nervously picked at her uniform apron. "That was long before my time. I have only heard rumors. Things that I don't give much credence to."

"Could you share what you do know?" Tiffany pursued. "I won't tell Clive what you tell me. Elizabeth, you have my complete trust."

"It's been said that his lordship's first wife took a lover and ran away one day." Her voice softened as she nearly whispered, "No one knows where she went or where she is now—all very mysterious. I was instructed by his lordship neither to bring up the subject nor to mention her name."

"Yes," Tiffany confirmed, "I recall the Duchess of Steffenfordshire mentioning something about that to me." She took a sip of coffee as she looked up at the young girl. "Can you tell me her name?"

"Penelope," Elizabeth barely whispered, "though, I don't know if she's known by a different name now. It's as if she dropped off the face of the earth."

"I imagine Clive was deeply hurt from such a loss," she concluded, "but he's got a funny way of showing love now. Maybe that's why Penelope left in the first place—tired of feeling like a possession."

"Milady, I wouldn't know anything about that." The servant girl asked, "At the risk of being forward, and you don't have to answer if you don't want to, is that how you feel about Lord Lantham?"

"You may ask." Tiffany breathed deeply. "Yes, Elizabeth. That's exactly how I feel. For some unknown reason, Clive doesn't share my bed anymore—sleeps in his bedroom. We're roommates now. He says my recovery shouldn't be complicated with moments of intimacy." Mild frustration and confusion came to her face. "For the life of me, I can't understand why intimacy would interfere with regaining my past memory. It's as if I'm one of those lab rats he's studying. Hell, I think Clive cares more for his lab subjects than for me."

"I think his lordship cares for you very much." Elizabeth warmly suggested, "Milady, I think you're having a blue morning. Why don't you ring your friend Karen or the Duchess of Steffenfordshire? A chat with one of your friends may be just the thing to cheer you up."

"Yes," Tiffany agreed with a sigh. "I'll visit the shop. I've been away too long. Karen is such a dear for letting me take some time off. I'd better let her know I'm still alive and kicking."

~~***~~

Larry sat in the vacant theater of the Dublin venue for that night's sold-out performance. This was his common practice to get a perspective of what the audience would see. Perfection ran deep in his soul and was a never-ending quest. He scrutinized the sets and various lighting effects. Joe occupied the seat next to him.

"Lar, have you called Taylor's daughter, Cindy?" he asked offhandedly.

"Where did that come from?" A look of wonder accented his knitted brow.

"Well, some of the British press must've reached the States," Joe explained. "Maybe she's expectin' a word from you. At the very least y' might let her know you're not cheatin' on her mother."

"I'm *not* cheating on Tay. I can't very well cheat on Tay *with* Tay." Larry casually brushed a wayward hair from his forehead. "You've got a point there. Why don't you call the others, Mark and Adrienne, Sonny and Robert for me. Don't give any details, just let them know there's a good hope that Taylor is alive and well. I'll deal with Cindy on my own. I don't need her blaming me for her mother's disappearance. She's only just recently accepted the fact that I had no hand in her father being out of her life."

"Guess you're right, Chief," Joe agreed. "When do you want me to call them? Before or after tonight's concert?"

"Better call them after." Larry adjusted his seat as he kept his eyes on the stage. The background singers and band went through their paces. "I don't want the distraction of phone calls to interfere with any show details. Gotta keep my head clear, if that's possible. Tiff, Tay, is all I've been thinking about. Her face is the only one I see in the audience. Sometimes I think I hear her voice—I turn around and find no one. Just another vacant moment filled with longing."

Joe patted him on the shoulder warmly. "I know, Lar. It's been damn rough on y'. Your pain gets to me. Just wish I could make it all right for y'."

~~***~~

A lazy afternoon. Tiffany and Karen strolled along the halls of the Victoria and Albert Museum in South Kensington. The weather was still too cool to spend much time on a park bench in the nearby gardens. Lady Lantham yearned for a kind and sympathetic ear. She related the confusion that grew larger with

96   *Cynthia B. Ainsworthe*

each passing day.

"Kar," Tiffany stated in a near whisper, "I have such restlessness running through me. My own thoughts torment me, as if I'm being pulled into a dark abyss with no strength to save myself."

"My dear, in what way?" Karen looked kindly at her friend.

"I don't think I love Clive." She bit her bottom lip, struggling to utter the words. "I've been living a lie—somehow, a lie that he created." She took a deep breath of dread. "I have no proof for my feelings—just a nagging intuition. How could I have loved a man so cold and controlling? I wish I could remember the beginning of it all."

"You remember nothing of your past with Clive?" her friend inquired.

"It's a complete blank—not even a glimmer." *Why does Kar want to know my past?*

Tiffany stopped in front of Tippo's Tiger in the South Asia gallery and gazed at the form of a man being mauled by a tiger.

"That!" She pointed to the exhibit. "That's how I feel. Clive is the tiger, and I'm his victim with no power."

Karen touched her friend's arm. "Tiff, I had no idea. Stupid me. I thought you had a life anyone would envy."

"Only a masochist would envy me." The two women ambled along the halls aimlessly noticing the exhibits. "I feel I'm hanging onto a great precipice with no one to pull me back. A life of endless social commitments with no substance—a shell hiding the person screaming to be set free."

"Oh, my poor dear," Karen offered softly, as one would to a sister. "How distraught you are." She paused a moment. "Is there not one person or thing that makes you happy?"

A weak smile curled at Tiffany's lips. Her expression took on a look of seeing a loving face before her. "Yes, Kar." A heavy sigh escaped. "Larry Davis makes me happy. His music and the truth I find in his genuine feelings touch my heart—as if he's been a part of my life in the past. I know this is silly talk … but that's how he makes me feel—wanted and loved."

"Crikey!" Karen cleared her throat. "That is a lofty goal. You leaving Clive to take up with Larry Davis?"

"Now, I didn't say anything of the kind," Tiffany defended.

"He makes me happy, that's all. His music is my safe

REMEMBER ? 97

haven …. A place of my own creation."

"What about his kisses?" her friend probed. "That was a nice bit of reality, wasn't it?"

"Yes," she acknowledged. A devilish twinkle settled in her eyes. "A forbidden reality, but definitely worth the risk."

"How much risk are you willing to take where Larry is concerned?" Karen delved, "Are you willing to take the chance of chucking away your royal marriage to his lordship?"

"Kar, you're making too much of my misguided judgment." She explained, "That was a girlish response on my part. I should've remembered my position and Clive." Her voice took on a wistful quality, "Yet, it was magical to me. When his lips met mine, I was someone else, free to be my own person with my own thoughts—no fear of being judged or reprimanded."

"Sounds like you're in love with this bloke."

"In love with his music." Tiffany conceded, "In love with him as a man? Well, that would be delightful to explore." She breathed deeply. "I'll never have the chance to find out. In a month, Larry will be finished with his tour and then heading back home to the States, I expect. Besides, I'm not sure I'd have the nerve to cross the stonewall existence of my marriage."

Karen replied knowingly, "You'd have the nerve. I'm sure of that." She smiled as if hiding a deep insight of her friend. "All you need is the opportunity."

"Maybe," Tiffany paused. "… an opportunity that will never present itself." *Our will it?*

TWELVE

"CINDY," LARRY STATED to Taylor's daughter on his cell phone, "don't get your hopes up, but I wanted to keep you in the loop."

"Is it about the headlines in the rags lately? This Tiffany Bradford woman looking like Mom?" He heard the cautious fear in her voice. "Is she really the Countess of Lantham?"

"Yes. I've met with her a couple of times during my concert in London. Funny thing though, Tiffany has no memory of her past—a pure case of amnesia." Larry started pacing in his Dublin Hotel room. "I can't go into details, but I feel I've found Taylor! Hell! I'm nearly one hundred percent certain of this. If it's not Taylor, then it's her twin."

"Mom was an only child like me," Cindy reminded firmly. "I don't remember her or Grandma mentioning a sibling."

"Exactly," he agreed. His palms grew moist with excitement. "All of this is so confusing. At least there's a flicker of hope. I know there has to be a logical explanation—just haven't found it yet."

"Interesting that this woman can't remember her past. Why is that?" she inquired.

"Seems Tiffany took a nasty fall, went into a coma, and woke up with no memory."

"Lar," Cindy pleaded, "if there is any way you can find out the truth, keep digging. I haven't had a day's peace since Mom disappeared."

"You can bet on it." Larry nodded as Joe entered the room. "I'll keep you posted. Please call the others and update them."

"Sure will," she agreed. "I'll call Mark and Sonny today."

Larry ended his call and directed his attention to Joe, who was at the bar getting himself a cold beer, one of the American beers the wet bar was stocked with per his request. The distraught singer slowed his pacing as he watched his friend flop into the comfortable brown leather wingback chair.

Joe began, "I take it you were talking with Cindy?"

"Yeah. I wanted to update her. Gave an explanation for

those pictures in the rags."

"How she's takin' all this tabloid stuff?" Joe popped the top from his beer; his eyes narrowed as he brought it to his lips.

"She's optimistic," Larry admitted. "I didn't want to get her hopes up—yet, I felt she should hear my side of things."

"Good idea." Joe watched Larry settle on the matching leather sofa. "After all, she *is* Taylor's daughter and should know the score."

"That's how I feel," Larry agreed. "I didn't want her to get the idea I was stepping out on her mom."

"Lar, you did right." Joe took a swallow of his beer. "If she got the idea y' gave up on findin' Taylor, Cindy might never speak to y' again." Deep in thought, Larry didn't respond. "Chief, got any ideas floatin' around? How y' gonna find the truth? This Tiffany dame just a look-alike, or is she really Taylor?"

"Don't know, Joe," he pensively stroked his chin. "There has to be a way—just haven't figured that one out yet."

~~***~~

Piers Andrews poured Johnnie Walker Blue over the precise number of three ice cubes into the finely cut crystal tumbler. Clive demanded his instructions be followed to the letter with no deviation. He served his employer the refreshment on a flawlessly polished silver tray. Lord Lantham enjoyed his prestige and title. He clearly held his own esteem in high regard in spite of his royal family relatives viewing his mediocre status on the heritage tree limbs.

"Your lordship, will you be requiring anything else?" Piers asked with the utmost of proper decorum.

"Andrews, I would like to ask you some questions about Lady Lantham," Clive sported cool indifference.

"I'll gladly tell you what I know, milord." He smiled, plainly pleased he may further secure his position in his employer's estimation. "Though, I don't know any details that your lordship doesn't most likely already know."

"Don't play coy with me, Andrews," Clive said firmly as he swirled the contents of his glass. "The hired help always know the secrets—being the proverbial fly on the wall." Piers remained stone-faced as Lord Lantham asked, "Tell me, has Lady Lantham been taking her medication as I instructed?"

100   *Cynthia B. Ainsworthe*

"Yes, yes she has." He stood ramrod straight with conviction. "All the medication envelopes you provided are empty. Your lordship, you can check for yourself."

"Andrews, I didn't ask about the ruddy envelopes! Anyone could empty the envelopes down the loo." Clive sat straighter as his face took on a cold hard stare at the butler. "Did you *see* her swallow the medication or not?"

Nervously shifting the weight onto his other leg, Piers stammered, "Elizabeth, she ... she mentioned that Lady Lantham took her medicine."

"I told you. *You* were to give the medicine to Lady Lantham!" Clive forced himself to keep his voice calm. "Why did Elizabeth give her the medicine when it was my express wishes for you to carry out that function?"

"Lady Lantham was indisposed." Piers fidgeted with his tie as if he felt Clive's fingers around his throat. "I didn't think it would be fitting for me to see Lady Lantham in her bed clothes."

"Quite." Clive took a swallow of the warming liquid. "Sorry, Andrews. I didn't intend to come down on you harshly— however, I demand my instructions be followed to the letter.... To the letter. Do we have an understanding in this?"

"Yes, milord." Piers swallowed hard, as if a golf ball occupied his throat. "Do you want me to be firm with Elizabeth and insist I give Lady Lantham her medicine in the future?"

"No, that won't be necessary," Clive replied coolly. "Elizabeth was right. It might upset her ladyship if the routine is changed. She trusts Elizabeth and is less likely to put up an argument."

Piers' quizzical look posed a question. Clive immediately noticed the butler's expression of mild wonder.

"Andrews, you are relatively new to this household. Although I don't have to, I feel I must explain a few things— things you are to keep in the strictest of confidence." Clive's voice took on a solemn quality, as if he was about to expose a dark family secret. "Her ladyship took a nasty fall while on holiday after our marriage. She fell into a coma and when she awoke, her past memory was obliterated. She had various tests while in hospital that showed she has a heart condition. Now you can fully appreciate why it is imperative she continues her medication as ordered. Her survival is dependent on that very fact." Clive stared into his drink. "My life would end as I know it if anything should happen to her. She's very valuable to me If she doesn't take her medicine as prescribed—then I can't monitor her progress properly—the results would be invalid."

"Invalid results, you say, milord?" Slight confusion veiled Piers' face. "May I inquire, is your lordship referring to an experiment of some kind?"

Clive's eyes grew wide with concern. "Experiment? Heavens, no! Don't be impertinent! All the medication for Lady Lantham is proven. You forget your place, Andrews." His tone turned to one of authority, "Not a word of this to anyone. Otherwise, you will promptly lose your situation here without a character, and won't be able to get work anywhere else. Have I made myself clear?"

"Perfectly, your lordship." Andrews took a few steps backward. "Is there anything else you require?"

"No. You may leave." Clive emphasized his orders, "Remember, not a word—not even to Elizabeth."

Piers nodded, left the room, and softly closed the double doors of the library.

Clive mulled over Tiffany's new obstinate nature as he sipped his scotch. Rodney remained curled on the rug at his feet. *Why is Tiffany so damn out of control? She's been taking her medication. I even doubled the dose. She should be more docile—not more animated. Just what the hell is wrong with her? She was happy with her humdrum existence. Now it's as if she's searching for more than her lost memory. But what? What is Tiffany looking for? If she finds it—then what? Will she leave me? Never! She'll be chained to a bedpost before I'll let her go!*

~~***~~

Larry's eyes opened with a hazy focus. He rubbed them to clear the image he saw through the bedroom window. *Am I seeing right? Who is that woman peering at me?* He moved closer to the foggy vision. Still in bed, it was as if he floated effortlessly toward the window by an unknown force. His heart pounded faster as the blue-green eyes sought his. Instinctively, he reached for her. As she came closer, her face emerged through the frost-covered pane. His hand reached for her. He felt his fingers run through her dark brown hair. Their lips were close. He could feel her breath.

102 *Cynthia B. Ainsworthe*

He said softly, "I love you so very much. At last I've found you. You've come back to me."

She didn't utter a reply. Love emanated from her eyes. Their lips met. He felt her warmth. Joy filled his entire being. Gone! The beautiful vision was completely erased. Now just a memory to take its place with all the others.

Larry awoke abruptly with a heavy breath. A heaviness of longing filled his heart. *It was only a dream! A beautiful dream—Tay was mine, if only for an instant. How can I go on without her? For a brief moment I was so happy, but now I'm desperately sad.* In the darkness, he stared at the vacant window, as if by focusing on his dream, he could make her reappear again. *Should I go against the advice of my PR people and seek out Tiff? It could mean the end of my career. Speculations of Lady Lantham and me are still a hot topic in the tabloids. Maybe there's a way I can see her again and still maintain privacy—but how? Yeah, this is the ugly price of fame—a price I've been paying for nearly my entire life! When in the name of God will the bill be paid in full?*

~~***~~

An hour passed. Larry sat in a chair as he gazed out the hotel window. The view from his suite's living room offered a vacant damp street that mimicked his mood. Gentle raindrops trickled down the pane and echoed the despair in his soul. The clock chimed one. He took no notice. Tormented memories of himself and Taylor occupied his thoughts. *I have to find a way to see Tiff. I must get her to remember her past. If she does, I know she'll remember who she really is—my wife, and she belongs by my side.*

Larry stared at Joe's scruffy uncombed hair on end as he entered the room. Even though it was one o'clock in the afternoon, his appearance indicated it to be much earlier in the morning. The deep lines on his face, his slow gait, and rounded shoulders paid testimony to Joe's advancing years. Larry thought Joe's spirits still seemed young, and in direct opposition to the various aches and pains that he complained of daily.

Joe glanced offhandedly at Larry in the chair. He didn't mention Larry's sullen expression. He gave an enormous yawn with a large gulp of air before saying, "Lar, how come you're not dressed yet?"

"For the same reason you're not." Larry gave a sideways

glance to Joe before returning his gaze to the gold wedding band on his finger.

"I got somethin' that might cheer you up," Joe offered with the hint of a smile.

"If it has to do with Tay, I mean Tiff," Larry sat straighter in his chair, "I might be interested."

"I don't know if it has anythin' to do with that countess friend of yours." Joe's chubby fingers combed through his hair. "But there's a possibility."

Larry's face lined with frustration. "Joe, just come out with it. Stop beating around the bush."

"Okay, I will," Joe agreed. "Just got off the phone with your agent in New York. Seems you have a kinda command performance request from a member of the royal family." Joe yawned again. "Good thing she called or else I might still be sleepin'."

"Get on with it, Joe," Larry said emphatically. "What did Nancy say?"

"You're to give a private performance at some manor house north of London. Since they will have their own personal security guys, you're only allowed to bring one security person. You can't bring any band members or background singers. Have to sing a cappella for this gig. Might have a piano player for y'." Joe paused a moment. "Guess they don't want strangers in the mix. Besides, it's after this tour, and y' got three or four weeks off before you return to Vegas for the Chambord stint." He ambled to a chair and flopped down directly facing Larry. "I told Nancy it was a 'go'. Figured this was too big an opportunity to pass up. Y' need some good press, considerin' all the negative stuff out there between you and Lady B."

"You said *yes*?" he questioned with surprise. "It would've been nice if you'd asked me first."

"I thought you'd jump at the idea." Joe upturned his palms. "Especially, since you might see Tiff. Her ladyship is connected to the royals. She just might show up."

"Y' know, Joe," his eyes sparked with a flicker of hope, "you might be onto something. Tiff could very well be there. That would be wonderful."

Joe gave Larry's hopeful expression a dose of cold reality. "If she does show up—she'll probably be with her husband, Lord

Lantham."

"I don't wanna hear it!" The singer's eyes thinned with frustration. "You're always pouring water on my hopes and dreams where Tiff is concerned. You did the same thing when I first met Tay years ago, and that turned out okay."

"Yeah, it turned out okay—at the expense of Paul," Joe reminded.

"Stuff it!" His jaw set. "No more talk of Paul. That's something I will always regret and will never forget!" Larry leaned closer with elbows on knees. "Back to the bad press. I thought most of the negative talk had died down."

"It has," his friend agreed. "Good PR is worth its weight in gold—can never get too much of that."

He nodded in agreement. A smile emerged as the prospect of seeing Tiffany entered his mind.

Larry stood up and started pacing. *My God, if Tiff comes to this private party, I could speak with her. I might have a chance to jog her memory. I have so many questions. I'll have to keep them to myself. I'd love to show her the photo of us. Nope. I can't risk scaring her off. Still, just to be near her again ….*

THIRTEEN

THE MERCEDES LIMOUSINE traveled slowly along the immense winding driveway. Larry looked out the window at the expansive brown tinged lawn as the driver commented on the history of the manor house he was about to visit. Joe appeared less than interested and sported a look of boredom with eyes that never focused on one single object as the scenery passed by. Larry felt ill at ease. The absence of his security men left a wary feeling in his gut. *I hope I won't regret this decision to do this private performance without my security.* Lines formed on his forehead. *Guess I'll be safe. How risky could it be performing for the royals? I hope they'll at least have a piano. I wonder if the Queen will be there. Can't get my hopes up. Probably just a bunch of royals who barely know my name. This is Thursday. I wonder if all the high muckety-mucks enjoy long weekends.*

The car pulled up slowly to the entry of the sprawling limestone mansion. The sun hung low in the February sky and was overcast with clouds, giving the illusion that the day was later than two o'clock in the afternoon. Meticulously groomed boxwood hedges adorned the foundation softening the austere façade. Tall, white towering columns flanked the entrance of two massive doors. Larry's eyes widened in awe of such an impressive sight. The driver quickly exited the car and opened the door for the famous guests. As Larry and Joe got out of the vehicle, the welcome of the head servant softened the crunch of gravel as he approached.

"I am Mr. Beddingfield. Butler to the Duke and Duchess of Steffenfordshire." His rigid posture spoke of the utmost decorum. The driver proceeded to retrieve the luggage. "It's an honor to have you as a guest at Hollingsworth Manor. I trust your stay will be enjoyable."

Larry nodded in agreement. "Thank you very much. I feel honored to have been invited."

"Me too," Joe chimed in. "Looks like a fine place. Somethin' I won't forget."

Following the butler, Charles Beddingfield, the two climbed

106   *Cynthia B. Ainsworthe*

the steps to the entry. As the door opened, the footman, greeted the famous guest with a warm and dignified smile.

The butler made a brief introduction, "This is Oliver, our first footman. He will be attending to your personal needs."

Oliver blurted out, "Oliver Pritchard, sirs."

Charles gave a disagreeable glance. "Please excuse Oliver. He is relatively new to service and is still learning."

The footman and butler immediately assisted in removing their coats and hung them in a discreet closet off the foyer. Oliver then exited through an obscure door.

Larry noticed the quiet in the room. "Am I the first one to arrive? I hope I didn't get here too early."

"Not in the least," Beddingfield replied. "Please, sir, follow me to the drawing room." The servant led the way to a room on the left and parted the heavy wood paneled doors to expose the large, lavishly appointed room. "Only one other guest has arrived. Please have a seat and make yourself comfortable. May I offer you a brandy?"

"No, thanks," Larry answered. "A cup of tea would be nice."

"Certainly, sir." the butler turned to Joe, "And, sir, what may I serve you?"

"A beer if y' got it," he replied as he glanced around the room.

"Will Guinness be suitable?" the servant inquired.

"Yeah, whatever y' got." Joe eyed the immense ancestral portraits decorating the twelve-foot high walls.

Larry made a face at Joe's common everyday approach to the butler.

His friend upturned his palms. "What? He asked me a question and I answered it."

"Don't speak so common," Larry whispered. "This is a royal residence."

"Yeah, I know," his friend grumbled.

Beddingfield left the two and quietly closed the door behind him. Hands in his pockets, Larry walked softly on the expensive Aubusson carpet as he surveyed his surroundings. His eyes immediately focused on the piano. A broad smile emerged. *I guess that's where I'll be sitting tonight—playing and singing my heart out. I wonder how many will be here. This is a large room.* Meanwhile, Joe had settled down on a comfortable wingback chair near the looming marble fireplace.

A soft knock came at the door. Larry assumed it was the footman, Oliver. The doors slowly parted. Larry looked up with surprise that quickly morphed into an expression of delight. He pulled on the cuffs of his black shirt—a long-standing nervous gesture.

"I didn't know you were invited, too," he commented with boyish glee.

"The same for me." Tiffany displayed inexplicable embarrassment. Color that was intensified by her dark green turtle-neck sweater came to her cheeks. "I thought this was a week-end just for the girls. That's what Amelia told me."

"Amelia?" Larry asked.

"She's my cousin-in-law, Amelia—the Duchess of Steffenfordshire," she explained. "She should be arriving later this afternoon." Tiffany acknowledged his friend and adopted brother, "Hi, Joe. Nice to see you again."

Joe nodded as he silently observed this interchange with a sly smile.

"Tiff, do you know how many guests are coming?" Larry raised his eyebrow endearingly.

"No, I don't." She walked to the long beige brocade sofa across from Joe. Larry followed as she sat down. "I thought this would be a quiet weekend. I'm only here through Sunday. I leave for London on Monday."

"Since this is Thursday, we'll have a nice long weekend to chat," he mentioned casually. Joe rolled his eyes. Larry and Tiffany's, gaze remained locked onto each other's stare.

Oliver entered the room carrying a silver tray with a full sterling silver tea service and small tea sandwiches for their enjoyment, as well as Joe's Guinness in a tall crystal pilsner.

"I'd like coffee, please," Tiffany commented softly.

"Of course, Lady Lantham." He smiled politely. "I anticipated your preference. Coffee is already prepared."

A grateful smile emerged as the servant went about his duties serving the Hollingsworth's guests.

"So, I guess you and the duchess are quite close?" Larry inquired charmingly as he watched Tiffany sip her coffee.

"Somewhat," she agreed. "I envy her free spirit and love for adventure."

108   *Cynthia B. Ainsworthe*

"Do you share that same zest for adventure?" He inched closer to her.

"You could say that." A devilish smile crossed her lips along with a spark in her eye.

"Hmm, this weekend could be interesting." Larry's hand gently grazed the top of hers.

Joe gave a loud cough. "I think I'll find Oliver to show me where my room is. Give you two some privacy. Besides, I need a nap."

Moments later, Charles quietly approached the guests. He carried a silver tray that held two small white envelopes.

"If you please, Lady Lantham and Mr. Davis, I have a message for you both from the Duchess of Steffenfordshire."

Larry and Tiffany exchanged quizzical glances.

"Amelia is rather mysterious," she commented.

The two hastily opened the envelopes and read the identical message.

Hello my pets,

I trust you've settled in quite nicely. Please enjoy all the amenities of the manor. My servants are at your disposal. Unfortunately, I will not be joining you this weekend as I have a social commitment of a similar nature.

Please forgive my little ruse. You are the only two invited guests. I thought you could both use a bit of rest and relaxation.

I'm sure you will find something to amuse yourselves. Please trust in the discreetness of my servants. They are very loyal and discerning. Mum's the word in their regard.

Have fun! The weekend is yours to explore!
My best regards,
Amelia

"My, my, my, my, my!" Larry spoke rapidly. His mind went into overdrive. *This could be a most interesting weekend. Amelia is quite a lady! I wonder if Tiff had any inkling of Amelia's plans. If she did, she's not showing it. She's acting just as surprised as me.*

"I don't know what to say," Tiffany exclaimed as color came to her face. "Seems Amelia expects us to get to know each other better."

REMEMBER ?   109

"A lot better, I would say." Larry put the note on the ornate inlayed coffee table. He extended his arm across her shoulders, as if he had Lady Amelia's unspoken approval.

"It appears so," she replied softly. "I'm afraid I'll be poor company for an entire weekend. You already know my past from our previous meetings."

"Poor company?" His fingers played along the softness of her slender neck. "I hardly think so. I find you fascinating."

"That's nice of you to say." She breathed deeply. "That's not how Clive thinks of me. He's bored with me."

"He's a fool." *How can he be bored with you! No other woman can compare to you.* "Sorry, I shouldn't have said that."

"No need to apologize," Tiffany offered as she sipped her coffee. "I find him a bore. Always more interested in his research, royal protocol, and his club. Maybe if I was his science experiment, I'd see him more often."

"Sounds like you're married in name only?" he inquired.

"You've summed that one up perfectly." Tiffany's tone embraced a touch of sadness.

"That's too bad," he agreed. "If you were in my life, you'd never be second place."

"Since I'm married," she mentioned softly, "that will never happen."

His fingers tilted her chin upward. *I want to kiss you so badly. Tiff, you're my wife!* Larry's lips came close to hers. She gently moved away to avert his advances.

Another soft knock sounded on the door. Oliver entered and cleared his throat to make his presence known.

"Excuse me, Mr. Davis. I will be pleased to show you to your room," he offered. "I took the liberty of unpacking for you, as per the duchess' instructions."

Tiffany reacted with relief from the tense moment. She immediately stood up, and Larry followed close behind her. He went to place his hand on her waist but aborted the effort. *Better not move too fast. I can't risk scaring her away. I might never get another opportunity to spend a weekend with her.*

Tiffany and Larry followed the footman. "Oliver, do you enjoy working in this big house?" Larry asked.

"Very much, sir. Someday I might work my way up to butler." Oliver paused on the landing.

110   *Cynthia B. Ainsworthe*

"Charles will have to watch his step," Tiffany chimed in.

"Milady, I mean me being a butler in another house. I would never presume to replace Mr. Beddingfield," he clarified. "He's a wonderful teacher."

The sharp sound of footsteps echoed on the white Italian marble as they climbed the long, spiral stairway. Oliver proceeded to comment on the various portraits that lined the walls showing the Hollingsworth ancestry and the importance of each.

Coming to Larry's room, Oliver opened the door and invited the two to enter. It had a masculine and refined feel with dark heavy Georgian furniture and walls papered in burgundy damask. Contrasting heavy brocade drapes of burgundy and forest green stripes accented the windows overlooking the vast English gardens and the countryside beyond.

Larry turned slowly in a circle as he eyed the lush décor. Not allowing him to comment, Oliver mentioned, "If you would like, sir, I can draw your bath before dinner."

"No need. I can do that for myself." He asked, "When are we expected for dinner?"

"At whatever time you desire, sir," Oliver replied. "Although, eight o'clock is traditional."

Larry gave an easy smile. "Eight o'clock it is." He glanced at his watch and then looked at her. "We have at least a couple of hours to kill. Tiff, what would you like to do?" *I know what I'd like to do—take you in my arms and make passionate love all night long!*

"I'd like you to sing to me." She blushed as a schoolgirl. "Though, I suppose you might want to take a break from performing."

"Not in the least!" He beamed. "I love music. Singing to you would be a treat for me." Larry turned to the footman. "Oliver, what's behind that door?" He pointed to an access near the bed.

"That door, sir?" the servant inquired. "That door adjoins Lady Lantham's room." Oliver slipped a sly smile.

"I see," Larry replied softly. *This can be a very interesting weekend. I wonder if Tiff would lock the door.*

Tiffany glanced from the door to Larry with wistful adventure.

FOURTEEN

LARRY SAT AT the baby grand piano playing all his famous love ballads. Tiffany's folded arms rested on the top as she looked at him dreamily. He charmed her heart with every lyric and facial expression. *I can't get this man out of my mind. Why does he captivate me so? I'm married. I shouldn't be feeling this way. But I don't feel married anymore—not since Clive has turned away from me. He treats his relatives better. I'm nothing more than his pet.*

"Tiff, you're so quiet." His easy smile tugged at her vulnerable heart.

"I was just thinking." She breathed deeply to hide her stirring emotions. "Your music takes me to beautiful places …. Places and feelings that are warm and comforting."

"Sounds like a woman in love." He tilted his head in a boyish fashion that eroded her defenses bit by bit and affixed his image firmly in her mind.

"In love, you say?" Tiffany played lazily with the gold necklace at her throat. "In love with the music?"

"The music, or the man?" Larry finished the song with a flourish as he hit the last note.

She giggled girlishly. "Definitely the music." Her pause punctuated her next comment as the tip of her tongue toyed along her upper lip. "Maybe the man too …. Who knows? The weekend is young."

Larry's sly smile met her question. Clearly, he hoped for more. "You don't say? Well, Lady Lantham, that's a very interesting proposition."

Her face brightened as she continued to look directly into his eyes. "A proposition? I never said that." Her hand went from her necklace to the top of the piano and traced an unseen image. "I don't know if I'm venturous enough for such abandoned fantasies."

"It would be fun to find out," he remarked in a soft intriguing voice. "The possibilities are endless, and …" he looked around the room briefly, "I don't think the hired help would say anything—not with all the proper protocol that's observed."

112   *Cynthia B. Ainsworthe*

"You're correct on that one. The country is saturated in protocol—at least where I come from." Tiffany nodded her head in the direction of upstairs. "What about your friend, Joe? Can he be trusted?"

"Definitely!" Larry assured. "I'd trust him with my life. He only betrayed me once—and then it was indirectly. Poor guy didn't know there was an eavesdropper around."

"Did that cause you harm?" Her brow marked concern.

"Not real harm to me." His expression turned to sadness. "But another good man paid the ultimate price."

"Do you want to talk about it?" she probed gently.

"Not really." He leaned closer and stroked the top of her hand. "I'd rather get back to the subject of where this weekend might go—your room or mine?"

"Hmm …. That does sound inviting," she replied in a coquettish manner. "But who said it would be my room or yours?"

"Where then?" Larry's eyes twinkled with anticipation.

"I don't know if there will be, a 'where' or 'when'." Tiffany faked a pout.

"You will let me know when you decide, won't you?" He employed his onstage charm to soften her reserves.

"You mean with words …" she paused to dramatize the moment, "or something else?"

"Tiff, you're driving me wild with distraction." His smile broadened with obvious anticipation. "I love every coy and teasing innuendo. You've always known how to get to me— right from the very beginning—at the Tampa concert." He caught himself. "I mean in the dress shop."

"You still see me as your lost wife, don't you?" Her laughing eyes turned serious.

"No, Tiff. I see you as who you are now. I misspoke. Sorry."

She stroked the side of his face as a slight smile of forgiveness emerged. "No harm done. I just don't want your heart to confuse me with someone else."

"Don't worry, Tiff." He gently moved her hand to his lips and left a warm loving kiss on her palm.

~~***~~

Candles flickered and gave the exclusive hotel bedroom a soft feel, accented by the dim light on the nightstand. Amelia

REMEMBER ?   113

stared at the cream damask covered wall. Her slow, satisfied breathing was coupled by another's.

"A penny for your thoughts, Lady Amelia," the deep masculine voice questioned, as he gazed at her full breasts barely hidden by the luxurious sheet.

She didn't look at him before answering as she stretched her naked body and extended a bare leg off the side of the bed. "Oh, I was wondering what two people I know are doing at this moment."

"Maybe, what we just shared?" He traced a line of kisses down her upper arm.

"Yes. Quite right—if I have anything to do with it." A delighted smirk emerged from her full lips.

"Who might these two would-be lovers be, if I may ask?" His hand supported his head.

"You may not." She turned slightly to see the candlelight illuminate his strong, youthful features and intense deep brown eyes. "Stephen, remember one thing, if you remember nothing else. You are mine for as long as I decide. Don't flatter yourself with the misguided notion that you are privy to my private life." His expression sullied. She ran her fingers through the thick brown hair on his muscular chest. "I am here with you because I can't resist your young virile body and the fantastic athleticism you can endure during our lovemaking. You are with me because you love the lifestyle my money provides. When, or if, I tire of you, you can move on to another. Although, I doubt they will provide you with the fine things you now enjoy thanks to my beneficence. Besides, any other woman with my standing may have the money, but can you really picture yourself mounting all that wilting flesh and caressing their road map faces?"

"Agreed." His kisses traveled up her neck to her earlobe. "But I would still like to know what you have planned for this mystery couple."

"It should be an interesting weekend for them." A devilish smile graced her striking face. "Oh, what I would give to be a fly on the wall. I bet the servants will have plenty to tell."

"Amelia, you are so very wicked—that's what I love about you—always full of surprises." His hand fell to her breast with a firm, teasing caress as her nipple grew taut.

"Full of money you mean," she quipped. "No matter. As long as you keep pleasing me in such a delicious fashion, you can stay."

"Will the servants tell you all the details?" Stephen probed.

"Definitely. They're loyal to me—first and foremost," she replied confidently.

"Amelia, why do you talk so callously to me?" he asked. "Do you talk to the duke with such a tone?"

"I talk to you the way I do, because I can," she countered. "And you love it."

He made a face. "How can you get free of him so easily? Doesn't he get suspicious?"

"I really don't think he cares much. By marrying me, his bank accounts bulge. Besides, young Stephen, he has his own diversions and I have mine … like you."

"Other women you mean?" Stephen softly kissed her full breast.

"Not likely. His taste runs alongside mine—young lads with fine loins that ache to be satisfied." Her hand reached down below his waist.

Stephen raised an eyebrow at this new revelation and feigned hurt feelings. "You make me feel like I'm a stallion in your stable, merely to serve your lustful needs."

"Well, Stephen … I *did* find you in the stable grooming a horse." Her eyes twinkled with renewed desire. "And, I must say, I wasn't disappointed. I love the way you rein in your mare."

"I love to ride my mare long and hard." His open mouth graced her lips. Stephen breathed heavily as he spoke with mounting desire. "Are you ready for another ride through the countryside? Or have I satisfied you enough this evening?"

"My, my … you *are* feeling randy tonight, aren't you?" Amelia's hungry lips met his in a passionate kiss.

~~***~~

Cindy Hastings sat at the breakfast table. She read the Arts and Entertainment section of the Tampa Sunday newspaper. Her long sandy blonde hair cascaded across her shoulders and feathered bangs flirted with her brows. She had inherited her mother's intense blue-green eyes along with an innate sensuality.

REMEMBER ? 115

The rustling of paper as Vic leafed through the sports section was the only noise that punctuated the silence.

The intrusive cell phone rang and brought her to the present. She made a face as she reached for the phone.

"Hello?" she greeted.

"Cindy, it's Mark," the male voice announced with a tone of concern.

A yawn escaped before answering, "Yes, I know. What's up?"

"Have you been keeping up with the entertainment news lately?" he asked with an air of importance.

"Not really." She took a sip of coffee before continuing, "I find it too depressing. I keep hoping to hear of some news about Mom, but there's nothing. I'm in constant fear I'll see a headline that they found her body somewhere—I don't want to face the fact that I probably won't ever see her again."

"I completely understand," Mark agreed. "Larry called me the other day from the UK. He just finished a tour there and is staying a little longer before he returns to his Vegas gig."

"Yes, so what does that have to do with Mom being lost?" Cindy inquired with a furrowed brow.

"He thinks he might've found Taylor." His voice rang with hope. "It seems Larry came across this woman who can't remember her past and is living as Tiffany, married to the world-renowned Clive Bradford, Lord of Lantham, the famous neurosurgeon. Larry's convinced this woman is Taylor but can't put the pieces together yet."

"I know." She explained. "He called me with the same info. I don't dare get my hopes up."

"Larry told me she's the spitting image of Taylor—the talk, walk, style, likes and dislikes—all of it." A few seconds of silence followed as Cindy digested this incredible news.

Vic, overhearing his wife's conversation, put down his paper. He studied her face as she spoke.

"Mark, I was beginning to accept the fact that I might never see Mom again—now all this could change—feeling hopeful and then finding out it was all for nothing." She bit her bottom lip as a renewed worry came to her.

"I hear you. The rags haven't put the pieces together yet. They're running on the premise Larry's seeing Tiffany and has

116   *Cynthia B. Ainsworthe*

given up on finding Taylor." Mark relayed his assumptions, "Papers sell quicker if there's a dark side to the storyline instead of coming to the conclusion that Tiffany *is* your mom. The tabloids are drenched with the sensational slant that Larry is cheating on Taylor." She heard a sipping noise over the phone. "I *know* he would never knowingly cheat on your mom."

"If he is, wouldn't that come full circle?" Cindy said with emphasis, "Considering that Mom cheated on my dad with him."

"I thought you were beyond all that."

"How can I ever really be 'beyond that'?" She sighed as her voice choked. "Especially after what happened to dad."

"Don't dig that all up again," Mark said with sincere kindness. "Nothing can be gained from it. The main thing to focus on is—your mom might be found. Larry is certain of it, and I can't see him grasping at straws—he's too levelheaded."

"Sorry, Mark," she replied in a low tone. "I can't go there. I won't get my hopes up only to be crushed again."

"I understand."

"Thanks." Cindy paused. "How is your wife seeing all of this? What's her take on it?"

"Adrienne agrees with me. People can suffer amnesia for a number of reasons, an illness, a blow on the head, anything is possible. Personally, I've seen the photo of this Lady Lantham or Bradford in the papers, and she's a dead ringer for Taylor."

"When you get a chance, would you drop them off to me?" Cindy asked softly. "I've been avoiding all those rags since Mom went missing. I'd like to see for myself."

"Sure thing," Mark agreed. "I'll bring them over tomorrow."

After all this time, nearly two years has passed, and now there's a chance Mom has been found. But what if Tiffany isn't Mom? Then what? My heart breaks all over again, all because of mistaken identity? I hope Larry isn't foolish enough to get involved with this woman. If he does, he'll be cheating on Mom and that would break her heart—might even give her another heart attack she wouldn't recover from—I would never forgive Larry for that!

Vic got up and grabbed his jacket from the coat rack. He fished the car keys from his pocket. Cindy didn't notice her husband ready to leave. He startled her from her thoughts.

"Cindy, I've got a poker game with the guys. Don't wait up. I

REMEMBER ? 117

feel a winning streak coming on."

"Don't bet too much. Remember the fifty dollar limit." She stood to hug him goodbye.

Vic kissed her cheek. "Yeah, yeah. I know the rules."

~~***~~

Tiffany sat at the dressing table freshening her makeup and combing her hair before going downstairs for dinner. She glanced at the door in the mirror—the door that connected her bedroom to Larry's.

After a long moment, she stood up, paused, and walked directly to the portal that could leave her in a compromising position later that night. Placing her hand on the key, she slowly turned it and heard the tumblers fall into place. *I know this is the proper thing to do—close my heart and body to temptation, but why is it so difficult for me? Locking this door feels like I'm going against my true nature. Just what is my true nature? Being shut away by Clive— is that where I'm destined to spend the rest of my life, or should I unlock this door and open the path to living and a real sense of freedom? Why does something so wrong feel so right? Yet, in a strange way, it feels familiar, too.* Without further thought, Tiffany unlocked the door. She took a deep breath, straightened her posture, and glanced one last time in the mirror before making her way to dinner. *Well, Mr. Davis, I have no idea what this evening will hold in store, but I'm ready for the adventure—an adventure I might regret—but, at least I'll know I'm alive and not a puppet on a string.*

FIFTEEN

TIFFANY FOUND LARRY staring through the expansive window of the manor's library. Although little of the formal gardens were visible at eight o'clock in the evening, he gave the impression he enjoyed the view. With a knitted brow and hands casually in pockets, it was clear Larry's thoughts were focused on more than shrubs and trees.

Plush Persian carpeting muted her footsteps. Slight rippling of the antique glass panes enhanced the charm of the old Hollingsworth estate. She cleared her throat to make her presence known. He turned and took a long hard look at her slim, enticing form enhanced by the red crepe sheath dress with a sweetheart neckline. Tiffany blushed as his eyes traveled from her cleavage to her sparkling blue-green eyes.

"Do you think I'm overdressed?" Her seductive voice cooed.

"Not in the least," he said with a smooth voice that made most women melt. "On the contrary," Larry offered as he started to walk toward her, "I'm only wearing a turtleneck and sports jacket. Maybe I should change."

"Don't change a thing." A smile curled the corners of her mouth. "I find nothing more appealing than a man in a cozy sweater. It gives me a warm feeling inside."

"A warm feeling?" His unmistakable charm showed through naturally like the sun kissing the sky. "If seeing me in comfortable clothes gives you a warm feeling, what would you feel if I embraced you?"

"My, my, Mr. Davis." She coyly looked at him beneath her long black lashes. "I don't know if I should venture into such a situation. I remember all too well our brief, passionate kisses in your dressing room."

"Please, call me 'Lar' like you did before," he requested softly.

"I didn't know if we were being overheard by the staff." Tiffany turned her head briefly to see if they were alone.

"I thought you said the staff was completely discreet?" Larry raised an eyebrow in a boyish manner.

REMEMBER ?   119

"Yes, I know." She fumbled her words. "I, I guess I'm just a bit self-conscious, especially with Joe in the house."

"Don't worry about him." Larry confidently moved closer and placed his hands on her shoulders. "Joe's really beat. He's having dinner in his room. This last tour took a lot out of him. He's not only my right-hand-man, he's also my confidant, brother, and personal security guard."

"I don't mind Joe being around," Tiffany explained with a tone of apology. "I rather like him. He's like a comfortable old shoe."

Larry laughed. "Now you've summed him up perfectly. Yes, Joe is a wonderful old shoe—one I would trust my life with—there's none better."

"I don't know why, and I shouldn't feel this way," she revealed, "but I feel as if I've known not only you, but Joe before in another place or time."

"Go on." Larry drew her closer and looked intently into her eyes, as if to communicate a truth only he knew and wanted her to realize.

"I know this sounds silly." The words choked in her throat. "I have absolutely no reason to feel this way—but, I sometimes know what you or Joe are about to say before you say it—as if somehow I've heard those words before."

"Tiff, I don't want to scare you off. Please hear me out on this. I feel with all my being that you do know me and Joe very well. Not because you are intuitive or have some far-out powers, but," he hesitated, "but because you are someone I know…have known. You're my past that is now my present. I know this all sounds crazy and mixed up. Just trust me in this. I can show you your past, if you give me the chance."

"I want to trust you," she admitted. *Can I trust him? I want his arms around me where it's warm and safe.* "I'm afraid if I let you into my life, what I have known as a certain degree of security will be lost forever."

"Does that security bring you happiness?" His hands slipped down her arms as his lips came close to hers. "Can it love you on long dark nights?"

"No," she whispered. Their lips met in a soft lingering kiss—a kiss more of love than lust. *I can't see any other man kissing me but Lar. This is wrong, yet I think I love him.*

120   *Cynthia B. Ainsworthe*

Their kiss lasted a long moment. Plainly, a kiss of never-ending love and devotion. Larry kissed her fingertips before holding Tiffany in a long embrace. An expression of deep contentment came to her as his strong arms encircled her and provided a moment of sanctuary from the harshness of Clive's world.

~~***~~

Clive and Alistair shared research ideas over a brandy in the hotel's lounge. Decorated in deep hunter green with dark wood paneling and accented by framed lithograph reproductions of various hunting scenes, it was quintessentially a very British and proper atmosphere for the patrons of well-to-do origins, be it by birth or not.

"Clive, have you listened to a word I said?" Alistair studied Lord Lantham's reaction. There was none, save for the steely cold stare at his drink.

"Quite." Clive finished his scotch in one determined gulp. "Yes, I've been listening to you. I just can't agree with all the bloody rules for this project. All those bureaucrats want us to do is drag our feet. We could be so much further along if they would give us the green light. Don't they realize who they're dealing with! I'm the Earl of Lantham, a world-renowned neurosurgeon, winner of numerous awards for advancement of neurosciences—not some ninny working on his first thesis!" His jaw tightened. "They should trust my suggestions and tramp full steam ahead. How dare they question my judgment? Damn the bloody protocol! I know I'm on the right track. We need to start human trials—we need to start them now!"

"Calm down, ol' man." Concern drew lines on Alistair's face. "I've never seen you so unraveled. Ripping at the seams it looks to me. Is there anything else bothering you?"

"Tiffany, for one. And her obstinate nature for another." Clive indicated to the bartender that a refill was in order.

"That sweet little flower you're married to?" His friend eyed the handsome bartender with a nod to replenish the drink.

"Well, 'sweet' and 'flower' are two words that no longer apply," he responded gruffly. "Self-determined and fiercely independent fit the bill when referring to her ladyship. If I had known almost two years ago what I know now," his voice became nearly inaudible as he continued, "I would have left her

REMEMBER ? 121

rotting in that Paris hospital."

Alistair's ears perked up. "Clive, what did you say?"

"Never mind. It wasn't worth repeating." His jaw set firmer as seething anger brewed. "She's not worth any words or my time." Clive paused a moment. "I owe you one ol' chap. Because of your wife planning a weekend in the country with Tiffany, I don't have her around my neck during this conference—no obligations to see her or speak with her."

"Sounds like you're down on women," his friend concluded. "Maybe you need to try a diversion along my tastes."

"Not a chance." Clive turned to face his friend. "I see nothing wrong with you and the boys—just not my cup of tea. Don't get me wrong, I couldn't care less who amuses you. For me, my research is all the bed partner I need. Sex dulls the senses and inhibits my intense theories—theories that could change the world and win me the Nobel Prize."

"Whatever works for you, ol' chap." Alistair wrote his room number on a cocktail napkin and pushed it toward the young man behind the bar. "Personally, I come up with my best ideas after the pipes have been cleared of rust. It invigorates me." The bartender gave a slight appreciative smile.

"Be that as it may, I find the lady of the house a ball and chain. She's too damn proper to take a lover—if she did, I could get rid of her. She's of no use to me now, not now when I can't control her."

"Would you really consider a *divorce?*" Alistair raised his eyebrows. "You of all people, so concerned with ruddy protocol and social position?"

"There are other ways. She could run off with a lover. My last wife did. No complications, everything was cut and dried, and I was the poor misunderstood and abandoned husband. Everyone at the club felt so sorry for me…. For a while, I was invited to all the best social gatherings. Oh, you should have heard them all say, 'Poor Clive, his wife left him, however will he cope?' and 'We must invite him to all the truly important functions to cheer him up.'" He stared vacantly at the wall while continuing, "I didn't have a free weekend for months. It was bloody well lucky for me that Penelope left during the beginning of hunt season. I made some very important contacts during that time—got me connected to MI6 and a very lucrative salary."

"I can see you're not in the best of spirits." Alistair raised his voice a decimal to be overheard by the bartender, "I'll call it a night, ol' man, and leave you to your scotch. Don't ring my room until morning." He winked at the bartender. "I have a feeling I may be otherwise engaged for the night."

~~***~~

After dinner, Larry stood by Tiffany in the drawing room as they gazed into the darkness of the English garden illuminated by a hazy moon, partially hidden by wandering clouds. Her mood was pensive. Feelings long suppressed rose to the surface. *Why do I feel this compulsion to make love to him? I have only met him a handful of times, and already he fills my entire being.*

"A penny for your thoughts," Larry whispered in her ear as his hands caressed her shoulders. Clearly, he wanted to be close to her.

"Oh, you don't want to know." She let out devilish giggle.

"Try me," he answered seductively as his gentle kiss rested on her earlobe.

"Hmm …" Tiffany paused with half-closed eyes. "That could be dangerous … for both of us."

Her allure drew his body closer. "I'm not afraid." Larry inhaled the fragrance from her hair. He placed his arms around her waist as if wanting to turn her to face him. "You can tell me anything, anything, Tiff." His soft voice played music to her ears, melting her resolve drop by drop.

"I was wondering how a woman of my status could possibly entertain such forbidden thoughts—thoughts that make me shudder knowing the possible consequences and yet thrill me to my very center." She turned to face him. His embrace grew firmer. "These are thoughts I shouldn't have—they're tantalizing and so very wrong."

He frowned with unvoiced concern. "Why don't you tell me," he suggested in an irresistible endearing tone that would melt his many devotees. "You might feel better and discover your thoughts aren't as forbidden or dangerous as you think."

"Yes," Tiffany looked into his soul-searching blue eyes, "but once I say them, they can never be taken back."

"Tiff, please don't tease me like this." His fingertips lovingly caressed her cheek.

REMEMBER ? 123

"Lar, I think," she paused. "I think I want to—"

The butler came into the room cutting off her words. "Mr. Davis and Lady Lantham, your beds have been turned down for the evening. Is there anything else you will be requiring?" His suave manner was polite and efficient.

Larry replied quickly, "Thanks. Lady Lantham and I would like to be left alone."

"As you wish, sir." Charles promptly left the room.

He turned back to Tiffany. Her former dream-like expression turned to one of concern as she fingered her wedding band.

Soothingly, he asked, "What is it, Tiff?" He framed her face in his palms. "Tell me what's on your mind."

"I want to. But, I …" She paused and bit her bottom lip with worry.

"Maybe this will convince you." Larry drew her closer. His lips gently met hers.

They shared a long, loving kiss. Her mind whirled. *I feel I've shared a million kisses with this man. Can I continue to resist him? His embrace makes me feel whole and alive. What is wrong with me?*

"Won't you share your feelings?" Larry's hot breath caressed her ear.

"I want to be with you," Tiffany confessed. "That can't happen. I'm married. You can't have me."

"I've heard those words a long, long time ago. I didn't believe them then, and I won't believe them now." His eyes searched hers as if for any glimmer of recognition. Her confusion rested on her face. "Somehow, everything will become clear to you." He kissed her again, more firmly this time as her body yielded to his embrace and desire. "I know in my heart, you'll see we were lovers—lovers that no one can pull apart. The truth always comes out."

"I know you think I'm someone else." Her eyes wandered about his face. "Please, Lar, accept me for who I am now—not who you want me to be."

"I don't want you to be anyone but who you are." His finger traced her lips. "You are the one I love."

His words tugged at her heart and soul. *Can I risk getting involved with this man? Do I want to stop? He's so irresistible. Have I the strength to say no yet one more time? Is Clive in a compromising position at this very moment, giving into impulse, while I'm struggling to remain faithful? God! I want Larry! What should I do?*

SIXTEEN

THAT EVENING, TIFFANY pondered Larry's words as she lay in her bed. She had resisted him again. Unsatisfied desire and confused emotions made her restless. *This is torture. I want Lar like no other. I have never felt the same passion with Clive—his approach to me is almost clinical, a chore expected of a husband. But Larry, he's warm and loving. His kisses stir a fire within me I thought was long dead. Clive had me believing I was little more than those mannequins I dress in the shop. If I do succumb to my wanton feelings, can I stop? Will I have started on a rollercoaster ride with no end? Am I ready to leave Clive and start an affair with Lar? If I do, will he grow tired of me and move on to someone new?*

Gentle tapping came from the connecting door of her bedroom. It jarred her from tortuous thoughts.

"Tiff, are you asleep?" His loving voice had an unspoken need, a soft urgency, and wistfulness.

She turned her head to the door. In a low tone, Tiffany replied quietly, "It's unlocked. I'm still awake."

The door slowly opened. She extended her long legs over the edge of the bed and grabbed her dressing gown. "Guess you couldn't sleep either." She slipped the lavender satin garment on her alluring form.

"No. I couldn't." Larry, in black silk pajamas, stood at the foot of the bed taking in her loveliness. "There are so many things I want to say, but words elude me." He approached her with an unnatural tentativeness, as if he saw her for the first time.

"Yes. I understand." Tiffany stood and reached for a carafe of water on the bedside table. "Thirsty?" She offered him a glass.

"Thanks." His hand came to rest on hers. He looked deeply into her eyes. "That might help, though I'm not thirsty for water."

"What are you thirsty for, Lar?" Her eyes spoke of forbidden dreams.

He let out a huge sigh. "Oh, what a loaded question. Are you

REMEMBER ? 125

trying to tease me again?"

"No. Not really." She looked away from him to hide the truth she dared not reveal. "I know I shouldn't be so playful. That's wrong of me." She looked up at him as emotions took control. "When I'm with you, I can't help myself. You bring out a zest for life in me that I never imagined existed before."

"Then, let it out," Larry advised. "Life is far too short, for it not to be enjoyed."

"I wish I could believe that," she commented softly, as if it was a beautiful apparition. "For me, life is one dull routine of protocol, social appearances and the like—everyone with false smiles and lovely comments, and the deadly whispers behind your back."

"Sounds like the entertainment biz to me," he acknowledged. "Y' see Tiff, our lives aren't all that different. I have the same negative things in my life."

"Yes, but the people who are really close to you, like Joe, are there for you." She sipped her water. "I don't feel that way. Yes, I have Karen's support, and now Amelia's, but it's not the same for me. I'm not certain that they would be there for me one hundred percent of the time."

"You didn't mention Clive," he observed. "Why is that?"

"Clive?" She arched an eyebrow. "Not likely. I'm just window-dressing to him. Someone to show up at all the mandatory functions. I think he loves our dog, Rodney, more than he does me. He's always acting as if I'm a source of embarrassment to him."

She sat down on the edge of the bed. Larry sat beside her. His arm drew her close to him.

"Why don't you call it quits with him?" he asked softly.

"And where would I go? What would I do?" Tiffany faced him. "I have no real skills to support myself."

"Think about it. I'm sure I can give you whatever you need." His voice rang true to her ears. "If you haven't realized it before, I care for you very much."

"Do you care for *me*, or the woman you think I am? I'm not Taylor. I can never be someone else, no matter how much you want it."

"It's you, Tiff." Larry paused a moment. "Please don't feel I've fallen for an illusion. My eyes are wide open, and I like what I see."

"But—" she started.

He answered her comment with his lips on hers. Her mouth parted as his tongue sought hers—a kiss mixed with love and passion. Larry ended their long kiss with more gentle kisses along her neck. His lips caressed the hollow of her throat. Gentle little moans escaped from her , plainly spurring on his advances. Larry's fingers tangled in her hair as he guided her to lie on the bed. Passionately kissing her once more, his hands caressed her breasts. Her nipples grew taut beneath the satin fabric. Her breath quickened between hungry kisses. Her mind was lost in the moment of love colored with lust that she had long forgotten. Larry's fingers gently worked on the sash of her dressing gown. His hand glided underneath her gown to her breasts. He caressed them more firmly.

Desire took over her body, she arched her back in sheer delight. Tiffany felt his mounting, firm desire against her thigh. He pulled the straps of her gown down her arms to expose her ivory mounds. She sought his mouth in heated passion. Their tongues mingled ardently. He broke their kiss. His tongue traveled down her neck, sending delicious sensations running through her. His mouth teased her erect nipples as his tongue encircled each one. Her panting quickened. His touch fueled a raging fire within her. His hand slipped down to her thigh, sending a tingling sensation that lit her inner essence. As his gentle caress slowly traveled up her leg, his mouth continued to tease her breasts, heightening her desire.

"Lar," she said breathlessly.

"Shhh," he replied. "Don't say a word. Give in to your feelings."

"I can't," she whispered.

"Yes, yes you can," he mumbled. His fingers sought her hidden recesses. "Don't think, just feel."

"Stop it," Tiffany replied more firmly. "I can't do this. I won't do this!"

"Where have I heard those words before?" He begged, "Please don't refuse me. I need you so badly. You were meant to be in my life."

She pushed his hand away as she sat up abruptly. "Lar, this isn't right. I can't be a mere fling to you. You'll leave for the

States and then what? I'll be back to square one, only with a broken heart."

"It doesn't have to end." Tears formed in his eyes. "Come back with me. Forget Clive. He doesn't love you. You admitted as much."

"It doesn't feel right." Her eyes glistened with sadness and a tear trickled down her cheek. "I have a strange feeling that I've been in this same situation with you, in another place and time."

"Bel-Air, maybe?" Larry kissed her temple. "I heard those very same words you spoke from my lost wife when she visited me there."

"That's just it!" Tiffany wiped away the tear. "You see me as Taylor. Every time we're together, you're reliving your past with her. That's not fair to me. You want a replacement, not the real me."

"Tiff, that's not true." Tenderness filled his eyes. "I see you, as you are now. It's uncanny you have a feeling that we shared moments before. Open your heart and mind, and let's find the answers together. I'll never leave you."

She apologized meekly, "Lar, I'm sorry I led you on."

"Your heart will tell you when the time is right." He gazed into her eyes. "I can wait."

~~***~~

Seated in the dining room, Larry asked, "What should we do today?" He smeared butter on his toast. Joe gave him a sideways glance and then looked at Tiffany. "It's a bright sunny morning. There must be some interesting diversions in this mansion." *I want to take Tiff to my room and make love to her.*

While the butler refilled his coffee he suggested, "If I may be so bold, sir, there is a full library with a chess board set up, various movies you may watch in the cinema room, and there's a full stable should you feel like a morning ride."

Swallowing his last mouthful, Larry took a napkin to his lips before saying, "Horses? I haven't ridden since I was a kid in Central Park. That does sound like fun." He looked at Joe and Tiffany for their opinion. "Everyone up for a ride to soak up some of this British culture?"

Joe coughed into his napkin. "Chief, I've never been on a horse." He upturned his palms. "How hard could it be?"

128   *Cynthia B. Ainsworthe*

"Sure, Lar," Tiffany agreed. "Sounds like fun. I don't jump, but I can manage a decent trot."

I just bet you can. I remember plenty of "rides" we shared—nights of passion.

"Somewhere in my past I must've learned to ride, though I don't remember it—among other things." She took a bite of her eggs.

Those eggs and ham could drive her cholesterol up. She should know better. Best not say anything.

"Clive was relieved to know I wasn't a total dolt on a horse. Must maintain the proper image, you know—can't be a disappointment with the horsey set." She paused with a quizzical look to the butler. "Charles, I didn't bring any riding clothes with me. What will I wear?"

"That should not be a problem, milady. His Grace maintains a complete selection of proper riding attire for his guests." He stood straight. "Shall I select your clothing and lay them out for you?"

Larry replied for the others, "Yes. That will be fine."

Beddingfield bowed. "Certainly, sir. Everything will be done to your liking." He promptly left the formal dining room.

"Sounds like an adventurous morning," he commented to Tiffany as Joe looked on.

Slight concern lined Joe's face. "Just as long as the damn animal don't go too fast."

Larry smiled. "Don't worry, Joe. I'm sure all the horses are quite tame."

Tiffany agreed, "Exactly, Joe. It's not like we'll be running a steeplechase."

Joe rubbed his chin in thought. "Don't know 'bout that. There's snow on the ground and pretty damn cold out there. Even an old nag might feel frisky."

I almost had my ride last night. I wonder if she'll ever see us as the way we were, or forever live in this fog of lost memory?

~~***~~

The crisp, exhilarating air brought chills to Joe as he stood near the mare. Larry and Tiffany were well-seated upon their respective horses. The groom had assured that Joe's horse was the tamest in the stable. Joe eyed the horse with suspicion. *She looks tame, but how will she be when I get on that saddle?*

REMEMBER ?   129

"That's one damn big horse," Joe observed.

"Yes, sir," the groom confirmed. "She's sixteen hands of love."

Joe walked to the mare's right side.

"Sir," the groom advised, "you need to mount her from the left."

"Right or left," he replied, "what difference does it make?"

"Whisper, that's her name, is accustomed to being mounted from the left." The groom went on to explain, "That practice has been done for centuries."

"Whatever," Joe mumbled as he walked to the other side.

The groom quickly added, "Better come around to the front, lest you'll be kicked from her rear."

"Left, front," he muttered, "all these damn rules just to get on a damn horse."

Tiffany and Larry exchanged glances as bemused smiles came to their lips.

Joe raised his right foot to place in the stirrup. The groom stifled a laugh as Larry offered, "Gotta use your left foot, Joe, unless you plan on riding backward and hold onto the tail."

"Lar, don't be a wiseass." He continued, "You think you're so damn smart 'cause you've ridden before."

"No, I don't, Joe." Larry glanced at Tiffany. "You'll do fine. We'll just go for a nice ride at a slow pace."

Having put the correct foot in the stirrup, Joe tried his hardest to lift his body up high enough to clear the horse's back. As hard as he tried, it was no use. He tried again, and again, six times over, and still no luck.

The groom suggested, "Sir, instead of trying to stand straight up in the stirrup, grab her mane with one hand and the saddle with the other, then pull yourself to the saddle as you raise your free leg, in one swift movement."

Joe followed the instructions. With the aid of the groom pushing up on Joe's derrière, he was finally seated in the saddle. The groom gave him a brief tutoring on how to hold the reins.

"Don't pull back on the reins too much," he advised, "she's got a sensitive mouth and might run away from the pain."

"Yeah, I'll remember that," Joe replied. "How hard could this be? I battle traffic in LA and New York—can't be as bad as drivin' in the city."

130   *Cynthia B. Ainsworthe*

The servant gave an expression of subdued skepticism. "Certainly, sir. Have a nice ride. Stay on the path, lest you should get lost. Never fear, the horses know their way back to the stables."

Larry led out on his gigantic black horse while Tiffany followed on her smaller red mare. Joe brought up the rear on the dapple-gray. *What did that the horse guy say its name was? Oh, yeah, she's Whisper.*

The light dusting of snow softened the sound of the horses' footsteps. The would-be lovers appeared to be well-seated and comfortable, while Joe felt wobbly in the saddle as his weight shifted from side to side with every stride, making his seat less than secure.

"You doing okay back there?" Larry asked.

Joe answered, "Yeah, I'm fine. Why are we goin' so fast?"

Tiffany replied, "Fast? We're still walking. Haven't even started trotting yet."

"Trottin'? Who in hell said anythin' 'bout trottin'?" he questioned. "Walkin' is enough for me."

"Come on, Joe," Larry interjected. "Where's your adventurous spirit? Don't you want to feel her kick up her heels?"

"No. I don't. Never been on a damn horse before. This is fast enough." Joe noticed a small detail. "Where is the horn thing to hold on to? I don't see one."

Tiffany let out a small chuckle. "There isn't one, Joe. You're riding an English saddle. You're thinking of a Western saddle." She advised, "You hold on with your legs and stir with the reins."

"Legs and reins!" He furrowed his brow with worry. "Don't sound too secure to me."

Joe tightened his grip on the horse's side as his hands tightly held the reins. Fear crept through his body. He pulled his arms closer to his sides shortening the reins. As tame as Whisper was, she apparently disliked something about what he was doing. In one quick movement she broke into a trot, then a few strides of a canter, before lurching into a full gallop. Joe desperately tried to maintain his balance as, with each ensuing stride, Whisper raced past Larry and Tiffany, kicking up snow in the wake.

"Don't pull on the reins like that," he heard Tiffany yell as he passed. "You're hurting her mouth!"

Damn it! My foot's out of one of those stirrup things! Then he lost the other. Now his legs dangled free and he couldn't stop his weight from shifting from side to side. *Where are those fuckin' stirrups? I'm gonna fall and break my neck!* Having lost his grip of the reins, they flowed freely about Whisper's neck.

In one last attempt to stay on the runaway mare, Joe flung his arms around her neck yelling, "Stop! Damn it! Whisper, just fuckin' stop!"

Larry came up from the rear in a full gallop. In a frantic bid to save his friend from possible injury, he grabbed the flying reins and managed to bring the mare to a gradual halt.

Breathing hard, Joe slowly regained his composure and released his death-grip on Whisper's throat.

"Joe, did you forget what the groom said?" He reminded, "Whisper doesn't like a tight rein."

"Yeah," he admitted. "I remember that now. That groom guy, Grant, said she was tame, but she's a wild beast. Bet he gave me the fastest horse in the stable."

Tiffany came up to them. "I don't think so, Joe," she commented. "Are you okay?"

"I'm all right." Joe felt the color rush to his cheeks. "Feel like a damn fool. Should've left the ridin' to you two. Gonna get off this horse before she does any damage to me."

Larry steadied Whisper as Joe ungracefully slid off the sweating mare. Once on firm ground, Joe added, "If it's all the same to you, I'll walk back to the stable. Enjoy your ride. Don't end your outin' because of me."

"Are you sure, Joe?" Larry asked.

"Damn sure, Lar." Joe looked at Whisper's fearful eyes. "I'll be all right. She'll do better if I'm not ridin' her. I'll walk her back to the stables."

Larry and Tiffany turned and continued their ride as they trotted off in the distance.

Whisper gently rubbed her forehead against Joe's shoulder as if to say she was sorry. He patted her neck.

"I'm sorry ol' girl. I don't know how to ride. You probably didn't mean to scare the crap out of me like that. You're really a nice horse." Whisper rewarded his kindness with a small whinny.

132   *Cynthia B. Ainsworthe*

Walking leisurely back to the stables, Joe noticed a helicopter flying overhead. *Bet that's some fancy ride for tourists, showin' 'em all the highfalutin estates 'round here.* The mare didn't appear to be bothered by the distant intruder in the sky.

He poured out his thoughts to the mare, "Y' know, Whisper, I work for one pigheaded guy. Lar made up his mind that this Lady Tiffany dame is Taylor. I've told him constantly not to get involved, but no—wouldn't listen to me. Don't know if he's bedded her or not. Hope he don't. He's already got a PR nightmare started. Told him 'bout the tabloids back in the States. They all but say he's cheatin' on his estranged wife and now questions why Taylor came up missin'. He's got his head in the clouds—so damn heartsick 'bout losin' Tay that he's graspin' at straws. Lar wants Tiff to be Tay, so he's now convinced himself she is."

Whisper's big brown eyes stared at him as if she understood every word. "Thing is, if Tiff is Tay, well that's okay—but if she ain't, then he's diggin' a hole to hell. How's he gonna live with the guilt when he finds out she's not Taylor? That could ruin his career, zap his creativity, and put him in a pit of despair. Lar could stop performin' and writin' music. Taylor's his main drivin' force—has been since he first saw her at the Tampa concert." Joe sunk his hand deep in his pocket for added warmth.

The tame mare whinnied as if to comment on his words. "I love Lar. He's my brother and friend. It tears me up inside to see him in such a mess. I can only hope Tiff has more common sense and can resist his charms. Very few women can resist him—that's why he's still on top. Besides havin' great talent, he's got those blue eyes the ladies love and thowin' in those hip moves don't hurt." Joe paused. "I fear the worst tonight. My gut tells me Lar's gonna make Tiff his. Once that happens, the fallout will make the A-bomb look like a smoke bomb. The way she looks at him, I don't think she wants to say no. Yup, Lar's headed down the wrong path, and there's no way I can stop him."

SEVENTEEN

AFTER A GOURMET dinner, Larry and Tiffany relaxed on a rug by the fireplace in the library, enjoying robust red wine in delicate crystal glasses. Joe had decided to go to bed early to find solace for his aching muscles. The roaring fire lent a romantic glow as popping embers accented the ambiance.

"It's been a nice day, hasn't it?" Tiffany's finger glided around the delicate rim of her wineglass. Her eyes sought his reaction.

"Yes, it has been nice. But it's not over." Larry took a sip of wine as his eyes probed her unspoken thoughts. "We have the rest of the evening to explore."

"Just what are you planning?" Tiffany's sweet, intriguing smile encouraged him.

His grin was wistful. "Nothing definite. That all depends on you, Tiff."

Larry's arm reached around her shoulder. His fingers played delicate caresses on her neck. Her eyes were half-closed as if enjoying his touch.

He cocked his head, taking in her beauty. "Where did you learn to ride so well? It's as if you were born on a horse."

"I don't really know. Somewhere in my past, I guess. But, like the rest of my past, I can't remember."

I don't recall Tay ever mentioning she rode horses. Hmm, was this a subject that never came up, or is Tiff merely who she says she is? Ridiculous! I know she's Tay. "Too bad. I bet you have a fascinating history—one I'd like to explore with you—if you'd let me try."

"Try away." She casually let out a laugh. "There's nothing I'd like more than to recall my roots. It's very frustrating to go through every day not knowing who I really am or where I'm from. Somehow, Clive's answers leave me with more questions."

"How would you react if you found out you had a past that included a marriage to another man?" He leaned closer and looked earnestly at her face for any indication of recognition.

134   *Cynthia B. Ainsworthe*

"Would you be willing to explore that with a lost husband?"

"I really can't say, Lar." Her pensive expression made him pause. "I don't know if I'd want to return to those times. I might find out facts I don't want to revisit."

Momentarily, Larry's face grew sullen. He placed his glass down beside him. His fingers lifted her chin. He gently kissed her lips. It was a kiss of deep love and warmth. She kissed him back as if feeling equal emotion. He ended their kiss as his fingers stroked her hair and then gently rolled Tiffany onto her back. He gazed into her soft eyes, still searching for the identity behind the face. *Why do I keep questioning my gut instincts? She is Taylor. A lapse of memory is the problem here—it's one I have to help her with. I know if we spend one night together, then she'll remember.*

"Tiff," his voice loving and sincere, "are you willing to try to regain your memory?"

A look of surprise came to her eyes. "Of course I am."

"Then, I might have the answer." *I hope she doesn't shoot me down on this.* "I truly believe that our intimate moments taken to a higher level will answer all your questions." *Damn! Did I just say that! I sound like a cheap jerk making a pass with a cheap remark! I've blown it now! Why couldn't I keep my mouth shut?*

"Mr. Davis, are you making a pass at me?" Her eyes danced with delight by his flattering comment. "It does open up possibilities, doesn't it?"

His face colored. "Tiff, I really didn't intend it to sound crude. It was a poor choice of words. I'm sorry. But I do like the fact that you're thinking of possibilities."

"Lar, don't worry about it." A sigh of relief escaped from him. "I know you really want to help me. That touches me very much." She kissed his cheek and toyed with his hair as her hand drew him closer to kiss her lips.

"I wanted this to be your decision with no regrets," he whispered tenderly. "This has to come from your heart."

Clearly overflowing with emotion, her eyes filled as a single tear graced her cheek. Larry kissed the drop from her face and followed with a passionate kiss of enduring love. She wrapped her arms around him as if he was a life raft that had rescued her from the seas of a confused abyss. Her breathing quickened as his embrace drew her closer. Lingering kisses on her neck aroused his libido. Tiffany made him heady. He wanted to know all of her.

REMEMBER ? 135

~~***~~

Amelia sat on the sofa reading a travel magazine in her lavishly furnished townhouse. Numerous fashion magazines covered the coffee table along with her cup of tea. An expensive area rug accented the highly polished wood floors.

Her cell phone rang. She picked it up from the side table at the end of the sofa.

"Hello, Amelia." The voice came from the phone. "I hope I'm not disturbing you. I had to ring you to see if there is any news of Tiffany."

"I haven't been back to the manor this weekend. Been spending my time in London with other diversions." The Duchess of Steffenfordshire sipped tea, then stood up. "I imagine things are going smashingly with Lady Lantham and that luscious singer. They have the house to themselves—a little thing I arranged."

"Sounds right cheeky of you and simply marvelous," Karen replied. "How did you get them together in such a compromising position?"

"Oh, it wasn't difficult for my devious mind." Amelia walked to the window and looked out to the street below. "It's rather fun. I think people should be happy."

"Yes, but what about Lord Lantham?" she asked cautiously. Amelia eyed a good-looking gentleman reading a newspaper. Instinctively she licked her lips as her hunger rose. "I don't think Clive will be a problem. He's busy with one project or another. In my opinion, he deserves whatever he gets in the end. Has all but ignored Tiffany."

"Did she tell you that they're not sleeping together anymore?" Karen sounded eager to reveal this fact.

"No. I didn't know." *I dare say, Tiffany will be ripe and ready for her singer-lover. I couldn't have picked a better time for this!* "Well, won't that just speed things along a bit. Clive stopped sleeping with his first wife months before she took a lover and then came up missing." Amelia paused a moment. "It's rather odd when I think of it. Before Penelope left, she was having lapses in her memory—very similar to Tiffany's situation. We all assumed she ran away with her lover. After the legally appointed time, Clive was awarded a divorce on the basis of abandonment."

136   *Cynthia B. Ainsworthe*

"Amelia, since Tiffany is no longer taking those tablets Clive is giving her, has she shown any improvement?" she asked with a hopeful tone.

"None that I can discern. Who knows how long it will take for the effect to wear off." Amelia eyed a man standing on the street. *Wish there was a way I could meet him. He is very dashing. I wonder who he's waiting for.* "I assume Elizabeth has taken care of switching the tablets with the sugar ones."

"I certainly think so," Karen assured. "She's very competent and only wants the best for Tiff."

"That may be, but I don't trust that new man of theirs, Andrews. I feel he's definitely on Clive's side." Amelia's hopes were dashed when the young man smiled at the approaching young lady. *Looks like he's engaged. She wouldn't be his mistress—not meeting on the sidewalk in public.* "He could've discovered what Elizabeth did with the tablets."

"I don't think so." Karen commented, "She's very loyal and bloody careful. Sorry, but I have to run back to the shop. Ring me up if you get any news."

"Certainly. You'll be the first to know." Amelia ended the call. She envisioned the two would-be lovers at her country estate and wondered if there would be a way to neutralize Piers Andrews' loyalty to Clive.

~~***~~

"I'll have one of the servants start a fire for us," Larry offered with a flare as he closed the door to his room. "I think the occasion calls for champagne and strawberries, if they're available."

"Seems like you've done this before, Mr. Davis," Tiffany remarked coyly. She strolled to the big leather chair near the hearth and sank down into its deep cushion.

"How do I call the servant? I never paid any attention to the butler's instructions." Larry sported a little-boy-lost look that was one of his onstage trademark expressions.

"You pull the servant bell cord hanging on the wall," she answered with a slight smile, clearly enchanted with his helplessness at this small task.

"See. You're indispensable to me." He exuded an irresistible charm that could melt any woman's heart.

"Lar, you flatter me. I can't ever remember being irresistible to anyone—least of all my husband ..." She paused as if wanting to unburden her soul. "Yes, Clive buys me nice things, but it's all for show. I'm nothing more than arm candy. I fit the mold he put me into. I'm sick of it and sick of him and his controlling ways. I don't even think he likes my American accent, and I'll be damned if I'll change for his liking. My accent is one of the small things I have left of my identity—I refuse to let go of it."

"Calm down, Tiff." He approached her and knelt on one knee facing her. "Keep yourself just the way you are. Don't change a thing. You can be yourself with me." His hand held hers as he kissed her

A knock came to the door that broke their kiss. Larry stood up and answered it directly.

"You rang, sir?" Beddingfield asked in a professional tone.

"Yes. If it is possible, Lady Lantham and I would like some champagne and strawberries sent up—that is, if it's not too much trouble. And we would like the fire started."

"Certainly, as you desire, sir," the servant responded. "They will be sent up straight away. Oliver will be here directly to start the fire."

Closing the door, Larry turned and walked back to the woman he adored. He paused as his eyes took in her beauty. *In the morning, will she regret what we do tonight? Making love to Tiff could be the end of our relationship or, the beginning of a wonderful life together. Do I dare risk it?*

~~***~~

Mark Barnes, a longtime friend of the family, sat at Cindy Hasting's kitchen table. He had exciting news from Joe Winton about her mother's disappearance.

"I can't believe what you're telling me." Her eyes narrowed with a hint of disbelief. "Surely you don't really think this Tiffany person is Mom?"

"I know it sounds incredible, but I seriously think there might be something to this." Mark went on to explain, "Joe called and said this woman is a dead ringer for Tay. She even has your mom's sense of humor and mannerisms."

"I've glanced at the tabloids in the stores—even bought one." Cindy shook her head not wanting to believe his words as she nervously twirled the dark blonde tendril falling to her shoulder. "If this person is Mom, then why did she leave Larry in the first place?"

"That's one question I can't get out of my mind." Mark knitted his brows with concern. "Tay and Larry were so much in love and fought an uphill battle to be together." He took a sip of iced tea from the glass. "I can't imagine why she would leave him and then deny any memory of her past."

"Exactly, Mark." A look of near horror came into her eyes. "If this woman is Mom, then she's guilty of bigamy. That's a very serious offense. I can't imagine Mom doing anything as crazy as that. No, she's always been totally upfront about most things in her life." Her determination grew. "I won't believe it. I can't. As far as I know, or anyone knows—Mom is lost somewhere. She's *not* this Tiffany person."

"You're entitled to believe what you want, Cindy." Mark said earnestly, "But, I think otherwise. Yes, the whole thing reads like a soap opera, but I'm nearly convinced Lady Bradford, Lantham, or whatever she calls herself is Taylor Davis."

Cindy studied his face. She wanted to believe his words, but common sense won her mind.

~~***~~

Tiffany and Larry sat on the cozy loveseat in his room by the warming fire, sipping champagne from the delicate crystal flutes. His eyes took in every inch of her alluring form. He enjoyed the way the flickering light played across her face. The belief that he had found his long-lost wife erased all remote feelings of guilt.

"You're so very quiet, Lar," she commented softly. "Are you having second thoughts?"

"I was relishing your beauty." He took a strawberry from the nearby silver tray and teasingly grazed her lips with the enticing fruit. "Why? Are you questioning yourself?" He paused a moment to see her reaction.

Tiffany opened her mouth invitingly and playfully took a bite of the strawberry. She brushed her lips against his fingertips, leaving a coy kiss that spurred him further.

She looked directly into his eyes and said with soft determination, "No. I have no questions left unanswered. I know my heart."

"There will be no going back in the morning," Larry reminded softly.

"I know, Lar." She leaned closer, inviting his kiss. "This is my decision—no one else's."

He kissed her lovingly with all the pent-up passion of the lost months as his arms encircled her shoulders. He could feel the heaving of her breathing and imprinted this moment in his heart.

She clung to every passionate kiss as a life preserver that sustained her very existence. Larry broke off their kiss as his hand caressed her waist and reached under her sweater where his palm found the fullness of her breasts. Her gentle sigh of pleasure signaled her approval and desire for more. Tiffany pulled away from his embrace. She quickly released the hook fastener of her bra. Larry's hungry hand found her firm mounds and caressed them softly. His fingers toyed with her taut nipples while his lips traced the delicate curvature of her neck. Her head leaned backward to expose more of what his mouth sought. A small, teasing "ah" escaped from her lips as his tongue teased her ear. His hot breath caused her to push her breast to his palm. Encouraged by her response, Larry whispered, "Do you want us to go to your room?"

"I don't care what room we go to." She kissed his ear breathlessly. "I don't want to break this magic—this feeling I have with you."

Larry stood up. Extending his hand out to hers, she took it willingly as he led her to his bed. His heart pounded as he watched Tiffany slide onto the big bed. He fumbled with the buttons of his shirt and removed the remainder of his clothing while Tiffany quickly cast off her sweater. He joined her on the bed and showered multiple kisses on her face, causing her breathing to deepen even more. Her hand gliding across the rippling muscles on his chest thrilled him. His hand caressed her leg, begging for her complete love. Still in a loving embrace, Tiffany slipped out of her skirt, leaving only the flimsy fabric of red thong panties. He quickly pulled the hindering garment down her thighs. Tiffany's hand met his. In one movement, she flung her panties to the floor.

He kissed her wildly—passionately. Their tongues mingled, sending a surge of pleasure through him. Her body arched, as if begging for Larry to caress her breasts. Eagerly, his hands cupped her. He relished the beauty of her body. *She is Tay. I know every inch of her body. She is my wife. We are finally together again. Nothing else matters.* Larry's hand moved down the delicate curves of her abdomen as his fingertips teased her. *I want tonight to be perfect for us—to be perfect for her.* His hand traveled further and clearly gave her a sensation of utmost pleasure, causing her to murmur, "Lar, I want you so badly."

He replaced his fingers with frenzied kisses. Her excitement rose as she moaned with desire and parted her thighs further, inviting him to enter her.

She wailed out loud as his erect manhood grazed along her thigh and his velvet member teased her silken folds. "Oh God, oh God!" Tiffany reached out to her lover. She opened wide to receive his love. He forced himself to be slow and controlled and felt her moist warmth envelop him—an experience he had only lived in his memories. Now it was his reality. They moved fervently to the ebb and flow of love's passionate rhythm. Her movement quickened as her pleasure plainly increased. He remembered all the times he had made love to Taylor, and now he was with her again—as one. Each lingering stroke drove him closer to satisfaction. She grabbed his firm buttocks and drove him deeper into her. His movements accelerated as ecstasy flowed over his senses, controlling his rhythm. She cried out, "Lar, I love you." Spasmodic movements followed as the lovers reached the pinnacle of bliss. They lay there limp, wet, and panting, satisfied in the soft glow of love.

When he could breathe again, he lifted his head. "Did I satisfy you?"

"You have to ask?" she cooed. "No one has satisfied me before. Not even Clive—not like this."

"Tiff ... you said you loved me." He kissed her nose. "Did you say that because we were making love? Or, do you mean something more?"

"I have always loved you—I don't know how, but I feel we have been like this before. I can't explain it, and I know it sounds crazy, but I feel you are a part of me."

"I understand completely. I feel the same," he replied softly as he kissed her temple. *I can never go back to guessing who you are. You're my wife. Convincing you is my goal—a loving goal. Will you have regrets in the morning?*

EIGHTEEN

THE JARRING RING of his cell phone woke Joe. He squinted to look at his watch. *Who in hell is callin' me at this hour? It's six o'clock in the mornin'.*

"Yeah, Joe here," he said groggily as he reached for his glasses.

"Brent, Brent Stern, Lar's business manager." The male voice came from the phone with a sense of urgency. "This is important, Joe. Wake up!"

"Yeah, what's so damn important to wake me up now?" He rubbed the sleep from his eyes. "Emergency or somethin'?"

"I got a call from this sleaze ball freelance tabloid writer. His name is George Charkin." He spoke with celerity. "Seems he's been digging around—very interested in Lar seeing Lady Lantham. Pictures of them together have been all over the papers in the US. Even new photos taken from the air with the two of them out riding horses over there."

Joe sat straight up in bed as he listened. *That must've been the helicopter that was flyin' around. I thought it was just a bunch of tourists.*

"He's been investigating the public records."

"Yeah, so what of it?" Joe asked nonchalantly. "Lar's got nothin' to hide."

"Let me finish," Brent insisted. "This lowlife has found not only Taylor's birth certificate, but also the certificate of her *twin* sister!" Joe's mouth slacked wide open. "He's threatening to take this to the papers for big bucks—telling the whole world that Lar's messing with his sister-in-law!"

"Hold on, Brent." Joe extended his legs to sit on the edge of the bed. "How do you know he's not blowin' smoke up your ass?"

"He faxed a copy of the document to me here at home. I have no idea how he obtained my fax number," he explained.

Joe rubbed the stubble on his chin in deep thought. "Documents can be forged. What you have, don't mean nothin'."

"I have the log info and page number here from the town of Mahopac, New York," his colleague remarked. Joe could hear

142 *Cynthia B. Ainsworthe*

the fear in his voice.

Larry's brother grabbed the pen and pad from the night table and quickly wrote down the important information.

"Brent, you did right in callin' me," he commented. "I'll do some checkin' on my own. Got my PI friend, Sal in New York—he'll check this out." Joe asked quietly, "Did he ask for hush money?"

"Oh, yeah! You know it!" Bren emphasized, "Two million strong in unmarked one hundred dollar bills with non-sequential numbers. Wants the money deposited anonymously into a Swiss bank account in two weeks by midnight. He's got balls, I'll give him that much."

"When Lar's legal team finishes with this shithead, he'll lose more than balls!" Joe affirmed. "Thanks for callin'. I'll pass this on to the boss as soon as I can. I'll call Sal right away and get him on this. Call the PR people. They'll know how to spin it to cut down on any damage. Tell them to play up that Lar is over here lookin' into doin' a charity thing with the royals."

"Don't know if that will fly for very long," Brent commented. "We'll do our best."

Joe ended his disturbing phone call. New worries consumed his thoughts.

~~***~~

Larry woke Tiffany with a loving, gentle kiss. She lazily opened her eyes and gazed at him. The fine lines that showed when he smiled amused her. She reached up and fingered his hair. *I've done something I thought I'd never have the courage to do. I've crossed the line and it's wonderful. Clive doesn't love me. Larry does. I know he loves me for me—not who he thinks I am or might be.*

"What's running through your head?" His smile warmed her. "Any regrets?"

"None," she cooed and snuggled into his chest. His strong arms around her shoulders gave a sense of safety and security. "For some odd reason, I feel completely guilt free. I want to sing from the rooftops and tell everyone we're lovers."

"Keep a lid on that one." He let out a small chuckle. "At the moment, that would be more than my career could endure. It'll be our secret."

"Yes, I know," she agreed blissfully. "It feels so deliciously wicked knowing that I have a lover." She ran her tongue lazily along her lips as if savoring her sweet transgression. "Lar, you're more than a lover to me. I feel we belong together."

"You don't know how long I've waited to hear those words," he admitted.

Raising an eyebrow, she pointed out, "But you haven't known me very long."

"It seems like a lifetime to me." He kissed her fingertips lightly. "The task at hand is to figure out how we can stay together."

"That is something I don't want to think about," she commented sullenly. "We only have the remainder of this weekend together."

"Tiff, I'll find a way. Leave that to me," Larry reassured.

He took her in his arms and kissed her passionately. With limbs intertwined, the lovers found themselves sharing the expression of their commitment as they did the previous night.

~~***~~

Preoccupation bugged Clive during the Neuroscience Convention held at the prestigious Dorchester Hotel on Park Lane in Mayfair, London. His thoughts ran to the frustrating results of the MI6 project. He sipped his brandy in the hotel's lounge during the lunch break. Although his cousin-in-law, Alistair, plodded along at a slow and methodical pace, Clive was impatient to see the conclusion of this research. He believed his reward would be a Nobel Prize to benefit his social standing.

The head of the newest endeavor to be undertaken by MI6, Derrick Miles, approached and tapped Clive's shoulder briskly. "I say, ol' man, I hope your deep thoughts are bringing new insight to the project. It seems Alistair is making a bit more headway than you. Any explanation?"

He looked at his supervisor's narrowing and inquisitive eyes, assuming his less than favorable opinion.

"I'm devoting my entire time to this research," Clive avoided eye contact with his inquisitor. "I don't want to come forth with any results until I'm certain of the facts."

Derrick commented with an undertone of warning, "I trust you'll have some concrete results soon. JL is becoming rather impatient with your less than sterling performance. I suggest, instead of going it alone, you share your findings with Alistair.

144 *Cynthia B. Ainsworthe*

Remember, we *did* team you together. Are you having a problem working with others?"

"Never! I have my own way of conducting research, and Alistair has his." *I wish this prig would mind his own business.*

"Quite," his supervisor mentioned with reserve. "Fine, as long as the results will be forthcoming before the end of the next century." His sinister chuckle was followed by a sardonic smile, which emphasized the unspoken meaning. Derrick left Clive to ponder his words.

Why does that bastard have to pressure me now? I've followed every procedure to the letter. Is it my fault that my subject is obstinate? Why can't she be the simpleton she was before? What has caused such a change? I increased her dosage—now I get the reverse expected response. This is all so paradoxical. There has to be a factor I haven't considered? Maybe she's not taking her medication as I ordered? How can that be? Andrews knows he'd be immediately terminated if he didn't follow my instructions to the letter. Elizabeth is too simple not to obey me. Should I conduct this research in a more controlled environment? Why did I ever let her leave for the weekend? There's no one to keep an eye on her. Clive finished his brandy in one large gulp. *She's always been obedient, except recently when she went to that concert and befriended that Yank. He seems to be harmless—merely looking for good PR to promote his music here in the UK. Having Tiffany on his sleeve is a self-serving ploy. I won't intervene at this point. Let her dig herself deeper with Larry Davis. That will give me more ammunition to get rid of her. No one in the family will fault my decision. I'll be the injured party.*

~~***~~

A knock came to Larry's bedroom door. "It's Joe. Lar, open up." His voice held a ring of urgency.

"Joe, I'm busy with Tiff. Not now. Whatever it is, it can wait," he answered as he held her in his arms in the comfy king-sized bed. He kissed her temple gently as his hand gently stroked her shoulder.

"Just wanted to speak with you about somethin'," he commented.

"Whatever it is, take care of it." His eyes rolled with annoyance. "This is my weekend with Tiff—no interruptions, Joe. You got that?"

"Yeah, Chief. Got it," he replied with resignation. Joe mumbled, "Right. No sense goin' off half-cocked until I get all the facts." His muffled footsteps trailed off.

Larry focused on his love. He relished the beauty of her face as daylight enhanced her complexion. His fingers ran through her silken hair. His eyes roamed about her face. She returned his look of love, clearly caught up in the same emotional whirlwind of desire laced with confusion over her identity.

"Lar, don't you think you should've heard what Joe wanted to talk to you about?" Her fingers ran along his bare chest, obviously enjoying the feel of his sinuous muscles.

"Don't worry about it …. Joe has a way of overreacting at times. Probably a detail about my Vegas gig or some idea my PR people came up with." He took her hand from his chest and kissed her palm seductively. "Whatever it is, it's not more important than us and what we have now."

"What do we have?" she asked gently.

"Love." His eyes searched hers.

"Is it? Or, lust?" Plainly, she searched for truth in his words and heart.

"For me, it's love for no other," he declared with a kind determination.

"I feel I love you, Lar, but," she hesitated, "but how can I know if what I feel is truly love—not when I have so many unanswered questions about my past. How can I really know myself? Why do we have to put a name to what we feel?"

"Ah, yes," Larry replied as he looked out into space, "a rose by any other name…"

"Something like that," she agreed. "Labels confine and smother. What we have is too beautiful to be put into a tidy little box and placed on a shelf. Keep it free, let it grow. Let the wind take us where it will."

"What if that wind pulls us apart, Tiff?" He looked deep into her eyes to search the depth of her soul. "What then?"

"I don't believe that will happen. What we've shared this weekend—our hearts and bodies have created a bond that no one can break." Her eyes watered.

"I hope so," Larry replied. "I truly hope so. My gut tells me our road will be far from smooth. Can you weather the bumps?"

She snuggled into his chest. "Yes. Having you in my life, I can go through hell and back."

"I pray those words never come true," he whispered softly. *She means those words now. How will she feel when I'm back in Vegas? Will time and distance change her heart? We only have two days left to fill a lifetime.*

NINETEEN

JOE PACED IN his room with his cell phone pressed to his ear. He waited anxiously for his old street buddy, Sal Mourtos, from New York to answer. Worry etched his face.

"Sal, y' there?" Joe asked.

"Yeah, I'm here." Joe heard his friend's fatigue. "What's up? Got a job for me?"

"Lar has a big problem I want you to help him with." He continued with pressured speech, barely taking a breath, "Got this freelance jerk tryin' to blackmail him with some fact that Taylor has a twin sister. He's makin' accusations that Lar's messin' with his sister-in-law while his wife is still missin'. It's all very ugly stuff. If it gets out, his career could tank. Wants two mill cash, unmarked, and no sequence numbers."

"Got a name?" Sal asked coolly.

"George Charkin," he sounded urgent. "I won't say anythin' to Lar until I get the facts."

"I'll get on it right away," his friend assured. "This is far more interestin' than the usual stuff I've been workin' on."

"Thanks, buddy. I knew I could count on you." Joe warned, "Be careful. Don't know if this guy has dangerous connections. Don't put your ass on the line."

"No problem. Talk to you later." Sal ended the conversation.

The phone call gave little reassurance to Joe. His mind tumbled into a myriad of tortured thoughts. *What if Lar nailed Tiff, and this George character is speakin' the truth? What then? It will devastate Lar to know he's sleepin' with a long-lost sister-in-law. What a damn mess! Might be an elaborate hoax by this jerk to fill his pockets. Sal better find an answer. Hope nothin' comes from these threats.*

~~***~~

Larry and Tiffany walked aimlessly, arm in arm around the grounds of the vast estate. Heavy coats staved off the harsh damp cold. Their bond had grown stronger with the strength of iron, and yet held the delicacy of a whispered dream, she mused. The freshly fallen snow reflected the purity of the moment—their moment and their truth.

148   *Cynthia B. Ainsworthe*

Thoughts of him filled her mind. *Does Lar regret last night? He's so quiet. Is he afraid to speak his feelings? Or is he formulating what to say to let me down easy? I pray he doesn't want to turn me away.*

"Penny for your thoughts," Tiffany kept her gaze on the snowy path, afraid to see rejection in his eyes.

"Nothing deep or novel, Tiff," he commented softly. "I was wondering how you felt about last night. Am I traveling down this path alone?"

"Path alone?" Her eyes twinkled. "Not likely. Unless I'm invisible, I'm right here with you."

"Aren't you being coy." He looked directly at her. "You know what I'm referring to—this emotional path we've charted—a wonderful path that can be fraught with mishaps and obstacles."

"Bring 'em on," she encouraged. "After last night, I can handle anything, except ..." she paused. "... you turning me away. I feel alive and free. It's marvelous and I never want it to end."

"I have no intention of ending what we have." Larry stopped walking, turned to face her, and held her hands. "Since you've come into my life, I can't imagine anything could take me from your side." He lifted her chin. His eyes probed her heart. "Tiff, I know I shouldn't ask this, but," the words caught in his throat, "would you return with me to Vegas?"

"Vegas?" Her eyes wandered about his face. *Is he serious?* "What about my life here? There's a problem——and his name is Clive. I can't just pick up and leave him out of the clear blue. Things have to be discussed with him—though the way he's been treating me, he might feel relieved to be rid of me." She bit her lip. "If I ask for a divorce, it would save his precious ego. Clive would like that—to garner the sympathy from the royals."

"You really think it would be that easy?" His eyes widened.

"Oh, he'll make a fuss at first, but then he will come around to see it's for the best." *Is Lar really serious? Does he want me, or the woman he thinks I am—Taylor.* "I don't know the British laws, so all of this could be a moot point until I discover the particulars."

"Leave that to me." His smile screamed triumphant. "I can hire some good British lawyers for you."

"I think you call them solicitors," Tiffany corrected.

"Solicitors," he conceded, placing a kiss lovingly on her lips.

~~***~~

In his heart, she was his long-lost wife. No one, or any circumstance could convince him otherwise. His perspective brought his dream to life. That dream had flesh and blood and was lovingly in his arms with a pounding heart and panting breath.

He slowly broke their kiss and said hoarsely, "Let's go back to the manor. We can spend the rest of the afternoon in your room or mine."

"My, my, Mr. Davis," she teased, "aren't you the hungry boy."

"Hungry for your love, Tiff." With a sincere expression, he added, "I don't have to make love to you. You're not a conquest to be met. You're the love of my life. I'd be happy to hold you for a lifetime." *I hope she knows I'm speaking from my heart. Am I moving too fast?* "Tiff, if you don't want to make love—I understand. I don't ever want you to do anything you're not comfortable with. Your happiness is all I want."

A strange look came over her face as though she had a flash of another time.

"Say those words again." Concern thinned her lips.

"What words?" He was baffled.

"About my happiness." Her fingers went to his face as a blind person would to trace his features.

"Your happiness is all I want," Larry repeated. *Is she remembering something? Did she make a breakthrough of some kind?*

"Funny, those words seem so familiar to me—as if I've heard them from you before." She shook her head in dismissal. "Silly of me. That can't be. We never met before, except that time in the dress shop. I guess I'm grasping at straws—straws to a past I'll never discover."

"Tiff, together, we'll find your past." *I know she's so close to the truth. All it takes is one remembrance of an event—all the pieces will begin to fit.* "Now, let's get back to the house." He looked up at the sky. "Seems another storm is brewing. A cup of hot tea would do us both some good."

"Not to mention the loving, too," she coyly suggested.

"Yes, the loving, too." His arm wrapped around her shoulder.

150   *Cynthia B. Ainsworthe*

They walked in pensive silence. The sound of crunching snow beneath their feet punctuated their unspoken bond.

~~***~~

"Piers, who was that on the phone?" Elizabeth asked coolly as she placed the groceries she had just purchased onto the kitchen table. *I refuse to call him Mr. Andrews.*

"Lord Lantham. Not that it's any concern of yours." His tone was sharp with an authoritative ring. "I have his lordship's complete confidence. However, you can't say the same. He knows I follow his instruction without question—save for that little incident of allowing you to give Lady Lantham her medicine. That, Elizabeth, will cease! I can't afford to lose my position because of your tiresome meddling." His posture stiffened. "And I remind you again, in the future you will address me as *Mr. Andrews.* Clear?"

Elizabeth raised a curious eyebrow in response as she stopped emptying the shopping bag. "Yes, *Your Majesty.* How much extra quid did his lordship grace your coffers with, for you to show such undying loyalty, might I ask?" *I don't like him and his haughty ways. He's getting above himself.*

"That is none of your business. You are quite over the mark. I shall not tolerate such interrogation and cheek from one who is obviously not schooled in the fine art of service."

"You sound more like the *lord of the manor* and not one of his employ," she commented tersely. "Mind you, Lord Lantham won't take to such an attitude, and you'll find your situation as redundant." *What is he up to? I have to protect Lady Tiffany.*

"If I were you, holding one's tongue would be of better service." He smirked confidently, showing perfect white teeth. "One word from *me* and you'll be back on the street where they first found you."

"You know nothing of how I came to this position or where I'm from," Elizabeth added. She felt the hair on her neck bristle. "Besides, her ladyship is on my side."

"Yes, Lady Lantham," he commented coolly, as if it was of little consequence.

"She's not the only royalty I know." *Wouldn't he like to know about the Duchess of Steffenfordshire? I'd better not mention that.*

"Really?" His narrow scrutinizing gaze froze on her. "To whom are you referring?"

REMEMBER ?   151

"I am not going to share with the likes of you," she curtly remarked.

"No bother then. I have to make arrangements for a party his lordship wants to host," he commented with cold detachment. "I'll write everything down and will give you your instructions in a few days. I'll keep the directions simple, so even you can understand them." Piers swiftly left the room with a royal air.

Of all the bloody nerve! He's the new hire here—not me! How dare he treat me as some gutter snipe! If milady was here, he'd be right out on his arse! There's another problem. He wants to give Lady Lantham her tablets directly. How am I going to work around that one? How can I switch the real tablets for the sugar ones? I fear those tablets are harming her. What if she goes back into a coma! My God! I have to do something.

TWENTY

DINNER WOULDN'T BE served before eight o'clock. Larry and Tiffany had over three hours to enjoy their time together.

She casually strolled in his room, looking over the various objets d'art on the fireplace mantle, while Larry freshened up in the adjoining private bathroom. Her eyes spied a small Eiffel Tower fashioned in ceramic and delicately highlighted in gold. Tiffany picked up the fragile item carefully and turned it over. Inscribed in delicate script was the word *Limoges*. She stared at the hand painted decoration. *Strange that such a little innocuous figurine should seem oddly familiar. Why do I know this name? I don't recall Clive having any items about the house with that signature. Hmm…what does this all mean? How I'd love to visit Paris and see this tower up close. I guess that will never happen—not if Clive has anything to say about it. If I can get free of him, Lar might take me there. Silly thoughts. He'll be out of my life when he returns to Vegas. I'll be back to the same dull routine of mandatory social engagements with the same boring people. If I'm extremely lucky, Lar will come back to me—I can always hope.*

Larry entered and stood there looking at her for a moment.

"As you once asked me, I pose the same to you." Larry looked incredibly charming in his navy blue cashmere turtleneck. "A penny for your thoughts?" He inclined his head while raising an eyebrow with a little boy smile that could melt any woman's heart.

"Just how nice it would be to travel." She placed the small ceramic piece back on the mantle. "I'd love to go to Paris some day."

"Why don't you?" He effortlessly poured Chardonnay in a glass and handed it to her.

She accepted the glass and traced the rim with her finger. "I doubt Clive would like that idea. He can barely stand the thought of me leaving home to go to the dress shop, let alone traveling across the Channel to France."

"Ah, but once you're free of him, we can go anywhere you want." Larry watched her sensuous lips take a sip of wine.

REMEMBER ? 153

"You make it sound so very simple," Tiffany replied with wistful wonder.

"It can be," he offered. "Life doesn't have to be any more complicated than what people make it."

"You said 'we', Lar. Do you really mean that?" *God, I pray he's saying the truth.*

"Tiff, I don't say things I don't mean." He stepped to face her and placed a gentle kiss on her forehead. "Least of all to you. My heart's an open book for you."

I want to believe you so badly. Please don't ever let me down. "I think you mean those words now." Her voice changed to one of despondency. "We're together in this beautiful romantic setting with none of life's day-to-day worries at hand. Come Monday, all that'll change. You'll return to your world and I to mine."

"Why spoil the rest of our time together with such sad thoughts?" he offered. "The time we have left is so precious and brief—till we can meet again."

He lifted her chin and leaned down to kiss her full, inviting lips. She met his kiss with equal passion of her own. Her body reacted with a lifetime of yearning that went deeper than mere physical attraction. As he held her, she felt his growing arousal against her as his encircling arms kept her safe from the reality of the outside world. Larry trailed teasing kisses along her neck. Small coos of pleasure escaped from her, begging for more of his touch. His eager hands reached for her firm, full breasts. She sighed deeply for more of his exciting caresses. Tiffany's fingers ran through his hair as desire took her senses to a new height of pleasure, making her want him as much as he obviously wanted her.

In one swift movement, Larry picked her up in his cradling arms and gently placed her on the bed. Her hands tugged at his turtleneck to remove the cumbersome garment. He reached at her sweater to release her from its constraints. Moments later, clothing lay in disarray on the floor. Two naked bodies were in the throngs of heated passion shrouding their deep, abiding love. His mouth slowly blazed a trail to her erect nipples, as his tongue teased her with encircling caresses and a gentle movement that brought her desire higher. Tiffany's hand sought his manhood with gentle stroking that drove him to moan with unrequited lust. She knew he wanted her, and she became intoxicated with her power It was a heady experience—one she had never known before. His warm, inviting kisses traveled down to her abdomen, sending sharp sensations of delight throughout her. The seat of her pleasure throbbed for more as she arched her back. Larry obliged as his tongue went further to the pinnacle of her desire and explored her soft surrounding velvet folds. Her thighs parted as she wanted more of his delicious, sensuous kisses at the rosebud leading to her inner being. He continued to tease her with his warm lips, she responded with gentle kisses on his firm arousal. His moan of delight let her know she gave him pleasure that equaled hers.

Breathlessly, she moaned, "Lar, I need you. I need you now." He quickly kneeled between her thighs and clearly took in her loveliness.

There was no darkness of night to obscure his view. He gently entered her depths a little at a time to prolong her desire. Tiffany responded with raised hips to meet him. "Please, Lar. Don't tease me. I want you so badly." She could feel his fullness as her soft folds surrounded him and the first thrust created a divine sensation. Slowly they moved to a rhythm of sublime bliss. Each bathed in the satisfaction of the other. Each time she cried out for more, the more he held back prolonging her ecstasy, the tighter her grasp became around him. Clearly, he could hold back no longer as the lovers moved with increasing urgency, being lifted to the pinnacle of ultimate pleasure. Limp and moist bodies clung to each other in the afterglow of satisfying rapture. Tiffany knew in her heart this man was her soul mate, a man she had to spend the rest of her life with—no matter what the cost. He had won her heart. She could no longer fool herself with thoughts that lust was her motivating factor.

Larry's voice was soft and warm, "Tiff, are you satisfied?"

"Delightfully so," she replied as he brushed a tear of pleasure from her cheek. "You make me feel alive. I don't ever remember feeling so in touch with my body."

"I'm glad I was the one who could do that." He kissed her eyelids lovingly. "You mean everything to me, Tiff. I can't see myself spending my life with anyone but you."

"Lar, I may be premature in saying this …"

"Go on," he encouraged.

"I think … I think I love you," Tiffany whispered. "I know I've had reservations before about expressing my feelings."

"Oh, Tiff. You have no idea how long I've waited and yearned to hear you say those words—words I've held in my heart and echoed in every song I sing."

His lips lovingly met hers. She opened her soft mouth to receive his kiss. Slowly, Larry rolled off from her. The two lovers lazily gazed up at the ceiling, each in their own private thoughts of happiness. Light slumber brought dreams of a wondrous future to Tiffany. A future she may not be ready or willing to face.

~~***~~

Longtime friend of Taylor and Larry, Sonny Fugatzzi swept the hair cuttings from the floor of his salon as he talked with his lover, Robert Stevens, before closing.

"Rob, I don't know what to make of all the publicity in the tabloids about Tay." He bent down to pick up a wayward hair roller. "It all seems too bizarre to be believed."

"Yes, but how can this Lady Lantham not be Tay?" His lover pointed out, "It's not like Tay ever mentioned having a twin."

"Yes. I understand. But why would she leave Larry and then turn up with a lord?" Sonny stopped sweeping for a moment and leaned on the broom. "Plus, how did she get a divorce without Larry knowing about it? There has to be some type of notice served—unless she's committing bigamy."

"That doesn't sound like Tay at all," Robert commented. "She's always been very upfront, except when she was having her affair with Larry when Paul was still around."

"That's true," he agreed. "No. This woman must be a damn good look-alike."

Robert assumed, "He must be convinced that Lady Lantham is Tay. That's the only explanation. What a mess he's created. When Tay does show up again, how will Larry explain that one? Very few women will accept the excuse, 'I thought she was you.'"

"Tay will be crushed. Could throw her into another depression, like she felt when Paul left." Sonny set his jaw. "A depression—worse than before."

"Exactly," Robert agreed. "And this time, she might not recover from such devastating news. Larry was—*is* Taylor's

156   *Cynthia B. Ainsworthe*

soul mate. How could anyone recover from such betrayal?"

~~***~~

"Joe, have you heard anything yet?" Brent asked impatiently.

He closed his bedroom door while firmly holding his cell phone. "I only called my PI friend the other day. These things take time. What's the rush? Didn't that slime ball give us a couple of weeks to come up with the money?"

"Yes, I know. But Larry's PR people are having a tough time putting a positive spin on the tabloid's exposé. It's only a matter of time before this all blows up in our faces."

"Just keep puttin' out that Lar's interested in Lady Lantham's charities." Joe reasoned, "The fans and press eat up the fact that he's supportin' worthy causes."

"That will only fly for just so long." Brent tensely explained, "When that bottom-dweller spills the beans, the flood gates will open—heaven and hell won't be able to hold back the fallout. Contracts will be dropped and ticket sales will plummet."

"Brent, don't assume the worse." Joe paced. He sunk his free hand into his pocket and nervously jingled his loose change. *What a damn situation for Lar!* "When we find out this is some elaborate hoax, he'll be in the clear. There's also the matter of extortion. I'm sure the police would love to investigate. That could be spun in our favor. Who wouldn't love to read about the wonderful, humble Larry Davis who has always tried to reach out to others through his charity performances and donations, and then he is victimized by a money-grabbin' blackmailer? If he contacts you again, and I'm sure he will, stall for more time. I may need two months to get all the facts. Tell him that two mill is difficult to get together on short notice, especially in unmarked bills. Then there's the little detail of makin' a deposit into a Swiss account with no identification of the depositor as he demanded. That would take additional time."

"I'll do my best. I hope it all turns out as you say, Joe." He heard Brent's doubt. "If not, we're all going down a black pit—one we may not be able to climb out of."

"Leave it to me," Joe assured. "My gut tells me he'll come out of this smellin' like a rose." *I hope I don't have to eat these words.*

~~***~~

REMEMBER ?   157

It was Sunday. Their last day together. Tiffany listened as Larry played the piano. Their night of love had forged another unmistakable bond in his heart, and he already felt the pangs of loss before their forthcoming farewell. His mind recalled other farewells he shared with Taylor. *How I wish this was different. When I married Tay, I thought the torture of goodbye would be our history and not a recurring future. Why in hell didn't I insist on going with her to Paris? I could always cancel a show or concert. How could I've been so shortsighted! I feel we're back to square one. Instead of dealing with Paul, now I have Clive keeping us apart. What type of nightmare am I living?*

He effortlessly sang the song "Taylor", written for the love of his life. Larry wanted to change the name to Tiffany, but thought it sounded contrived and awkward. He hoped Tiffany would understand the message, especially after sharing their bodies, and that maybe it would help her to remember her past with him.

"That's a beautiful song you wrote for her," she commented. "I know it was written from your heart." Tiffany looked out the window. "Lar, what happens when Taylor comes back into your life? I don't want to be a mere mistress to you. Someone you fit into your busy schedule whenever you're back in the UK."

"Don't you remember our talk?" He stopped playing and reached for her hand. "I have every intention of you joining me in Vegas. I don't feel Taylor will return as I knew her." *How can Tay return when I'm looking at her right now? Tiff, you are Tay.* "We have nothing to worry about on that score. In time you'll understand and put those groundless worries behind you."

"Those are easy words, spoken in the moment of melting hearts and growing desire." He could tell she was trying to restrain her sadness. "I won't hold you to them. That wouldn't be fair."

"Never doubt my feelings, Tiff." He saw her tear-rimmed eyes. "I won't be the one saying goodbye. For you, those words don't exist."

Larry stood up from the piano and took her in his arms. She nuzzled into his chest. He inhaled her familiar fragrance "Forbidden". *How much longer before she realizes she's my wife? Saying goodbye will be hard on us. I'd give anything to keep her by my side and not release her to Clive. I can only imagine what her tormented life must be like. Should I push her to come to Vegas with me tomorrow? Hang the damn tabloids! If she agrees, that's all that matters. I have enough money to support us for the rest of our lives. Come this time tomorrow, I will either be ecstatic or extremely sad. It's all up to Tiff.*

TWENTY-ONE

THE LIMOUSINE WAITED in the driveway of the Hollingsworth estate. Joe had checked the luggage with Oliver and waited for Larry to join him in the backseat for their lengthy ride to Gatwick Airport. Tiffany would drive alone to her London townhouse.

They stood in the massive doorway of the manor and held hands while gazing deeply into each other's eyes. Choking emotion filled Tiffany's throat. She wished she could find the right words to say to him, but they eluded her.

"Lar, you will call, won't you?" her whisper pleaded.

"That's a given." His finger erased her careless tear. "Please come to Vegas with me. You won't ever have to see Clive again."

"I can't. I don't have my passport with me—I don't even know where Clive stows it. In fact, I don't remember seeing my passport. He's most likely stashed it with other legal documents." *How I wish I could go with him and forget my life with Clive.* "I'll always remember this weekend. Those memories live in me."

"This isn't the end, Tiff," he said softly. His fingertips caressed her cheek. "It's the beginning, if that's what you want."

"Don't ever doubt that I want you in my life." *You really mean those words? Or, are you merely being polite? I want to believe you.*

"I'll come back. Soon." He ended with a deep and loving kiss.

"If you don't return, I'll understand." More tears rimmed her eyes. She took a deep breath for courage. "I'll make no demands on you, ever." *Oh, God. I want to go with him so badly. I fear I'll never see him again. How can I go back to Clive?*

"I'll return, Tiff." He held her tightly in his arms. "And when I do, we'll never be apart. I'll take you to our home."

He gave Tiffany a passionate kiss. Her body trembled with sadness and longing for his love. She wanted his arms to hold her forever, with their promise of safety and a haven from her reality.

160   *Cynthia B. Ainsworthe*

Larry gave her a parting kiss and put his hands squarely on her shoulders. "I'll be back. I swear I will."

He released her and turned to the waiting car. The harsh crunch of gravel under his footsteps accentuated her feeling of despair. She bit her lower lip to fight back the tears. *Tonight I'll be back in London. London, where lies nothing but emptiness for me—my prison of meaningless social engagements cloaking a loveless marriage.*

~~***~~

The car traveled down the long driveway from the manor. Joe observed Larry's downcast eyes and watched him finger his gold wedding band.

"Lar," he began, "I have somethin' to tell y' that can't wait."

Larry turned his head toward the passing landscape. *Can't you leave me to my thoughts? I don't want to talk business now.*

"It's about Tiff." He paused a moment. Larry turned his head with full attention. "Your manager, Brent, received an extortion message from a freelance rag writer sayin' Taylor has a twin somewhere, and he's threatenin' to leak this news—suggestin' Tiff is her twin, so you've been carryin' on with your sister-in-law."

Larry took a deep breath of disbelief. "How can that be? Taylor always said she was an only child. In all the years I've known Tay, she never hinted at a sister. I know her as well as I know myself."

"Hold on, Lar," Joe quietly reassured, "we don't know nothin' for certain yet. I got a PI workin' on it. I'm sure it's a big misunderstandin'. Still, if Tay's parents couldn't afford a second child, they might've put her sister up for adoption and never said a word to Taylor—that would be somethin' they'd be ashamed of and not want anyone to know."

"Do you know what this means?" he blurted out to his brother. "If this is true, then I've been cheating on Tay with my sister-in-law!" *This can't be true! It has to be a horrible misunderstanding. My God, what have I done?* "How much does he want?"

"Two mill deposited in a Swiss bank account," Joe replied softly. "He faxed copies of birth certificates as proof. All very neat and tidy. Has the same date of birth, same parents, and location as Taylor's. Looks like Taylor was the older sister by five minutes. Doesn't look good for y', Chief. If it's true—

REMEMBER ? 161

could hurt your career real bad."

"I couldn't give a damn about my career right now!" His hands balled into tight fists showing white knuckles. He clenched his teeth as the veins in his neck bulged with rage. "I don't care what it takes—Joe, you've got to get to the truth! How can I live with myself if I actually slept with my sister-in-law?"

"Don't worry," Joe consoled, "if y' did, no one will have to know. I'll take care of everythin'."

Larry looked at him with pain in his eyes. "*I* will know."

~~***~~

Elizabeth busily polished the silver trays in the kitchen, which was one of many preparations for the forthcoming Friday night cocktail party. Her grocery list rested on the table. She glanced at it. *Before I do the shopping, I'll stop by Karen's shop. She may have some news of milady. After all those terrible photos in the daily papers, I'm sure Lord Lantham will be writhing with anger. I feel so sorry for Lady Tiffany. I wonder how she'll handle all this. His lordship hasn't said a word to me or Piers. What will he say when milady returns home today? My skin crawls at the thought. I hope there won't be a terrible row.*

Piers entered the room. Elizabeth paid no notice of him as she focused on polishing.

"What is the meaning of this?" He said sharply. He tossed the envelope Elizabeth thought she had hidden onto the table. The one with the tablets she was supposed to give to Lady Lantham inside it.

Elizabeth abruptly stopped polishing. She felt color come to her face. "Those, those are extra tablets," she stammered.

"Don't lie to me!" he shouted. "Lord Lantham instructed me to give these tablets to her ladyship. Foolish me, I let you persuade me in going against my better judgment and allow you to give them to her. Did you ever entertain the thought you might be doing her more harm? Don't you think that Lord Lantham knows what is best for his wife, or is that too complex for you to comprehend?" He paced back and forth in front of the table. "You have jeopardized my position here." Piers grabbed her wrist firmly. Elizabeth grimaced and tried to pull away. "If I lose my situation—you will as well! No simple-minded wench will do this to me—not without paying a price!

162   *Cynthia B. Ainsworthe*

I'll inform him how you've deceived me—deceived us all with your mindless meddling in his affairs."

She twisted her wrist free. Fear came to her eyes as she bit her bottom lip. "I have not done anything wrong! I told you, they were extra tablets—tablets that milady refused to take for one reason or another. I saved them in case they were needed." *I hope Piers believes me. He must! I can't tell him the truth. I have no guarantee Lady Amelia will give me a position if I'm sacked.*

Piers said with staunch determination, "When Lady Lantham returns today, I'll make certain she takes her medication because, my dear mindless urchin, *I* will be the one giving them to her."

Oh, poor lady, she'll return to living in a fog. How can I help her now? "You'll see that I've been telling the truth," she lied. "I would never do anything to harm her. I'm just as loyal as you—if not more so."

Piers turned to leave, then paused in the doorway to face her. "Mind your step, Elizabeth, I'll be watching you."

I just bet you will. Well, you don't know who I've got on my side. Lady Amelia is no match for you. I'll definitely share this with Karen. She'll ring up the duchess for me.

Out of Piers' sight, Elizabeth quickly removed three tablets from the envelope and placed them in her uniform pocket. She stowed the concealed medication back in the cupboard.

~~***~~

In the backroom of her shop, Karen checked the new arrival of dresses against her inventory list. It was the spring line that she hoped would generate new sales for the upcoming social season. Since the Duchess of Steffenfordshire's influence, her revenue was on the upswing. She increased the quality of her merchandise accordingly. Her mind was preoccupied with the news Elizabeth had relayed not more than one hour ago. *I'll ring the duchess privately. Can't risk shop employees eavesdropping.*

~~***~~

Karen sat in the Hare and Hound enjoying a cup of tea before heading home. Deep in conversation with Amelia, her finger nervously traced an imaginary image on the tabletop. The duchess enjoys a glass of wine.

"I wanted you to know. This all sounds a bit devious to me," she commented.

REMEMBER ?   163

"It was right of you to tell me." Karen sensed Amelia's abject anger despite her outward appearance of calm. "Clive's going too far. Leave Piers to me. I know how to deal with his sort."

Karen breathed deeply. "I knew you'd know what to do. Tiffany is so kind. I hate to think any harm will come to her."

"Don't fret. Clive wouldn't dare drug her before his party—that would be too obvious." The two women glanced around for eavesdroppers. "Has Tiffany returned home yet?"

"If she has, she hasn't contacted me." A blinding realization came to Karen. "What if his lordship read the news in the papers? He could bloody well have put her away somewhere."

"I doubt that, my dear." Amelia smiled knowingly. "The only news he reads is his medical and research journals. Just the same, I shudder to think of the backlash all this negative publicity might cause Tiffany. What was I thinking? I thought the manor would be a safe retreat for them."

"Don't blame yourself," Karen consoled. "You had no idea that the rags would be following Mr. Davis. It was an honest assumption."

"Be that as it may, I still feel sorry for her." Amelia sipped her wine. "Have you received an invitation to Friday's party?"

"Me?" Karen let out a chuckle. "Not bloody well likely."

"Don't worry about it," she commented. "My car will pick you up around seven thirty. Cousin Clive won't say anything to me, especially since I've always questioned him for the real reason Penelope came up missing." Amelia continued, "Tiffany needs all the help she can get. After Elizabeth gives you the tablets, give them to me when I pick you up, if we don't meet before then."

"Quite right. I have a feeling those bloomin' tablets are for more than nerves." Karen looked around for rumormongers among the pub's patrons. "Can you have them analyzed?"

"That's my plan." She cautioned, "I need to be careful. Can't have my name connected to any of this. There's an unspoken royal rule—family always covers for its own—no matter what the offense."

~~***~~

Tiffany arrived back late in the afternoon. She was thankful Amelia's driver offered little conversation as it allowed her to focus on the past weekend's events. She neither thought about

164 *Cynthia B. Ainsworthe*

Clive nor cared what his reception might be, but she was relieved to see her husband hadn't arrived home.

Rodney comfortably settled in her lap as she rested on her bed. Her thoughts ran to Larry. *Should I call him? Did he really mean his words? How can I be certain? If he loves me, he'll take my calls.* Her internal monologue continued as fear of rejection crept in. *If he won't talk to me when I call, he could be busy. He's a famous entertainer. Maybe his time isn't his own.*

She went for her cell phone on the night table and looked at her watch as she dialed. *It shouldn't be too late to call him. He's probably just taken off.* After four rings, she got his voicemail. She left her message, "Lar, I know I shouldn't be calling so soon. Sorry I missed you. Maybe you're already in the air and couldn't receive this call. You have my number. Please call me when you land. I do love you."

~~***~~

About to board his private jet, Larry looked at the caller ID of his ringing cell phone. He knew it was Tiffany. He turned his phone off with a heavy sigh of resolve. His somber look spoke of darkness. He made a decision. Good or bad—it was what he felt he had to do.

TWENTY-TWO

"I DON'T WANT to take my medication, Andrews," Tiffany said firmly in her dressing gown. Her bright eyes showed defiance as she sat on the edge of her bed.

"Your ladyship, it's for your own good." His quiet determination held steadfast. Morning light sharpened his features. "I have my instructions from Lord Lantham. He was very insistent." He handed her a glass of water with one hand and offered the tablets with the other. "Do you want to see me lose my situation?"

"Of course I don't," she admitted. "I don't feel I need them."

"If I may be so bold, I think your husband, the doctor knows what's best, Milady." His tenacious approach unnerved her. "Please, Lady Lantham, do as his lordship requests. Surely there is nothing to fear."

"Odd you should bring *fear* into it. Whoever said I should fear my husband?" *Andrews is a pompous ass. No wonder Clive likes him—two birds of a feather. I haven't been feeling so tired and washed out lately. Could it really be true that the medication is bad for me?*

"No one, milady." Piers unremitted.

Against her better judgment, she took the two tablets and swallowed them with a gulp of water. Fatigue rapidly took over as she rested her head on the pillow and promptly fell asleep.

~~***~~

Clive said little to her during the few days before Friday. On the evening of the party, Tiffany aimlessly walked around his room while he dressed in the adjoining bathroom.

He called out to her, "Tiffany, please get me my cufflinks and studs from my jewelry box. The key is in my jacket pocket."

"All right." She fought the sensation of moving in slow motion. *I feel so very tired. Why is that? I thought that was behind me. I didn't feel like this with Lar, and I was still taking my medication. Why should it affect me now? Maybe I'm coming down with something. I hope it's not my heart problem.*

The box sat on a tall dresser. Fetching the key she unlocked

166   *Cynthia B. Ainsworthe*

the box and lifted up the lid to get the items he had asked for. *What was that? Something jiggled in here.* She examined the jewelry box more closely. The wood at the bottom definitely moved. *Why would it do that? A hidden compartment?*

Clive's irritated voice rang out, "What's taking you so long? Do I have to do everything for myself?"

"I'll be there in a moment," Tiffany replied with false cheerfulness.

Clive burst into the room before she had expected him. She stopped dead in her tracks, feeling like a child caught with her hand in the candy jar.

"What the …? What do you think you're doing!" he shrieked. "Those are my things and none of your business." Color and indignation covered his face.

In her upturned palm, Tiffany held a three-row pavé diamond wedding band and a heart-shaped diamond engagement ring she had pulled from the secret compartment. She stared at him, her brow furrowed.

"Now you've done it." Clive's speech was pressured and rapid. "I planned to give them to you for our anniversary. It doesn't do for the Countess of Lantham to wear a plain gold band—not someone of your standing."

"Why didn't you give me diamonds when we married?" *I wish I could think clearly. Everything seems so vague.*

Clive approached her. "There was no time, you little moron. It doesn't matter. We were married, and that's all you need to know."

He took the rings from her, placed them back into the jewelry box, and then securely locked them up. He placed the key in his pocket.

"Why can't I wear them now?" Tiffany inquired with a childlike simplicity.

"Because," he said with condescension, "it is not our anniversary. You will get them when I decide the time is right." Beads of perspiration dotted his forehead. "Remember, my simple-minded pet, I know what is best for you in all things. Now, go down and ready yourself for our guests. Don't do or say anything to embarrass me. My superior will be here, so you must make the proper impression. Merely smile and keep your opinions to yourself. No one is interested in your idle thoughts

REMEMBER ? 167

and childish chuntering. These people are my colleagues with intelligence. No one needs to know you are lacking in that department. And stay away from Amelia—she's purely royal decoration for the party."

Tiffany clamped her lips shut. *No sense in upsetting him. Clive always wins. Maybe one day it will be my turn.*

~~***~~

The party gave the appearance of success for Clive, as appropriate euphemisms and false bravado hummed in the Bradford's living room. Compliments abounded where there was no basis for the comment. Forced smiles were met with insincere handshakes that signified meaningless formality. Polite conversations with no clashing of opinions, save for the mundane talk of Parliament issues, kept temperaments in check.

Tiffany glided from one circle of guests to another saying the same rehearsed words, "It was so nice of you to come It's a lovely night. We're very pleased you accepted our invitation." After Amelia observed her saying this same greeting for the sixth time, she pulled her friend aside to the corner of the room.

"Tiffany, what's wrong with you?" she whispered. "You're acting like a mechanical doll—saying the same thing over and over again. Aren't you feeling well? What has Clive done to you?"

"Amelia, I'm fine." Tiffany's eyes searched the room without focus.

"The hell you are." She grabbed her shoulders firmly. "You can't even focus. Tiffany, you look like you're in a bizarre trance."

"Merely very relaxed, that's all." She pulled away from her friend's grasp. "Really, nothing to worry about."

"I thought that weekend at my estate would've done you some good," Amelia commented. "You look worse now than when I last saw you. Didn't you have a nice time with Mr. Davis?"

A glimmer of life came to Tiffany's eyes. "Oh, yes. We had a wonderful time." She muttered, "Lar told me he loved me and wanted to take me to his home." Her downcast eyes hid a waiting tear. "I tried calling him every day since he left, but he

168   *Cynthia B. Ainsworthe*

hasn't returned my calls. I was nothing more to him than a pleasant diversion."

"Don't say that, Tiff." Amelia encouraged, "Keep calling him. He's a big celebrity. Any number of reasons could have prevented him from speaking to you."

Karen caught sight of the two women talking quietly and started toward them.

Amelia continued her gentle probing, "Did you and Larry make love—is he your lover?"

A bashful smile emerged before Tiffany replied, "Yes. It was wonderful. He was wonderful."

"I knew you were meant for each other. It was only a matter of time," she confidently assured.

Karen approached. "Is this bloody private or can anyone join in?"

"So sorry, my dear," Amelia answered. "I didn't mean to ignore you. I wanted to talk to Tiffany about her holiday with Mr. Davis."

"Shush," Karen warned, "someone might 'ear you." She took a long look at her friend. "My word, Tiffany, you look like you're a bit off your feed. Not feeling well? Is that why Piers Andrews called and said you would be away from work indefinitely?"

"I didn't know he called." Tiffany struggled to focus her thoughts. "That must be Clive's doing." She continued monotonically, "I haven't been well. I've been very tired. I take several naps during the day. I truly can't tell the difference between what is real, or if I remember some dream I had and think it's real."

Karen and Amelia exchanged amazed and concerned glances.

"Can't you leave Clive? Being shut away is not good for you," Karen checked to make certain nobody had heard her.

"No, I don't think so." Her meekness and reserve hinted to helplessness.

"Besides, Andrews is acting like a watchdog. I don't have the energy to avoid him."

"You leave Piers Andrews to me." Amelia held a sly glint in her eye as she glared at the male servant. "He won't be a problem for long. I know how to deal with him, and I dare say, it will be jolly good fun." She started to leave Karen and

REMEMBER ?   169

Tiffany, then turned back and said, "Please excuse me. I have a game to win."

~~***~~

Larry pensively stared out the window at the desert landscape of Las Vegas from his opulent suite at the Chambord Hotel. His mind was a million miles away from the present. Everywhere he looked he saw Tiffany's face. Her fragrance lingered with him. She was there, but wasn't. The torment drove him to distraction. His cell phone rang. He didn't look at the caller ID. Voicemail was his servant, and he used it often. Joe enters the room and heads for the bar.

"Aren't y' gonna answer it?" Joe reached for a beer from the refrigerator. "It might be Lady Tiff."

"Yeah, I know," he answered flatly. "Let it ring. I have nothing to say—nothing can possibly help now."

Joe handed him a bottle of water. "For what it's worth, I think you're bein' a damn fool. For all we know, there's nothin' to this twin identity scam. I got my man workin' on it."

"What if it's not a scam?" Larry looked squarely at Joe. "I slept with my sister-in-law. My God, you know what that means!" His eyes grew large with fear. "If Tay ever comes back, it could ruin our marriage."

"Chief, now don't take this the wrong way … but your marriage doesn't look too good at the moment. Considerin' the time we've spent in the UK, it's been almost two years with no sign of Tay. Why chase a ghost when you've got a woman who loves you now?"

Enraged at Joe's words, Larry said through clenched teeth, "If you weren't like a brother to me, I'd flatten you. How can you say such things! This is Tay we're talking about—the only woman I've ever loved—can't you understand that!"

"Calm down, Lar," Joe pleaded. "Don't go off the deep end. I was only tryin' to help."

"That kind of help I can do without."

Larry took his phone from the coffee table and listened to the recent message. "Lar, it's Tiff. I don't know why you aren't taking my calls. I can't talk long. I don't know when Clive will be back. Please call me, even if it means goodbye."

His throat grew tight with emotion. *How can I ignore her pleas? I feel she needs my help. No, it's better this way. No tearful goodbyes to get in the way.*

Joe broke the momentary silence. "Chief, I gotta tell y' 'bout an issue with the Chambord."

"What is it? Upset that the house isn't full for every performance?" he asked, feigning interest.

"No, it's not the ticket sales," he began. "It's all the cancellations for nearly the past two years. They're sayin'…sayin' you're more interested in playin' elsewhere than honorin' your contract with the Chambord. Even you're fans are sayin' some nasty things—that you don't care 'bout 'em anymore. They don't like the idea of spendin' bucks to travel to see y' and then y' cancel on 'em."

"What in hell do they expect!" He sounded incensed. "For God's sake, my wife is missing. I took time off to look for her, and booking other concerts was more convenient for my quest. The Chambord can take their bottom-line attitude and shove it. My fans will *have* to understand."

"Getta hold of yourself." Joe placed his hand on Larry's shoulder. "I'm on your side, but if y' can't be depended on, ticket sales will suffer. People won't be bookin' rooms at the hotel to see your show. *You* were the big draw to get 'em in the casino. Y' have to give up this Taylor search. Your career can't stand another hit. The news media has been all over this thing with you and Tiff. Your PR people can only do so much—the charity spin is gettin' old. How much bull do y' think your fans are gonna swallow? They're not dumb y' know."

"I've heard that all before." Larry paced around the room. "I didn't like hearing it then, and I don't like hearing it now."

"Let it sink in this time." Joe sunk his hands deep into his pockets with exasperation. "You need to understand. You can be your own worst enemy."

"If it's one thing I know—I know the woman I made love to last weekend responded exactly like Tay. A twin would not respond the same way. There would have to be differences." Exasperated, Larry upturned his palms.

"Don't know nothin' 'bout that stuff," Joe said with a sigh. "What y' gonna do? Gonna cut Lady Lantham loose, or risk your career? Risk your marriage if Taylor does return?"

"I don't know, Joe." He added, "Get a replacement passport for Tay. I don't care if you have to forge her signature to get

REMEMBER ?   171

it—just get it done and quickly. Something tells me I'm gonna need it."

Joe gave an agreeable nod.

Larry buried his hands into his pockets and paced faster. *I hope to hell Joe finds out something about that blackmail issue with that scumbag writer. He should be shot at sunrise.* His pacing paused a moment. *Should I cancel more shows and go back to London? Is Tiff in danger or merely misses what we had? I know I love her, or I love the idea of her being Tay. For one glorious weekend, I had my wife back. Now she's gone again—maybe gone forever. Should I call her?* He looked at his watch and mentally calculated the time difference. *I wonder if it's too late to call Tiff.*

~~***~~

Amelia Hollingsworth edged her way through the other guests a she approached Piers Andrews. He immediately turned to her and offered a glass of champagne from the silver tray he held.

"Champagne, Your Grace?" he asked charmingly, with a broad smile that showcased his white teeth. His dark eyes lingered on her cleavage for a moment.

She noticed his glance. "Thank you, Andrews." Amelia lifted the glass and touched the rim to her lips before taking a sip. "Tell me, are you happy here under the employ of Lord Lantham?"

He raised an eyebrow and replied, "Yes. Why do you ask, Your Grace?"

"It's a shame that someone with your obvious talent should be employed by such a staid and boring employer," she coyly remarked. "If you were in my service, the benefits would be far more interesting, not to mention more enjoyable."

"Your Grace, are you suggesting I terminate my situation?" he said after subtly clearing his throat as he edged to the periphery of the room.

"Of course I am." Amelia held a playful glint in her eye. "I promise my terms will be very agreeable to us both. If you please me—there will be hefty bonuses for you."

Intrigued, he asked, "Please you how?"

"Any and all ways imaginable." Her hand lightly touched his sleeve. "Whatever Clive pays you, I'll double it." She glanced to see if anyone had noticed her conversing with the servant.

172   *Cynthia B. Ainsworthe*

"You'll even have the use of the car and a new wardrobe from a personal tailor."

"Quite," Andrews replied softly. "That does sound interesting. How may I contact you?"

Amelia retrieved a calling card from her small purse and slipped it into his jacket pocket. "Don't take too long, my dear. I don't like to be kept waiting for *anything.*"

After placing the half-empty glass on his tray, she whispered, "Ring me tomorrow. Why waste time with formality?"

Piers gave a devious smile and she felt him watching her as she made her way to the powder room off the foyer.

~~***~~

Tiffany excused herself from Karen, "I'm sorry, but I feel I must call Larry."

"I thought you said he hasn't been receiving you." Karen looked mildly confused.

"That's true." Tiffany's forehead lined with worry. "I can't help it. If I don't get in touch with him, something terrible might happen. I know it sounds silly, but I need to hear his voice while I'm mentally clear enough to think. Sometimes my thoughts are so foggy, I can't communicate with anyone."

"Oh, Tiff. I had no idea things were this bad," Karen replied with genuine concern. "Yes, run along. If Clive asks for you, I'll tell him you went to the loo or something. Don't worry, I'll cover for you."

Karen watched Tiffany leave the living room through the hum of party guests. *I wonder where Tiff's going. I hope she isn't feeling ill again. Would she make her escape during a party? It's certainly a perfect time, if she does. Clive wouldn't miss her until the guests go home.*

TWENTY-THREE

IN HER BEDROOM, Tiffany hastily dialed her cell phone. It rang once, twice, three times. *Please, Lar, pick up. I need to speak with you.*

Someone picked up but didn't say anything. "Hello," Tiffany said.

"Hi, Tiff," Larry replied. "It's good to hear your voice."

"I've called many times but only got your voicemail. I … I hope I'm not calling at a bad time."

"No, not really." His tone was reserved. "Things have been crazy here. I've been busy putting a new show together," he lied. "Everything okay with you? Any problems?"

"None," she replied quietly. "I miss you, Lar."

"I know, Tiff …. Look, I wish we could talk longer, but I've got this press conference to get to," he lied again. "Call me tomorrow, and we'll have a long chat."

Her heart sank. "Yes, I'll call tomorrow." She sighed deeply. "Much success with your press conference."

"Thanks. Bye, Tiff." The phone went dead.

She stared into space with a vacant look that matched the sinking feeling in her heart. *He seemed hurried and never once said he loved me. Has his feelings changed? Was I so hungry for love that I wore my heart on my sleeve—only to be tossed away like yesterday's news? Maybe he's busy, or people were around and he couldn't talk freely? I want to believe that. Must I forever be chained to a loveless marriage?*

Tiffany mustered her courage. She looked in the mirror, took a deep breath, and smiled back at her image. She spoke to the woman in the mirror, "Well, I can't let Clive know how I truly feel. Must keep up the appearance of happiness and the dutiful wife to all of his colleagues."

Moments later, she made her way back to the guests, smiling politely, and commenting on the lovely dresses the women wore. Her controlled demeanor was in keeping with Clive's expectations. Karen spotted her and came to her side, clearly eager to learn of the result of her phone call.

"Lady Lantham," Karen started, "may I speak to you for a moment?"

174   *Cynthia B. Ainsworthe*

Tiffany excused herself to talk with her friend. The guests gave Karen a slight disapproving look with raised eyebrows, clearly indicating she was not of their social strata.

Out of earshot Karen continued, "So, tell me. What did 'e say?"

"He's busy. We didn't talk long. He had a press conference to get ready for." Heartache rimmed her eyes with moisture.

Karen placed her arm around Tiffany's shoulder and gave a reassuring squeeze. "Don't worry, ducks, all will turn out well in the end. Remember, 'e's a right famous bloke with many duties—not much time for a personal life."

Amelia came to join them. She saw Tiffany's sullen look. "Tiff, I take it you didn't talk to him, or if you did, he didn't say anything encouraging. Am I right?"

"Yes." She twisted her tissue. "That sums it up. He's busy and couldn't talk. Told me to call tomorrow."

"See that you do then." Amelia encouraged, "Chin up, my dear. Things aren't as bleak as you might think. At least Piers Andrews won't be a problem for you anymore." Tiffany raised an eyebrow. "Soon he will be in my employ. All the better for you and quite better for me. I hope he won't be a disappointment. He is easy on the eye, and it's so tiresome to find a handsome package with no fortitude to last the night. No mind though, if he's not up to the task, I'll pass him off to one of my friends who would be happy just to look at him in the all together." She added, "They're a bit older, but I'm sure if the price is right he won't mind lying next to a few wrinkles and such."

Karen whispered, "You are so very wicked."

"Thank you," Amelia smiled smugly. "I'll take that as a compliment. I merely know what I want. I have no idea what I would do if my wishes were refused …. But with my money—that's not likely."

Tiffany commented softly, "I'm trying to keep my spirits up, but Lar said so many beautiful things about wanting a life with me. Now his tone has changed—distance was in his voice." Her fingers fidgeted. "I felt he would rather I didn't call at all—as if he couldn't wait to get off the phone."

"I shouldn't think that," Amelia advised. "You have no idea who was in the room with him. Most likely, he couldn't speak freely."

"I suppose you're right," Tiffany conceded. "I hope when I call tomorrow, he'll give me some more encouraging words." She weakly smiled at her two friends, took a deep breath, and blinked repeatedly, fighting back the tears. "It's getting late for me. I must retire to bed. Clive will understand. He doesn't like me to stay up too late and risk boring his friends. It's an understanding he has with me. I must say good night to everyone."

~~***~~

As she left her friends to make apologies to the other guests, Karen commented to Amelia, "He's a ruddy bastard, 'e is. Making her act as a bleedin' puppet, doin' 'is will. I'd like to see 'im in the tower, I would. The rack would be too good for 'im."

"Calm down now," Amelia advised. "He'll get his comeuppance in good time. We must support Tiffany. I have a feeling she'll need us in the future."

"Quite right," Karen agreed. "We must think of 'er. What are you goin' to do with the tablets Elizabeth gave me that you've got now?"

"I need to get them analyzed, but it might take some time," she spoke softly and checked to make sure no one else would hear her. "I have to be careful Clive doesn't suspect a thing. Discretion is the keyword. I need to locate a laboratory he's not connected to—that might be a problem." She watched Karen take a drink. "Go easy. You're dropping your h's."

~~***~~

"Sal, what have you got for me?" Joe asked from his cell phone. He sat on a chair in Larry's Las Vegas suite enjoying a beer.

"The guy doin' the blackmail job is goin' by a fake name— guess he's too smart to use his real one." Joe heard the New York City traffic rushing by as his friend continued, "He's dead on with the birth certificate. There were two births five minutes apart, both girls—born to James and Elizabeth Baker in Mahopac, New York. First was named Taylor Cynthia Baker, second was Stephanie Elizabeth Baker."

Joe stroked his chin. Worry came to his face. "Any idea what happened to Stephanie? Any school records, employment records, voter's ID, anything?"

176   *Cynthia B. Ainsworthe*

"Nah, nothin' s far. Still lookin'." Sal puffed on his cigarette. "There has to be somethin'. A person can't come up missin' with no record. I just started scratchin' the surface."

"Scratch a little deeper and hurry it up," he remarked in a commanding voice. "This scum ball isn't gonna wait forever before spillin' the beans. Extortion has an ugly taste to it, and my boy can't afford to have this crap hit the fan."

"Hold on, Joe," Sal replied. "I'm doin' the best I can. Have I ever let you down?"

"Don't make me remember that conversation we had in the lobby of the hotel," he reminded. "That little talk cost Paul big time."

"Will you let that go, for Christ's sake!" Sal remarked. "You didn't have jack shit to do with that. It wasn't your fault."

"Yeah, whatever." Joe continued, "Just get some results—and *soon*."

"I'm on it."

Joe ended the call. *I hope to hell Sally comes through. He has to—too much is ridin' on Lar's career.*

~~***~~

In the kitchen, Piers pulled out the card from his pocket while Elizabeth refreshed the silver platters of hors d'oeuvres with various delicacies. He smiled slyly as he read the duchess' full name and title with her cell number below.

"Aren't you looking like the bleedin' cat what ate the canary," Elizabeth commented.

"Not yet. But soon," he replied intriguingly.

"What you have there, may I ask?" she queried.

"You may not." He swiftly placed the card back in its hiding place. "All things in good time—a very good time."

Piers picked up the waiting trays, turned on his heels, and strode back to the waiting guests.

Elizabeth muttered, "What has caused his new level of cockiness?" *I hope it doesn't involve milady. I know he's thick as thieves with Lord Lantham. Wish I could speak to the duchess or Karen.*

Karen entered the kitchen. Elizabeth looked up in surprise.

"What are you doing here? How did you arrange this? Did Lord Lantham invite you?" she asked the shop owner.

"Not bloody likely. The Duchess of Steffenfordshire invited me." She casually picked up a cracker laden with sour cream and caviar. "Should've seen 'is lordship's face when I entered—could've frozen the Thames with that look, mark my words. 'e was polite but not bleedin' 'appy about it." She looked at Elizabeth. "Why aren't you serving with Piers?"

"Never at a posh affair. It's just not done." Elizabeth placed parsley on the canapé tray.

"Karen, please don't take this the wrong way, but you're dropping your h's." The young girl wiped her hands on a towel. "Had a bit of the bubbly?"

"Just a few." She chuckled. "It feels good to let my hair down. In the shop I have to be right proper for the clientele. After hours, the ol' Karen cuts loose."

"This being my first 'posh do,' I wouldn't know." Karen continued, "I must say, there's a bunch of bores out there. All talking about the royals, who's 'osting what, and all that rot. Not a lively one in the group, save for the Duchess of Steffenfordshire and Lady Tiffany. Bit too uppity for me."

"Exactly," Elizabeth agreed. "If it wasn't for Lady Tiffany, I'd find another post, I would. I worry about her so." She placed the last sprigs of dill on shrimp canapés. "Did you get the tablets to the duchess?"

"Yes. I think she'll have them analyzed somewhere." Karen helped herself to a tidbit from the waiting tray. Elizabeth quickly placed another in its place.

"What do you think she'll find?" The young servant glanced at the doorway, fearing Piers might enter.

"Nothing good, you can bet on that." Karen added, "I wish there was some way to get Tiffany away from here."

Elizabeth heard approaching footsteps. "Karen, you'd better return to the others. I'll be in trouble if Piers sees us talking—he might get me sacked because I was socializing with the guests."

Her eyebrows arched in awe. "Go on, will y'. What a pompous lot. Don't get your knickers in a twist." Karen turned as she left and said, "I'll ring you tomorrow."

~~***~~

Tiffany lay on her bed. She listened to the last guest bid their goodbyes. She knew Clive would follow his usual routine and return to his room to take a shower. He never altered his habits, one could nearly tell the time by where he was or what

178   *Cynthia B. Ainsworthe*

activity occupied him.

She anticipated silently for his footsteps down the hall. He had the key, and she wanted it.

Hearing his bedroom door close, Tiffany waited for the sound of the shower. *In five minutes he'll be in the bathroom congratulating himself on another successful social event—ever cementing his bonds to business or society.*

Tiffany heard the shower running from her adjoining room. She opened Clive's door a crack and spied his shadow going into the bathroom. Stealthily, she glided to his tuxedo neatly hanging on the wooden valet. Carefully, she slipped her hand in the jacket pocket. She was in luck. The small key was there. Quickly, Tiffany went to his jewelry box and silently unlocked the treasure-laden chest. Lifting the platform and exposing the false bottom, her fingers plucked out the two diamond rings. *I don't know why, but I know these are mine—from my past. Why else would Clive keep them here and not in a gift box?* She securely locked the container, then slipped the key back into his jacket pocket.

The shower abruptly stopped. Tiffany scurried back to her room and quietly closed the door. Fearful Clive might have heard her movements, she climbed into bed fully clothed, pulled the covers up to her chin, and closed her eyes in a semblance of slumber. She laid still as a corpse.

Her door opened. Tiffany heard his muffled footsteps on the carpet. *God, please don't let him pull the covers. Please make him leave. I'm so afraid. I don't know what he might do if he thinks I'm spying on him.* She sensed his close presence at her bedside and noted the large shadow he cast over her body as she clenched the rings tighter in her fist. The prongs pressed deep into her flesh, as she ignored the pain. *Why didn't I turn out the lights! Oh, no! He's going to know I'm not asleep! What will I do?* The shadow didn't move for what seemed to be an eternity to her. *Why is he just standing there looking at me? What is he going to do?* She controlled her breath. *He mustn't know I'm awake. I have to breathe slowly. Can he sense my pounding heart? Clive, please go and leave me alone!* Minutes seemed like hours to her. With every passing moment she feared his discovery of her motives. The memory of him taking her in the library raced to her mind. *What if he assaults me again? How will I react? I dare not fight him—he might kill me.*

"Tiffany, are you awake?" His voice loomed ominously. No

answer came as she nearly held her breath.

"Can't you hear me? Tiffany, I asked you a question," he persisted.

She remained quiet. He leaned closer to look at her face. She gave no reaction, not even a wince.

"Hmm, just as well," Clive scoffed. "You're of little use to me as a wife. As a subject, well, that's quite a different matter."

Her throat went dry with fear. She heard him walk away and close her door. She stayed there for what seemed like an hour with the covers to her chin. Never had such terror gripped her very soul. *I have to get in touch with Lar. I hope he can talk. He's my only hope. She looked at her watch. I'll call him now. I'm convinced he'll know what to do.*

TWENTY-FOUR

PIERS AND THE Duchess of Steffenfordshire sat in the Dorchester's fashionable tea room at a secluded table, enjoying their drinks and assorted finger sandwiches. He was aware of her reputation. She neither flaunted nor tried to hide her various liaisons and had become known as the royal rogue with the social set of high society—a reputation she apparently relished. Nonconformity was her byword.

"Piers, I expect you to start tomorrow," Amelia stated matter-of-factly as she raised the cup to her lips.

He immediately coughed politely. *She doesn't hedge the obvious.* "It's customary to give two weeks' notice to my present employer."

"'Customary' is not a word I recognize, as you will soon discover." She reached across the table and lightly touched his hand. "For the amount of your salary, you will meet my needs at any time I desire. I will not be refused."

"I expect to have time off." He placed his hand on top of hers. "No one should be expected to work 24/7." *She must be joking. What an ego!*

"Oh, don't worry," she cooed. "You'll welcome the rest. You'll have little energy for anything else."

"Are you posing a challenge?" Piers inquired charmingly.

"No, merely the facts." Her tongue ran across her bottom lip teasingly.

"Really?" he encouraged.

"Let the tournament begin." She suggestively bit her bottom lip. "I have a room reserved. Can you meet my expectations?"

Meet your expectations? I'll surpass them. I leave no lady unsatisfied!

~~***~~

Tiffany looked out her bedroom window. Gentle rain left lingering droplets on the pane. She felt unsettled from the previous evening. Clive didn't return to her room, though she stayed awake most of the night fearing he might. Piers hadn't even knocked on her door with her scheduled medication. That was a relief, and she wondered if her husband had another

REMEMBER ? 181

strategy planned for her treatment. Two white tablets waited on the plate with her glass of orange juice Elizabeth had left. She pulled the rings from the pocket of her robe and looked at them in her palm. *I know these rings hold a key for me—but what? Why should these diamonds mean so much to me? Surely Clive purchased them just for show so everyone will think he's such a generous husband. I wonder if Lar will take my call. He never answered last night.* Her heart began to ache with grief of an imagined loss. *Has he forgotten about me? Am I no longer who he wants? Our weekend was so beautiful and perfect. Perfection never lasts—as a rose must die at its end.*

A gentle knock sounded on her door.

"Yes," she replied as she continued to gaze through her window. The dismal weather mimicked her forlorn feeling.

Elizabeth entered and gave a brief curtsy. "Milady, I was checking on you to see if you are feeling poorly or might be taken to your bed."

"I'm all right …" her voice trailed off. Her vacant stare remained fixed to the horizon, as if a lonely dream had captured her interest. "I have little in my life anymore. Though, not so long ago, I felt the world was at my feet with glorious possibilities. Now I'm not so sure. I'm merely going through the motions of life with no real substance—adrift with no direction, only torment."

Elizabeth approached quietly with kindness and concern. "I see you haven't taken your medicine. No matter then. I'm sure no harm will come if you skip a dose now and then."

Surprised, Tiffany looked at her. "Why did you say that? You've always insisted I take my medication. What's changed? Has *His Majesty* cut your salary, and you're less than pleased with him?" Immediately she regretted her words. "Sorry, I shouldn't have said that. I'm not feeling very optimistic at the moment."

"No harm done, milady …. Would going to the shop make you feel better? It's been some time since you've been there. Karen would like to see you. She calls nearly every day to see how you're getting on." Elizabeth looked closely at her mistress.

"No. I don't think so." Tiffany sighed deeply. "I don't feel like working or having to put on a cheery face for the sake of others. Maybe in a few days." Elizabeth started to leave.

182   *Cynthia B. Ainsworthe*

Tiffany said, "Tell me, have you ever given your heart to someone who disappointed you?"

"Yes. Once," Elizabeth replied in a near whisper.

"How did you get over it?" Tiffany inclined her head.

"I still am ..." The words nearly stuck in her throat.

~~***~~

Larry sat on the leather sofa in his dressing room. He reviewed the notes he had made on changes to his show. As hard as he tried to concentrate on the scribbled words, his mind kept wandering off to the love of his life. Rehearsal would start in fifteen minutes.

"Joe, did you get Tay's passport replaced yet?" He tossed the papers onto the small coffee table.

"It's in the works, Chief." His friend scratched his head with his short thick fingers. "What's the hurry?"

"I just want it. I don't know when we might need it." His brow furrowed. "Have you heard from that bastard blackmailer? What's up with the investigation? I need to know if Tay really has a twin. Not knowing the truth has been eating at me."

"I've got some people on it," Joe replied casually.

"Well, speed it up." He added sarcastically, "I'd like to know sometime before next year."

"Chief, what y' gonna do if you find Tay does have a twin?" Joe got up and took a bottle of water from the bar. "Y' gonna break it off with Tiff?"

"What else can I do?" The thought sickened him. His eyes filled with sadness. "If she's not really Tay, how could I possibly continue any relationship with her? Tay's the only woman I truly loved. When I think of all we went through to be together, and now to end up like this—not knowing where she is or how she is—it tears me up inside. I'm not whole anymore. Just a mere shell waiting in the wings to go on and play the role women fantasize about—an illusion of love and happiness." Larry shook his head in despair. "It's a helluva way to go through life. My music doesn't have much purpose anymore." He reached for an open bottle of water from a side table and took a large gulp. "I'm a prisoner to my own career— trapped in a life with little meaning. Sometimes, I wish I could just chuck everything and say the hell with it. No more tours, no more Chambord or recordings."

REMEMBER ?   183

"Y' can't do that, Chief." Joe emphasized, "Think of all those

people who rely on you. All those people you'd be puttin' outta work!"

"That's the only reason why I keep going." Larry inhaled deeply.

Joe patted Larry's shoulder kindly. "Don't worry. All good things come to those who wait."

"Yeah, Joe. Heard that one before. Why don't I believe it? Rings a bit sour for me now." His eyes held disbelief.

Larry gathered up the tossed papers from the table and headed out to join the rehearsal.

~~***~~

Brent glanced down at the passenger seat of his red Mercedes convertible when his cell phone rang. He maneuvered through the congested Los Angeles traffic. Reluctantly, he picked it up. The ID displayed "Caller Unknown." *Who the hell is this? I'm in traffic!*

"Yes," he said angrily. "Make it short. I'm driving."

"Don't get your shorts in a knot," the male voice countered. "You nor your boss are in no position to talk to me like that."

His jaw tensed. "I can't talk right now."

"Yeah, I know. You're driving." There was silence as he paused. "Just a friendly reminder call, ol' buddy. Your boss has two weeks to pay up, or the whole ugly mess will hit the papers—and he can kiss his plush lifestyle goodbye. His career will be in the sewer."

"Don't worry about the date. I'm not so sure you have anything at all." Brent's eyes darted from the rearview mirror to the traffic ahead. "How do I know the documents aren't forged?"

"Don't try to play me. You know better. If you found out the records aren't legit, you would've said so at the beginning and hung up on me." Brent heard the smug assuredness in the man's voice. "They're legit all right. I don't deal in fraud."

"No. You deal in blackmail!" he replied with disgust.

"Oh, such ugly words coming from a man with no balls in his corner. I prefer to think I deal in forceful persuasion." The man paused. "If I were you, I'd choose my words more carefully. After all, you wanted me to extend the deadline,

184   *Cynthia B. Ainsworthe*

didn't you?"

"Yes. Two mill is a lot to come up with on short notice—even for Larry Davis." Brent hedged cautiously.

"Tell you what, just to show I'm not heartless," the blackmailer continued, "I'll give you another two weeks then—the price goes up to three mill."

"Three mill! If he can't get a hold of two mill in two weeks, how in hell is he gonna come up with three in four weeks?" Brent continued, "You're fucking crazy!"

"He can take it or leave it—doesn't matter to me," he offered with a false, controlled warmth. "Either way, I come out of this lookin' pretty good. The Tabs will pay big bucks for an exclusive story on the pristine Larry Davis two-timin' his ol' lady with his royal sister-in-law."

"I'll call you back with what Larry wants to do," he replied.

"Very crafty. You can't call me, you don't have my number. I'll call you. Tell your boss not to wait too long. The clock is ticking. With every tick—the price goes up," the male voice retorted. "Look at it this way, I'm doing you a favor. I could've leaked this little gem to the Tabs as soon as I discovered the twin situation, but being the sweet guy I am, I decided to give Mr. Davis a break—give him a chance to keep it all nice and quiet. Hell, man, he should be thanking me." His arrogant comment rang in Brent's ears. "You might say I'm Larry's best friend. Another reporter wouldn't have thought of making such a generous offer. They would've tipped off the rags, taken the money, and ran."

Brent bristled. "Don't hold your breath waiting for a thank-you."

"No thanks expected—just money."

The call ended abruptly. Brent tapped his fingers nervously on the steering wheel. His mind envisioned Larry's career ending in the toilet. *If I can't stop this guy, and Larry doesn't want to pay him off, what in hell is gonna happen to my job? It's not like there are tons of celebs out there clamoring for a manager. Why did I ever agree to make Larry my exclusive client? I've got nothing to fall back on.*

TWENTY-FIVE

CLIVE MADE CAREFUL notes in the laboratory as he observed his primate subjects. Walking from one cage to the next, he noted every nuance of movement and behavior between the control group and the ones who had received the experimental drug. Results progressed nicely for him. He discovered the monkeys that received the drug showed promise. Their short-term memory blacked out until the drug wore off with no side effects. Once this chemical combination lost its effect, their natural behavior and memory returned. *Why aren't these results the same with Tiffany? She can't be more complex than a primate! She's an empty-headed half-wit. Soon we'll be ready for human trials. I can taste the sweetness of a Nobel Prize. It's almost within my grasp.* Engrossed in his research, he didn't hear Alistair approach.

"I dare say, ol' man," Alistair began. "I have some smashing good news, smashing indeed."

"What of it? I'm busy with my findings. If I'm right, we'll be able to start human trials soon." Clive continued to make notes and didn't look at his friend.

"'What of it', you say? I'll tell you what," said Alistair, beaming. "The royal gossip is, Her Majesty is very pleased with you. You may receive an honor of sorts from the royals. How do you like putting that in your cuppers?"

Clive abruptly halted his scientific notation and walked to the center table. "What did you say? Me?"

"That's right, ol' man," he said, smiling. "Seems she's been following you. Quite impressed with the time you donate at the clinic, not to mention that bit of impressive surgery you did for that three-year-old boy from the orphanage a few years back."

"Alistair, do you know how long I've waited to hear this? I've dreamed of this for so many years." He could feel himself smiling from ear to ear. "At last, I'll get the recognition I'm entitled to. I was afraid my marrying a commoner would have put Her Majesty off. Seems poor judgment in my personal affairs was overshadowed by my professional achievements."

186   *Cynthia B. Ainsworthe*

His eyes gazed up at the ceiling. "Do you think I'll be elevated to a duke? If I am, I'll be invited to all those social engagements I only read about. I will have respect as a duke—long overdue. At last, I'll be a duke like you. What a brilliant occurrence!"

"Steady on," Alistair warned. "Nothing is settled yet. You haven't received any notice in the post—and it's been decades since anyone was elevated to a duke to show the queen's favor."

Clive cut him off, "Yes, I know—mere formality. It will happen soon enough." He rubbed his chin. "I suppose I will have to take Tiffany to the ceremony. Hopefully she'll take to her bed for the event."

"I say, ol' man," Alistair responded looking curious, "why would you not want her there? Seems she would add to the moment."

"She's always been a bit awkward with propriety. Speaking out of turn and her irritating American ideas." Clive contemplated out loud "No one would think it odd if she was indisposed. Common sickness wouldn't raise any eyebrows. I might be able to arrange that, if needed."

Alistair remarked slyly, "As long as she doesn't come up missing like Penelope." He patted Alistair's shoulder.

"Don't worry about that. I'll keep her under control. She won't be anywhere I don't want her to be." Clive continued, "As long as she doesn't create a scandal—that would never do."

"Wish I could say the same for Amelia." He looked bewildered. "I don't know where she is or what she's up to half the time—but then again, I really don't care." Alistair added, "Tiffany's supposed little mishap with that Yank, Larry Davis, was never taken seriously by the royals. At best, they all had a bit of a laugh. Given her background, they didn't really find it scandalous as Tiffany can be quite lacking in the social ways of the upper class."

"Quite right," Clive agreed. "I fell in love with her beauty. I should have searched what's between her ears—dare say, not much more than a primate." He looked at one of his subjects in the caged enclosure. "She's just as impulsive with no thought of consequence. How can someone of her fifty years be so bloody thoughtless?"

REMEMBER ?   187

"Fifty, you say?" Alistair inquired. "She doesn't look a day over forty."

"I know. That's why I married her," he conceded. "She makes a lovely adornment on my arm at public functions."

~~***~~

Joe sat in a comfortable black leather chair in Larry's Las Vegas living room. He enjoyed his downtime reading the latest sports stats. His phone rang. He noticed it was Brent. *I wonder what he wants now. Hope it's not an idea for a damn tour. This travelin' is wearin' me out. Gotta retire one of these days. Don't know where Lar gets his energy.* He put down the newspaper and reached for his cell phone on the coffee table.

"Yeah," Joe answered. "What's up?"

"Got a call from that scumbag," Brent answered with exigency. "He'll give us two more weeks, but the price goes up to three mill."

"Three mill! What? Is he out of his fuckin' mind? He's a greedy bastard!" Joe shouted.

Brent agreed, "He's hungry all right. You got any info from your PI contacts? Time is gonna run out, and I hate to think of the backlash when this hits the stands. The media will be all over it."

"I got a guy workin' on it." Joe turned his head to see if Larry still sat on the patio. "I'll get in touch with him to see if he's learned anythin'."

"Better make it quick," Brent advised. "Time's running out. How's Larry dealing with this hanging over his head?"

"As well as can be expected. Kinda washed him out—doesn't care about the show much and even less about his music," Joe remarked. "He's hopin' against all odds the documents aren't real—that the whole thing is a phony scam."

"I've been hoping for the same." He added softly, "Joe, if this does come out 'cause Larry refuses to pay, his career could be up in smoke. Even his PR people won't be able to find a way out for him."

"Yeah, I know." Joe stared at the carpet. "Though, I don't think Lar would mind a bit."

"I would care. I care a lot." Brent added, "Larry is my *only* client. I've nothing to fall back on."

"Don't worry 'bout that," he answered. "I'm sure Lar would

188　*Cynthia B. Ainsworthe*

fix you up with some up and comin' new talent out there. He wouldn't leave you in the lurch."

"Joe, that's a nice thought," he offered, "but I'd rather not have to start all over again from square one—not after all these years."

"Don't sweat the small stuff," Joe advised.

"It's not small to me." Brent emphasized, "This isn't just about Larry's career—it's about mine, too."

"Look, I gotta go, Brent. I'll call my contact as soon as I can," Joe reassured.

"Thanks, man. I'm counting on you." He heard Brent's fear.

~~***~~

Joe's stomach knotted and twisted like a ball of half-done spaghetti in a stew pot as he sat in a booth of his favorite pizza parlor. He knew if there was no way to prove the birth certificates were fraudulent, then Larry's career and reputation would be at stake. He raised the beer bottle to his lips and took a thirst-quenching gulp and made a face as his mind mulled over Larry's current dilemma. *It's damn hard to watch Lar in a tough spot. How I wish he never spotted Tiffany in that shop window. He was better off wonderin' where Taylor vanished to. Now, he's a damn fool chasin' a ghost! My gut told me all along Tiffany wasn't Taylor—would he believe me? Hell, no! Got it in his head this dame has to be his lost love! If he listened to me in the first place, Lar wouldn't've slept with Tiffany. Now the news media got wind of that scandal—speculatin' what goes on behind closed doors. What a mess! His fans are gonna quit buyin' his music if he don't straighten up. This all started with Taylor—Taylor started with that concert. Would Lar make the same choice if he had seen the future? Where's that damn crystal ball when y' need one?*

The annoying ring of his cell phone broke his train of thought. Joe never looked at the caller ID and assumed his boss was on the line.

"Yeah, Lar," he answered. "What do y' need?"

"It's not Larry," the voice replied. "It's Sal. Got some news for y'."

Joe adjusted his seat and leaned closer with eagerness as if Sal was sitting in front of him.

"Better be good news. Things can't get much worse. Lar's manager been tearin' his hair out with worry, and there's talk the Chambord might wanna break Lar's contract."

REMEMBER ? 189

"It's good news—very good news." Sal sounded smug.

"Sal, out with it. Don't tease me like one of those dames on the street." Joe took another swallow of beer.

"That crack reporter didn't do a very good job of investigatin'," his friend boasted. "Seems he only looked into things halfway. Not very good for a reporter."

"Sal, quit stringin' me on. Tell me what you know." Joe heard the city traffic through the phone. He envisioned his old haunts in New York City where he and Larry grew up.

"Here it is, ol' buddy." Sal took a deep breath. "Yes, there are two legit birth certificates. One for Taylor Cynthia Baker born on June 9 at Mahopac Hospital at 11:06 in the evenin', and another for Stephanie Elizabeth Baker born on June 9 at 11:12 that same night—six minutes later—same parents with same address. What this sleazebag didn't do was check further—which I did."

"Go on," Joe encouraged. "What more did y' find out?"

"Like I said, I looked further and found a death certificate for Stephanie Elizabeth Baker dated June 10—she died four hours after birth at three in the mornin'. Your man has no worries."

"Are y' sure about this?" Joe questioned earnestly, "No mistakes?"

"Not a one. I double checked everythin' myself." He added, "I'll fax you the documents tonight."

"Where's Stephanie buried?" Joe quickly jotted down the newfound information that would release Larry from the extortionist's plot.

"She's not." Sal's drag from his cigarette permeated Joe's ears.

"What do y' mean *she's not?*" *These pieces aren't fittin' together.* "Bodies aren't left layin' around."

"Keep your shirt on," Sal advised coolly. "No, she ain't buried 'cause she was cremated. Seems her parents were short of cash in those days and couldn't afford to bury the baby."

Joe glanced at his watch. "I gotta go and tell Lar 'bout this news right away." He added, "Y' did good, buddy. Talk to y' later."

"Glad I could help. It was kinda nice to do some investigatin' that's not routine for a change."

The dial tone sounded in Joe's ear. He quickly called Brent to relay the good news.

TWENTY-SIX

SITTING IN A comfortable upholstered chair in his lavish suite at the Chambord, Larry nervously tapped his fingers on his knee. He worried about the dropping ticket sales and the fact he was no closer to being with Tiffany than he was a month ago. *I've got to see Tiffany. How? I'm booked for the next four weeks. Four weeks! That's when that scumbag wants his money! If I don't pay, can my career take a hit like that? I've tried so hard for so long to keep my nose clean, and now a scandalous rumor could bring me crashing down on the pavement. I'd like to think people come to hear my music, but if the affair with Tiffany gets out, they'll buy tickets out of morbid curiosity, whispering among themselves about my exploit—my music won't matter a damn!* He bit his bottom lip. Worry drove furrows on his forehead. *The hell with all of it. If I have a chance to see Tiff again and convince her she's Tay, then I will. My music is a poor companion on a lonely night.*

Larry grabbed his cell phone from his pocket. Looking at his Rolex watch, he estimated London time. He hesitated a moment, then dialed her number.

"Hello?" the female voice answered tentatively.

"Tiff, is that you?" he joyfully asked.

"Yes, Lar." He heard her yawn. "It's me. Why haven't you returned my calls? I lost count of how many messages I left you."

"Been busy with the show," Larry explained. "Had to schedule additional shows. Fans don't like it when I cancel."

"I understand." Tiffany added, "I'm sad when you don't return my calls."

"I told you, Tiff," he apologized, "I've been busy."

"Busy with your music or busy making music with someone else?" Her tone had an icy edge. "What was I, some diversion while you were in London—a way of killing time between rehearsals and press conferences? Did you find some new lady to hang on your sleeve?"

"No! Never! Don't think like that," he pleaded. "There's been no one else." *Her words are nearly identical to those Tay said to me so many years ago. Her anger sounds like Tay's.* "I don't ever want to say goodbye. Don't even think it."

"Talk is cheap, Mr. Davis," she retorted. "You took me to your bed and made love to me. I feel like I've been thrown out with the dirty bed linen." *Tay said those same words.* "You can't make a fool of me. I put everything on the line for you—risking my husband's reputation, not to mention his wrath."

"Let me explain." His heart ached. He wanted to take her in his arms and feel her lips on his. "Please, I'm begging you, Tiff. Don't say these things. There's a situation I have to take care of first—it's complicated—trust me."

"Is that situation a blonde or brunette—or have you moved on to redheads?" she quipped. He heard her hurt and anger loud and clear.

"That's not fair, Tiff." He implored, "There is no one else—believe me."

"Not even your lost wife?" *You are my wife. I wish you could remember.* "Where will I be when she returns? Just a fond memory of a weekend dalliance? Someone to fill in the void until she returns? I think not. I won't be treated like this. You were my one hope of salvation from the life I've known—a life that has been dark and dismal. Now I have nothing—nothing but a broken heart and days wondering when I'll have to suffer the brunt of Clive's rage."

"Has he hurt you?" Larry's words caught in his throat.

"Would you care?" she asked coolly.

"Of course I care," he said with an urgency that swelled from his depths.

"I expect to see you in two weeks," Tiffany replied. "If you don't come, then I'll have my answer."

"I'll be there," Larry affirmed. "You can count on it. I won't let you down."

"What about your shows?" she asked cautiously.

"The hell with them." He added, "There will always be shows, but there is only one woman for me and her name is Tiffany."

"What about your wife?" she asked softly. "Will you leave her for me?"

I don't have to leave Tay. You are Taylor. "Yes, Tiff. You've got me—all of me."

192   *Cynthia B. Ainsworthe*

~~***~~

Larry sat on the sofa in his dressing room. Tiffany's words rang loudly in his mind. *What must I do to get through to her? When will her memory come back? What if it never returns? Can Tiff love me the way she did? How will Cindy react to all of this? Can she accept Tiff as her mother? Will she be able to see the Taylor within when Tiffany doesn't recognize her?*

Joe entered the room and looked pensively at his boss. "Chief, got good news," he began. "We don't have to worry about that jerk-job anymore. He didn't do his homework—Taylor had a twin named Stephanie Elizabeth Baker."

Larry looked amazed and crestfallen at the same time. "Joe, what do you mean *nothing to worry about?* You just told me Tay has a sister! That's not good news. That means I've been sleeping with my sister-in-law!"

"Calm down, Lar. Let me finish." Joe handed Larry a bottle of water from the bar. "Yes, she *had* a twin. The twin died hours after birth."

"Taylor never mentioned she had a dead sister." Larry rubbed his chin in thought. "Are you sure about your facts? There can't be any foul-ups."

"My PI buddy will fax the docs to me tonight," he assured. "It'll be in black and white. That sleazebag didn't look for a death certificate. He only did half the job thinkin' he was gonna make a ton of money." Joe grabbed a bottle of water, opened it, and took a large gulp. "Y' want me to contact legal and bring extortion charges?"

"Better not." Larry's eyes narrowed. "Let sleeping dogs lie. Could be stirring up a hornet's nest." He paused a moment. "Did you call Brent?"

"Yeah, he knows all about it. I'll give him a copy of all the docs. When that scumbag calls him again—and he will, looking for his three mill—Brent will burst his bubble," Joe said, smiling with satisfaction.

Larry went on, "Are you sure about the death certificate? Why wouldn't Tay's parents mention her twin? Why keep it a secret?"

"Don't know 'bout that one." Joe stroked his chin. "Could be it was too painful for them." He placed his hand on Larry's shoulder. "Chief, don't go lookin' for trouble. Just be thankful

REMEMBER ? 193

the truth is out. Nothin' but smooth waters ahead."

"I have to get Tiff to remember she's Tay," Larry commented determinedly.

"You still goin' on 'bout that?" Joe raised an eyebrow. "Tryin' to make Tiff into someone she's not could blow up in your face. Y' could end up losin' her—then you'd be without Tay and Tiff."

"Enough!" Larry replied sternly. "You're not gonna bring me down. I *know* she's Tay. I won't believe anything else."

"Have it your own way," Joe conceded. "You usually do."

~~***~~

Tiffany and Karen enjoyed their London lunch at the fashionable Auberge de Provence at Buckingham Gate in Westminster near Victoria Station. It was a high-end, cozy, and cavernous restaurant attached to the St. James Court Hotel. Karen's eyes rolled when she looked at the menu and noticed the cost. Tiffany acted nonchalant when she placed their orders.

"Kar, don't you like your fish?" Lady Lantham took a bite of her Coq au Vin. "You've hardly touched your food."

"It's lovely," she assured. "I don't know how to act in such a posh restaurant. I've never been to such a fine place."

"No worry." Tiffany took a sip of Moet champagne. She savored the delightful flavor. "You deserve to be here, just like everyone else."

"That may be, but I'm not certain my manners are befitting such grandness." Karen discretely eyed the other diners. "I might be using the wrong fork."

"Ridiculous!" She confirmed, "You are just as good as anyone here, and in most ways better." Questioning, Karen tilted her head as her friend continued, "You are a true friend with no pretense. You're upfront, honest, and can be counted on." Tiffany looked briefly at the people enjoying their meal with an air of quiet superiority. "Most here would leave their friends at the drop of a hat if there was any hardship or social disgrace—you wouldn't, so that makes you far better than any of them."

"Tiff, you say such kind things," she commented in gratitude. "By the way, what's the occasion? Why treat me to such a fancy lunch?"

194   *Cynthia B. Ainsworthe*

"We need our strength for an afternoon of shopping," she explained. "I need a whole new wardrobe, and it must be stylish. Only the best will do."

"That sounds smashing. What stores do you have in mind?" She added, "You do know you can have anything in my shop at cost, don't you?"

"Karen, that's very kind of you." Tiffany explained with delight, "These clothes must be not only fashionable, but expensive, too—very expensive." A devilish smile came to her lips. "I'll give Lord Lantham something else to worry about besides his test tubes."

"Go on, will you. You plan on getting him riled up?" Karen warned, "I wouldn't do something like that, he could bloody well ship you off somewhere—saying you've gone bloody daft."

"That doesn't concern me." A light laugh escaped. "For some reason I feel alive and in control. I don't think I've ever felt this full of life, except for that wonderful weekend."

"Ah, you're talking about that escapade you had with that Yank, Larry Davis," she surmised.

"Yes, I am." Her eyes glowed. She remembered the warmth of his embrace and the delightful roughness of his beard the morning after love and passion. "It was glorious. I love him very much. No one has touched my heart like him." She took a bite of her chicken. "I have a sinful secret to share."

"How can it be more sinful than…" Karen continued in a whisper, "your affair with Larry? What are you doing—giving Clive his comeuppance with slow acting poison? Serve him bloody right if you did."

"Not as dreadful as that." Tiffany leaned closer. "Larry is coming to see me in two weeks. He said so in his last phone call."

"You believe him, then?" Slight skepticism colored her eyes. "You don't think he's keeping you dangling on a string—wanting you for a bit of slap and tickle whenever he's in town? It's a bleedin' feather in his cap to have Lady Lantham in the wings, if you get my drift."

"Kar, I know you mean the best." She touched her friend's hand lightly. "This is a chance for me to have real happiness. He said if his wife returns, he would choose me over her."

REMEMBER ? 195

"He said all that, did he?" Her jaw slacked in astonishment. "Who brought up that subject about his wife? You or him?"

"I did." Karen looked kindly with a hint of pity as Tiffany continued, "What does it matter. He chose me and I couldn't be happier."

"Tiff, I'm happy for you. Truly I am." She took a sip of champagne. "On to happier things—where are we going to? What shops do you have in mind?"

Tiffany's eyes lit up. "I thought we'd start at Fortnum and Masons, and then go to Harvey Nichols. If there's time, we can drop into Harrods. I'm sure we can find something you might like, as well."

Karen coughed politely. "I dare say, Tiff, you don't do anything by halves. What are you planning to do? Spend six months of his lordship's wages in one afternoon?"

She replied smugly, "No. Not six months—a year's worth." *A hefty bill at the end of the month will be a nice gift for him to remember me by. By then, I'll be long gone. Larry, I'm counting on you. You can't let me down—not now! The fat is in the fire—there's no going back for me!*

TWENTY-SEVEN

SONNY FUGATZZI BUSILY made drinks for his guests at their evening cocktail party. In the kitchen, his lover, Robert Watson, refilled the hors d'oeuvre trays with the help of Cindy and Vic. The gathering was in full force with spirited conversation among the mix of gay and straight partygoers. Mark and Adrienne Barnes enjoyed the diverse topics of discussion. Sonny had a knack for inviting different personalities that meshed well at his gatherings.

In the living room, individual clusters of guests chatted on various topics. Except for Vic and Adrienne, the group was unaware of Cindy and Mark's personal relationship to the world-renowned Larry Davis. Before long, the topic of interest focused on the famous couple.

"All the rags are full of Larry's exploits with his wife's look-alike, Tiffany Bradford," Ted Martin commented as he swirled the wine in his glass. "I would have never thought Larry would take up with someone else."

"I agree," Glen Locke concurred. "The lame excuse has been these meetings were for," his fingers made quote signs in the air, "'*charity*'. I wonder whose charity they were referring to— Larry's or Lady Bradford's."

"Yes," Giselle LeBlanc remarked from the corner of the room with a slight French accent. "It's Lady Lantham to be correct. Just who was the beneficiary of the charity? What exactly was the charitable gift—a private performance?" She gave a light chuckle, then glanced at her partner, Ellen, seated adjacent to her. "Though, I prefer my charity to be of the female variety."

Ellen smiled back with an amused glance.

"Unlike Larry," Giselle continued, "when I make a commitment to someone, I remain faithful."

Sonny piped in, "In defense of Larry, we don't know what is really going on. It could be his association with Tiffany Bradford, I mean, Lady Lantham, is truly charity and nothing more."

REMEMBER ?   197

Mark agreed, "Exactly. I've known Larry for a few years, and have never found him to be anything but honest and very much in love with Taylor." He reached for a morsel from the silver tray on the coffee table. "My God, he rescued her when she was at her lowest. They're soul mates—perfectly matched."

"That's right." Adrienne added, "I saw with my own eyes how much in love they are."

Ted chimed in, "*Were in love* might more aptly express what's going on now. Taylor's been missing for nearly two years." He savored the bacon wrapped scallop before continuing, "Seems to me, Taylor is from his past, and Larry is looking to fill his future—at least until she returns—if she returns."

Sonny couldn't refrain from making a point. "I can't believe, and won't believe, Larry would be unfaithful. He's not one to jeopardize his situation—with his marriage or career."

"Speaking of his career," Robert announced as if he had privileged knowledge, "the tabloids are saying he's all but washed-up. With all the cancellations since his wife came up missing, he's considered a very risky commodity. I'm surprised the Chambord hasn't let him go."

Glen reinforced this last comment, "On one entertainment TV program, there's gossip he might lose his recording contracts and his fan base is waning. Promoters aren't certain he could sell enough tickets to fill an arena for any new road tours." He held out his glass to Sonny for a refill. "Let's face it, he did it to himself. If a celebrity can't be counted on to meet his commitments—how can he or his management expect to sell tickets? No tickets equals no money for the venue providers."

Mark interjected, "You can't put a price on love. This is the woman he loves. He's merely trying to find her. Possibly, he feels Lady Lantham *is* Taylor. It sounds crazy, but stranger things have happened."

"I know it sounds far-fetched," Adrienne remarked. "There could be a bizarre reason for Taylor being Lady Tiffany. Until we know the truth, we should give him the benefit of the doubt."

Sonny changed the subject. "Let's talk about something else. Larry's been run into the ground enough." He lowered his voice a decimal, "I don't want Cindy to hear negative stuff

198   *Cynthia B. Ainsworthe*

about her mother and Larry."

Cindy and Vic, along with Robert, came from the kitchen. Those who had been unaware of Cindy's relationship to the famous entertainer stared at her with awe.

"I hear what?" Larry's step-daughter asked, "What am I not supposed to hear?"

Sonny turned colors. "We're discussing how Larry is still searching for your mom."

"I miss her very much," Cindy said sadly. "I want to believe that wherever she is, Mom is safe. I pray every day she'll turn up. As for Larry—I really don't want to discuss him."

Vic gave his wife a kiss on the temple. "I know you're upset. One day she could turn up with a logical explanation."

Cindy turned to Sonny and Robert. "I'm sorry. We need to leave. I'm not in a party mood at the moment."

"Please don't go," Robert encouraged. "Some of our guests had no idea Taylor was your mom."

"*Is* my mom," she corrected.

"Yes," Sonny agreed. "It's our fault for not cluing our other guests in. I'm so very sorry."

The roomful of partygoers sported a look of embarrassment that punctuated their plea. They commented in near unison, "Cindy, please stay. You don't have to go."

"Maybe another time." She walked to a chair and retrieved her pocketbook. "C'mon, Vic. I want to go home."

The hosts walked them to the front door. "I'm so very sorry," Sonny consoled. "I apologize for my guests."

Robert added, "We never expected the subject of your family to come up."

"That's okay," she replied meekly and gave them each a kiss on the cheek and a hug. "I don't blame you two."

~~***~~

Tiffany folded her newly purchased garments in a suitcase on her bed. She had a plan. She was determined to get away from Clive at the earliest possible moment, but she couldn't stop the doubt that crept into her thoughts. *I pray Larry doesn't change his mind. He sounded so convincing when we last spoke. Ridiculous! Of course he'll return to me. He said he'd be here in two weeks. What if work keeps him away? No, he won't let that happen. He can't! When the bills come in from my shopping spree there will be no living with Clive! Will he kill*

REMEMBER ?   199

me and say I ran away—like Penelope? Did Penelope really desert him, or did something happen to her? Coldness ran through her core and jabbed at her heart. *I must get my imagination under control. I can't let fear cloud my judgment.*

A light knock sounded on the door. Elizabeth quietly walked into the room with a cup of coffee and a plate of small cookies. Rodney followed her in, and jumped onto the bed. With a curious sniff at the suitcase, he sat up and raised a paw to Tiffany begging to be noticed. Tiffany gave him a loving pat on his head. His tail wagged appreciatively.

The young servant eyed the partially filled suitcase and Tiffany's hurried movements of folding newly purchased clothes. Elizabeth placed the beverage and plate on the small table by the window.

"Milady, are you going on a trip?" she inquired.

"Hopefully … if not with Larry, then by myself." Tiffany looked at the young girl. "I can't stay here any longer. I don't know where I'll go, but it will be somewhere—somewhere safe, in another country, where Clive won't find me."

"If I may be so bold, do you have proper traveling documents?" Elizabeth asked meekly. Tiffany's eyes posed an unspoken question. "A passport, milady. Won't you need a passport?"

Her eyes grew wide with realization. "You're correct. I have no idea where Clive stashed it." She sat down on the edge of the bed with a hopeless expression. Her shoulders slumped forward. "I'm trapped. I'm stuck here in England. Clive would eventually find me." *Why did I go off half-cocked? I never thought this through.* "Larry will have to help me—he must!" A look of desperation clouded her eyes.

"Don't fret, milady," Elizabeth comforted. "I'm sure he'll come through for you. Anyone can tell he truly cares. That look he gives you says it all."

"How do you know the way Larry looks at me?" Tiffany asked.

Elizabeth turned colors. "I've seen the two of you in the papers, milady."

"What did those papers say?" Tiffany was intrigued.

"Nothing I'd care to share." Elizabeth wrung her hands nervously. She clearly regretted having brought up the subject.

200   *Cynthia B. Ainsworthe*

"Milady, those papers are busy making up stories—all for the sake of sales. Take no mind of them, I certainly don't."

"Elizabeth, you haven't answered my question." Tiffany probed, "What are they printing about Larry and me?"

"Speculation mostly, that you and him have more than a friendship," she answered with downcast eyes.

"I don't care!" Her posture stiffened. "Words can't hurt me." A small devious smile came to her. "Though, I think Clive would be upset." *I wonder why he hasn't mentioned this to me.*

"I suspect Lord Lantham doesn't read those types of papers," the young girl mentioned. "All I've seen him reading are his medical journals."

"That's a relief," Tiffany said with a sigh. "I don't need his interrogation." *Something's wrong. Clive may not read those tabloids but he must have heard about them. What devious plan does he have in store for me? I might be in more peril than I thought! Lar, save me. I don't want to share Penelope's fate!*

TWENTY-EIGHT

BRENT SAT IN his office. His cell phone rang. He jumped at the sound. The ID showed no useful information. The male voice started before he could speak a greeting.

"Got the money yet?" The caller spoke with a steely, authoritative tone. "Time is money. The price rises with every passing day."

"Not so fast, scumbag." Brent's controlled irritation triumphed. "You haven't done your homework. Very sloppy investigation if you ask me."

"Careful, you're raising the price," he replied confidently. "Though, with the deep pockets of your boss, he can well afford it."

"You won't be getting one dime," Brent retorted. "There's no living twin. She died hours after birth. Your extortion plot is kaput! If you do intend to run with this fabrication, we'll sue the pants off any rag that publishes it—and that, my dear friend, will end your career."

"Not so damn fast!" the blackmailer nearly yelled. "How do you know all this? You have verifiable proof?"

"Check it out yourself," Brent commanded. "It's all in black and white in the records of Mahopac, New York—plain as day. Records of births and deaths don't lie. Leave us alone. Be thankful we won't take this any further. Go back to the scum you dwell with!"

"You can't sue me," the male voice replied with a malicious sneer. "You don't know who I really am."

"That's the only good luck you have, bastard!" Brent hung up the phone.

~~***~~

Larry paced in his Las Vegas home. His thoughts centered on Tiffany—not the show. Ever since his wife never returned from Paris, his career had taken more of a backseat in his life— a career teetering on ruin—one that took a lifetime to build.

Joe entered with the poodles Gigi and Jacques. He had just returned from the grooming salon. The two pups ran to their "daddy" with wagging tails, begging to be picked up. *They miss Tay, too, and the way they used to nap on her side of the bed.* Larry bent down, picked them up, lovingly petted their curly heads, and gave them brief kisses.

"Joe, call the Chambord. I'm cancelling the next six weeks," he directed coolly. "Tell them I have to see the doctor or something." Joe was ready to object. Larry cut him off. "Don't start. I'm firm about this. The fans will have to understand— the Chambord will have to understand. I *must* get Taylor back. Tiffany *must* remember who she really is and who she belongs with."

"Chief, you're jeopardizin' your career—everything you've worked so hard for," Joe pleaded with open palms. "Don't throw it all away on someone who may not be Taylor—that's too high a price. The odds are in the house's favor. You're playin' roulette with your career—the house will win."

Frustration and anger began to wax. "I don't give a damn. The bottom line—either you're with me or not. You choose."

Joe's eyes widened with the ultimatum. "Chief, of course I'm with you." He casually walked to the kitchen. "So, when do you want to leave for London?" He opened the refrigerator for a cold beer.

Larry chuckled. "You know me so well, Joe."

"Always have." He handed a bottle of cold mineral water to his friend. "By the way, Taylor's passport arrived a few days ago."

"Why didn't you mention it before?" Larry took a large gulp of the cooling liquid.

"I wasn't sure if you'd change your mind." Joe's expression indicated displeasure at what he clearly thought was Larry's folly.

"Not a chance. Tell the pilot to gas up the jet. I want to leave this evening." Larry walked out to the pool patio. He glanced at the chaise lounge where he and Taylor had shared so many romantic evenings. A warm smile of remembrance came to his lips.

Joe came up behind him. "That's short notice. Lot of fans will be upset—includin' the Chambord. Lost revenue for all concerned."

"Can't be helped," Larry replied. "Tiffany is expecting me.

Somehow, I feel she's not safe with Clive. I've nothing concrete—just my gut."

"More like your heart," Joe commented knowingly. "Definitely not your head. I can't prevent you from wreckin' your career and reputation."

"Fuck the whole thing," he stared at his reflection in the pool. "No amount of fan adoration, record sales, or concerts can take the place of Taylor. You can't put a price on happiness. Without Tay, nothing is fun anymore—just a job—going through the motions—and for what? To feed the fantasies of fans and fill the pockets of others? I'm sick of it."

"I'll call Brent and the pilot," Joe said solemnly. "The Chambord might break your contract."

"If they do," Larry's jaw tightened with determination, "so what! I can't go on like this. No one should have to suffer like this."

"What about all those people losin' their jobs?" Joe again tried to speak reason. "You could be puttin' a lot of souls outta work."

"Can't be helped," he remarked softly. "I might be able to find them work through my contacts."

"Yeah , if you have any contacts left." Joe left the room to make his required calls.

Larry called out to him, "Bring Taylor's passport. Tim can babysit Gigi and Jacques."

~~***~~

After returning home from the club, Clive climbed upstairs. He was pleased. No light peeked from Tiffany's closed door. Elizabeth approached, arms full of stacked linen to be put away.

He called her name; "Elizabeth." She peeked over the pile of towels. "Has there been any change in Lady Lantham?"

"Milord, she is requiring more rest than usual."

Clive gave a slight smile of approval. He mumbled to himself, "It must be working." His attention returned to the servant girl. "You're giving the medicine to Lady Lantham every day?" He raised a questioning eyebrow. "Exactly as I instructed?"

"Yes, milord," she replied. "I followed your instructions to the letter."

204   *Cynthia B. Ainsworthe*

Before opening the bedroom door, he turned back to Elizabeth. "You best brush up on your curtsy—soon I'll be Duke."

"Oh, I say, milord," she said as she gave a brief curtsy, "that is so grand. You must be very pleased indeed. When will that be?"

"Quite." He looked at her squarely. "I must say, it's high time and well overdue. Nothing is official yet, but my accomplishments are being noticed by the royals. I'm certain the queen will make an exception and favor me with an elevated title." He added, "Good night, Elizabeth. I shan't require anything further."

Clive entered his room. He started to walk to his wife's adjoining bedroom, then stopped. *No. I won't wake her. She's of little use to me. I'm not certain she can understand anything at this hour—the drug must have taken hold by now.* Clive sat on the edge of the bed and began to undress.

His slender fingers loosened his tie, then slipped off the expensive Italian leather oxfords. *Hmm…must be careful she doesn't receive too much. I can't afford any mishaps like last time. If I could only find the key to making the effect reversible at will—only erase negative memory. The answer just might lie with Tiffany…baffling. Her reaction is so atypical—nothing at all like the primates. It's almost as if she was taking a damnable sugar tablet. Can't be. Elizabeth would never disobey me—she's too simple-minded, like Tiffany.* He changed into silk pajamas and climbed into bed. *If Tiffany proves to be a failure as a subject—there's always Switzerland.*

TWENTY-NINE

AT CRUISING ALTITUDE, Larry stretched his long legs. He stared at the black void through the window. Six weeks of cancellations resulted in a firm warning from the Chambord. He had to agree to reschedule all shows, plus favor his fans with a special meet-and-greet for six Chambord charity events. He felt that was a small price for the chance to bring his love back into his life. *In nine short hours I'll be with Tiffany. I know I can make her remember.*

He looked at Joe seated across from him. "Joe, call the Regina in Paris. Do it now. I want reservations for the day after we arrive in London." His posture straightened.

Joe glanced at his watch. "At this hour? It must be five or six in the mornin' in Paris."

"Just do it," Larry commanded. "I want the same Presidential Suite. It must be the same. Everything must be the same, even the dozen red roses."

Joe took his cell phone from his pocket and fulfilled Larry's request. The singer closed his eyes. Images of Taylor traveled through his love-hungry brain. Joe's voice faded into the distance. The wafting of her fragrance, "Forbidden", came from his treasure trove of memories. Only during his daydreams or sleep was his lost wife with him once more. Music was no longer his safe haven to escape life's pain. His dreams now held the key to his sanity. Slumber took over where his consciousness left off.

~~***~~

"What the hell is going on?" the man demanded to the Chambord's concierge. "We've traveled all the way from London for my wife's birthday so she could see Larry Davis' show—now you tell me it's cancelled! What type of scam are you running here?"

"Sir," the hotel employee implored, "this was out of anyone's control. He's taken sick indefinitely and has cancelled his shows for the next six weeks. No one can control when they will be ill."

206   *Cynthia B. Ainsworthe*

"No," the man sniped, "unless you're Larry Davis and think you're bloody bigger than God!"

A lengthening line of irate ticket holders for the same show cheered the British customer on with grumbles of their own.

"What about all the money we spent to come here?" the tourist asked. "Flying from the UK is not like taking a taxi to the nearest pub."

"I'm very sorry for any inconvenience." The concierge offered, "Your ticket will be refunded. There are many fine shows here in Las Vegas. Your wife might enjoy seeing one of those. I've been told Mr. Davis will be rescheduling all his cancelled shows. You can use your tickets at a later date."

"I'm not flying across the pond to take my wife to see another Larry Davis show. I should have known better with his track record—all his previous cancellations. She won't want to see any Vegas show—not when her heart is set on seeing Larry Davis." The gentleman sarcastically patted his paunch. "Though I can't imagine why. He's skinny as a stick." He turned and looked at the others in line. "A woman likes a man who has something to hold on to."

The hotel employee cleared his throat at this last comment. "Sir, I will refund your money right away." He produced two small pieces of paper on the counter. "Please enjoy two free drinks at any of our bars with our compliments."

"Two free drinks—mighty poor compensation for spent money and disappointing my wife," he remarked as he took the beverage coupons.

Swiftly, the concierge refunded the disgruntled customer, then waited to greet the next ticketholder with a polite and efficient smile. His work was cut out for him. There wasn't a pleasant smile in the entire line.

~~***~~

Joe stood on the front door stoop. He rang the bell to the Bradford's townhouse. Rodney's barking greeted him when Elizabeth opened the door. He immediately started talking before she could utter a word.

"Is Lady Lantham home?" His pressured speech screamed of urgency. "Gotta speak with her. Mr. Davis wants to see her right away."

Tiffany's voice came from the sitting room. "Elizabeth, who's

REMEMBER ?   207

calling? Is that Joe?"

"Yes, milady," she responded. Her mistress entered the foyer.

Elizabeth stepped aside. Tiffany stopped briefly, then went to Joe and gave him a warm, welcoming hug. "It's so good see you, Joe." She briefly looked past him to the waiting limousine for any possible glimpse of Larry in the backseat.

"If you're lookin' for Lar," he offered, "he's not with me— waitin' for y' at the hotel." Her eyes narrowed questioningly. "He doesn't want people to know he's here—cancelled his shows to see y'. The word's out he's laid up in a hospital somewhere."

"Oh, no!" She realized the implications. "I didn't want Lar to cancel his shows. All those poor fans. What must they think?"

The servant closed the door as Rodney begged for attention. Joe bent down and gently patted the loving pup.

"Don't sweat it." Joe's easy smile swayed her fears. "His fans'll understand—they always have—they always will. When he does give a show, it's always top rate. Nothin' will change." He lowered his voice a decimal, "Can you pack quick? I think Lar has a surprise for y'."

"No need to whisper." She glanced at the young girl. "I have no secrets from Elizabeth. She has my complete trust. I'm already packed."

"Tiffany, you're one unpredictable lady," Joe commented.

She turned to the servant. "Please get my bag. I have it in the back of my closet."

Elizabeth swiftly went up the stairs. Tiffany led Joe into the sitting room. His words stopped her. "Tiffany, we don't have much time. I'd love to visit with you, but I think y' better be gettin' to the hotel. Lar's waitin'. I think he's got plans."

They returned to the foyer. The young servant came downstairs with her ladyship's bag. Joe took it quickly. Tiffany said her goodbyes to Elizabeth and gave an extra ear rub to little Rodney, a tear glistening in her eye. She whispered to the pup, "I love you, Rodney. Elizabeth is your new mommy now." They scurried to the waiting car. Her stomach clenched with trepidation as the vehicle started moving.

~~***~~

The moment Joe opened the door to the hotel suite, time

stood still for Tiffany. Larry looked tall, strong, and commanding. He approached with an easy stride and smile that could bring sunlight in the middle of the night. Her heart ached with overwhelming love as her eyes met his—eyes filled with so much desire that she thought glaciers would melt to turbulent rivers of passion.

His voice was mellow and inviting, "It's been too long, Tiff."

"That's an understatement." She eased out of her coat and handed it to Joe. Her hands shook so much she was afraid he would notice.

Joe hung up the garment. He nodded at Larry's gesture for him to make an exit and promptly headed for his room.

"So, tell me, Mr. Davis," Tiffany strolled over to the dark brown leather sofa, "after this visit, will you put me on the shelf?"

"Not a chance." He sat down on the couch and offered his hand for her to do the same. She obliged, effortlessly sliding beside him. "I wasn't certain you would return. There were always moments of doubt."

"Never. You're the only one I've been thinking of, even in my dreams." He took her hand and caressed her fingers gently. "You're trembling."

She blushed. "It's been the same for me," she confessed. "I believe there's only one person for me—that person is you." She diverted her eyes from his gaze. "I'm sorry if I made it sound like an ultimatum. I had a desperate longing to see you, feel your arms around me, feel your lips on mine."

"Like this?" His fingers tenderly touched her chin. She sighed deeply in anticipation. His lips caressed hers. Her heart and soul melted. She was one with him. The long, warm kiss spoke of eternal adoration and commitment.

Tiffany pulled away slowly. Her fingers ran though his hair and moved to the back of his neck. Her gaze settled on his face. She wanted this moment to last a lifetime. A loving smile graced her face. She really was free—free from Clive's tiresome conversation and boorish manipulating ways. Time stood still for her, and she savored this moment as new, beautiful memories etched into her being.

"I took the liberty of ordering dinner for us," Larry remarked.

REMEMBER ? 209

"I hope you didn't order fish," Tiffany eased back on the sofa. "The only fish I eat is out of a can and that's tuna." She paused a moment as if her own words sounded odd to her. *I feel as if I said those same words to him before. What's happening to me? I don't remember a similar situation. Is my mind leaving me?*

"And I bet you consider eating a whole fish with the head and tail still attached as barbaric?" he probed.

"Why, yes." Her eyes, full of confusion, met his in wonder. "How did you know?"

"A lucky guess." He stood up, reached for the chilled bottle of champagne on the coffee table, poured the dancing liquid into two crystal flutes, and offered her the glass. "Let's toast to beautiful beginnings—to our beginning. This will be our night to remember. You will never have to return to your former life with Clive." Her eyes welled up as her glass met his. "To the future—our future and wonderful possibilities."

She sipped the pale yellow liquid and savored the delightful taste that tickled her tongue. But it was more than that. It was something they enjoyed sharing.

"Lar, you make everything seem possible and the impossible surmountable." Her hand lightly touched his knee. He cleared his throat. His charming smile enticed her. She needed him more now than ever, yet she hoped he wouldn't rush her to the bedroom. She wanted this night to last forever and to engrave every detail in her memory.

An odd feeling entered her, almost as if from an alien force. Softly, she mentioned, "I am changing inside, and I don't know what to do about it. An exciting confusion mixed with adventure. It frightens me a little."

"Don't fight it, Tiff," he encouraged. "Go with it. You're feeling your past—a past that is crying to be released—that may be the key to your memory."

"That's what I'm afraid of." She paused before saying, "Lar, what if I find out I was a horrible person who did horrible things—hurt others?"

"Tiff, there's not a hurtful bone in your body." He cajoled, "I love every single one of them."

"Of what?" she asked innocently.

"Your bones," he smiled, then added, "and your mind, eyes, hair, face, body, all the way to your toes."

"I love your compliments," she cooed. "You know how to sway a lady." Her fingers stroked the stem of her glass. Larry noted this suggestive gesture and grinned. "I don't suppose you have more champagne in the boudoir?"

"Whatever the lady wants." He stood and extended his arm in the direction of the bedroom.

"This lady would like to have dinner first," she teased, "then we'll see if further activities might lead elsewhere." She ran her tongue along her bottom lip. "Love is never good on an empty stomach—ruins the moment. I wouldn't want you to focus on my stomach groans instead of my moans."

"Then, by all means," he agreed. "Let's have dinner. I'll call room service."

She eyed his long legs as he strolled to the phone across the room. A devilish feeling churned in her stomach. *I wonder if he's feeling playful. I am. How intoxicating he is, or is it because I'm free of Clive? Do I love him because he's my lifeline to a new life? Is Lar really the one I want? Will I still want him if I regain my memory? I mustn't think of this. Tonight is ours.*

THIRTY

"WHAT DO YOU mean she's gone on holiday?" Clive glowered at Elizabeth as his voice echoed off the foyer's walls. "How long has she been gone?" He continued in rapid-fire fashion, "Did Lady Lantham say where she was going? Did she leave alone or was she with that tart, Duchess Steffenfordshire, or even worse—that strumpet Karen from the dress shop?" Rodney cringed in the corner as Clive's voice grew sterner. "What about her medication? Did she pack her medicine? Not just her heart pills, but the special ones I prescribed?"

"Milord, Lady Lantham, left by herself," she timidly lied. "She has her tablets, both the ones you ordered and her heart medicine." Elizabeth offered quietly, "She shouldn't be longer than a fortnight, I imagine."

His eyes widened. Rage smoldered deep inside him. "Indeed? A fortnight, you say? And without my permission! For God's sake, Elizabeth, why did you let her go? Are you so simple-minded not to know she's not safe on her own? You should have called me—called me! Do you understand!"

The young girl nodded meekly with wide eyes and a fearful, frozen expression.

He raised his hand in preparation to strike her. Judgment took over. He gritted his teeth. His open palm clenched. The skin on his knuckles drew tight and white. Elizabeth stepped back with eyes shut, clearly fearing a fierce blow. With his hand at his side, Clive's near loss of control manifested itself as he repeatedly opened and closed his fist. *I can't take this out on Elizabeth. If she tells anyone of my reaction, it might get back to the royals—that could ruin my forthcoming title of Duke. I know the queen will make an exception for me—how could she not? Acting out in anger could sabotage my research.* He scowled at the pup cowering in the corner. Deliberate angry steps took him to the library for a stiff scotch. Rodney did not follow. Clive noticed Elizabeth had picked up quivering Rodney and reassured the pup with loving kisses. *Why did I ever get a dog for Tiffany? At least he's not a poodle as she wanted. She should have taken that beast with her. He's not even good for hunting.*

212   *Cynthia B. Ainsworthe*

~~***~~

In Larry's suite, the waiter placed their dinner on the waiting table by the window overlooking London's skyline. Tiffany eyed the lavish table setting complete with a single red rose in a silver vase. She licked her lips in anticipation of a delicious feast.

"I hope you like what I ordered," Larry remarked. The waiter waited patiently in the background. Larry pulled out a twenty pound note from his pocket and handed it to the young man. "Thank you. That will be all. If we need anything else, I'll ring."

"Certainly," the man replied and left the room.

Larry invited her to sit down by pulling out her chair and gestured, "Your throne awaits Lady Lantham."

"Now you're making fun of my title." She sat down. "I don't like being called Lady Lantham. It doesn't fit me at all."

"Sorry, meant no harm." He gave a slight smile.

Larry lifted the silver dome from the plates with a flourish. Tiffany's eyes widened.

"Oh, Lar," she exclaimed with delight, "filet mignon! I haven't had beef in so very long. Clive makes me stick to my diet—he says I have to watch my cholesterol."

"I can order something else, if you'd like?" He sat opposite her.

"No. I think I can afford to deviate this once," she commented. "After all, this is a celebration—my being free, and I'm with you."

"It's definitely a celebration," Larry concurred. "What would you like to do after dinner?" He felt her foot moving against his in response. Her coy smile affirmed her intentions.

"Oh, Mr. Davis," she teased, "I'll leave that up to you. You can't give me a tour of London—we might be seen by the paparazzi." Her finger ran around the rim of her champagne flute. "You could give me a tour of this lavish suite. I've never been to any of the Dorchester's guest rooms." She heightened her teasing banter by adding, "Of course, if you'd rather not—I can always busy myself in front of the TV."

"Not on your life." Hunger was in his voice. "If you think I came here to spend a casual night with you—think again." He sipped his champagne as he looked longingly at her. "This will be a night neither one of us will forget."

"Hmm, and what activities do you have in mind—a repeat of our weekend at Amelia's manor?"

"Do you have an objection to that idea?" he queried.

"Since I accepted your invitation, what do you think?"

"Tiff, you like word games, don't you?" Larry flashed her a suggestive glance. *She's toying with my emotions.*

"Maybe. I like all games. Mostly I like games of a physical nature." She looked at him coyly.

"What might those physical games be?" He took a bite of his chicken.

Tiffany seized a piece of beef and chewed with obvious sensuous relish. "I love the taste of meat in my mouth, feeling the firmness of the flesh, and the delicious hint of saltiness on my tongue. Merely stroking the substance is sublime—an experience I could savor well into the morning hours. It's been so long since I've had a good piece of meat."

Larry swallowed hard while not taking his eyes off her. He grabbed his water glass and gulped the cooling liquid. Her foot slid up his calf and back down again. She slipped her shoes off under the table, and her toes traced up his leg to his thigh. He coughed and took another swallow of water.

"What's wrong?" she purred. "Are you at a loss for words, Lar?" Her fingers slid up and down her water goblet slowly. "I've never seen you without a retort of some kind."

"Oh, I can think of plenty *retorts* as you term it." He took a deep breath to calm his churning emotions. "Retorts that are better suited for the bedroom." He extended his hand across the table. "Shall we? I hear the sheets at this hotel are of the finest quality."

"So, you want to check out the sheets?" Tiffany licked her lips. "I didn't realize you were interested in thread count. I seem to remember your interests lie elsewhere. There were other things you like to feel besides bed linen." Her tongue ran across her upper teeth. Despite her delaying tactics, her heaving breasts and slight breathlessness told him her hunger ran as deep as his. "I think we should have our coffee first. Waiting always intensifies the senses, don't you agree?"

"I don't need to prolong the waiting. My senses are as sharp as nails." His fingers caressed the top of her hand. "Do you need more playful banter to set the mood?" His clear blue eyes

214   *Cynthia B. Ainsworthe*

bore into hers. "I can make you sweat in the middle of winter without barely trying—I remember what the lady likes."

"Well, aren't you full of yourself?" Obviously, she didn't want the game to end.

"It's not myself I want to fill." He used all his onstage charm to weaken her. "I can think of another way to fill something."

"You 'remember what the lady likes', and you want to *fill* something? My, my, Mr. Davis, now who is prolonging the moment?" She turned her hand upward and slowly ran her fingers against his palm. "Seems to me, you're enjoying this just as much as I. Am I right?"

"Not exactly." *How much more does she expects me to take? I want to pour the coffee, but I don't dare stand up now—she'll know how ready I am.* "Why don't you pour the coffee," he suggested. "Then we can move on to more exciting activities." Eagerly he added, "We can have coffee in the bedroom."

"What's wrong, Lar?" she teased. "Why don't you want to leave the table? Is there something you don't want me to see?"

"You're a little vixen, and I love you for it." He vaguely hinted at her assumption. "Yes, it would be less embarrassing for me if you poured the coffee."

Clearly pleased with her feminine powers, Tiffany poured the coffee and brought the cups to the cocktail table. She sat down in one smooth movement.

Patting the sofa, she said softly, "Lar, don't leave me alone. Come over here. I won't look if you don't want me to—I'll keep my eyes on yours the entire time."

"Tiff, you are such a damnable tease," Larry said as he strode over to her.

"And you wouldn't have me any other way," she remarked.

"Definitely not," he agreed with bated breath.

He promptly sat down, nearly crushing her skirt. His hand caressed her cheek as he drank in her beauty. Larry's arm drew her closer. Their lips met and his tongue searched for hers. She coyly evaded his touch. Her tongue met his and electric shocks ran through him as they mingled their passion. She gave love bites on his lower lip. He ran his tongue slowly along her neck. Tiffany let out a soft "ooh" as his mouth caressed the small of her throat. She guided his hand to her breast. He gasped when he felt the firmness of her beneath her clothing. She sighed heavily. "Oh Larry more. Please," she panted. With her hand on his, she encouraged his touch. Larry felt her chest heave with every breath. His mouth sought hers with a hunger she matched.

He spoke breathlessly between passionate kisses. "Let's continue this conversation in the bedroom."

Tiffany slid her hand onto his firm manhood and gave a gentle squeeze.

THIRTY-ONE

"KAREN," ELIZABETH SAID hurriedly on the phone. "I'm afraid for Lady Tiffany."

"What's wrong, my dear?" she answered.

"His lordship went into a rage when he found out Lady Lantham went away on holiday, and he expected me to stop her." She caught her breath. "He nearly hit me, he did. If I didn't need my position, I'd give him what for."

"Now, now, Elizabeth. Lady Tiffany will be just fine," Karen soothed. "Her time away from *His Majesty* will be good for her and will give him a chance to smooth his pompous ruffles." Elizabeth worried, *I pray it won't be worse for Tiffany when she returns home.* "Elizabeth, did she pack the medicine Clive gives her?"

"No. She has her heart pills." She continued with a triumphant tone, "I conveniently forgot her special tablets Lord Lantham insists she take."

"Good for you." Elizabeth heard the smile in Karen's voice. "I don't know what's in them, but I do know Tiffany is far better when she's forgotten a dose or two. Where did she go?"

"I don't know. Mr. Joe came for her in a black limousine, he did. Right proper it was," the young girl answered.

"Tiffany might need an alibi." Karen paused a moment. "Amelia should know about this. I don't like the bloody sound of his lordship's temper. Tiffany could end up in danger—deadly danger if Clive feels he's losing control over her."

"Maybe I should look for service at another household," Elizabeth said softly.

"Better stay where you are for now." Karen added, "He has no row with you. You can keep an eye out to protect Tiffany."

Elizabeth heard the front door open. She quietly ended her call with whispers and picked up Rodney who waited at her feet. Petting the dog, she thought, *I won't let anything happen to you or Lady Tiffany. Lord Clive isn't the ruddy King of England!*

~~***~~

Tiffany looked at the Eiffel Tower through the limousine window as the driver maneuvered the congested Parisian streets.

REMEMBER ?   217

Larry sat next to her and looked for any reaction that might indicate recognition. She smiled briefly but didn't appear awed by her surroundings as would be expected by a first-time visitor.

Larry inquired, "Anything look familiar?" *She must remember something.* "The streets or cafés?"

"Not familiar, more of a comfortable feeling." Tiffany hesitated, "Like almost returning to a dream."

"Or it could mean the return of a memory?" he suggested.

"Well, Clive told me he and I fell in love in Paris and married here." She nervously fingered the strap of her pocketbook. "That *is* the most logical reason."

"No matter." Larry said softly. *Maybe a place, smell, or taste will bring her out of this darkness.*

Soon, the limousine was on Rue de Rivoli heading toward Place de la Concord. The car came to an abrupt strop as a pedestrian stepped off the sidewalk into traffic. The driver muttered French curses at the offender and inquired if his passengers were unscathed. Without forethought, Tiffany replied in fluent French. She looked amazed at Larry.

"Did that come out of me?" Confusion replaced her wonder.

"Yes, you spoke in French." *Is it all coming back to her?* "Haven't you spoken French before? I seem to remember you said you spoke French."

"That's true, but only a few words and simple phrases." Her eyes darted about his face. "I didn't hesitate, not one bit. I immediately *thought* in French. That has never happened before."

"Don't try to explain it," he suggested. "Let your mind guide you. This could be the breakthrough we're hoping for."

The car pulled up to the entrance of the Hôtel Regina on 2 Place des Pyramides. The doorman immediately opened the back passenger door and gave the greeting, "Welcome to Hôtel Regina. I hope you have an enjoyable stay."

Tiffany froze for a moment as her eyes gazed over the hotel's façade. Her reaction caught Larry's breath as he studied her face.

"Have you been here before?" he asked.

"I might have been," she answered. "Perhaps with Clive."

Larry left a sizable tip to the driver and then the bellman who

218   *Cynthia B. Ainsworthe*

gathered their luggage. He led the way through the massive brass revolving doors.

The click of her heels echoed on the ornate marble tiled floors. At the reception desk, the concierge sported a broad smile and warm welcome.

"Bonjour Monsieur and Madame Davis," Jean-Luc greeted. "It has been a long time since you were our guests."

Tiffany immediately explained, "I'm not Madame Davis. I merely look like her."

Jean-Luc's confusion played on his face. "Pardon, Madame," he apologized. "I, I had …."

Larry quickly explained, "Madame has suffered a fall that affected her memory." He added, "Here are our passports. I trust the same suite has been reserved for us?"

"Bien sûr, Monsieur. Suite Présidential, as you requested." He handed the room keycards to Larry. "Sylvie will escort you to your room."

Sylvie promptly appeared from the back office and waited at the gleaming brass elevator doors. Larry smiled as he handed her the room key. Tiffany walked as if in a daze, intently looking around at her surroundings for some recognition.

The ride to the septième étage was swift. The plush red carpet muffled the sound of their footsteps. Larry entered first, followed by Tiffany. He took her hand and guided her to the double-wide tall windows. Sylvie excused herself and closed the door.

Parting the sheer curtains, he asked, "Have you ever seen a sight more beautiful?"

"It's lovely. The Eiffel Tower and you said that was the Jardin des Tuileries in front of the Louvre." She bit her lip. "I feel so uneasy about all of this. Things are familiar But I can't put a memory to any of it. What if I'm developing other mental issues besides my memory loss?"

He embraced her tenderly as a father would a frightened child, and tried to calm her fearful trembling. "Don't be afraid. We're in this together. I think you're going to start remembering very soon."

"I hope so, Lar." She buried her cheek against his chest. "I truly hope so."

~~***~~

REMEMBER ?   219

Clive placed his umbrella in the stand near the door, removed his coat and hat, and hung them on the nearby coat rack in the foyer. He held The Times newspaper firmly in his hands.

Still holding Rodney, Elizabeth waited fearfully for her master's command. The knotted brow and clenched teeth indicated his foul humor.

"Where might Lady Lantham be during her fortnight excursion?" His tone demanded a definitive answer.

Elizabeth held trembling Rodney closer. "She's out, milord."

"That is no answer, Elizabeth." Clive placed a hand on his hip with a cold calmness. "I repeat. Where is Lady Lantham?"

"I don't know, your lordship. She didn't say, you see. I didn't think it was my place to ask." *I hope he won't hit me, or do worse to little Rodney.*

"Quite." Clive glared coldly into Elizabeth's eyes. "Did she have any bags with her?"

"No, I don't think so, milord," she lied. *I've got to keep Lady Tiffany safe.*

"You don't think so?" Clive clenched his fist. "You stupid girl." He mumbled, "First Andrews quit and now Tiffany isn't home and you don't know anything. What nerve! She leaves for a fortnight with no luggage! Outrageous!"

"Milord, I didn't actually see her ladyship leave." *If he strikes me, I'll go directly to the police.*

Clive strode to the study and settled into the leather wingback chair. He briskly opened the newspaper. Elizabeth peeked through the doorway. He took no notice of her. Quietly, the servant girl tiptoed back to the kitchen. She dialed Amelia's number. Her back was to the door leading to the hallway.

"Duchess," she whispered, "I can't talk long. Lord Lantham asked where Lady Tiffany is. I didn't tell him I knew, but he's jolly cross and I don't think he'll be satisfied until he gets an answer. I'm also afraid he'll do something to hurt the dog, Rodney. What should I do now?"

"If you feel unsafe, leave and go to the police," Amelia advised. "On the other hand, if Clive is merely grumpy, watch him and report back to me."

"Yes, of course." Elizabeth turned to keep an eye on the kitchen door dreading a possible intrusion from Clive. "I'll

220   *Cynthia B. Ainsworthe*

watch and see what he does next."

"Elizabeth," she offered softly and with kindness, "you can always come here with Rodney. You don't need to take this one on. If I must, I can deal with his lordship on my own terms."

"I understand, Your Grace—I mean, Amelia." The young girl took a breath of courage. "I want to help Lady Tiffany. If I can find evidence that will help her, then that's what I'll do."

Rodney gave a low, slow growl with his big brown eyes fixed on the door.

Elizabeth continued, "I need to go. Lord Lantham might be nearby."

~~***~~

Larry and Tiffany walked along the quai of the Seine. He hoped the uneven cobblestone way would seem familiar to her. She looked pensive.

"Penny for your thoughts," he remarked.

"Not worth a penny. More confusion—nothing concrete. Why can't I remember anything?"

"Give it time, Tiff. Give it time." Larry lovingly embraced her waist as they strolled. "Rome wasn't built in a day. Where would you like to dine tonight?"

"That dinner cruise, Bâteaux Parisiens, seems a nice idea. I wonder if Laurant and Suzanne still work there."Astonished, she asked, "Where did that come from? Have I been there? Who is Laurant and Suzanne?"

"They work for the dinner cruise." A knowing smile spoke of hope. "When we get back to the hotel, I'll check to see if we can make reservations." He stared at her with a optimistic curiosity. "What about now? Visit a park, shop, or something else?"

"I'd like to sit and watch the boats go by." She walked to a nearby bench. "It's relaxing here. I can let my worries float away with the flow of the Seine."

"I need to make a call to Joe," he explained. "I'll be right back."

Larry walked a short distance away. He dialed Joe's number and watched Tiffany as he waited for Joe to pick up.

"Yeah, Chief," Joe answered.

"I want you to fly back to Las Vegas and get the poodles, Gigi and Jacques," he requested.

REMEMBER ? 221

"What for? Don't they need papers to travel?" Joe inquired.

Larry made a face. "It wasn't that long since they traveled out of the country. My houseman Tim, knows where the documents are. I think if you bring them here, and Tiffany sees them, she might remember who she is."

"Lar, why don't we keep searchin' for info here in Paris?" Joe reasoned, "We can look up Taylor's friend, Frédéric Millet, at that little shop not far from the Regina."

"Guess you're right." Larry's glanced over at Tiffany. "I'm damn frustrated. She mentioned that dinner cruise and the two people Tay knew who work there."

"I hear y'," his brother agreed. "Keep your shirt on for a while longer. Don't get your hopes up. Remember, Tiffany said she met Clive in Paris, so they could've been on the same boat."

"Leave it to you to keep my feet on the ground. Talk to you later." Larry ended their call.

Tiffany watched him return. Her serene smile spoke of peaceful thoughts and an inner calm.

~~***~~

The kitchen door swung open with a ferocious force. In Elizabeth's arms, Rodney trembled and skinned his teeth as his growl simmered deep and low.

"I thought I'd find you here." Clive's voice was fierce with control. "We would like our tea now in the library, if you can pull yourself away from that flea-bitten mongrel."

Will he strike me or worse, hurt Rodney? "Yes, milord. Right away, milord."

Elizabeth timidly placed Rodney on the floor. The loveable pup cowered under the wooden kitchen table.

His lordship left with a seething rage that hung in the air. The servant girl took a deep breath as his footsteps faded down the hall. Elizabeth quickly put a kettle on the stove and opened a cabinet for the special tea blend Clive demanded as the household staple. *Will he be as angry as before when milady stayed out late? Should I give up and leave now?*

Elizabeth held the silver tea service firmly in her hands. She took a deep breath for courage and gingerly walked just into the library's entrance. Rodney stayed close to her heels.

Clive didn't look up from his medical journal. "Elizabeth, are

222   *Cynthia B. Ainsworthe*

you serving the tea from the doorway, or do you expect me to get up and serve myself?"

She swiftly entered the room, placed the tray on the low table before him, and poured the tea into a fine porcelain cup. Rodney stayed in the hall. Clearly, the pup had learned when to give his master a wide berth.

"Is there anything else, milord?" Elizabeth backed up slowly.

"No. I'll ring should one require anything." Slamming of paper against leather indicated his displeasure. "Let me know as soon as Lady Lantham returns from holiday."

"Yes, milord." Elizabeth fidgeted. "If I may, milord, Rodney needs walking."

"By all means take that beast out. He's more of Tiffany's charge than mine." He huffed. "She's rarely around lately. The dog pound or RSPCA might be a better place for him."

"Please, sir." Her eyes pleaded. "If you don't want him, I know of many fine families who would love to take him in."

"Careful, Elizabeth," Clive warned with steely eyes, "you're treading very close to the window. You may not be well suited to service. Do not ever suggest what one might or might not do."

"Beg your pardon, milord. That was never my intention." Elizabeth inched backward closer to Rodney. "I will make certain Rodney is no bother to you. He can stay with me in my quarters."

"Right." He took a sip of tea. "Remember, good service is seen and not heard."

~~***~~

At Café Carousel across from the Hôtel Regina, Joe sat in deep conversation with Frédéric Millet. He enjoyed his French beer. His French friend sipped Lillet Blanc wine. The gold statue of Jeanne d'Arc provided a commanding view to the hotel's entrance.

"Bottom line is this," Joe said in between swallows of beer, "Lar is certain this Tiffany woman lost her memory and is really Taylor who has somehow assumed a different identity and is living as a wife to this earl, Clive Bradford, in England. I have all the dates written on this paper when Taylor disappeared and the last place she was seen. She was stayin' here at Hôtel Regina and workin' freelance for Gérard's. It's

REMEMBER ? 223

not like Taylor to pick up and disappear—not when she fought so hard to be in Lar's life."

Joe slid the paper across the table to Frédéric. He took it and studied the information. His eyes widened with recognition.

"Yes. I remember Taylor being here very well. We shared a couple of drinks together and went out to dinner a couple of times. She never showed up for our last dinner date the night before she was due to fly home. I thought business made her change her plans. I even checked with the hotel, and they said she had requested her luggage to be sent to the airport for her flight departing the next day—I have to admit that was unusual, but not unheard of." He took a sip of wine. "I can check a hospital that treats the homeless That would be a start and then go from there."

Joe beamed. "That might just be the ticket. How will you be able to get the records? Isn't that confidential stuff?"

"Yes. I have a friend who is, how you say … in investigation with the police." Frédéric gave a typical French shrug. "There might be a record of an accident during that time. I'll give him a call, and then we can go visit Hôtel-Dieu on Île de la Cité. They care for persons in the first nine arrondissements in Paris."

"Thanks, Fred." Joe took a last swallow.

Frédéric dialed his friend and spoke in French while Joe paid the bill.

~~***~~

At an outside café near Pont de l'Alma in the eighth arrondissement, Claude sat in deep conversation with his old friend and confidant, Frédéric Millet.

"This is very important to me, dear friend," Frédéric emphasized as he took a sip of his wine. "I need to discover what happened to my American friend, Taylor Davis. I have a photo of her."

He retrieved the picture from his wallet and slid it to his friend across the table. Claude studied Taylor's image briefly.

"She's a very beautiful woman. How long has she been missing?" his friend asked.

"Almost two years now." Frédéric leaned forward in earnest. "She was on a business trip for Gérard's. She would shop in the fabric district—mostly Montmartre. She never returned to her

224   *Cynthia B. Ainsworthe*

hotel—completely vanished. There must be some explanation."

"That depends," Claude cocked his eyebrow with a cynical smile.

"Maybe she wanted to vanish—leave her husband for one reason or another?"

"Never. They fought too long and too hard to be together." Frédéric lit a cigarette. A passerby gave a disapproving look at the lingering smoke. He chose to ignore the criticism. "I *know* Taylor. Believe me, this is not her style."

"I'll have to dig though the old records." Claude took a sip of his black espresso. "It will take some time to do all this research. She wouldn't be recorded as a missing person."

"Please, don't take any longer than necessary." Frédéric sipped his wine. "Larry needs to know the truth."

"You do realize that it is possible, if not probable, that she is dead?" He looked directly at his friend. "Frédéric, don't get your hopes up."

"Yes, Claude. I understand." His eyes moistened. "Alive or dead, we need to know."

~~***~~

Tiffany and Larry sat in the quaint L'Écu restaurant. He studied her reaction as she looked around at the rustic décor of horse harnesses and copper pans on the stone walls, and the timber lined ceiling. She turned her attention to the menu.

"See anything you like?" he inquired after a little while.

"Bœuf Bourguignonne looks interesting." Her French pronunciation was flawless. "Too bad we couldn't get reservations on that dinner boat."

"Well, at least we were able to make reservations for this week." Larry hoped L'Ecu would jog her memory. "It'll give us something to look forward to—a treat for us."

"Yes, I know." She coyly licked her lips. "What made you think of this place? It's charming."

"I was here once before, a long time ago." *This is the restaurant you took me to.*

"My guess is, you'll have the fish or chicken. Right?" Her smile was playful.

"You know me so well." *Tay said those same words to me.* "How did you know my food preference?"

Larry reached for her hand. Tiffany responded by trailing her

REMEMBER ? 225

foot along the inside of his calf.

"A lucky guess." Her eyes held simmering desire. "I know we don't share a past. Yet,. somehow I feel we do."

He smiled. *We do share a past. A beautiful past.* "I won't pressure you. Memories return when there is no stress. Let's enjoy our meal and have a wonderful evening."

"Yes." Tiffany suggestively ran her fingers up and down the stem of the wine glass. "And a wonderful ending to this evening."

"You're on," he asserted. "Anytime."

"Any place, anytime." She bit her lip. "Why did I say that? Feels like I said those words before."

You did when I proposed to you. "I don't know. However, I like your choice of words."

~~***~~

Joe was nearly asleep when his cell phone rang. He looked at the travel alarm clock on the nightstand. Midnight. *Who is callin' now? Lar or the Chambord?*

"Yeah," Joe answered.

"This is Frédéric. I apologize if I'm calling too late." He explained, "I have some news. I spoke with my friend, Claude. There is an unsolved case about a mugging in Montmartre on a backstreet. Seems a woman was hit on the head and left unconscious. She had no purse, passport, nothing to identify her. They sent her to that hospital I mentioned on Île de la Cité. We can go there tomorrow to see if there are any more details. Maybe there are photographs."

"Sounds like a plan." Joe sat up and took notes. "When do you want to meet up?"

"I'm free tomorrow. Nine in the morning is convenient—at the same café in front of your hotel?"

"Great. I won't say anythin' to Lar until we know more." Joe stroked his chin as his eyes narrowed. "No sense givin' him false hope. You think this Brit guy had somethin' to do with this?"

"I won't know more until I speak with my friend." Frédéric added, "He told me he would review all the details tomorrow and then contact me. I thought we might hurry this along if we could ask our own questions. We might meet someone at the hospital who remembers something."

"Yeah, but I don't speak French," Joe reminded his friend.

226   *Cynthia B. Ainsworthe*

"No problem." Frédéric chuckled. "I'll translate."

Joe laughed. "I should've figured that one out. Guess I'm too stressed to think clearly."

What if this woman who was mugged is Tay? How did she get to England? How did she end up with this Clive bastard? What if Clive was stalkin' her? Would a prestigious doc and royal do such crap? Why is Tiff goin' so long with this lost memory? Drugs? Does Clive have anythin' to do with that? If he does, then why?

THIRTY-TWO

AMELIA HELD THE analysis report in her hands. She couldn't believe what she had read, yet the words were true—all of it. It listed technical chemical names that would require a scientist to interpret. She scrolled down the page. The words caught her breath.

> … *substance known to lead to permanent neurological injury through prolonged use; in particular, cognitive abilities associated with various memory functions. Not approved for human consumption at this time pending further clinical studies* …

Her hand trembled. Restrained rage brewed. The duchess grabbed her cell phone. The ring tone sounded repeatedly. *Pick up! Pick up!* Amelia lit a cigarette and blew the smoke upward.

"Hello," answered the girl.

"This is Amelia. Don't talk if you're not alone." Fear veiled her voice.

"I'm alone." Elizabeth said softly, "What's wrong?"

"How long has it been since Tiffany took one of those pills Clive gives her?" Amelia began to walk around the room.

"Weeks. I haven't given her ladyship those pills since before she went on holiday at your estate up country. At least three or four months, maybe longer. I have those pills hidden. Why? Is milady in harm?" asked Elizabeth.

"Can you leave?" Amelia feared for the young girl. "I can meet you at Green Park in thirty minutes."

"Right." The duchess heard Elizabeth's trepidation. "I can say Rodney needs a walk."

"Bring those pills," she instructed. "I might need them as evidence. Only take what you can fit in your purse. You won't be returning. You and Rodney are staying with me."

"Are you certain?" Elizabeth's surprise echoed in her ears.

"Quite." Amelia spoke with desperate urgency. "Clive has

228   *Cynthia B. Ainsworthe*

lost all reason. He can't be trusted. I'll call Joe with this information. Tiffany can't return to England—at the very least she can't return to Clive. There's a fine line between genius and insanity."

~~***~~

The clock on the marble mantle chimed seven. Consternation hardened Clive's jaw. There was no aroma of cooking food wafting from the kitchen. *Where is that idiot girl? When she returns, I'll tell her she's redundant without a reference. I'll make certain no one will have her in service.*

He picked up the phone. Passing minutes fueled his frustration and sparked his anger. *Answer the damn ruddy phone!* The ringing tone continued.

"Alistair, where are you?" Clive commanded.

"At the club, ol' boy." His cousin-in-law sounded amused. "What's the problem?"

"Tiffany has taken off, and now that wench Elizabeth hasn't returned from walking the dog. Hasn't even started cooking dinner." Clive walked to the bar and poured straight gin into a cut crystal glass.

"Simmer down," Alistair advised. "Come down to the club. The food is good—there's a ripping roast beef on the menu."

"I don't give a bloody fig about the roast beef. I'm concerned about Tiffany's defiance." He took a mouthful of gin. "She's acting far too American and free-spirited these days—has been since she met up with that Yank."

"Throttle down." His friend suggested, "It's a new age. All females want to think they're free. It works quite well for Amelia and me."

"I'd hardly say our situations are similar, Alistair," Clive pointed out. "Your private interests don't resemble mine in the slightest."

"Have a taxi bring you. I'll be waiting in the lounge," Alistair directed.

"Right. Be there straight away." Clive ended the call. *I can't understand it. The medication is supposed to keep her drowsy and easy to manipulate. And I've doubled the dosage. That servant wench had better not be lying when she says she's been making Tiffany take them.*

~~***~~

Fewer than a dozen people occupied the club's lounge and

gave the immense room an impression of near vacancy. Bankers and lawyers seated in plush wingback chairs relaxed with expensive brandy and Cuban cigars. In the air, hushed conversations whispered of lucrative deals won or lost.

Clive Bradford spied his friend at the mahogany trimmed bar, seated on a matching stool. He sat down beside him and then gesticulated to the bartender.

"So, have you lost your anger?" Alistair took a swallow of his gin and tonic. "Got those mountains pared down to a proper molehill?"

"Not really." The earl put the glass of brandy to his lips. "Tiffany is bloody infuriating. I could control Penelope, but not her. Why in hell did I ever fall for an American?"

"Life is never simple," answered his colleague.

"It is for you and Amelia." Clive stared at the black marble bar top. "She's always where she belongs. Not causing possible trouble with you and the royals."

"If you call having clandestine affairs out in the open as *where she 'belongs',*" Alistair said chuckling, "then you're operating from a different dictionary than mine."

"Yes. However, the family understands her and accepts it," Clive reasoned.

"Only because they know she won't change. Besides, one can't criticize too heavily since there have been many before in the royal line who have conducted themselves not too far afield from Amelia's antics." His friend clarified, "It would be the proverbial pot calling the kettle black." He paused a moment. "How's the research coming along?"

"Nearly to a bloody stop." *Alistair drop it.* "Still working out the kinks."

"I wish they hadn't pulled me off it." Puzzlement covered Alistair's face. "I thought we worked well together—might have found the next best thing by now, instead of you at a standstill. I wonder why they sacked me from that research."

"I have no idea, ol' man. No idea whatsoever." *Leave it alone. You got in my way. Always running your mouth. I couldn't trust you.*

"I hear MI6 is getting antsy for results." Alistair took a few nuts from the dish on the bar and placed them on his napkin. "You got any communication from them? Wanting to know when they can start the human trials?"

230   *Cynthia B. Ainsworthe*

"I'm not at liberty to say." Clive's irritation rose to the forefront. "And you shouldn't be speaking of the project where anyone might hear."

"I didn't mention the details." He fingered his napkin and looked curiously at Clive. "What are you hiding?"

"Have you heard anything about my promotion?" he asked, eagerly. "Couldn't a queen raise an earl to the level of a duke?"

His friend rubbed his chin as if in thought. "That honor hasn't been carried out, apart for the immediate royal family, for many years. We've had this conversation before, old chap. What you're asking for is highly irregular."

"Yes, but still. There isn't a law against it." Clive took a large swallow of his drink. "It could still happen, especially considering the positive impact on society as a whole with this ground-breaking work." *I don't care what he says. I know I'm in favor with the royals.*

"I can snoop around a bit for you. A carefully dropped word here and there, ol' man," Alistair replied. "Wouldn't an Order of Merit for your medical and research work be enough for you?"

Clive clenched his teeth. "An O.M. is no comparison to becoming a duke."

Alistair's eyes narrowed. "You didn't answer my question. What are you hiding?"

Clive's jaw twitched. "When you tell me I'm to be a duke, you'll have your answer."

His friend took a deep breath. "Clive, your work at the walk-in center and previous accomplishments in the advancement of neurosciences has certainly put you in their esteem. However, I think they are waiting for your research results for MI6. That would be a real coup for Crown and country."

"So, my marriage to an American is not viewed as a blight? An embarrassment, if you will?" *I'm still in the running. I can taste the venison now, seated at the grand table at Balmoral.*

"Not in the least. Of course, it would have been better if she was a subject and not a foreigner." Alistair elaborated, "I mentioned to the viscount that Churchill was half American. He countered with the fact that Churchill's best half was English." Clive listened intently. "All joking aside, I truly don't feel the royals could give a flying fig as to your wife's nationality."

REMEMBER ? 231

He snickered. "You're not King Edward and Tiffany isn't Wallis Simpson, not to mention the escapes of Princess Margaret and her photographer chap—may she rest in peace." Alistair took a swallow of his drink. "Get a grip, ol' man. You're making too much of this. Times have changed. Far more lenient these days. You could be duke in good time, with an enormous amount of luck."

"Just as long as it's not given posthumously," Clive emphasized.

~~***~~

After dinner at L'Écu, Tiffany and Larry walked arm in arm down a small side street toward the hotel. She looked in the closed shop windows at the various artistic displays. The previous rain left shallow puddles reflecting the quaint streetlights. Nobody encroached on their solitude. She took comfort in the calm and enjoyed the fact that they no longer needed to speak to break an awkward moment of silence.

"What do you want to do?" she asked with an unspoken suggestion. "Walk a little longer or something else?"

"Depends." Larry smiled boyishly.

"Depends on what?" She toyed with his emotions.

"We could continue our walk till dawn." He purposely paused, "Or we could partake in other activities till dawn."

She mused before saying, "What might those *'other activities'* consist of?" *He wants to make love to me.*

He paused walking. "If I tell you, there are no surprises." His boyish smile turned devilish as he turned to face her. Larry touched the tip of her nose. "Surprise and wonder is half the fun."

"I see you love life as much as I do." Tiffany had a glint in her eye. *He's so mischievous. I wish I had met Lar before Clive.*

"I know this, Tiff." He paused, "I love you. You have always been there deep inside," he said poignantly.

"I love you, too." Her fingers reached for his hair. "I was drawn to you from the beginning. I didn't know why or how. I know you were meant to come into my life." *I wish I could remember my life before. Was I really a part of Lar's existence? Or am I merely an unfortunate who looks like this Taylor he refers to?*

The couple rounded the corner to the hotel. The doorman smiled and tipped his cap as they approached. A group of

232   *Cynthia B. Ainsworthe*

tourists waited in the lobby near the entrance, clearly anticipating an evening tour of Paris at night.

At the elevator, Tiffany mentioned, "There's a piano at the far end of the lobby behind those gates. You could ask if you can entertain the guests."

"You're joking, aren't you?" he inquired.

"Yes, of course," she replied.

"Tiff, how did you know about the piano? It's hidden behind those tall palms." Larry pointed out.

"I don't know. I have no idea why I even thought of a piano." Confusion veiled her face. "Why do I say things and then can't remember why? I have no recollection of this hotel, and yet I feel I know this place and the people who work here." *Will I ever remember? Am I destined to live in this void forever?* "The other day when I was standing in the hall, waiting for you to come out of our room, I had the funniest feeling as if I saw myself walk the same hall before, almost like seeing my own ghost." Tiffany shivered. "It was a very creepy feeling."

The elevator arrived. They entered and remained silent. Lines of worry came to her forehead. Larry looked at Tiffany and squeezed her hand.

"I can wipe your negative feelings away," he assured.

"How?" She looked at him with childlike eyes.

"With this." Larry kissed her gently as the elevator doors opened.

Just before the doors close, two hotel guests enter and greeted them with bemused smiles.

The man remarked as the doors closed, "Yup, we're in Paris."

"Be quiet. They're honeymooners," his wife retorted.

At their floor, Tiffany and Larry left quickly. A different tourist couple swiftly entered the elevator, and the brass doors closed silently.

"Honeymooners?" She tilted her head with a hidden invitation as they walked to their room. "Sounds like fun."

"We are in a way, y' know." He expounded, "We are in love and have discovered our feelings for each other through long trials—"

She finished his sentence, "And tribulations."

"Yes," Larry said chuckling, 'and tribulations'."

He reached into his pocket, found the keycard, and placed it expertly in the slot. The familiar buzz sounded. Upon entering, Tiffany removed her jacket and handed the garment to Larry. She walked to the sofa and sat down before kicking off her shoes. She wiggled her toes and massaged the soles of her feet while he hung his coat up in the foyer closet. His seductive smile was not lost on her. Tiffany raised her arms above her head in a stretching movement, aware that it emphasized the outline of her breasts.

He went to the minibar, grabbed a bottle of mineral water, and raised it in her direction. "Thirsty?"

His stride was easy and confident. Tiffany took the quenching liquid from his hand. "Thanks. This will do for now. But it won't satisfy my deeper thirst."

"Really?" He eased himself onto the sofa beside her. "What thirst might that be?"

"You have to ask?" Tiffany arched her back as she gave a yawn hidden by the back of her hand. "My, my. I thought you knew me better than that."

"I know you better than you realize." His lips mouthed kisses on her ear. "Want to test my statement?"

"Hmm ..." she purred at the touch of his hand on her breast. "You know how I like to be touched."

"And kissed ... like here." Larry's kisses explored her neck. He ventured further to the sensuous hollow of her throat. "What about here?"

Tiffany played with the hair at his neck. She wanted him desperately and yet enjoyed the playful game she'd devised.

"Don't you think we need to go to the bedroom?" Tiffany took a deep breath as she pushed his hand away.

"Wherever and whenever, I'm yours," he replied.

She slid off the sofa and sashayed to the bedroom. Larry obediently followed. Tiffany didn't stop by the bed. She undressed, item by item, as she moved to the bathroom. He did likewise. Strewn clothing marked their path.

Both naked, Larry adjusted the water temperature. He pulled the curtain aside, entered first, and Tiffany followed. With soap in hand, she lathered his back. Her fingers went to his firm buttocks and massaged him. She reached around his waist, found his already-erect manhood, and stroked him to greater

234   *Cynthia B. Ainsworthe*

arousal. Larry turned to face her. His mouth sought hers. Their tongues mingled and sent her desire from smoldering to blazing. While she fondled him, his hands caressed her taut nipples, then traveled down to her most sensitive area, bringing her to a raging fire of desire. Her entire body ached for him. His fingers continued to tease her, bringing her higher before caressing her breasts again. Tiffany moaned louder each time his fingers found her area of utmost pleasure. Larry guided her to the shower wall, lifted her hips, and eased her onto him. Her legs encircled his hips. She felt his hot firmness throb deep inside her inner being. His movement was slow at first. She moaned with each new sensation and grabbed his buttocks to intensify the fiery passion. Fervor raced through her body and spurred on the desperate need for an ultimate conclusion. Tiffany's breath quickened. His rhythm grew faster and faster until at last, ecstasy was hers. Her inner spasms caressed his manhood. He let out a moan as his spasmodic movement within her exploded. He held her there for a while, basking in the loving afterglow before she lowered her legs to the shower floor. Affectionate kisses on her neck spoke of love—not mere passion. Larry kissed her warm mouth. She loved the feel of his lips.

"You took me by surprise." Her eyes searched his. "This was something I've never done before."

"Are you referring to our spontaneous position?" Larry kissed the wet hair at her temple. "This is far from our first time."

"Yes." Tiffany looked at him with a hint of self-awareness.

"I didn't plan it." He turned to shut off the running water. "Spontaneity can be a good thing. At least, I feel it was for us."

Tiffany pulled the shower curtain aside, stepped out, and handed Larry a towel. "Yes, spur of the moment works. I'm usually up for most anything."

"How well I know that one." He smiled while briskly toweling off his soaked hair and body.

"Are you saying I have no surprises up my sleeve?" Tiffany seductively dried her long legs.

"Oh, I'm certain you have more surprises." He wrapped the towel around his waist, leaned toward her, and left a kiss on her nose. "And I'm looking forward to discovering every single one

REMEMBER ? **235**

of them."

An inner sadness veiled her face. He lifted her chin. A questioning look came to his eyes.

"What is it, Tiff?" Larry asked with a velvet tone. "What's wrong?"

"I don't want to return to London and Clive. I can't." Her words bled a deep pain. "Knowing him, I can only imagine his reaction."

"I thought you knew you wouldn't return to him when we left." Her eyes searched his faced as he spoke. "Wasn't that the original plan? Did I miss something? Is there a detail you're not telling me about?"

"Yes. I know it sounds that simple." *Lar, you have no idea how Clive can be.* "He has a temper. I don't know what he might do."

"All the more reason to remain with me." Larry embraced her as a protective cloak might. "I'll take care of you."

"What if your wife appears?" *You're not thinking this through.* "What then? I'll have no other choice but return to London and *His Majesty.*"

"I know this makes no sense," he explained softly, "I don't feel Taylor will return. She's living another life—the life I have is here in my arms."

"Don't Lar." Tiffany pulled away. "You still don't see *me.* When you look at me, you see Taylor. When you make love to me, it's Taylor."

"No. Tiff. I see who you are … I only pray in time you'll realize your true self."

Should I return to Clive now before I make matters worse? He might not be too bad. Maybe I ought to return tomorrow. He's never hit me, at least not yet.

THIRTY-THREE

JOE AND FRÉDÉRIC stood in the hallway of the Hôtel Dieu Hôpital, located on Île de la Cité, the oldest healthcare facility in Paris. A middle-aged nurse answered Frédéric's questions. Joe listened as if he understood.

"Madame, are you certain?" he asked in French.

"Bien sûr, Monsieur." She continued, "I remember this very well because she was well-dressed in haute couture, Nearly all the patients here are homeless, or at the best very poor." The nurse looked briefly down the hall to see if she was needed before continuing, "This pretty woman came in unconscious, in a coma. Thugs on a backstreet in Montmartre, near the garment district, mugged her. Blood was at the back of her head. She had no purse, no identification. Doctor Clive Bradford took over her care as charity. He was here giving lectures to Paris doctors. Since she showed no improvement, he decided to transfer her to London for further care."

"How long ago was this?" Frédéric took notes.

"Oh là là," she said, as she knitted her brow. "Must have been about two years ago, maybe less."

Joe asked, "Was she wearing any jewelry?" The nurse looked confused. Frédéric translated.

"Oui. A beautiful ring with a heart-shaped diamond and a wedding band with pavé diamonds. Très magnifique .... Like I said, her clothing was extremely expensive, true couture." She looked at the two men. "Do you know this woman? Is she better?"

Frédéric responded, "We think we know her. Why did Doctor Bradford take interest in this unknown woman?"

She explained, "When he first saw her, her beauty must have taken his heart. Doctor wanted only the best for her. He stayed by her side nearly night and day hoping she would recover. He was very devoted to her care. He transferred her to London after a week to ten days."

"Did he say where or what hospital in England he was moving this woman to?" Frédéric probed.

REMEMBER ? 237

"I really don't remember, Monsieur. I think it was the famous neurological hospital he worked at." She wrung her hands. "I'm sorry I can't be of more help."

Joe and Frédéric thanked the nurse for her assistance. They walked down the hall toward the exit. Joe tried to fathom all he had learned. *If this is Taylor, and Clive Bradford took her under his care, why on earth did he lead her to believe she was someone else and give her a different identity? He saw her rings. He had to have known she was married. What was in it for him? This makes no sense. Or is Taylor not this woman the nurse described? Nah, that doesn't fly. It's too far out there that a woman who looks like Tay would wear the same rings and dressed in designer clothes. Still…the impossible might be the case.*

~~***~~

Amelia made certain Elizabeth and little Rodney were comfortable in their new quarters, and introduced her to the other servants of her posh townhouse in Mayfair, which wasn't far from Lord Lantham's residence. *Ever since childhood, he's been secretive. What secrets has he hidden from the family?*

The Duchess of Steffenfordshire drove to the neighborhood bank on a mission. She parked her Rolls Royce, crossed the street, and entered the very old establishment. The doorman nodded to her in recognition. A low-level bank executive led her to the bank president's office.

"Mr. Graham will be with you momentarily, Your Grace." He pulled out an upholstered chair for her comfort.

She smiled automatically without genuine emotion. Her feathered, flamboyant hat with silk flowers obscured her view of art prints hanging on the damask lined walls. Amelia checked her watch. A short, balding man briskly entered the room. His well-tailored, snug suit was evidence for his love of food. She looked up and extended her hand.

Mr. Graham shook her gloved hand. "So sorry to have kept you waiting, Your Grace. How may I be of assistance? Transfer of funds perhaps?" He wedged himself between the overstuffed arms of the swivel chair.

"No. I need to see the activity on my account." Amelia leaned forward with intense determination. "In particular, my account with Lord Lantham. Before you continue, I fully realize he is the primary owner of this account. However, my money did set this up prior to my marriage to the duke. I am

238   *Cynthia B. Ainsworthe*

fully aware of the laws and ownership of funds. Should I succeed the earl, barring any of his issues, which are none presently, then the money reverts back to me and then would belong to the duke." She paused a moment. "I want to see any transactions that have taken place since opening this account." Amelia reached into her purse and passed a small piece of paper to him. "Here's the account number."

"Certainly, Your Grace." A strained smile came to his face. "Of course, you realize this is most unusual—most unusual indeed. And, the earl will be notified of your inquiry."

"I wouldn't expect anything less." Her eyes never left his. "I have every right to know how my money is being used."

"I will just be a moment, Your Grace." Mr. Graham left the office. He went directly to the bank manager. Amelia turned to observe the bank president confer with his colleague through the large glass window. Her posture stiffened while she watched their gesturing, pulling on cuffs, and straightening of ties. *What's really going on? They both seem as nervous as a bag of cats held over the Thames. Did Clive close out the account and abscond with my money?*

Fifteen minutes later, Mr. Graham returned with computer-generated papers. He handed them to Amelia.

"That's the entire activity on the account from its opening some twenty years ago." He cleared his throat. "As you can tell, the interest earned compensated substantially for any withdrawals."

"Withdrawals?" She flipped the pages. "Clive knows I didn't designate my money to be spent. These are his funds in name only."

Mr. Graham placed one hand over the other and wrung them together anxiously. "Your Grace, if you notice, the opening balance compared with today's balance is approximately one hundred pounds more."

"Yes. I can very well see that. However, the interest has been depleted by my cousin." Her sharp eyes shot angry darts. "His lordship and I will have a very serious conversation about this."

"As you will," he replied timidly.

Amelia scanned the documents. One item was consistent. An automatic deduction every month payable to L'Hôpitaux de Suisse, Geneva, Switzerland. *What is Clive up to? Three thousand*

REMEMBER ?   239

pounds. Wait, these payments started more than five years ago, when Penelope left him. Is there a connection?

The duchess folded up her newfound information and placed it securely in her purse. She rose and extended her hand. "Thank you, Mr. Graham. You have been most helpful." She turned to leave.

"The pleasure was mine, Your Grace, anytime I may be of assistance." Taking his handkerchief from his jacket, Mr. Graham wiped his brow. A large sigh escaped his lips.

Swift steps took Amelia across the street to the black Rolls Royce. Seated in the front seat, she scrutinized the entries once more on the printout. *Was this something to do with Clive's research? If so, then why spend my money for it? The government funds his projects. What is he hiding? A charity case of some poor soul? He's always working at the walk-in center. Or something darker?*

~¡~¡***~¡~¡

Joe's cell phone rang at five in the morning. He fumbled for the device as he tried to focus on the bedside clock. *What the hell!* He looked at the caller ID. *What does he want now!*

"What do you want? Condoms?" Joe asked snidely.

"Very funny. That's not it." Larry whispered, "I don't want to wake Tiffany. Here's the plan. I want Mark to fly over here with Gigi and Jacques. Call Mark, Tim, my houseman, in Bel-Air, and my pilot. Tim knows where the vet documents are, so they can enter France with no problem. The poodles like Mark and will be okay with him. Do it now. It's eleven PM in Tampa."

"What the hell for?" Joe sat straight up in bed. "What can the poodles possibly do? And what if Mark can't leave?"

"The poodles might spark Tiffany's memory. Tell Mark I'll double any money he's losing by making the trip … Joe you still there?"

"Yeah, I'm here." He yawned loudly into the mouthpiece. "Not quite awake yet."

"Well wake up and get a move on," Larry whispered louder.

"Yeah, I will." Joe dangled his legs over the edge of the bed. "I'll call him and the others as soon as you hang up. Then, can I go back to sleep?"

"Call me back with the details," he asserted.

"Boss, you're graspin' at straws. I'll do as y' want, but don't

240   *Cynthia B. Ainsworthe*

think anythin' will come of it." He stood up and walked to the bathroom.

"None of the negative stuff, Joe. I don't need to hear it. Gotta go."

Joe heard the dial tone. He went to the bathroom, looked in the mirror, splashed water on his face, and took care of nature's needs. *Lar's barkin' up the wrong tree again. Will he ever learn? She's not Taylor … Or is she?*

~~***~~

Fire glowed in Clive's minatory gaze.

Amelia purposely ignored his protests. She sat reading a fashion magazine on the sofa in the drawing room of her townhouse.

"Well, are you going to give me a proper answer or not?" Clive demanded, his hands on his hips.

"I don't have to answer you. I answer to no one, including Alistair." *Guilt gnawing at your bones?*

"Where is Tiffany? I am her husband and have a right to know." He took a step closer. "You've put her somewhere. You always fight the system—wanting to change things."

"The only time you don't like change is when you don't benefit from it." Amelia stood up to meet him head-on. "You've been like that since childhood. When things didn't go your way, it was someone else's fault and never yours. Pampered Little Lord Fauntleroy could do no wrong and was preened by the nanny because you were a boy and would inherit."

Clive grabbed her wrist. She yanked free and stared at the red mark of his fingerprints. "Is that how you treat Tiffany? Yield or else? No wonder she wanted to break free! Wherever she is, she is safe."

"I have a right to know where my wife is. One won't put up with this temerity. You tell me this instant where she is!" His fists repeatedly clenched.

"You gave up those rights to any woman when Penelope left," Amelia replied with steely calm. "Your wife is Penelope—not Tiffany."

His teeth clamped tight as his jaw twitched. Eyes full of stifled rage glared at her. "Too many gins have softened your brain along with your toy boys. I am divorced on the basis of

REMEMBER ? 241

abandonment and adultery by that tart." Clive stepped closer with a raised fist.

Amelia drew a small revolver from under a sofa cushion. He stopped. His eyes narrowed.

"One more step, dear cousin, and I swear I will stop you." Her hand held steady.

"I'll leave." He walked backwards. "You're not worth the bother. Neither is Tiffany. One wife left me, why not another?"

"That's the first time you've said something that wasn't self-serving in years." Amelia chuckled. "Keep it up. Maybe you'll realize doctors are trained to be healers—meant not to do harm."

~~***~~

Clive sat at the back of the club nursing his bandy. His thoughts swirled like the contents in his glass. *When I get a hold of Tiffany, I'll …. As for Amelia, she's no better. She married a title, but far from earned it! Alistair is a spineless idiot, always bowing to those higher up. Tiffany is the problem. She must be dealt with, and soon. If only I could find her. Accidents happen all the time. Poor Clive Bradford, the Earl of Lantham, to lose such a pretty wife under such horrible circumstances.* A sardonic smile emerged. *Yes, that's it, a perfect solution—and the loss of my dear cousin the Duchess of Steffenfordshire.*

THIRTY-FOUR

"CHIEF, CAN YOU talk?" Joe asked from his cell phone. "You alone?"

"Hold on a minute." Larry closed the bathroom door while Tiffany showered. He walked to the living room. "I can talk now."

"Got a call from Amelia." He took a deep breath. "Gotta keep Tiffany away from Bradford at all costs. She said he's probably been givin' Tiff these experimental pills that cause brain damage, somethin' to do with wipin' out memory for good. He's been stealin' Amelia's money and sendin' it to a hospital in Switzerland—most likely for his estranged former wife, Penelope. Guess he was actin' kinda threatenin' with Amelia. She pulled a gun to get him to leave. Me and Frédéric gonna take the TGV today to Geneva and check this out. The train will get us there in less than four hours. Amelia faxed me the info here at the hotel. I'm at the front desk. Fred should be here any minuet."

"A gun? Are you sure?" Concern clouded his eyes. "This man must be very dangerous."

"Calm down, Chief. He has no idea where you and Tiff are," Joe explained. "You okay without me for a day? I might be back late tonight."

"Yeah, I'll be okay." Larry paced the room as he connected the facts. "When is Mark due in?"

"Not until tomorrow mornin' … Lar, you good with this?"

"I'll deal." He signed heavily. "Joe, what if Clive gave Tiffany these pills, and she'll never remember her past?"

"Don't think that way. I'll have more news when I return. We uncovered some stuff yesterday," Joe said cautiously.

"Tell me now." Larry pleaded, "Don't keep important information from me."

"I haven't said anythin' 'cos I don't know if the patient the nurse described was Taylor," Joe said, softly. "Lar, Fred is here. Gotta go. Talk to you when I know anythin'."

"Joe, call me on the cell," Larry instructed. "Don't wait till you get back."

REMEMBER ?   243

"Got it," he replied.

The line went dead.

Tiffany stood in the doorway to the bedroom. She walked behind him and encircled her arms around his waist. She reached up on tiptoe to kiss the back of his neck. Larry turned around, embraced her, and kissed her forehead.

"What was that all about?" she questioned. "Business?"

"You could say that." Larry looked out the window at the golden statue of Jeanne d'Arc. "How about we spend the day in Montmartre? Wouldn't it be nice to soak up some French culture?"

"Fine." She turned on her heels. "I'll get dressed."

~~***~~

"Mon Dieu!" Frédéric exclaimed. His eyes grew large in disbelief. "Incroyable!"

"What terrible condition this creature is in," Joe agreed.

They stood in the hallway of L'Hôpitaux de Suisse in Geneva, a renowned facility for those afflicted with mental disorders. The two men peered through the small window of the patient's room. All surfaces were padded and was absent of furniture save for a bed. A thin institution gown covered her frail body. Thin muscles covered her bony structure with nearly transparent and bluish skin. Sunken hollows held scared black eyes with wild side-to-side movements. She huddled in the far corner. Her angular arms hugged knobby knees as she rocked back and forth like a frightened child.

"Messieurs," the nurse stated, "this poor person has been as you see since she was admitted some five years ago."

"Do you know how she came to be admitted?" Frédéric inquired.

"Mais, oui. I was on duty when she came in. Doctor Bradford brought her. He explained he found her in a hospital in London. She has never spoken a word. No reaction to those around her." The nurse continued, "Everyone thought she had no name. I discovered the truth." She moved closer to the men, then whispered, "All she had were her clothes and an empty purse. I looked closer in that purse. The lining had a tear, and I found her expired driver's license. The photo was of her, and the name was Penelope Bradford."

"Did y' ask Dr. Bradford about what you found?" Joe fidgeted,

244   *Cynthia B. Ainsworthe*

waiting for her answer.

"The doctor was already in London when I discovered her identity." She shrugged her shoulders. "We contacted him many times. He never responded. Payment for her care continue. If not—she would be transferred to another hospital. I don't know if this poor woman is a sister, wife, or sister-in-law of the doctor."

Joe piped in, "I think she was one of Clive Bradford's experiments gone wrong."

"Madame," Frédéric said as he glanced at Penelope, "is there any hope at all for this woman?"

"There is always hope, Monsieur." The nurse shook her head as she looked at the floor. "I'm afraid the doctors believe hope is beyond her grasp." She sighed deeply. "We keep her clean, feed her through a stomach tube, and try to get her to move. It is a struggle, nearly impossible. Some days are better, others are worse." She looked sadly pensive. "This poor woman delivered a baby boy six months after her admission. We called Doctor Bradford. The baby was put up for adoption as he instructed."

~~***~~

Joe looked out the TGV's window. Scenery flew by at incredible speed. Frédéric dozed next to him. In a few hours he would be back in Paris. *That poor woman. Still kinda young and to be put in that condition. Clive is a madman. Charges should be brought. Did he give pills to Tiffany that damaged her brain? Is that why she can't remember nothin'?*

~~***~~

Tiffany and Larry strolled the uneven cobblestone streets of Montmartre. She appeared relaxed. Larry looked at her with optimistic curiosity, ever keen for the slightest indication that someone or some old shop would spur her memory. *Tiff, please recognize something. A face, a place, anything! I want you to know you're Taylor.*

"Madame Allen, pardon, Madame Davis!" A plump woman stepped out from an art shop. "It has been so long," she stated in French.

"Bonjour, Madame Gautier. Ça va?" Tiffany asked how the older woman was doing.

"Très bien, Madame." She shook Tiffany and Larry's hand.

A customer entered the woman's shop. She turned and waved

REMEMBER ? 245

her hand. "Au revoir, Madame et Monsieur. À bientôt."

Larry stopped Tiffany in her tracks. "You knew that woman's name. Do you remember her?"

"I'm dumbfounded. I don't recall meeting her, yet I knew her name." Consternation filled her eyes. "I speak French but don't know why. Jean-Luc at the hotel insists he knows me and that I know him, and now this. The harder I try to remember, the more lost I feel." She looked up at Larry as a helpless child floundering in a backstreet looking for a parent. "Will I ever be normal? Living like this isn't normal. It's living a nightmare within the solitude of a gray fog."

"Give it time, Tiff." Larry embraced her. "Give it time. Haven't you ever heard the phrase 'Time heals all'?"

"I'm afraid there isn't enough time to heal me. That's what scares me the most." He felt her shudder in his arms.

The old worn streets took them to Musée de Montmartre. The antiquities displayed brought a respite from the tourists and crowded streets. Although small, it held interesting facts in French with no English translation. Of notable mention were photographs of actors, directors, and crews filming scenes from the "War and Remembrance" miniseries. This caught Tiffany's attention. She stared at length at the black and white images. Her mouth moved as if to speak. Larry held his breath for an instant. *Was that a trigger for her?*

"Do you recognize someone in those photos?" He searched his memory for recognition of the famous personages at a charity or showbiz event.

"I'm not sure." She hesitated, still looking at the aged photos. "I feel that I've seen these actors in those exact costumes on the television. I can't place where, how, or when. I think I was rather young, maybe in my childhood."

"Are you certain?" He offered, "Do you want me to tell you their names? The actors, I mean? I've never personally met them, but I do know who they are."

"No. Please don't tell me, Lar." She sighed. "This has to come from my memory—not yours. Don't create an image for me—Clive has already done that. He put my past in a neat little box, explained my existence, and tied it up with a bow never to be opened according to his rules."

"Enough about Clive." Larry hugged her with a shield of

246   *Cynthia B. Ainsworthe*

love. "He's the past and will never be a part of your future. He'll have to kill me to get to you." He chuckled. "That won't happen. He hasn't the guts. Sneaky ways are more his style. He picks victims he can control, that is—until he met you. Tiff, you are one person whose will to survive has given you strength. Hang on to that. Never let it go."

"I hope so, Lar," Tiffany said, her voice as soft as a wisp of a cloud. "There are times I feel as weak as a kitten. That's when I'm scared the most. Dark confusion assaults my brain like a black seeping poison blanking out my thoughts—where the senseless is normal. I keep searching for the one key that will trigger my mind—that will free me—a sight, a smell, anything. Yet, there's nothing."

~~***~~

"They didn't wait!" he said out loud in his vacant library. "My work at the walk-in center was enough." Clive stood up from his desk, went to the bar, and poured a large brandy. His hand trembled while he studied the document a second time scribed in perfect calligraphy on the finest linen stationary. A gold embossed emblem headed the invitation.

> *By command of Her Majesty The Queen …*
> *The presence of Clive Bradford,*
> *The Earl of Lantham is requested …*
> *… for the ceremony and to hereby confer*
> *the title*
> *Duke of Bryningmead …*

Thoughts of heightened grandeur consumed his mind. A satisfying smile marked his face. *How many more invitations await me at Buck House At last, I won't be an underling to Alistair. We are now equals. Joining the hunt at Balmoral. I can almost smell the heather. Life is good and I'm on top.* His jubilation faded. His lips thinned. *Tiffany and Amelia could ruin this for me. Something must be done. But how? Dealing with my dear cousin should be artfully done—can't risk discovery. Where in bloody hell is Tiffany? It will be a grave embarrassment if my wife isn't there for the ceremony. I suppose I could explain her absence as illness—but that wouldn't be good form.*

~~***~~

"I'm all dressed." Tiffany twirled in the suite's living room. The emerald green skirt enhanced her shapely legs. "How do I look?"

"Perfect, as usual." Larry walked closer to embrace her and took a whiff of her hair. "Love that fragrance. Don't ever change."

"I won't." A coy pout made her lips look irresistible to him. "Even if I wore no perfume, you'd still think I smelled good."

"Ah, you know me so well." He released her. "We'd better get a move on. The concierge ordered the cab for six on the dot." He checked his watch. "We only have fifteen minutes."

Tiffany took her purse as Larry helped her on with her jacket.

"Am I overdressed?" Momentary concern crossed her eyes.

"Nah. You look fine," he assured.

They left the suite and headed to the elevator.

~~***~~

In the reception area of Bâteaux Parisiens, Tiffany and Larry waited in line to confirm their reservation and pay for the tickets. It was mostly tourists milling around—some over-dressed and many underdressed for the occasion.

"Madame Davis," a male voice sounded behind them.

They immediately turned around. Larry shook his hand and greeted the gentlemen. "Enchanté."

Puzzlement brewed in her eyes as she stared at the dark haired man.

"Madame Taylor, don't you recognize me? C'est moi. Laurant," he explained.

Tiffany smiled while desperately trying to recall if and when she ever met this person.

"Laurant," Larry clarified, "Madame hasn't been well. Her memory is not completely clear."

"C'est dommage." The French gentleman rutted his brow with concern. "That is too bad. I hope you feel better very soon." He paused as a cruise boat employee motioned to him. "Excuse-moi. I am needed. I will give your regards to Suzanne. Sadly, it is her day off." Laurant scurried off to his duties.

"Who is he? If I am Taylor, it's obvious I've met him before and that person he called Suzanne." Tiffany continued to look at Laurant from across the room. "I don't remember him nor this place." *Was I ever here before and with who?*

"I thought it best to let him think you were Taylor." Larry moved to the counter. He handed his credit card to the recep-

248   *Cynthia B. Ainsworthe*

tionist. "It's too complicated to explain, and my French isn't that good."

"You sound as if you don't think I *am* Taylor." She searched his face for his true feelings. "Have you accepted me as who I believe I am, Tiffany—Tiffany Bradford?"

"A name isn't important." Larry returned his credit card to his wallet and placed the tickets inside his jacket pocket. "I know I love you and that's enough."

Massive windows and a glass ceiling provided expansive views of illuminated Paris monuments along the Seine, as the dinner boat lazily made its way along Île de la Cité and Île Saint Louis. Music started, with a violinist playing Mozart classics. Later, a small band and French chanteuse entertained passengers. Larry waved his hand for the musician to come to their table located at the bow of the boat. He whispered he didn't want to be acknowledged and refused to sing under any circumstances.

The violinist replied, "No problem, Monsieur."

Various tourists took sneaky photos from their cell phones and cameras. Larry shrugged this off and didn't pay attention to their curiosity. Tiffany removed her cloth napkin from the linen covered table and placed it in her lap.

"Are you enjoying yourself?" He took a bite of his Dover sole. "I thought this would be a nice diversion. Clear some of your disturbing cobwebs away."

"It's a lovely cruise. I don't think I've ever been on a boat like this before." Tiffany pushed the green beans around her plate and left half of her chicken entrée uneaten. "At least I don't remember an experience like this." She sighed heavily. "That's the story of my life. No memory. A hell of a way to live."

"Would you like to dance?" he offered. "I'm no Fred Astaire, but I think I can keep from stepping on your toes."

She brought the napkin to her lips. "Yes. I'd like that."

Larry took Tiffany's hand and led her to the dance floor when a slow classic recorded in the fifties played. His arms brought her close to him. She felt comforted and secure. As they danced, other guests took photos of them. *I'm in Lar's arms and it feels good. I don't care if Clive gets wind of this. He is my past, and Lar is my future.* She snuggled closer into his shoulder. *What if*

Taylor shows up? Where will I be then? Out in the cold? She's been away so long, it's not likely. Yet, it could happen.

"What's wrong?" Larry asked. "You're tense. You feel all right? Something wrong with the food?"

"No. I feel fine." She kissed his cheek. *Lar can read my every mood. I can't tell him my true worries. I love him too much to come between he and Taylor.*

The cruise ended with a resounding rendition of the Cancan, which made for a merry conclusion to the evening. After disembarking, they walked up the steps to the taxi stand at the foot of the Eiffel Tower.

The same tourists continued taking photos accompanied by hushed comments and assumptions. They overheard one couple say, "Looks like Larry found his wife and all is well."

I'm not Taylor. I'm Tiffany. I'm so tired of everyone's conclusions, even Lar's. Will he still want me when he knows the truth? Is he in love with an illusion or in love with me? And what about Clive? What if he finds me? He must be searching. She shuddered and swallowed hard. *Oh God, I'm so scared.*

~~***~~

Larry directed the cab driver to drop them off at Place Vendôme, not far from their hotel. Strolling along the closed storefronts with minimal jewelry displays, Tiffany enjoyed the grandeur and grandiose style of the square.

"So, this is where the rich and famous come to shop for a little bauble." A triple row diamond tennis bracelet caught her eye. She looked at it for a long while. "Funny, I've seen that before. Maybe in a magazine."

"Any place else?" he asked.

"Not that I recall." She chuckled sadly. "I suppose that's another detail from my past, or Taylor's, that I should remember?"

"I won't lie to you." Larry looked squarely at her. "I gave you that bracelet during our first time in Paris."

"You gave it to Taylor, not me." She pleaded, "Just let it be. If I ever was Taylor—I'm not her now. I'm Tiffany. I need for you to accept that, or—"

"Or what, Tiff?" Dead calm with anguish colored his eyes. "You'll leave me?"

"I don't want to. It may come to that." She implored, "Please understand. I can't fit into someone else's identity. If Taylor should ever return, I'm out of the picture. This lovely romance of ours would become a fleeting memory." *I hate saying these words.* "I should leave and return to London. Maybe tomorrow, if I can get a flight."

"No, Tiff!" He entreated her heart. "Please don't. I love you."

"You love Taylor, not Tiffany." She turned to walk back to their hotel.

THIRTY-FIVE

MARK UNPACKED IN Joe's room at the Hôtel Regina. The poodles, Gigi a white toy and Jacques a black toy, pranced around, jumping from the floor to the sofa and back again. Clearly, they were happy to be off the plane and out of their crates. Although Larry's jet provided the utmost in comfort, Mark felt more secure keeping them in their carriers.

"Gigi and Jacques, are you ready to meet a very nice lady? Hopefully, your Mommy?"

They wagged their tails at his words and moved in circles. He sat down on the sofa. *Is this Tiffany person really Taylor? God I hope so. I think of her as my "sister" in every definition of the word. The thought of Taylor gone forever is beyond my comprehension.* The two poodles curled up on his lap. His cell phone sang one of his own songs. Mark didn't look at the caller ID.

"Joe here." He stated, "Come over to the Carousel Café across the street from the hotel."

"Sure. What's the hurry?" Mark placed the poodles on the floor and then peered out the window. He spotted Joe at a table in front of the café.

"Need to fill y' in on some details. See y' in five." Joe ended the call.

Mark took his jacket from the back of the chair, attached the poodles' leashes, and left the hotel room.

The poodles scampered through the lobby. Jean-Luc called out, "Bonjour Gigi and Jacques" as the three headed for the massive brass trimmed revolving glass doors.

The traffic came to a stop. He picked up the poodles in his arms, crossed the street, and walked over to Joe.

"Good to see you, man," Mark began. Jacques crawled onto Joe's lap. "It's been too long."

"We'll catch up later. There's important things y' gotta know." Joe's chubby fingers ran through his thinning hairline. "You already know Lar thinks this Tiffany person is Taylor. Well, Frédéric and me been doin' some investigatin'." He took a long breath before continuing, "Seems this doctor dude, Clive

252   *Cynthia B. Ainsworthe*

Bradford, took in a woman who was mugged someplace in Montmartre after he saw her in a charity hospital ward here in Paris. Found out Bradford has a wife, or had a wife, who is catatonic in an asylum in Geneva, Switzerland. She gave birth to a son six months later—he was adopted."

"What does this have to do with Taylor?" Mark eased closer in his seat.

"Gettin' to that." Joe motioned to a waiter for another beer. "Bradford's workin' on a drug that erases memory for some big hush-hush project for the Brit government. He told Tiffany they met in Paris, fell in love, married on a boat in the Mediterranean, she slipped and fell, hit her head, and lost her memory. His cousin Amelia thinks he's been feedin' those experimental pills to Tiffany—looks like his first wife Penelope suffered the same ugly consequence, too."

"Are you certain about all this?" *This is too far-fetched to be believed.*

"There's no marriage certificate registered in France for Clive Bradford and Tiffany, Taylor, or anyone else." The waiter brought Joe's beer. Mark ordered coffee.

After the server left, Joe continued, "Bradford, the bastard, already has this fancy title and thinks he's gonna get promoted from earl to duke for his contribution to a medical advancement of some sort. At least, that's what Amelia told me in the information she sent through. He's also been payin' for Penelope's care out of Amelia's earned interest from her bank account."

The waiter served the beverages and promptly moved to another table of tourists.

"He sounds like a real piece of work." Mark stirred his coffee in thought. "How can I help? And why bring the poodles?"

"Lar seems to think the poodles might spark Tiffany's memory—make her remember she's Taylor." He brought the beer to his lips and took a long swallow. "Seems like a crack-ass idea to me, whistlin' up a rain pipe."

"I agree." Mark sipped his coffee. "Then again, stranger things have happened. Taylor was always devoted to these little fur kids." He petted Gigi affectionately. "Joe, what do you really think happened with Taylor? Haven't you ever wondered?"

"Sure. I wondered." Joe fingered his paper napkin on the

tabletop. "I hated to think it, but I always felt she was mugged and murdered. Taylor was always fearless—had this outlook nothin' bad would happen to her."

"Yeah. That sums her up all right." Mark's eyes narrowed. "Nothing bad happened to her until she met Larry and all that business with Paul." He sipped his coffee. "Deep down, I don't think she ever got over that guilt."

"You got that one right." Joe stroked Jacques. "She must've gone to her death with that burden. Never letting' anyone know her troubles—always happy."

"When is Tiffany supposed to see Gigi and Jacques?" Mark inquired.

"After our drink. We'll go to the park across the street. I'll call Lar from there." Joe gestured for the check.

~~***~~

Tiffany haphazardly packed. Larry removed each article of clothing as quickly as she placed it in the suitcase.

"Stop it!" she demanded. "We can't go on. I have to leave. I can't be someone else. How can I be? I don't even know who I am."

"What's a day?" He grabbed her shoulders forcing her to look at him. "All I'm asking for is one day. I fell in love with you as you are now. Not a dreamed version of you. You, Tiffany, the person."

Let me go and find out who I really am. "No you didn't." Her determination was steadfast. "You fell in love with Taylor and want me to fill her shoes. As much as I love you, I can't live with you—not like this—not now." *We have no future.*

Larry's cell phone rang. While he talked quietly, Tiffany continued to pack. Her tear-filled eyes blurred her vision. Heaviness filled her chest as she fought deep sobs. *I must remain strong. I can't give in. Amelia will help me. She'll know what to do to keep Clive away from me.*

He ended the call, then pleaded, "Humor me in this, Tiff, Let's go to a café, a museum, or a park. Anywhere where it's peaceful."

She stopped packing with shoes in her hands. "A new location will clear my head? Is that what you're saying?"

He firmly cupped her shoulders bringing her close. Tiffany let her shoes fall to the floor. His lips gently caressed hers.

254   *Cynthia B. Ainsworthe*

They kissed a long moment. It was a kiss of love and not of passion. After, still in his arms, she looked up at him.

Her mouth opened to speak. "Lar, this doesn't change a thing. I'm still leaving today."

~~***~~

"I don't know what you're going to prove by taking a walk in the park," Tiffany insisted.

She and Larry strolled along a well-worn path in Jardin des Tuileries. "You won't change my mind. I'm leaving today on the next flight to London."

"Understood." He led the way to a park bench. "Have a seat and enjoy the view."

She sat on the end of the green bench. Behind her, the sound of small barking dogs drew her attention. Tiffany's eyes squinted at two poodles pulling their leashes from Mark's hands. He let them run free. Gigi and Jacques galloped to her, yipping joyfully the entire way. She placed her hand on Larry's arm and gave a tight squeeze.

"I know them!" Her voiced heightened with joy. "Gigi and Jacques. My babies! I remember them! My God. It's true. How can this be?"

At her feet, the poodles begged to be picked up. She lifted them. Poodle kisses showered her face. They wiggled incessantly as their tails wagged to show their happiness and excitement to see her.

Joe and Mark approached the bench.

Mark's eyes filled with tears. "Remember me? I'm Mark, the guy you adopted into your family—your unofficial brother."

"Mark, I'm so sorry. You look familiar, but I'm … just not there yet." *I seem to remember him sitting on a patio with me. This is scary!* She looked at Larry. "I want to be alone with you. Can we walk?" To Mark she asked, "Will you stay here with the kids?" She hugged each poodle.

Tiffany walked with Larry out of the park. They crossed the street to Pont Royal over the Seine.

She stopped at the center of the bridge to face him and held both his hands. *This place is special to us. Why? Could it be? This was … I remember now. It was our turning point.*

She paused for a few seconds before saying, "This is our bridge. Our moment. No one can take this from us."

REMEMBER ?   255

"Those words I said to you a long time ago." His misty eyes searched her face.

"Yes. I know. I finally remember. I think …. No. I know. I *am* Taylor. I really am her. It feels so strange, but now I see that you've been right all this time. I'm so sorry I ever fought you on this. Do you forgive me?"

"There's nothing to forgive." He held her close. The wind kicked up, cooling their tears.

"Lar, I found something in Clive's locked jewelry box. I've been meaning to show you but I wanted to remember something—anything first." She reached into her purse. Her hand revealed a diamond pavé wedding band and an engagement ring with a heart-shaped diamond. "I think these are mine, and you should place these back on my finger."

Tiffany, who was now ready to accept she was Taylor, removed her old wedding band and tossed it in the river. *I've tossed Clive out of my life as easily as discarding his ring. I'm finally free! I'm Taylor Davis.* With trembling fingers, Larry placed the diamond rings onto her finger. He gazed into her eyes and bent to kiss her with so much love it brought tears to her eyes.

"Lar, I don't remember everything yet." She bit her lip. "What I do know is, I remember you're my husband, and I love you very, very much. It might take a while for everything to come back."

"Take all the time you need." Wonder glowed from his face. "You remember what is important, Tay."

"Tay," she said as her lips curled at the corners. "I like the sound of that. It sounds right. Please don't ever call me Tiff. That's an ugly past I'd rather forget."

"Don't worry," he assured with a firm hug. "You'll never hear me call you that name again."

"Shouldn't we get back to Joe, Mark, and the poodles?" She looked up at him. "I want to share the news."

"Yes. We have a lot to celebrate." They stopped at the crosswalk. "We could have a nice dinner at the hotel's restaurant?"

"Fine by me." *When will I remember all of it? All those precious moments that Clive robbed from me.* "Clive had something to do with me not knowing who I am, didn't he?"

The light changed. Larry took her hand as they crossed the

256   *Cynthia B. Ainsworthe*

street. "Yes. From what I've learned from Amelia and Joe, he fed you pills to suppress your memory. His first wife is in an asylum. Apparently Frédéric discovered you were mugged in Montmartre, hit on the head, and ended up in a coma. You were on a freelance trip for Gérard's. Clive spotted you in the charity hospital, took you under his care, and transported you to London as his wife. He created a past for you."

"Why would he do such a horrible thing to a person?" *He's a bastard!* "He treated me like a lab rat. Expendable. Not human at all."

"He's sick all right." Larry's jaw hardened. "I'll deal with him on my own terms."

"Lar," Taylor said as fear cloaked her face, "don't do anything foolish. Please. We can fly home and forget about all of this. Let's just put it behind us."

"Not until I have my say." His determined words highlighted his unyielding resolve. "No one, and I mean *no one*, gets away with what he's done. I want to confront that bastard—and soon."

Fear gripped her heart. *What if Clive pulls a gun! I can't let Lar see him alone. Oh God, what can I do to change Lar's mind. I'm terrified what might happen.*

~~***~~

Mark, Joe, Larry, and Taylor sat at the round table in the hotel's dining room. Others spoke in quiet voices about the sights visited or business deals. The waiter served coffee, while she chose demitasse. Larry restrained his frown, fully aware of Taylor's longstanding heart condition.

"Have you remembered anything else since the park?" Mark asked. He reached for the cream.

"Bits and pieces." She sighed with frustration. "Wish I could remember everything."

"Give it time," Joe stroked his chin. "The main thing is you remember who you are."

"That's the best thing." Larry squeezed her hand. "We're husband and wife. You'll have the rest of your life to put the puzzle together."

"I get glimpses in my mind." Taylor maneuvered the lemon twist in her cup. "I have a daughter, don't I? Cindy?"

"Exactly," Mark looked at Larry and then Joe. "She lives in Tampa with her husband Vic."

REMEMBER ?   257

"Mark, you're married to ..." Taylor's eyes narrowed as if in thought, "to Adrienne? She runs an art gallery. The gallery belonged to ..." Wretchedness dwelled in her eyes. "Oh my God! Paul!—It was my fault."

She abruptly left the table, scurried through the lobby, and took the spiral stairway to their room.

Larry followed quickly behind her calling out, "Tay, wait! Don't go through this alone. Let me help you."

At the door, out of breath and with tears streaming down her cheeks, he embraced her. His fingertips wiped her tears away.

"Tay, you did nothing wrong." Larry opened the door. "That's part of the past. Remember, Paul always wanted your happiness, as do I."

She hurried to their bedroom, sat on the bed, and stared down at the carpet. "I have such guilt. It's all so real, as if I lost him yesterday."

"Tay." He stroked her cheek tenderly and lifted her chin for her eyes to meet his. "Don't go back to the past. You and I are the future. Our future."

"I know." Mascara ran down her cheeks from her tears. "I do love you, Lar. More than you could know. Probably more than you love me."

"I'll fight you on that one." He handed her a tissue. "I loved you from the first concert in Tampa. That's when our hearts first met."

"I remember that. I sat in the front row center seat." She wiped her eyes. "Will you make my apologies to Mark and Joe?"

"I'll call Joe now."

Larry dialed his number and stated, "Settle the bill, Joe. You and Mark stay in Paris tomorrow with the poodles. I have to fly to London in the morning—unfinished business to settle. Later."

"I'm goin' with you, Lar," Joe insisted.

Larry ended the call.

Taylor grabbed his arm. "No. Let it be. Don't confront Clive."

"He's no contest for me." His eyes lined with determination. "I can handle him."

"I'm going with you." Her hand caressed the edge of his ear. "I insist. I know him better than you. He might get violent if you go there alone."

THIRTY-SIX

LARRY STOOD AT Clive's townhouse door in Mayfair with Taylor behind him. Joe waited in the hired limousine. Her hand trembled when he pushed the doorbell. No answer. He pushed the bell a second time. Muffled footsteps grew louder. The door slowly opened.

"Tiffany!" Clive's anger was evident. "Get in here. The neighbors will see you." To Larry he snidely asked, "What are you doing here? The personal escort for her ladyship?"

Larry grabbed the earl's necktie and simultaneously drew back a clenched fist with his other hand and punched him firmly on the nose. Blood splattered over Clive's white shirt as Larry pulled him by the tie to the open library. Taylor remained by her husband's side.

Joe left the car and quickly climbed the stairs only to have the door shut in his face by Taylor. Clearly, she didn't want anyone in the street to hear the commotion. He tried the doorknob. It wouldn't open.

"What is the meaning of this, Mr. Davis? You have the unmitigated gall to return when it's clear you have absconded with my wife?" Taylor followed the two into the library. "I have a very strong notion to call the police. And you, Tiffany. You will pay for what you've done and the embarrassment you've caused me. You never did know your place, nor how to act in it!"

"I wouldn't be so quick to call the police." Larry took a step closer. Clive walked behind his desk. He wiped the blood from his nose with the back of his hand. "Not after you hear what I know to be the truth."

"Rubbish!" Lord Lantham opened the top desk drawer. "You believe the ravings of a half-witted female?"

Larry pulled the papers from his inside jacket pocket and clutched them tightly. "I have the proof here! You and Taylor, Taylor Davis, are not married and never were married. You kidnapped her for your own sick purpose—a beautiful lab rat for your perverted research. She is *my* wife. Your true wife,

REMEMBER ? 259

Penelope, is rotting away in a catatonic state in an asylum. While there she gave birth to a son who you rejected." The veins in Larry's forehead bulged with a visible pulse. "You created a false past for your Tiffany—my Taylor. Tried to make her into your ideal for a wife."

Clive reached into the drawer. He picked up his revolver and pointed it directly at Larry's chest. Taylor gasped in horror. "You, my dear man, will leave this minute and leave Tiffany here. If not, I will kill you."

"Have you forgotten about your promotion by the royals? I doubt Buckingham Palace will look kindly at your forthcoming honor if you shoot me—a celebrated entertainer from the States." Larry motioned for Taylor to stand behind him. "Besides, if you do, your cousin Amelia will reveal your little secret. She knows all your ugly dealings—including your son from Penelope who was put up for adoption at your request."

Larry inched to the door. Clive held the gun steadfast. Their eyes fixed in a dead determination. *Tay's worth my life. If he does shoot, what will become of her? Will he kill both of us?*

"Rubbish!" He discounted Larry's evidence. "Amelia wouldn't dare."

"Are you willing to take that chance?" He was near the hallway. "Kill me and your future will be ruined. Or we can leave now and explain *Tiffany's* absence the same way you did Penelope's. If you do nothing to prevent our leaving, no mention of this horror will come from us."

Clive wouldn't put his gun away. "You have a bloody nerve. Steal my wife and one is supposed to react like one was on a walk in Hyde Park?" He looked at the official notice of his impending elevation to Duke on his desk. Blood droplets from his nose stained the prestigious document. He gritted his teeth at this site.

"I'm stealing nothing from you!" Larry glared while Taylor trembled. "You are the thief! An arrogant, pompous, holier-than-thou, self-appointed asshole!"

Larry and Taylor turned away. Breaths caught in throats as they waited for the sharp piercing bang from a bullet discharging. Nearly running to the front door, Taylor flung it open. Larry followed. Joe stood by the open door to the limousine. They quickly slid into the backseat.

Larry directed the driver, "Get me the hell out of here! Go back to the airport and my jet." To Joe, he added, "After we land in

260   *Cynthia B. Ainsworthe*

Paris, you and Mark book commercial flights back home. Tay and I will take the jet."

"I figured on that one." Joe voiced his assumptions. "Got your bags waitin' in the jet. Mark's still at the hotel. What about Gigi and Jacques? Want them with us or you guys?"

"Bring them to the jet," Taylor chimed in. "I've been away too long from those babies." She looked at Larry with consternation. "What about Rodney and Elizabeth? I'm afraid they won't be safe with Clive."

"Not to worry." Larry patted her hand and left a kiss on her temple. "Elizabeth and cute Rodney are living with Amelia. She'll take good care of them."

"Poor Penelope," Taylor mumbled. "Because of Clive, she's a prisoner of her own mind." She paused a moment. "Lar, that could've been me. You saved me. You never gave up. Clive could've killed us."

"For a brief moment, I wasn't sure he wouldn't." Larry's love radiated from him. "I'm glad he was more concerned with his royal title."

"Poor Cindy." Her daughter's welfare came to her. "After all this time she must've been frantic. I see glimpses of her wedding with Vic. She was such a beautiful bride. No mother could be more proud. For some odd reason, she always resented being half French." Taylor looked out the window at the passing London sites. "Did you call her?"

"Yeah, I did." Larry checked his watch. He was eager to be flying back to Paris. "She's on cloud nine. Said she might visit very soon after we settle back in Bel-Air."

"That doesn't sound like her." Taylor paused as if in thought, "I recall I had to drag her out to make a visit. Something must be wrong with her work or Vic. Hope their marriage is okay."

"I'm sure all is well." He turned to her as the car approached Heathrow. "Tay, do me a favor?"

"Sure." Her adoring gaze traveled around his face.

"No more working for Gérard's, freelance or otherwise." He squeezed her hand. "No more working, period."

"Agreed." Taylor kissed him lovingly. "I'll stay at home and be your own private pest."

"Pest all you want." He sighed with delight. "That's music to my ears."

REMEMBER ? 261

~~***~~

Larry and Taylor settled on his private jet headed to the States, relaxing on the comfortable sofa styled bench. The poodles curled up on plush leather chairs opposite them. He had notified the steward to remain in his quarters unless called. Half-consumed champagne flutes sat on the small coffee table in front of them.

"How long before we land?" Taylor munched on a cheese cube.

"At least five hours." He placed nibbling kisses on her neck. "We fly into JFK to gas up and do the customs drill."

"What about the paparazzi? You don't have Joe as a buffer," she pointed out.

"So." He chuckled lightly. "You're my wife. No big deal." His attention resumed on her neck while unbuttoning the front of her blouse.

She pushed his hand away. "The steward might come back."

"What's wrong?" His curiosity radiated from his smile. "It's no worse than what you did to me in my Vegas dressing room."

"That was different," she said pouting.

"No, it wasn't." He returned to the sensuous curve of her throat. His mouth sought hers. "Besides, don't you want to be a member of the Mile High Club?"

"We're not completely alone." She put up another objection. "Gigi and Jacques are here."

Larry glanced at the sleeping poodles. "They won't tell."

His hand maneuvered the last button on her blouse. Taylor kissed him back as her tongue sought his to mingle their mutual desire. His hand traveled up her leg to the top of her stocking and onto her bare flesh. His fingers shot a surge of fire through her innermost being making her want him more than she could have believed was possible. He released her firm breasts from the constraints of her bra. She sighed, eager for the heat of his mouth. Larry found her nipples and teased them with his tongue, bringing them to full tautness. Taylor unzipped his pants and stroked him to firm arousal. His hands slipped off her thong panties and pushed her skirt to her waist. His fingers fondled her velvet folds and settled on her area of most intense pleasure, teasing her with increasing caresses. Moist droplets came from him. She pulled his pants down his thighs. His manhood stood erect, ready for her. Taylor lay back on the sofa and opened herself to receive him. Larry entered her slowly, then pulled back to tease her. Her hips reached up to him as her hands grabbed his buttocks. She wanted him now. He thrust deeper; she felt her moist walls surround him. His rhythm quickened as desire took control. Taylor guided him to move faster. Her breath shortened as each delicious stroke made her crave another and another in a frantic motion of heated passion. Her legs wrapped around him to pull him in deeper. Damp hairlines and gasps signaled her ultimate pleasure. She gasped out loud as the ecstasy of climax together became theirs.

Lifeless limbs and panting breaths melted into love's afterglow.

"Tay," Larry whispered as he stroked the moist hair by her ear, "don't ever leave me. You are my reason for everything I do."

"Never." She kissed him softly. "I'll be by your side as long as fate allows."

Fate. Why did I say that? Surely nothing could ever tear us apart again. Could it?

She kissed him with renewed passion.

~ END ~

The following is a preview of "Forbidden Footsteps", the third book in the Forbidden Series. Release date yet to be determined.

Forbidden Footsteps
Forbidden Series ~ Three

Cynthia B. Ainsworthe

*"Fragile heart …
scattered pieces …"*

~~ C. B. Ainsworthe

ONE

(excerpt)

JEAN-CLAUDE SPOTTED his father, alone in the corner, enjoying his dirty martini. He walked up and asked in French, "How much do you know about Davis?" He took his handkerchief to his nose.

Charles raised an eyebrow. "I see your allergy is acting up …. It is rude to speak in French when our hosts speak English. I didn't bring you up to be rude."

"You didn't answer my question," he countered in English. *Is he hiding something?*

"I know he's more famous than me." Charles took a sip of his drink. "Why the interest? You want Davis to back your career? Haven't I done enough for you?"

"His step-daughter is of more interest to me." He glanced in Cindy's direction.

"Ah, that could be a problem." Charles discreetly gestured to her with his hand. "Did you not notice her wedding band?"

"Since when did that stop me, Papa?" A smug grin came to his lips. "She seems to be a delicious challenge." *An American woman is just what my appetite needs. I've been savoring French pastry for far too long.*

"Some challenges are best unmet," he advised.

"You play it too safe. Always have." Jean-Claude watched Cindy chat with other guests. "Taking a risk in uncharted waters is where the fun is, and can be the most satisfying."

"Don't be foolish, Jean. Have you forgotten about Monique in Paris?" Charles reminded him.

"I'm bored with her. She's so Parisian and entirely predictable."

He caught Cindy's eye and she responded with a coy smile. "Besides, I don't feel I have to marry my mistresses." He kept his eyes on Cindy as he talked. "You're paying alimony to what—four or is it, five wives now? I don't pay alimony to a single one. It's time I venture for new experiences."

REMEMBER ?/FORBIDDEN FOOTSTEPS   265

Charles chuckled "Your new experiences always result in the same old ending."

"Papa," he remarked, "I'm too old for you to be giving me advice about my personal life."

"At thirty-two, you still act and react as a child." His father continued, "Like it or not, I still worry about you. Besides, I don't want you to make trouble that would cost me this relationship with Monsieur Davis. He could be important to my career."

"Go back to your martini." Jean-Claude stated while looking at Cindy, "There's an interesting woman I need to know better."

~~***~~

"Who's that good-looking man?" Cindy asked. "He looks like a French Don Draper out of Mad Men—acts as if he knows the world and owns it." Her gaze focused on the hot guy talking to Larry's manager, Brent, in the periphery of the living room of her mom and stepfather Larry Davis' Bel-Air home.

"Aren't you rushing things, dear daughter?" Taylor replied. "You haven't decided if you want to stay married to Vic yet. Give yourself time."

There goes Mom—always giving advice. Cindy smoothed out the wrinkles in her black dress. "I was never one to put things on hold." She kissed Taylor's cheek. "Mom, I know you mean well. My marriage with Vic was over when he put me in debt and refused to get help for his gambling. I'm just glad I never put his name on the deed to the Tampa home you gave me."

"Want to talk about it?" Cindy felt her mother's scrutinizing eyes. "We can have a nice long chat after the party."

"Not yet." Cindy studied the man who piqued her interest. *His navy blazer looks expensive. I bet he knows how to treat a woman.* "I have other things on my mind." She fingered her hair then wet her lips slowly with her tongue. "Care to introduce us?"

"No." Taylor raised an eyebrow of motherly concern. "That's Charles LeGrand's son, Jean-Claude, and yes, he's drop dead gorgeous. He's like a fantastic pair of shoes—you want them, but they're not in your size."

"I wouldn't mind walking a few blocks in them though." Cindy edged closer to her quest.

"That's rich, coming from you. You always rebelled against anything French." Taylor grabbed a handful of nuts from the counter as she looked at the man her daughter fancied.

"I've changed." Cindy took a step closer to him. "People change all the time."

266   *Cynthia B. Ainsworthe*

"Maybe and maybe not." Taylor touched Cindy's elbow to get her attention. "Look, it's clear you're on the rebound. Take it slow. This is no time to be looking for a replacement."

Cindy spun sharply around as her eyes narrowed. "I don't think you're in any position to talk after what happened to Dad."

"That was a deep cut." Tears rimmed Taylor's eyes. "There isn't a day I don't think about what happened." A sigh escaped. "I thought you and I had moved beyond that—we had found some peace between us."

"I'm sorry, Mom." She hugged Taylor and kissed her cheek. "I shouldn't have said that. I never meant to hurt you." She bent to pat the white and black toy poodles, where they sat at Taylor's heels, as if seeking safety from the strangers' feet. "Good girl Gigi and you're good too Jacques," she said quietly.

"I know, Honey." Taylor kissed her daughter's hairline at the temple.

"Excuse me, Mom." Cindy broke away as her voice trailed off, "Introductions need to be made.

~~***~~

"Why tidying up?" Larry questioned. "Our houseman should be doing this."

"Tim and both catering staff members are busy serving guests and collecting abandoned glasses," Taylor said as she tossed used napkins and paper plates into the trashcan. "I can watch the party goings on from the doorway. LeGrand's son is handsome. That could be a problem for Cindy."

Larry picked up a sponge and wiped the kitchen counter down to help her clean up.

"Our party seems to be a success," he mentioned and noticed Taylor eying her daughter.

"More of a success for Cindy, if she has anything to say about it." She refilled the chip bowl.

"Really?" Larry grabbed a jar of nuts from the cabinet. "Anyone we know?"

"Jean-Claude LeGrand, of all people." She turned to face her husband. "Do you know his reputation?"

"Yeah," Larry affirmed, "the old 'love 'em and leave 'em' routine."

"Exactly!" Taylor opened a package of fresh cocktail napkins. "And Cindy's on the rebound. She's vulnerable—prime for the pickings of a roué."

"Roué?" he asked with raised eyebrows.

REMEMBER ?/FORBIDDEN FOOTSTEPS 267

"It's French for playboy." She stopped refreshing the party food. "And I bet he's been one for years. He's had plenty of lessons from his father."

"Careful, Tay," Larry cautioned. "Charles and I have a business deal in the works to put out a duet album. Keep a lid on your feelings. You could blow it for me." *I hope Tay doesn't worry too much about Cindy. They lost their closeness since Paul. I don't think Cindy's ever forgiven her mom.*

"Mum's the word." She kissed his cheek. "I'll be the perfect supportive wife with a wary eye on his son."

Joe entered the kitchen. "Great party, Lar. Your business deal with LeGrand could open the French market for y'" He brushed his short white hair back with his hand.

"That's the idea." He chuckled. "Who knows? I might actually learn more than two words of French."

Taylor smiled with approval. "You learning French isn't on my mind at this moment. Cindy's rebound reaction is what troubles me."

"C'mon," Larry suggested, "let's get out there and give Tim and the other servers a break." *I wish she wouldn't worry so much.*

~~***~~

Cindy stood behind Jean-Claude, admiring the tall dark-haired man with intense black eyes. Her eyes widened with a devilish glint and her hand quickly smoothed her hair before she casually bumped into him.

Jean-Claude turned to see the object of his disturbance. His smile slowly emerged, showcasing his white teeth.

"Pardon, Mademoiselle." He inclined his head with an approving look. "Have we met? I don't recall the pleasure of meeting such a beautiful woman."

I love his accent. Cindy extended her hand.

Jean-Claude lifted it to his lips and gently placed an enticing kiss on it. His eyes slanted up at her with a silent message.

"I'm, I'm," she stammered, "Cynthia Hastings, though my friends call me Cindy." *God! He's gorgeous!* "You speak perfect English." *Why did I say that? That's so lame.*

"Merci, Cindy." He still held her hand and rubbed his thumb slowly across the ridge of her middle finger. "Like my father, I sell more records in America if I speak the language. I understand from your step-father that you are half French?"

"Yes. My mom is the French one in the family." Her eyes evaded his gaze before continuing. "I avoided everything French

268   *Cynthia B. Ainsworthe*

most of my life—a rebellious phase—avoided the culture and language, until now."

"Ah, until now? And what has changed your mind?" He momentarily glanced about the room. "My father's music? I understand your mother is a fan of his, n'est-ce pas?"

Cindy felt color come to her cheeks. "I thought that would be obvious."

"Maybe you listened to a few of my songs?" He shrugged in a typical French fashion. "I know I'm not as famous as my father, but I have time to prove myself. My music is more contemporary than the legendary Charles LeGrand."

"Music isn't the only thing of a French nature that might interest me." She nonchalantly looked about the room.

"I should be mingling." Jean-Claude said. "Guests will think you are my new love." He discreetly pointed to the wedding band on her left hand. "I see you are married. He has a treasure to adore every night." Clearing his throat, Jean-Claude added, "Is he here? I would like to meet that special man who could whisk you away."

"Vic's in Tampa. I'd rather not talk about it. I've left him." Cindy sipped her drink. "When I make my mind up, there's no going back for me."

"Fini?" He gave an approving smile. "I like a woman who knows her mind. Are you certain there can be no second chances for your Vic?"

"Very certain." Her jaw set in determination. "No one takes advantage of me and will get forgiveness."

"Bien sûr, Mademoiselle." He made a small bow. "I now know your rules. Merci for that illustrious example." A light chuckle escaped. "I have rules, too."

"Want to share?" Cindy looked directly in his eyes. "Rules are meant to be broken—when it's fun."

"You are a true coquette, and delightfully beautiful." He finished his brandy in one gulp. "And with that, I must greet the hosts or they will believe we French are truly rude."

"No issues from Mom on that point. She raises the French flag at every opportunity." Cindy looked at him from beneath her long lashes.

Jean-Claude's light laugh trailed off as he walked in the direction of his father.

ABOUT THE AUTHOR

Cynthia B Ainsworthe and Barry Manilow

Cynthia has longed to be a writer. Life's circumstances put her dream on hold for most of her life. In 2006, she ventured to write her first novel, **Front Row Center**, which won the prestigious **IPPY Award** (Independent Publisher), as well as garnering numerous 5-star reviews, one from known **Midwest Book Review**, is the first book in the **Forbidden Series**, and a script is in development by her and notable Hollywood screenwriter, producer, and director, Scott C. Brown. Ms. Ainsworthe has been a guest on several talk radio shows. As a retired cardiac RN turned author, she enjoys her retirement in Florida, caring for her husband and their five poodle-children. Cynthia is currently writing **Forbidden Footsteps**, book three in the **Forbidden Series.**

Author Awards
2008 Prestigious IPPY Award in romance, *Front Row Center*
2013 Reader's Favorite International Award
in fiction anthology,
The Speed of Dark for two contributing stories:
When Midnight Comes and Characters.
2013 Excellence in Writing Award, It Matters Radio,
for short story
It Ain't Fittin'

VISIT CYNTHIA AT:

Amazon Author Page: http://www.amazon.com/Cynthia-B.-Ainsworthe/e/B00KYRE1Q8
Official Website: http://www.cynthiabainsworthe.com/
Facebook Fan Page:
https://www.facebook.com/pages/Cynthia-B-Ainsworthe/38240446635
Facebook Profile:
https://www.facebook.com/cynthia.b.ainswortheauthor
Twitter: https://twitter.com/CynB_Ainsworthe
LinkedIn: http://www.linkedin.com/in/cynthiabainsworthe/
Goodreads:
https://www.goodreads.com/author/show/4533371.Cynthia_B_Ainsworthe
Google+:
https://plus.google.com/u/0/+CynthiaBAinsworthe/posts/p/pub
Pinterest: http://www.pinterest.com/ainsworthe1/
Wordpress:
http://ainsworthe1.wordpress.com/2014/06/29/137/
Blogspot: http://cynthiaswordsandpassion.blogspot.com/
Book Trailer:
https://www.youtube.com/watch?v=qhK7prWYxhk
Publisher: http://www.wordsandpassion.com/

Made in the USA
Monee, IL
10 January 2020

20134706R00157